# The Love Academy

Belinda Jones's first paid job was on cult kiddy comic *Postman Pat*. Since then she has written for a multitude of magazines and newspapers including *Sunday*, *Daily Express*, *Empire*, *FHM*, *heat*, *New Woman* and *more!* magazine, where she was a features writer and male model scouter for four years. Belinda's widely acclaimed first novel, *Divas Las Vegas*, was voted No. 2 in the *New Woman* Bloody Good Reads Awards in 2001 and *On the Road to Mr Right* – a non-fiction travelogue love quest – was a *Sunday Times* top ten bestseller. *The Love Academy* is her sixth novel.

**Praise for Belinda Jones**

'You won't want to put this feel-good read down' *Company*

'Great characters . . . hilariously written . . . buy it!'
*New Woman*

'A riotous page-turner, full of witty observations about life and love' *She*

'Deliciously entertaining' *heat*

'A perfect, sunny read' *B*

Also by Belinda Jones

Fiction

*Divas Las Vegas*

*I Love Capri*

*The California Club*

*The Paradise Room*

*Café Tropicana*

Non-fiction

*On the Road to Mr Right*

*To embark on more fabulous journeys with Belinda Jones, visit her website: www.belindajones.com*

Belinda Jones

# The Love Academy

arrow books

Published in the United Kingdom by Arrow Books in 2007

3 5 7 9 10 8 6 4 2



First published in the United Kingdom in 2007 by Arrow Books

Arrow Books
The Random House Group Limited
20 Vauxhall Bridge Road, London SW1V 2SA

www.randomhouse.co.uk

Addresses for companies within The Random House Group Limited can be found at:
www.randomhouse.co.uk/offices.htm

The Random House Group Limited Reg. No. 954009

A CIP catalogue record for this book
is available from the British Library

ISBN 9780099489887

The Random House Group Limited makes every effort to ensure that the papers used in its books are made from trees that have been legally sourced from well-managed and credibly certified forests. Our paper procurement policy can be found at:
www.randomhouse.co.uk/paper.htm

Typeset by Palimpsest Book Production Limited,
Grangemouth, Stirlingshire

Printed in the UK by CPI Bookmarque, Croydon, CR0 4TD

For my brother Gareth
(and everyone with an inner Italian)

# Acknowledgements

IN ENGLAND: What stars you are at Random House – Justine, Kate, Rob, Susan, Ollie, Louisa, Claire, Ellie, Laura, Laurie, Anne, Lucie and Emma – I am so grateful to all of you, and the reception crew who always make me smile! Much Prosecco-chinking to Eugenie, Lucinda and Alice at William Morris Associates. My favourite jet-setter, Vicky Legg at Orient Express Hotels. Ma and Bro for boat-on-a-lake bliss, Chip and Sue for an idyllic writer's retreat, Samantha Pengelly for a hilarious misdummer night and James for leading me to the greatest secrets and treats of Venice!

IN ITALY: Maria Luisa, Simone and Sabrina at the wondrous Palazzo Abadessa with a special mention to Nicola, the inspiration for Dante. Cristina and Roberta of Walks Inside Venice, Danytza at Villa San Michele and Alessandro, formerly of the Dei Dogi hotel – you are one of the most heart-warming people I have ever met!

IN AMERICA: Thank you Ty for our beautiful home and giving me Auntie status to the outrageously appealing Mackenzie and Ethan. Wished you had been our neighbour, Shari! Big love to all Vegas visitors and to Tezz, you are the most uplifting being on the planet! Raeleen, thank you for your wisdom and infectious *joie de vivre*. The fabulous Dorian and Alicia at Stateside WMA. And finally to my awesome Little Sister Anamaria Canedo for being such a joyful and inspirational friend to me. Miss you!

# 1

*'If I can stop one heart from breaking I shall not live in vain.' – Emily Dickinson*

What if there was a place you could go to have your heart's longings fulfilled? A place that could give you a real, touchable person to love, not just some peppy pointers on how to attract The One? What if that place was in Italy? Better yet, Venice?

Would you go?

I leave on Monday. Not that I want my love life meddled with – I have a done-deal, joint-home-owning boyfriend in Joe, so for me this is purely business: my latest commission from *Hot!* magazine. Basically, there have been one too many euphoric reports of Brits finding their true Amore at The Love Academy and the interest in this place is interfering with our readers' appetite for reality TV stars and their skanky hair extensions. So now Ruth, my editor, wants one of those undercover pieces with a snidey, knowing tone (her particular forte but she's already booked on a freebie spa trip to the Bahamas), the idea being to undermine their credibility and prove her theory that The Love Academy is nothing more than a highly stylish escort agency.

My fingers drum on the matt-silver keys of my laptop.

I'm supposed to be writing the teaser for the next issue before I go – just a line or two to get the readers making a mental must-purchase but typically this proves to be a greater challenge to me than the article itself. I couldn't seem to get to grips with the story angle in the office, not least because at four o'clock yesterday afternoon we received a promotional set of cocktails served in martini glasses complete with their own lids to prevent spillage and spiking in clubs, and we decided to 'test' the concept in every flavour. So now it's the morning after and I'm hypnotised by the flashing cursor on my home computer.

I know Ruth will dismiss 'Lessons in Love', 'Hot for Teacher' and 'Can Romance Be Taught?' as too tame. I'm considering a shot of Madonna in her 'Italians Do It Better' logo T-shirt with an aside of: *Especially if you pay them!* But I'm concerned that might be libellous?

If only I really was as single as I am required to be for the article then I could simply exclaim, 'I Fell In Love With A Gondolier!' and have done with it.

I do a figure of eight in my wheelie desk chair in the hope of dislodging some inspiration.

Lately our magazine seems to be taking the scaremongering tack of US news: *Your future boyfriend could be spending the weekend with a Venetian Courtesan!* But I'm not big on that. Perhaps I should go with our old favourite of using song titles. How about: 'That's Amore! Or is it . . . ?'

There's a ring at the doorbell. Oh merciful distraction! It's my brother. My own little raincloud. There was a time when Joe and I relished our Saturday brunches with Kier because we always ended up laughing till hollandaise sauce spurted from our nostrils, but now Joe cries off in favour of fictitious squash games on account of Kier having become such a dirgy downer. It's not his fault; he's got a broken heart. And though I've tried every possible pep-up from spiritual retreats in the Orkney isles to invitations to the fashion department during model castings, it seems nothing can de-gloom him. Still I keep trying, even noting down platitudes from embroidered cushions in chintzy old-lady shops. I have this theory, if I could just find the right quote, that certain configuration of words that totally resonates, then something inside him will shift and let hope come pouring back into his life.

'I've got one for your brother,' Joe said before he left today. 'You know I was telling you about all the redundancies at work? Well, Pete says the boss quoted Tennessee Williams to him on his way out . . .'

'Go on,' I encouraged, pen poised.

'"*There is a time for departure even when there's no certain place to go.*"'

'Oh that's perfect!' I cooed. 'Did it make Pete feel better?'

'No, he punched him.'

'Oh.'

'See you later, baby!'

'Bye!' I waved him out the door, nevertheless deciding to give it a whirl over the almond croissant appetisers on the menu this weekend.

'You know, Kier, there is a time for departure even when there's no certain place to go,' I repeated, praying for some sign of recognition in my brother's hazel-flecked eyes.

*Au contraire*. Clearly sick of my quotations, he had one of his own to slap back: 'The saddest thing in the world is loving someone who used to love you.'

Now it was my turn to feel punched, right in the heart. I felt my eyes well up in sympathy. You can't argue with that. Although I would say it's pretty grim seeing someone you've loved for thirty-five years get so low. And then stay there, in the pit of despair for pretty much a year now.

'He just needs to get back on the horse,' Joe keeps saying, meaning: 'he just needs to go and shag another bird'. But Kier's not like that. His feelings are not easily transferable – his 'I love you' comes with a lifetime guarantee – and in this case he seems especially convinced that his heart was meant specifically for Her. Not that I know much about the her in question – Kier plays his cards close to his chest, and his relationships closer, always afraid of jinxing them if he were to acknowledge his hopes for their future out loud. More than once the first I'd hear of his latest girlfriend would be when it was all over. And even then the details would be sparing. This is very much a private issue for him, so it's not like he's driving us crazy sitting there going on and on about her, trying to figure out what went wrong or how to woo her back so much as just being distant and melancholy.

Or 'so hollow', as James Blunt was saying a lot around the time the split occurred.

Today Kier's actually reasonably personable; his clothes only look like day three of wear and his brow isn't rucked to its usual degree. Which is kind of a shame in a way because I can be certain I'm going to piss him off before we've even finished giving a greasy-spoon finish to the goodies he's brought over.

'Shall I get going with the swine or do you need to finish what you're doing first?' He nods to the laptop.

I quickly snap the lid closed in case he offers to help – he's actually much better at summoning the nutshell succinctness of a headline than me, one of life's natural wafflers, but this is a topic that needs to be eased into. 'Nah it can wait.' I make for the cupboard. 'Chai latte?'

'Don't mind if I do.'

I watch him unloading the shopping bag, to-ing and fro-ing between the fridge and the countertop. Perhaps this isn't the best time to ask him. Even his spine seems a little straighter today. But Joe would reason that he still hasn't shaved off his afro-esque beard and then remind me of what happened when I dropped by Kew Gardens earlier this week. (That's where Kier works, as a landscape gardener.) While he was finishing up in the waterlily house, his colleague Griff took me aside and said he feared Kier was at risk of losing his job because he was repeatedly caught staring off into space or sitting with his head in his hands when he should have been nipping assorted buds. I asked if he'd spoken to Kier about it but he said mere words weren't enough. Which is why I feel it is my duty to perform this one-woman intervention . . .

'What?' he catches me staring.

'Nothing.' I fall at the first hurdle, going back to frothing the milk. I don't want to incur his wrath or make him feel criticised in any way but it has to be said, and soon – I leave in less than forty-eight hours. The clock is ticking . . .

'You know when you were in Venice,' I finally blurt, pausing to let the blood drain from his face. Did I mention that that is where the heartbreak took place?

'Yes,' his voice is immediately taut, eyes trained fixedly on the frying pan.

'Did you ever hear of a place called The Love Academy?'

He gives a slight shrug and continues aligning the strips of bacon. 'I heard mention of it, but I couldn't tell you where it is. I never went there myself.'

'Well, I don't suppose you needed to, at the time . . .' Oh, that didn't come out right.

'You mean I do now?' He looks up, clearly affronted.

'No, well actually yes, but for different reasons than you might think.'

'What exactly are you saying?'

There you go – pissed off, good and proper. Masterfully done.

'It's just that I'm going there, to The Love Academy, next week. Monday, in fact.'

'You're going to Venice?' he clarifies.

I nod, already feeling disloyal. From his expression you'd think I'd made plans with Cinzia herself. That's her name, the ex. You say it with a 'ch' as in '*Cin-cin*!' Such a cheery name for pain.

'It's just for work,' I explain hastily. 'A few days, undercover on this course and I wanted to ask . . .' His eyes warn me off but I hurry out my words regardless, '. . . if you'd come with me.'

He looks at me in disbelief. Like I was asking him to fry his own hand in the pan.

'It's all expenses paid, as much provolone as you can eat, and you could see your old friends . . .'

Consumed with derision, he starts, 'Are you—'

'Kidding? Crazy? No!' I try to make a joke. 'The thing is Ruth – you know, my editor – has her heart set on a boy and girl angle to the article I'm writing.'

'So take Joe.'

'Well, I would but he's got a conference in Manchester and besides they need the boy and girl to be single.'

'But you're not single, you're going out with Joe,' he makes a valid point. 'Practically married to the guy,' he motions around him at our home, highlighting the joint toaster, joint sofa, joint cat.

'I know,' I whine. 'But for the purposes of this piece she's insisting I appear to be looking for love.'

He rolls his eyes, ever less impressed with tales from the magazine world.

'And anyway, she's now totally sold on the brother-sister angle and ever since I told her that you used to live there she won't consider any other option.'

'Well, you should never have told her in the first place,' he glowers.

'I didn't do it entirely on purpose!' I squeak, seeking mercy.

The fact is I was driven to it when fellow feature writer Fenton offered to go with me. He writes so cockily from the standpoint of the 'Real Man' but in person is ultra fey and preening; I simply can't bear to be around him and his 'manly' fragrances. That's when I opened my big mouth about Kier. And then Ruth got all excited – she liked the idea that he could ask around the locals, speaking just enough Italian to get the incriminating stuff. I tried explaining that the only dirt Kier digs is soil but she wouldn't be told. Besides she loved the brother-sister angle, saying it would be like getting the male version of me which is not true at all – Kier and I are about as opposite as two people with the same parents can be. Particularly in terms of love. He's always wanted to settle down, whereas I've always metaphorically covered myself in butter so no one can get a firm grip on me. I don't quite know how I'm the one who ended up in the committed relationship while he's still searching. The universe does have an absurd sense of humour.

Especially considering that Kier is the type of man who falls for the unique essence of a girl whereas I'm always hoping to find a match for some forgotten old-movie ideal of a leading man.

The other thing about Kier is that he's probably one of the few people left on the planet who doesn't want their face splashed all over a magazine. Although it's a very nice face and our Auntie Margaret is always saying that with his strong jawline and barrow-wheeling muscles he ought to be a model. Frankly, he couldn't think of anything worse. He needs fresh air not Ferragamo, to walk never ending open fields not narrow catwalks. 'Tis me with all the superficiality in the family.

That said, although as a teenager I wanted to *look* like the women on the beauty pages, I always wanted to *be* the writer who interviewed the pop stars. And so I did everything it took to make that happen. Initially it was so rewarding to see my words and character observations in print but lately I feel reduced to caption writer status. Investigative pieces like this one on The Love Academy are rare. Back in the day, I used to have to fight tooth and Rouge Noir nail to get an extra page so I could give a great story the wordage it deserved, now an entire spread gets devoted to Britney Spears emerging from Starbucks with – shocker! – a hot beverage. As a writer, that's so soul-destroying. And if that doesn't get you, editor Ruth will. Ever since she was promoted to head honcho she's taken full advantage of the fact that she can be as abrasive and belittling as she likes to her staff – knowing that they love the magazine so much they'll take it. It's strange to think that her barbed jurisdiction does not extend to the real world, least of all to my brother.

'You'll just have to find some other guy,' he shrugs, refusing to bend to her will.

'But I've only got one brother and now she knows about Venice—'

'Say it was all a mistake, tell her I actually spent six months gardening in Venezuela.'

'I can't do that.'

'And I can't—' he pauses to correct himself. 'I won't go back.'

'Wouldn't it be going forward?' I suggest, a little uncomfortable in my bullishness. 'We could create some new memories, some good ones.'

'I don't need any more good memories,' his face darkens. 'It's because the old ones are so amazing,' his voice cracks as he speaks, 'that they hurt so much.'

Again my insides wrench. I'd do anything to click my fingers and present him with a new love, make this old anguish go away. But it seems an impossible task. It was so much easier when we were four and five. If some other toddler was bothering him, I'd walk up and thump them – that extra year being all the clout I needed to scare them off. Now my instincts are equally protective but I can't steamroller in and make it all alright with a chubby fist. As Joe puts it, 'You can't chin Cinzia.'

'But there's got to be something I can do!' I'm forever howling.

And then along comes this trip, I blab Kier's Venice connection to Ruth and then convince myself that he needs to go back there to gain that all-too-elusive closure. (Such a neat little concept – a brief moment of unpleasantness before you dust off your hands and move on.) When I suggest this to him he laughs, 'What, so picking open an old wound is the best way to heal is it?'

He's over by the window now, looking out into next door's garden.

'You know, sometimes revisiting a place or a person can actually put things in perspective,' I address his hunched back. 'Remember when I had that totally illogical obsession with chunky Duncan who dumped me back in 1993 . . .'

'You never met Cinzia did you?' he challenges, turning to face me.

'No.' I can't lie.

'Well, thank you for asking but the answer's no.' Curt, polite, subject closed. He picks up his jacket and heads for the door. 'I'll see you when you get back.'

'What about brunch?'

'I'm not hungry.'

'But—' I'm dashing to his side, ready to block the doorway. I don't want him to leave and be alone with all these feelings that I'm responsible for bringing up.

'Kirsty!' he turns on me.

I get it. There's no persuading him. I've totally cocked this whole thing up. I have to let him go. All that remains for me to do now is marinate in my own misgivings.

Sitting there amongst the kitchen debris I think how ironic it is that in Italy family is all-powerful. In Islington, quite the opposite seems true. Right now I feel utterly ineffectual – I mean, what's the point in being related to someone and thus having all this extra investment in their well-being when you can't do a darn thing to make them feel better?

# 2

*'The desire of a man is for the woman, but the desire of the woman is for the desire of the man.'*
*– Madame de Stael*

'What about Jason Morris?'

'He moved to New Zealand,' I tell Joe.

'When?' He looks perplexed.

'Two years ago.'

'Well that would explain why I haven't seen him down the Crown lately.'

Instead of reading the Sunday papers, Joe and I are sitting in bed with our respective address books trying to find a man I can take to Venice.

I began with the men I know, narrowed it down to men I like and then asked myself exactly whom I would be prepared to share a room with.

I sigh out loud. 'The only ones left on my list are gay.'

'There's always Kelvin Sprat. No man on earth is more available.'

'He's got a girlfriend.'

'What?' Joe hoots. 'And more to the point, *how*?'

I shrug my shoulders. 'Maybe he did a stint at The Love Academy on the quiet.'

'Maybe.' He inspects a random business card. 'Jack Pinner & Sons?'

'Jack Pinner?' I repeat. 'As in the old plumber geezer?'

'Mmm, actually I think he died last year. We could try one of his sons?'

'Maybe I should just resign,' I cast my book aside, defeated. 'I've been talking about leaving for months—'

'You'd still have to work your notice,' Joe notes all too accurately, prompting me to adopt the pose of an aggrieved starlet. 'Ha!' he suddenly looks gleeful. 'I know one man who's always had a thing for you and would drop everything to go!'

'Who?' I enquire with caution, opening just one eye.

'My dad.'

I don't make an instant dismissal. Mr Simmons is actually a peach.

'He's single. Loves to travel. Always had a huge crush on Gina Lollobrigida . . .' Joe enthuses.

'You know, I almost would – but sharing a room with him . . .' I pull a face.

'Might be a little weird?' He looks disappointed.

'Not least because I'd be coming in from dates with *another man*.' I shoot Joe a sideways glance.

He chuckles at me, knowing full well what I'm angling for. 'You'd like me to be jealous, wouldn't you?'

'Little bit,' I concede. His confidence in 'us' is admirable but a tad blasé for my taste.

He turns on to his side. 'Look, it's work. I understand. I trust you.'

'But this man they're fixing me up with, he's going to be *Italian*!' I protest, exasperated.

'So?' Joe laughs, pulling me into his arms. 'It's not like you'd fall for that crap.'

And there we have it – the dud aspect to Joe: to him, romance equals crap.

I guess some men want princesses to worship and adore, others want buddies they can sleep with. And I know Joe's not alone in wanting the latter. I know there are innumerable men out there who are equally dismissive of Valentine's Day and anniversaries and I understand that they don't want to be told how to behave on a certain day and I wouldn't mind so much if they took it upon themselves to do something loving and celebratory on some completely random Tuesday but it never quite happens, does it?

It makes me wonder why women were made with such a capacity for swooning if so few men have the propensity to induce that state.

And you know the most frustrating part of all – just how easy it is to make a girl melt. Are men just being contrary? Lazy? Withholding? It feels like a kind of deprivation. That's it – I'm officially romance-deprived! It's a real condition, I swear. And it hurts.

'Hey! I bought you flowers once!' I imagine Joe protesting.

I remember the occasion well. He had come straight from the supermarket, plastic bags of fish fingers and loo rolls swinging from his arms as he handed me a cellophane-wrapped bunch of chrysanthemums with the heart-stopping sentiment, 'Here. For you.'

I enthused wildly, 'Oooh baby that's so lovely of you!' because I want to encourage him to do it again but at the same time part of me wanted to tsk, 'You couldn't peel the £3.99 price sticker off before you gave them to me?'

But in a way that's sweet, isn't it? Keeping it real. No show or pomp. Flowers are flowers after all. He was in Sainsbury's – or Stan's Berries as he calls it – and he thought of me. That's the important thing. Does the presentation of the gift really matter? Would it have meant so much more if he'd snuck up behind me, kissed the back of my neck and then brought the bouquet around to my chest husking, 'Read the card!'

I hear my heart yelp, 'Yes!' and then 'What does it say, what does it say?'

'*It's you and me baby, always you and me!*' or '*Thank you for loving me*' or '*You are so very special to me!*'

All those things he's said to me, so I know he's got it in him. What's stopping him from going that extra mile?

I've been thinking about this a lot since The Love Academy commission. Prior to that I've been pretty much resigned to the fact that Joe is Joe, he's not going to suddenly start quoting poetry or writing proposals in the sky but he's here and he's mine, and for that I'm grateful. Perhaps a little too grateful at times. It is possible I let too much slide for fear of being alone again? Kier is such a cautionary tale and Joe was such a long time coming – I'm thirty-six and he's the first guy I've lived with.

It's funny; all those single years I thought my problems would be solved if I had a boyfriend. I thought it was an automatic assurance that there was always someone there to love you and support you and that you would share everything and feel so close and secure. I wasn't at all prepared for the day-to-day wobbles and frustrations. Living together has certainly introduced us to a whole new world of humdrum. Phonecalls are no longer to say 'I'm thinking of you!' but reminders to pick up fabric softener. We used to go out to dinner at Italian restaurants with twinkly fairy lights but now it's, 'Well, we've got that leftover chilli to use up.' And despite all this extra home time, I swear we have less one-on-one time – when he would stay over with me there was nothing but the TV and me to entertain him and we'd spend our nights united on the sofa but now he's got his one-man recliner and his computer and his car to tinker with and a million little chores to tend to, I sometimes feel like an afterthought. He doesn't come home to see me, he just comes home.

Of course there are certain aspects I relish – there is nothing better than being embraced first thing in the morning. All I feel when his arms are around me is safe and warm and loved. It's like a hit of Valium and instantly I forget all the bad stuff. I only start to remember when I don't get my cuddle quotient. Basically I can see all of our relationship flaws from a distance and none of them from within his arms.

As for the thing that seems to make women despair the most – lack of commitment – that doesn't even apply. It was he who suggested moving in together, he who wanted us to buy a house. He's even now suggesting the next step – a baby.

At the moment that seems like a step too far for me. His sole concern appears to be financial whereas I worry about *everything* else. Not least the lack of a Big Ben-style donging from my biological clock. I'm certainly old enough but there's barely a sound. Maybe it's my hearing that's at fault. Or maybe my particular clock happens to be digital. Who knows? The fact is I can't bring myself to say that I *don't* want kids but I'm fairly emphatic that I don't want to *not* have kids. A life with no offspring seems a little bleak and finite. So, I suppose, by default more than anything else, I do. But is this something I want now?

Trepidation is normal I'm sure. The concept of creating

another human being is so terrifyingly huge. I mean, I worry about getting the mixture of vodka and cranberry right when I make a cocktail, so I'd certainly want some assurance that Joe and I would be a good blend for a child.

Perhaps these nine days apart are timely. Perhaps I will gain a little clarity. For now I'm just going to make the most of the fact that our last day together is a Sunday. He pulls me into a squeeze, murmuring, 'Mmm, you feel so nice!' and I sigh contentedly, settling in for hibernation only for him to swing his legs out of bed.

'Hurry back,' I coo, temporarily replacing him with the pillow, presuming he's nipping for a wee or a glass of water.

He looks at his watch. 'I'm going to try my darnedest to be back by 9 p.m., that way we can still have a bit of a night.'

'Wha— where are you going?' I shoot upright.

'Work.' Joe is head of internal events at a big corporate company in the City.

I bite back any protestation. It's all a bit of a pressure cooker environment there at the moment so I know he has to go the extra mile, especially with this week's conference coming up. All the same . . .

'Don't you want breakfast before you go?' I offer. 'There's a ton of leftovers from yesterday's farrago.'

'That's okay. I'm meeting Keith for a fry-up before we go in.'

'Oh.' Joe's still in the honeymoon phase of his friendship with new work colleague, Keith. He'll be all slumped and monosyllabic with me but when his 'boyfriend' calls, he's all perky and witty and energised. Makes me sick to see him using up the best of him for someone else and leaving the dregs for me.

'You don't mind do you, I thought you'd be packing . . .'

I look at the clock. 'For ten hours?'

'You've got a lot of clothes.'

'I know, seven and a half feet worth,' I quote Joe's moving-in measurement to me.

'You've added a few more inches since then.' He reaches for my bum. 'And I don't just mean in the wardrobe department!'

He gives me a roguish smirch of a kiss and leaves before I can throw the pillow at him. Always nice to start the day with a fat comment.

That's another recurring irritant – Joe's phenomenal lack of tact.

On my birthday of all days we were out to dinner and I was shimmering with candlelit satisfaction when he leant close and said, 'What's a woman your age doing getting spots?' I thought surely I must have misheard him, surely what he actually meant to say was, 'You've never looked lovelier!' but no, he was sitting there pointing to the angry bump on my chin. It was an amazing double-stab, spearing my age (I'm four years older than him) and my imperfect skin in one go. I barely made it to the restaurant loo before I erupted with tears and outrage. How could he say such a thing out loud? It seemed so deliberately spiteful and yet he sat there so blithely oblivious. I don't understand how such an intelligent man can be so incredibly ignorant. It's like last month when this new bimbo secretary at his work gave me a moment's insecurity. 'Oh baby,' he pulled me to his chest. 'I'm happy with you. I don't need hot and sexy.'

And it's not just me that gets it. The other day his seven-year-old niece was visiting and he commented, 'Wow, your arms are really hairy!' then walked off, leaving her forlornly assessing what was barely a hint of golden down. That's what annoyed me the most – it wasn't even true! I rushed up to her urging her not to take any notice, telling her she's perfect just as she is, whereas her uncle is an idiot and needs to have his tongue removed.

Suddenly I'm glad to be going away. Isn't there a theory knocking around that if you raise your game, your man will instinctively follow suit? You don't even have to beg or plead with him to step up, you just have to lead your life with more dignity and conviction. Yup, always a catch . . .

I roll over on to my stomach and press my face into the mattress. Well, I can lie here getting myself in a stew or I can be practical and pack. For once I choose the positive action, get out of bed and stand, hand on hips, in front of my wardrobe.

If I were going anywhere else in Italy I'd be thinking Capri pants and Pucci headscarves but what does one pack for Venice, other than stripy T-shirts and beribboned boaters? The only Venetian fashion shoot I can recall featured Julia Roberts in a selection of pouffy designer ball gowns, innovatively paired with Wellington boots as she waded through a flooded St Mark's Square. I think that was a winter edition of *Vogue*. Well, it's summer now and my primary concern is accommodating the inevitable pigeon poop. I don't want to feel anxious anticipation every time I'm sitting at some terrace café or posing for a picture with a chorus line of grey birds on my extended arm, later to be captioned, 'Will Kirsty have men flocking to her side?'

I begin pulling every item of a chalky white hue, scraping the hangers along the rail adding further metallic etchings to the slightly bowing bar, amazed at just how many garments still bear their tags. Jeez, even when it comes to fashion I have problems committing – I see something, I like it, I buy it but I can rarely bring myself to wear it because then that would mean I own it for good and then there's no going back.

I'm just chiding myself for not asking Anya, the fashion editor at *Hot!*, for a little assistance when I hear the glass chink sound from my computer alerting me to a new message. Funny isn't it, there's always that hope that *this* will be the email to kick-start the life you've been waiting to lead, even when you should be perfectly satisfied with the one you've got.

Oooh! It's from The Love Academy, telling me to pack something that would be appropriate to wear to a wedding. What, like a long white dress and a veil? Oh, 'as a guest'.

I return to the wardrobe and fumble for the three summer frocks that always seem trying-too-hard dressy for general daywear but are too candy-coloured girlie for night. One clearly has its sights on pulling the best man, one has a polyester lining so would most likely stick to my thighs during the ceremony and the third was acquired on a day where I'd spent four hours tramping down Oxford St and refused to go home empty-handed, no matter how impractical the purchase.

'Well, your moment has come!' I tell the slightly gaudy lilac-and-gold number.

Right. Now jewellery.

I suppose the ultimate Venetian accessory is a carnival mask but I imagine they're a devil for flaking glitter on everything, leaving gold dandruff on the shoulder of your dance partner, intermingling with the pepper flakes on your fusilli . . .

That's another thing with Joe – dinner! I set myself off again. I actually now prefer eating in front of the TV because when we sit at the table I know I'll be abandoned mid-mouthful – I honestly can't remember the last time he didn't get up and start cleaning his plate off at the sink before I'd finished my meal. I did suggest this was a little ill-mannered and asked him to wait until I was done but after a couple of times I thought I'd probably end up with an eating disorder the way he was staring at every morsel I squidged on to my fork, so I let it go.

'Okay,' I'd sigh. 'You can get down now.' Off he'd shoot and I'd sit there with my lone glass of wine wondering why they didn't clone Cary Grant when they had the chance.

Bzzzztt. Now I have a text.

It's all go here! Good thing Joe's at work – we wouldn't have a minute to ourselves.

I press the appropriate button and three words appear.

'Alright, I'll come.'

My jaw drops and I stumble back on to the bed in amazement.

The text is from my brother.

What could have changed his mind? A night spent poring over old photographs? The decision to go back and win Cinzia anew? The possibility that The Love Academy's rave reviews are for real?

'I called Tonio,' Kier explains when I call and ask. 'He's out of town for the first three days but when he gets back he needs my help with something.'

'Okay.' I decide not to probe further, I don't want him questioning his decision.

'And, you know, it would be good to see him.'

I smile delightedly to myself – see! There is some good to come out of this.

'And work have been encouraging me to take some time off . . .'

'Good, good . . . Well, don't forget—'

'To shave. I know. I will. I'm getting a haircut too.'

Gosh. This is really positive. He's been hiding beneath that bushy balaclava for way too long.

'Um, we need to pack something to wear to a wedding,' I wince slightly at the request.

'I've got the suit I wore to Dad's seventieth.'

'Perfect!' I cheer. 'Anything I should know to bring?'

'As little as possible. Venice is not the place to be manoeuvring great steamer cases.'

'Gotcha.'

'And comfortable shoes. You'll be doing a lot of walking.'

I hoik out the two most frivolous heels and replace them with flip-flops. 'I'm all set!'

I run through the meeting arrangements with him and then, still slightly breathless, thank him for changing his mind.

'I can't make any promises about my mood when we get there.'

'I understand,' I'm quick to soothe him. 'I'm just so grateful that you're coming and who knows, we might even have a good time.'

'Don't push it.'

'No, no, right. Well. See you tomorrow.'

I click off the phone and do a little dance – so happy I treat myself to an acapella rendition of 'O Sole Mio'!

Wow. Suddenly it feels like big change is possible. And not just for Kier. What if this is a life-changing phase for me too? I feel a stirring occurring. For too long I've been tolerating disappointment every day. It's become the norm for me to think, 'Is this it?' and answer with a simple, 'Yup, sorry 'bout that. Nothing I can do.' But what if The Love Academy can do something? I may be going undercover as a single person but perhaps there's a tip or two I can pick up about reigniting the passion in an existing relationship? Deep down I want Joe and I to work. I want him to be The One. The alternative, any alternative feels like way too much upheaval. And I already know from one break-up how much I'd miss him. I miss him right now. I look at the clock. Just two hours to go.

Perhaps I'll watch *Summertime* – my favourite Venice-set movie – while I do my nails.

At 8.25 p.m. no less, I hear the key in the door and in he walks with my favourite Thai takeaway, kissing me before he even sets it down and I think, 'He's come home. To me!'

By the time we head for bed I feel in a cosy cocoon of domesticity. I watch him strip off, revealing his wonderfully imperfect body and when he scoots beneath the duvet, I eagerly spoon up beside him. I take back everything I said before – I was just being over-sensitive and hysterical, like he says. This feels so right!

Lying there, gently grooving my nails along his scalp, he sighs the words, 'Love you.' And then turns around to give me a kiss.

'Love you too,' I breathe, resting my head on his chest, ready to surrender to synchronised slumber when he unexpectedly disengages himself.

'You okay?' I enquire.

'Mmm hmm, I'm just a bit hot.' And with that he retreats over to his side of the bed.

It's absurd to feel crestfallen, but I do. The night before I leave for The Love Academy I don't even want the whisper of a suspicion that I might not be in the perfect relationship for me.

He didn't want to hold you.

It's not personal, he's just hot, I tell myself.

Don't you want a man who'd be prepared to raise his temperature a few degrees just to be close to you? Don't you want a man who'd sneak a love note into your suitcase? Don't you want a man who always puts you first? Don't you want a man who treats you as lovingly as you treat him?

I pull the pillow snug around my ears, but it's not so easy to muffle a voice that's inside your own head.

# 3

*'Missing you could turn from pain to pleasure if I knew you were missing me too.' – Unknown*

'So, see you in nine days then . . .' I pretend to be blasé as we approach Victoria Station.

The prospect of leaving Joe always makes me feel queasy-uneasy. I have this craving for a moment of intense significance before we part – not to be morbid but just in case we never ever see each other again – but he's admitted to me that he generally doesn't register that I'm gone until the next day.

'I'm not going to miss you while you're still here, am I?' he reasoned last time I complained that he was all too unphased the night before a trip.

I asked him if next time he could hold me a little longer, a little tighter, just for effect but I'm guessing he's forgotten that conversation because he's pulled up to the curb but failed to unclick his seatbelt.

I look across the street to the station entrance and then back at Joe. 'Couldn't you get a little bit closer?'

'Well then I'd have to loop back on myself to be headed in the right direction for work.'

Oh yes, far easier for me to make a kamikaze dash across

a main road lumbering an unwieldy and over-stuffed suitcase. Did I mention it's also started to rain?

I sigh, biting back my snipes – I don't want our parting words to be terse and unpleasant. Instead I force a smile and reach to give his hair an affectionate ruffle.

'Babe!' he halts my hand.

'What?'

'I'm going straight to the office.'

I blink back at him. I can't even touch his hair now? My mouth opens but before I can speak his phone rings. He answers it. I sit motionless, feeling weightless and distant. This is pitiful. I wasn't expecting him to furnish me with a solid silver St Christopher and a set of love notes, one to be opened every hour we're apart, but a proper hug would have been nice.

'Yes, yes, hold on a second Keith, I'm just dropping the Kirster off,' he clasps his hands over the phone, leans over and pecks me on the lips. 'Have a good time sweetie.'

Still I sit there. 'Is that it?' I ask, addressing not just him but the universe in general.

'What?' he switches back to me.

Again all I can do is stare blankly back at him.

'Is there something else?' he enquires impatiently, holding the phone up to my face as if I might have forgotten that he had made another conversation his priority.

I step out of the car, open the back door, tug out my suitcase and as it hits the pavement with a thud, say out loud, '*I do hope so*.'

For a good five minutes after he's driven off, I stand on the roadside, mildly stunned. He couldn't pull it together to focus exclusively on me for five minutes? That's all I needed. In fact three would have been enough. One if he'd have cupped my chin and said, 'I'm going to miss you so much! Please don't run off with the man that binds the raffia on the Chianti bottles!' That way I would have left him with a spring to my step and a plumped-up heart but now I feel utterly deflated. There is simply no denying the lack of passion between us. If we carry on like this we won't even be doing the basic things required to make a baby in the first place.

Squaring my shoulders, I prepare to cross the road. I have to shake this malaise for Kier's sake and thus allot myself only the time it takes to reach the platform to indulge these pitiful feelings. I'm going to have to learn to compartmentalise my emotions, especially considering the nine days ahead. Besides which, I can fret and over-analyse all I want but the truth is that one 'hey honey' phone message from Joe could still totally turn things around for me – I really don't want to be mad at him, I want to be in love!

I stop suddenly and take out my phone, illogically optimistic. Nothing. He's probably still yakking to Keith. I'm tempted to call him but I'd basically be ringing to say, 'Love me better! Love me more! Love me the way I want to be loved! And then act like it was your idea!'

It's then I see two girls in WHSmith uniforms walking to work arm in arm practically holding each other up because they are so convulsed with giggles. That's who I want to be! Not the girl waiting by the phone – however mobile it might be these days. (So much for modern technology – at least when there was just the home phone you only had the second-by-second rejection when you were in the house, now you carry it with you everywhere you go.) I turn back to get another fix of the girls. What would they think of me letting the kiss-off from a boyfriend temper the excitement of going to Venice. *Venice,* for gawd's sake!

*'Stupid girl!'* Pink gets on the bandwagon taunting me.

I really must update the ringtone on my phone. But then I see that the call is from Mitzi on the celebrity desk and decide it's perfectly appropriate after all. Not that she is inherently stupid but I think her obsessive tugging at her hair in a bid to maintain her Eva Longoria flick has started to affect her brain.

'Morning Miss M, how was Dubai?' I ask as I make my way across the station concourse.

'Not bad, two Cs and a B.' She grades everything in terms of celebrity presence. 'I hear you're off to Venice?'

'En route as we speak,' I confirm, side-stepping a power-walking pinstriper.

'Right, there's a couple of things I need you to do for me while you're there.'

I take a bracing breath. For the last few months she's been trying to train us up as pay-roll paparazzi, insisting we go everywhere armed with the latest camera phone, obliging us to send the image back to the office quicker than you can say lychee martini, or onion bagel, depending on where the celeb-sighting has taken place. Every bona fide snap earns you a £10 Oasis voucher, saving the Picture Desk £50-200 a pop. So far I've earned £20 for taking 'candid' snaps of two reality stars who remembered me from when I interviewed them a few months back and begged me to take their photo outside Diesel and Jo Malone respectively, obviously hoping to get some free goodies.

And you know what, they almost deserve it for taking the pressure off some of the A-listers out there. I went on to spare Kate Winslet, Rachel Weisz and Jude Law that afternoon. Obviously I'll be getting their thank-you cards in the post any day now.

'Firstly, whenever you get the chance, hop aboard the private shuttle to the Cipriani Hotel,' Mitzi has already launched into her brief. 'It's where all the deluxe stars go – Jennifer Lopez, Gwyneth Paltrow, Harrison Ford, Georgio Armani . . .'

'Got it!' I cut in. I get the feeling she could be name-dropping all the way to the check-in desk.

'They have one of the only pools in Venice so it goes without saying that a celeb in a bikini means—'

'Yup, yup, I know the score. But are they really going to let me wander freely if I'm not a guest?'

'Just make a lunch reservation. Or dinner. Or tea, whenever you can get there.'

'I think my schedule's going to be pretty packed.'

'Mmm,' she says absently. 'How big is this piece you're doing, anyway?'

'Four pages at the mo. Depends on what I get.'

'You mean aside from herpes from all the male hos they've hired!' she hoots.

'What's the other thing you need?' I'm keen to get this conversation over with.

'Elton John.'

'Got it,' I pretend to be jotting down her bidding when in fact I'm eyeing a butter-raisin pastry. 'Sir Elton in a bikini.'

'No no no!'

'What then?' I play dumb.

She lowers her voice. 'Ruth has left me a note promising

me a bonus if we can get something on him and David at their Venice home.'

'But it wouldn't be you getting it, it would be me,' I state, somewhat plainly.

There's a short silence followed by, 'Alright, I'll split the dough with you. And I'm guessing it'll be a wedge cos she's got a bet going with Anastascia.'

'Oh god, those two,' I groan, sick of her petty competitions with the editor of *Flash!*

'Seriously,' Mitzi implores. 'I'm saving up to get a nose job so I could really use the money. Oh! Oh! And keep your eyes peeled for Patricia Arquette and Thomas Jane – they might be going back for their anniversary.'

'I didn't realise they were married.'

'This time last year. Vintage lace in a gondola, the works.'

'Is that everything?' I suddenly feel very, very tired.

'Well, obviously it goes without saying that if any celebs have attended The Love Academy . . .'

'Well, that information would be confidential.'

'Not for long when you get rooting around, eh?'

I grimace. If I wanted to feel this grubby in the workplace I'd simply offer the commuters lap dances amidst the sooty train exhaust.

'And tell that handsome brother of yours I'm still waiting for him to take me on a date!' she yelps before signing off.

I roll my eyes. 'I'm sure just as soon as his reservation comes through at Robouchon he'll be in touch.'

Here he is now at our designated meeting place, a neatly groomed vision in tan moleskin and ivory cotton. For a second it's almost like the whole Cinzia crash never happened but as I draw closer I see the transformation is only at surface level. It would seem this tendency to be at the mercy of our love lives runs in our family as I catch him scowling vitriol at a pair of teen lovebirds savouring their last precious moments together: her standing on his battered trainers, their long hair intertwining in the wind, foreheads together, eyes locked, lips alternating between sweet nothings and soul-searching kisses.

I can see Kier's objection – it seems terribly rude to flaunt such rapture when ninety per cent of the viewing public must surely be feeling some pang of envy or inadequacy. Or is that just my bitter skewing of the statistics?

I quickly poll the faces of the passers-by: some swiftly avert their eyes, others roll them, some stare longingly, others lasciviously. And then there's me, thinking tartly, Why didn't I get a goodbye like that? What exactly did I do to deserve the ejector seat of boyfriend farewells?

'Kier!' I throw my arms out with a bold exclamation, hoping to snap him from his dark thoughts like one might jolt another from their hiccups.

'Kirsty.'

His response is considerably more measured but his hug is heartfelt. I linger in his arms hoping to transfer any remaining traces of apprehension he might feel on to me, so I can later cast them into the canal. Along with my own.

'How are you feeling?' I ask, slightly concerned by his shadowy eyes as we step aboard the Gatwick Express.

'Tired,' he confirms, taking his fuzzy red seat and snoring lightly before we've even pulled out of the station. I can't help but marvel at men's ability to nod off however emotionally fraught the situation. Still, I'm glad for Kier – there's no better painkiller than sleep.

All too awake myself, I twist around so I can observe the long-haired lovers' anguished parting and then watch with amazement as they both board the train. They weren't even saying goodbye! That was just them having a 9 a.m. snog! Oh dear god. I slump down in my seat, praying they won't take the available pair opposite us.

As they walk past – phew! – I hear their accent. No mistaking it. *Italian!*

# 4

*'The gorgeous and wonderful reality of Venice is beyond the fancy of the wildest dreamer. Opium couldn't build such a place, and enchantment couldn't shadow it forth in a vision.' – Charles Dickens*

Four hours later, we touch down at Venice Marco Polo Airport. The wretched couple are still with us. I fear they'll haunt us the rest of the week but soon I realise they will be entirely indistinguishable from the hundreds of other ravenous lovers at large.

'I'm sorry,' I feel compelled to apologise to Kier as another couple attempt to devour each other in the line for Passport Control.

'There's no escaping it in the summer months,' he notes resignedly. 'You should see them at Kew on the weekend, especially in the Temple of Arethusa,' he shakes his head.

'Yes, but at least there you can turn the hose on them,' I grumble.

'We're up!'

As he nudges me forward, I get an inner twirl of nerves. The boothed guard studies my face and then my picture. It's almost as if he can sense the deception – that I am adopting a new undercover identity just as he inspects my certified one.

He mutters something to his colleague, perhaps: *What*

*insolence – daring to question the authenticity of love in Italy!* – then he looks back at me and clips, '*Il prossimo!*' beckoning the next in line.

I release a breath and walk on – my spy status intact.

After the usual tedious wait for our bags, we exit the concourse and head out along a sheltered walkway beneath a decidedly unsummery sullen sky, chased by gusts of chill air.

Only now does it truly hit home that this is no ordinary city – we must approach Venice by boat, or water taxi as my expense account allows.

There is already a queue at the jetty so I amuse myself by reading the Dos and Don'ts of the Veneziana Motoscafi:

Do not stand astride the boat and the landing stage (unless you are adept at doing the splits).
Do not smoke (unless you're angling for some action-movie combustion).
Do give your hand to the driver when stepping on to the boat.

I watch the woman before me do just that, envisioning her in white button-cuffed gloves, and decide the rule is both practical and genteel. Her husband seems less keen to hold hands with an Italian man, however.

'Here we are,' Kier nods to the next motor launch burring up beside us. It's unspeakably chic – sleek-crafted wood seemingly glossed with golden syrup, interior walls carpeted with velvety teal and seats of supple white leather. I sit back, running my hand along the stitching feeling like a movie star, even if the lighting department forgot the sun lamp.

Meanwhile, Kier is helping the polo-shirted driver heave my straining suitcase aboard. Somewhat embarrassed, I joke that I barely had enough room for the dead body, what with all my hair products and appliances but no one laughs. Hmmm. I'm mildly concerned that I've been in Italy for an entire hour and have yet to experience the infamous flirtation, but console myself that it's probably because I appear to be with Kier. No doubt the second my mock-single status is revealed I'll be overwhelmed with overtures and heart-shaped pizzas.

And we're off!

Skimming the water, the windows dribble with spray and drizzle giving me the feeling of being in an open-air car wash. After ten minutes or so I discern some land and scoot forward to take in the driver's viewpoint, but Kier tells me it's a false alarm.

'That's Murano, the glass island, not Venice.'

'The glass island . . .' I breathe, picturing dinky translucent buildings within a snow-globe dome. 'I hope I get the chance to go shopping. I'd love a set of wine goblets, you know the ones with the lacey gold band around the top?'

'They're pretty pricey,' Kier cautions. 'Glass is abundant here but not cheap.'

'Well, maybe I'll settle for a special occasion pair,' I decide as we surge onwards, already adapting to the idea of liquid roads, eagerly on the look out for my first gondola.

And then I see her – La Serenissima, as this ancient city is known. Could she spare a little serenity for we two visitors, I wonder?

Prior to our arrival I'd had visions of Kier and I slashing down the Grand Canal with Bond-chase fervour, his former cares being whipped away with the wind, but regulations restrict us to a dirge-like two miles per hour, slowing the world to the pace of an aged scene-shifter. Entranced as I am by the wading ochre façades with their prickly water-level borders of barnacles, mussels and limpets, my gaze returns repeatedly to Kier's angsty face. He looks at once leaden and empty, as if everything except his outer casing is indeed being held captive somewhere in this city. But where?

As we burble down a deserted waterway festooned not with carnival streamers but sodden laundry, I try to peer into the homes looking for some clue, but the wrought-iron doors seem ornately impenetrable and the window shutters deviously hooked. Despite this, there is a certain empathy to the architecture – buildings I would ordinarily have described as majestic show-stoppers assume a dejected, forgotten air, as if subduing their flamboyance in respect for his loss.

Suddenly I feel actively cruel – am I really putting him through all this just to satisfy a petulant editor or, worse yet, some need in me to feel like I can make everything alright for him? They say it's not over until the fat lady sings and one might presume Italy to be rife with large opera dames but is that reason enough to bring him here? Before I become entirely overwhelmed with guilt and defeatism I make a decision – if I can't put my faith in the justice of the world to bring him the love he deserves, I have to start believing in The Love Academy.

No sooner do I make this decision than our driver throws the boat into reverse and we retreat down an alley so narrow even our suitcases suck in their bellies. Now he decides to floor it?! The driver sloshes to a halt beside a small wooden platform and bids us disembark. Kier does so without hesitation but I'm not so sure the platform can support the two of us *and* our luggage. I try to use the delaying tactic of paying but the driver motions agitatedly to me to climb up and pull on a tasselled cord hanging down the side of the masonry. I do so nervously, half-fearing I may trigger the trap door and be plunged into the lagoon.

Instead, what I now see are two giant black panelled doors drawing back to reveal a sumptuous salon – marble floors overlaid with vast Persian rugs; ovals of jewel-bright stained glass; intricate antique lanterns on staffs standing sentry either side of an imposing double staircase; a hand-painted ceiling of pale gold and misty blue hexagons high above us . . . I want to pause and gawp and take in every pillar and portrait from here to the garden at the far end of this most dramatic entrance hall but *now* the driver wants paying. One hundred euros. Apparently the fare is calculated on a 'per minute' basis. No wonder they drive so slowly. Next time I'll stick my swishing feet out the back and save myself fifty quid.

'Welcome to The Love Academy!' a petite brunette with a soft gamine haircut greets us. 'You are Kier and Kirsty Bailey, yes? My name is Sabrina.'

I'm trying to be polite and return her sweet smile but I still have awe-jaw as I take my first steps inside a genuine Venetian palazzo.

I can't believe a place so grand can feel so instantly homely – the sensation actually makes me shiver.

'You must be cold,' Sabrina tuts the clouds as she drags the doors closed behind us. 'Would you like me to arrange for a cappuccino to be brought to your room?'

My eyes light up. 'Do you do hot chocolate?'

'Of course,' she smiles comfortingly. 'And for you, Signor Bailey?'

'Nothing,' he replies. What use is sustenance to a husk of a man? 'I'm going for a walk.'

'But—' I begin.

'I know, the welcome reception is in an hour. I'll be back.'

'Don't you want to see the room?' I sound plaintive as I address his back. How can he walk out on this bliss? Doesn't he at least want to look around?

'No need,' he gives me a dark look as he stalls by the reception desk. 'I've been here before.'

# 5

*'When I went to Venice my dream became my address.' – Marcel Proust*

Pomegranate pink wallpaper of lavishly embossed satin and a terrazzo floor polished to a slippable sheen, *that* I was expecting, but even by Venetian standards the chandelier taking centre-stage in Room 16 is a confection of the absurd – a twiddly-fiddly ice-sculpture tipped with lurid colours in tints of popsicle red and electric blue. I peer closer, never having seen anything quite so disturbingly gaudy – nubbed glass hoops hang from the extended arms like calamari bangles and garish glossy flowers last seen in the hat of a circus clown spring forth. All this and the ceiling sconce is seemingly suspended in mid-air courtesy of a *trompe l'œil* skyscape which, in turn, is trimmed with ever more elaborate painted borders giving the illusion of gilded wood inset with floral plaques and chunkily carved rosettes. I expected a little over-stimulation in the Doge's Palace, but in our own room?

I walk over to the edge of the creaky antique bed and rest on the tapestry-like counterpane as I take my first sip of Italian hot chocolate – the sensation is bitter-sweet with such a dense yet powdery aftertaste I have to alternate each sip with a slug from my water bottle, now lukewarm from the journey. Sliding myself back to match the headboard to my spine, I am amazed at the power of this room to invoke notions of illustrious assignations. I can quite imagine Casanova loitering on the street below and twice I have leaned out of the nearest window just to check I'm not keeping him waiting. I wonder what Joe would make of this place? Not that I really need to wonder at all, I know he would loathe it – we once stayed at an exclusive Italian-style guesthouse atop Richmond Hill for a friend's wedding and all the lavish flourishes that made me swoon were reviled by him as too busy and cluttered – the excess of fabric in the canopied bed made him feel claustrophobic; the scent of the designer candles was too sickly; the claw-foot tub beside the leaded window with a view wending down to the Thames was an impractical inconvenience. 'What do you mean there's no shower? How am I going to fit in that thing?'

I suppose baroque is the antithesis of straight-man style; they do seem to like their simple lines and minimalist monochrome, don't they? Few real men relish gold accents. All the same, I can't help but wonder what life would be like with one who did. For starters, I bet he would wear only strokable fabrics such as velvet and cashmere. His hair would have an untameable curl, his lips would taste of Shiraz and he'd always be happy to linger in bed, especially one such as this, no doubt tracing your outline with a peacock feather as he gazed upon you with wonder at all that had gone before. And all that lay ahead . . .

There's a knock at the door. My heart pounds. Is this how it begins? First the room seduces you and then a masked man with lacey cuffs! Oh. It's Sabrina with our registration forms. I can barely hide my disappointment. Even though she is shortly followed by a young man with a platter of nibbles in lieu of a formal dinner.

'Everything is to your liking?' she enquires perkily.

'Yes, yes, it's wonderful!' I hurry, eager to get back to my fantasy, now with the added bonus of snacks.

'Any questions?'

'Well, just one,' I concede, recalling Kier's parting comment. 'Has this always been the home of The Love Academy?'

'Actually no. We have been at this address just three months.'

'Oh, so this place . . . ?'

'It was, still is, a hotel,' she replies. 'The Palazzo Abadessa.'

'Palazzo Abadessa . . .' I repeat.

'The owner of the hotel, Signora Maria Luisa is a very special lady. You will meet her tonight at the welcome reception.' Sabrina smiles knowingly before she moves on.

I return to my nest of propped pillows and try to decide if the name is genuinely familiar, as in a place Kier has mentioned in the past or whether it simply has a pleasing ring to it. I suppose I'll find out soon enough, he's due back in twenty minutes. In theory. Of course it's perfectly possible he won't come back at all. He set off at quite a pace. I wonder where he is right now – chasing down backstreets trying to outrun old ghosts or standing, paralysed, beneath Cinzia's balcony?

I hold the registration form up in front of me and try to concentrate on the formalities of the situation.

Page one is a print out of all the details I have already given, including two lies – one that I am single and two that I write children's stories for a living. Not too much of a stretch seeing as so many of my magazine articles are shamefully immature. (See '*Match the hunks to the trunks!*' in our August beach issue.) My low-brow status seems all the more accentuated in a city with such a prestigious literary legacy – there's Lord Byron proclaiming:

> I saw from out the wave of her structures rise
> As from the stroke of the enchanter's wand

Whereas I'm busily noting down how the primary-coloured barber's poles of the canals resemble props from *It's A Knockout*.

While picking at the nibbles, I review the second sheet expecting it to be some kind of questionnaire – I've attended a few of these self-help workshops in the past and they typically request a statement summing up exactly what you are hoping to get out of the course, ostensibly so the organisers can cater to the specific needs of the group. In this case there is nothing more than a confidentiality agreement demanding I swear on my best pasta recipe that I won't reveal the details of my experiences over the next nine days to anyone outside of The Love Academy. I sign it with a flourish, bringing my lie quota up to three.

It's a good thing we're not in Sicily. Or Rome for that matter. I'm not religious but it just wouldn't seem right fibbing so close to the Vatican.

Once again I find myself leaning out of the shuttered window, the most wistful of poses, even if I am overlooking a graffitied wall and a noisy tour group. Trying to bypass the gaggle of Kagouls is an older woman in a cloche hat and grey cape-coat. She glances up at me but I can't quite read the expression on her face. What *do* the locals make of The Love Academy, I wonder? To her, am I just another gullible tourist falling for the line that Italians do it better? Perhaps she's all for it because it's bringing new employment to the community? I wish I'd seen the original recruitment ad for this place: *Lovers Wanted! Must be able to convince hopeless cynics that romance is real.*

I look at my watch and then make my way to the door as if Kier might simply be standing on the other side, waiting for me to let him in. He's not. I sigh as I slump against the doorframe and let my eyes wander the upstairs salon – it's just as splendid as the one below with damask chaises and heavy picture books displayed on long lacquered-gold tables. In seconds my inquisitive nature has me tip-toeing around the uneven floor, pausing beside each door hoping I might eavesdrop some revelatory comment, which would be lost on me even if I did, since the truly scandalous stuff would be delivered in Italian. I make a mental note to keep my tape recorder on me at all times so that if I catch anything secret-sounding I can get Kier to translate for me later.

Now this looks an intriguing nook, I peer into the darkness, startling myself by setting off the automatic light as I step into an ante-room. Three more bedrooms, it would seem, one marked PRIVATO. Could this be the room that contains all the secrets of The Love Academy? If I jimmied the lock would I find a big pop-up sign declaring, 'Yup, it's all a big con! This is the world's most stylish escort agency!'

I stare at the dark wooden door as if waiting for my X-ray vision to kick in. It doesn't sound like there is anyone inside. I take a step closer. It surely is absurd to be snooping at such an early stage in the game, if I'm caught now I'll have no story to tell at all. So why is my hand reaching for the door handle?

'What are you doing?'

I spin around, my right hand gripping at where my heart just leapt from my chest.

'You're back!' The element of surprise in my voice is all too apparent as I take in my brother's rain-dappled form.

'Shouldn't we be getting ready?' He's clearly in no mood to play lookout to my Miss Marple.

'Yes, yes,' I nod, still jittery as we retreat into our satin sanctuary.

As I watch him pull a change of clothes from his suitcase, a variety of sentences fidget on my lips, but I can't seem to find the one that best conveys, 'I'm sorry I brought you here, is there anything I can do to make this situation better and by the way, where exactly have you just been?' So instead I simply say, 'There's a registration form for you to sign. And help yourself to the food platter.'

Again, just a nod.

I feel so awkward, so ineffectual.

'Listen, if you want to leave—'

'Yes?' he looks at me, challengingly.

'Well obviously I don't want you to—'

'And it would get you into a lot of trouble at work if I did . . .' he cocks an eyebrow.

'That doesn't matter,' I try to sound laissez-faire about the £2,500 I would surely have to reimburse the magazine for his airfare and course fees, not to mention the botched brother-sister angle.

'I'll stay until Tonio returns,' he concedes. 'But after that I can't make any promises.'

'That's fine,' I shrug lightly, trying not to make any sudden movements for fear of sending him back out into the night. I'll take what I can get for the moment. With any luck this place will be a full-on cult experience and we'll both be drugged and slavishly obedient before bedtime.

*

We take turns in the outsize bathroom, neither of us making the kind of effort I imagine is taking place in neighbouring rooms – positive chemical labs of pomades and perfumes, I'll warrant. I can see them now, re-doing ties with increasingly clammy hands, hoiking cleavages, balancing precariously on the edge of the bathtub in order to try and get a full-length gander at themselves. If I listen closely enough I'm sure I can hear the buzz of a nose-hair clipper.

I inspect my travel-kinked hair and scold myself for not making more of an effort – too much time wasted concerning myself with Kier's fractious vibe, not enough time spent with the castanet clicking of my hair-straighteners.

'Your brother's love life is not your problem!' I try to ram home Joe's latest mantra to me but then catch myself – Joe who? There is no Joe. For the intents and purposes of this article I am single. Back in the game and at a point in my life where I need something surprising and hopeful to happen in my heart or I might simply expire.

Wow. How nervous must the genuinely lovelorn guests be right now? Could their new lover really be awaiting their pleasure downstairs in the reception room? Are they mere minutes away from an arrow through the heart? Though I've had quite enough years being single I can't help but envy them this anticipatory state tonight, for as lonesome as it can be without a partner, there's still the hope that all your romantic dreams might be fulfilled whereas when you're settled in a relationship there are so many ideals you have to let go of.

Or do you? Would I even be feeling that way if I was with the right person? Not that I'm sure my dream man exists in the twenty-first century. My ideal is more dinner-dance than lap dance; more hand-written letters from the plains of Africa than an abbreviated text from the local pub; more black-and-white movie fantasy than is ever likely to become my technicolour reality. Of course The Love Academy claims I can have all that I wish for. And more. And soon.

I set my toothbrush back in the glass and bite on my now minty lip. I can't believe I'm even buying into this enough to have this thought but what if he's here in the building – the man with whom there is no doubt? The one who I can just as easily picture swaying to Sinatra as see swinging our future offspring (little Max and Millie) high above his head?

And if he is downstairs, equally keen to meet me, am I really going to show up looking like this? The mirror reflects back a stricken face but it's 7.54 p.m. and there's no time for magical transformations now. All I can do is slick on my twinkliest lipgloss and reach for my trusty slinky wrap dress and highest heels. I wince as the latticed bronze nips at my toes. It's all about bravado now, starting with Kier. I accost him with forced jollity: 'So,' I cheer. 'Are you ready to meet the future Mrs Bailey?'

'Are you ready to cheat on Joe with a gigolo?' he snips back.

I feel smited. And not a little guilty. How did this ever seem like a good idea?

I sigh to myself as I head for the door no longer caring whether or not Kier is following behind – I'm done with being *Hot!*'s guinea pig. When I get back I'm going to ask for a transfer to the interiors magazine down the hall. Oh to be researching Murano glass right now instead of toying so carelessly with human hearts.

# 6

*'Venice is like eating an entire box of chocolate liqueurs in one go.' – Truman Capote*

As we approach the cranberry-carpeted double staircase, Kier instinctively goes left, as I go right. The segregation seems almost appropriate: men and women, different mind-sets, different needs, totally different ideas about the behaviour that demonstrates true love.

Regrouping at the bottom Kier barely manages a grimace in my direction. It's hard to imagine how easily we used to be able to trigger a laugh in each other – all that shared history gave us so much material for amusement, now a smile seems a far-fetched notion.

'You are first to arrive!' Sabrina commends us, directing us not to the lavish ballroom I had imagined, but beyond the reception area to the garden.

I'm tentative as I step out into the courtyard but the sky has cleared and brightened, highlighting each dew-bejewelled blade of grass. Kier is straight on to the lawn, dampening his trouser cuffs as he makes like a jungle explorer, foraging into the vines draping the tall surrounding walls. Fearful of sludging my shoes, I stick to the brick pathway encircling the central trees and pause to admire the elegant statuettes and abundance of bushy hydrangeas with petals like faded confetti.

'This is so beautiful!' I gush suddenly feeling very girlish. 'I didn't expect this at all!'

'Well, Venice is hardly known for its greenery.' He tramps back in my direction.

'I know!' I retaliate – is he still giving me tone? 'But you worked here as a gardener so I presumed there must be a bud or two to tend to. Are these fan palms?' I ruffle the whiskery bark before me.

He nods.

'And nasturtiums?' I address the lipstick pink blooms at the base of the trunk.

'Petunias. See how their petals are shaped like an old gramophone speaker?'

'Oh yes,' I nod, relieved that we seem to have found a subject he's willing to communicate on.

He even initiates a sentence: 'This is actually one of the stops on the *Secret Gardens of Venice* walking tour.'

'How enigmatic,' I comment.

'That's the nature of this city,' he notes, face clouding over. 'So much hiding behind high walls . . .'

Uh oh, there he goes, retreating again. Gotta keep things breezy! 'Perhaps you could show me where you used to work tomorrow, if we have time?' I suggest.

'Perhaps.'

I look at my feet wondering if it's time to get my jutting bunion seen to and then look back at him. 'Is it far from here, your old workplace?'

'No more than fifteen minutes walk,' he shrugs.

'Oh, that's great,' I enthuse. 'I'm sure we'll be able to sneak off at some point.'

Silence.

I can't believe I'm suffering stilted cocktail small talk with my own brother. Suddenly total strangers seem an inviting prospect, besides which I could be blocking the new love of his life. I need to move on, preferably trading places with an eligible woman. The courtyard bar is now bustling with prospects so I lure Kier back suggesting we grab a glass of Prosecco. As he reaches for a pair of slim flutes, I touch the arm of a passing temptress.

'That dress is absolutely stunning,' I coo, admiring her crimson satin sheath.

'Oh, you have no idea the trouble it's caused me!' she's instantly in a huddle with me. 'I chose red because I thought it would make me stand out but then I get here and discover I'm a perfect match for the wallpaper!' She re-enacts a look of horror which I duly mirror. 'I mean, who's going to love a disembodied head!'

I laugh out loud, delighted to have happened upon someone with an instantly discernible personality and, if I'm not mistaken, an American accent.

'You can imagine my relief when they decided to have the reception al fresco!' she continues.

'And of course green is opposite to red on the colour spectrum so you're totally popping!' I tell her.

She looks delighted then sighs as her eyes rove the garden, 'All I need is my *Principe* Charming to appear . . .'

'Seen anything you like?' I ask, as if we're shopping for clothes.

She gives a non-committal shrug. 'Nothing to get me reaching for the old/new/blue just yet.'

'What do you think of the palazzo?' I ask. Seeing as she's from the States, I expect her to go into raptures about how wonderfully ancient and authentic it is but instead she scrunches up her nose and whispers, 'Kind of creepy, isn't it?'

'Really? You think so?' I'm shocked.

'Did you see the porcelain dolls lined up on the chaise upstairs?' she shudders.

'I didn't mind them,' I reply. 'I mean, if they were ventriloquist dummies then I'd probably be checked-in somewhere else by now . . .'

'Oh, I wish I was staying at the Broccato,' she gives an exaggerated pout.

'Oh no you don't,' my brother chides, entering the conversation a little more brusquely than might be considered polite.

'Yes I do,' she counters, looking him up and down, wondering what business it is of his. 'It's meant to be by far the most sumptuous hotel in Venice.'

'It's a myth. The place is shabby and oppressive with hospital-smell corridors and an apoplectic duty manager.'

We both blink at him.

'Do you mean epileptic?' She leans in, suddenly fascinated.

'No. Angry. Uncontrollably so. *Threateningly* so.'

'What happened?' we both want to know.

'I don't want to talk about it,' he takes a glug of his drink.

'Oh you gotta say!' she urges, agog.

He hesitates for a moment then blurts, 'They call themselves a luxury hotel and charge seven hundred euros for a room with stained carpets and besmirched upholstery and black scuff marks on the walls and when you complain they tell you in the most patronising tone, "We're an old hotel, sir," as if you simply don't understand the history of the place and when you retort that these are twenty-first century marks and present-day neglect they tell you that all busy hotels are the same and then when you take photographs of the tatty paint and the abandoned ladder in the corridor because this really wasn't what you had in mind for your month's wages, the duty manager threatens to sue you and has a red-faced hissy-fit in front of the assembled lobby, all of whom, at this point are wishing they hadn't fallen for the hype and stayed instead at the Gritti Palace.'

'Wow,' I gulp.

'So, are you saying the Gritti Palace is better?' she asks, conspiratorially.

Kier snorts like a disgruntled donkey and excuses himself. Apparently these two are not a match made in Abercrombie & Kent.

'Who *is* that guy?' she asks as she watches him march over to the bar for a refill.

'That would be my brother, Kier,' I sigh, hoping it is not his intention to offend every woman in the room. 'I'm Kirsty by the way.'

'Tiffany Chase from Miami, Florida. Oooh, chocolate,' she's happy again as a silver tray of shiny brown baubles stalls beside us. 'What's in them?'

'These are the liqueur chocolates,' the waitress informs us. 'Particular to Italy we have limoncello, grappa and moscato inside.'

'Excellent, now we can get twice as drunk!' I cheer as I pop a random selection into my mouth, chasing it down with a slurp of Prosecco.

'It is my theory that they have aphrodisiac properties,' the waitress tries to tempt Tiffany but she's resolute.

'I can't have them,' she retreats. 'It's part of my detox. No alcohol, no wheat, no dairy. Are these ones plain dark chocolate?' She points to some coin-size discs on another passing tray.

I look around for the hidden cameras. She's got to be kidding.

'You're detoxing in Italy?' I feel the need to re-state and clarify. 'You realise that means no Valpolicella or Chianti or ice-chilled Soave? No linguine, no gnocchi, no pizza all crispy and charred from a wood-fired oven?'

She shakes her head.

'No mozzarella, no ricotta, no parmesan!' I feel myself gathering momentum as I move on to the desserts: 'No tiramisu, no panna cotta, *no gelato*!' I'm now quite shrill.

She shrugs, seemingly unfazed.

'Wouldn't it make more sense to detox somewhere where the food is bad?'

Before she can reply a cute young wine waiter cuts in offering us a top-up on the Prosecco.

'Do you have any champagne?' Tiffany enquires, quickly countering my bemused look with a glib, 'Well, I can give up all alcohol but that.'

'Actually I think Prosecco is pretty much the same thing,' I advise her, 'they just can't call it that because it's not from the Champagne region of France.'

The waiter awaits her response, on pins and needles as if he's waiting for permission to bestow a personally chosen gift upon her.

'No,' she stands strong, 'I only like champagne.'

I can't help but wonder if she's as particular about men as she is about her diet? No bakers, no milkman, no sommeliers?

Perhaps she'd make an exception for this wine steward? He has just promised to summon champagne exclusively for her.

'He was rather handsome,' I comment as he scoots off on his mission. 'Very eager to please . . .'

'Oh no, I don't do waiters!' she looks scandalised, as do I by what seems a positively sacrilegious declaration in Italy.

'You know it's not just a temporary job to tide them over until something better comes along, here it's considered a valid career.'

'Next you'll be suggesting I date a gondolier,' she scoffs.

'Well, it's funny you should mention that but on the way over my brother was explaining that they're actually the richest men in Venice. They earn more than all the lawyers and businessmen in town!'

'Really?' Now that has her eyes lighting up.

'It's true,' a deep Italian voice intones. 'They have big wallets, but small brains.'

We turn to find a man in a white moulded mask and black cape. For a second I flash to *Phantom of the Opera* and wonder what scars lie beneath, but then I realise he's not the only masked figure to have infiltrated our group – I spy jester-type affairs dangling little silver bells, pretty filigree numbers twinkling Swarovski crystals, gilded kitty designs and several featuring the traditional hooked proboscis. We must number at least forty now with these new arrivals. Though we're down a man in terms of Kier – nowhere to be seen.

'I thought the Carnival was in February,' Tiffany frowns, recoiling from a design with a disturbing resemblance to one of those creepy S&M style wrestling masks.

'Are we supposed to be wearing one?' I ask the Phantom, thinking I'd probably go for feathers and sequins. In red and gold. Maybe with a stick.

He shakes his head. 'Only the Amores.'

'The Amores?' I repeat, intrigued. 'You mean . . . ?'

He nods.

So these masked men and women are our matches for the week? Talk about keeping us guessing!

'The Love Academy likes to see who is naturally drawn to whom, without the distraction of the physical, at least initially,' he continues.

Well, that would explain why all of them are sporting capes in lieu of traditional costume – no chance of falling for a woman's hoiked cleavage or a man's satin-clad buttocks. I make a few mental notes with regard to the article – not least that this is something of a departure in terms of typical escort agency practice where surely all choices are based upon looks?

Eyeing the Phantom, I have to confess there is something rather sexy about not knowing the form or features of these people. It's that secrecy motif again. And the possibility that as you remove the mask you could reveal the face you've dreamed of your whole life . . .

I want to mingle some more to maximise the thrill but Tiffany's got old Phantom-face back on the subject of the gondoliers and I find myself lingering as we learn that there are only four hundred registered in Venice and the number of licences is limited, typically passed down from generation to generation.

'Do you know any personally?' Tiffany enquires, seemingly unconcerned that she might be ruining her chances with this potential Amore.

'Oh yes, they are fine to eat pizza with or to go to the casino or the disco but for conversation . . .' He shakes his head. 'You can't speak something important about the life, about the marriage, about the growth of a person inside . . .'

As I'm thinking how deep this fellow seems, Tiffany goes the other way.

'How much are their gondolas worth?'

I have to imagine that under his mask this man is raising an eyebrow or two. She hasn't asked one question about him.

'Well,' he replies patiently. 'They are all handcrafted locally, so about twenty thousand euros.'

'Hmmm. I suppose, seeing as they are so traditional, they only marry fellow Venetians?'

'On the contrary, they mostly have to look to foreigners for dates – the last man a Venetian father wants his daughter to be dating is a gondolier.'

'Oh that wouldn't be a problem for me,' Tiffany chirrups. 'I haven't spoken to my father in twenty years.'

As we're talking I notice Tiffany's hand repeatedly stealing to the seconded plate of dark chocolate discs – one for her mouth, one for her handbag, one for her mouth, one for her handbag . . .

Apparently I'm not the only one who clocks this.

'They say chocolate is a substitute for love,' a pint-sized forty-something smarms close, his bare head barely coming level with Tiffany's shoulder. 'I'm Melvin.'

She assesses what little there is of him – from stacked shoes to moist-dough complexion – and then reaches for another chocolate, making her preference abundantly clear.

He turns his attentions to me. Doesn't he get that he should be chatting up the ladies in the bedazzled papier mâché?

'You know, this is my second time at The Love Academy,' he tells me.

'Oh dear, didn't it work out for you the first time?' I sympathise.

'Quite the contrary,' he sleazes. 'It's because it worked so well that I'm back. If you know what I mean.'

He appears to be giving me a visual strip search so I turn away with a shudder, only to collide with the doting waiter and a silver ice bucket containing Tiffany's champagne.

'For you!' he steps past me, acting as if he's brought her the head of the dragon that has tyrannised her village for centuries.

I expect her to carry on talking as he fills her glass but instead she fawns, 'Oh you do spoil me!' deliberately touching his sleeve as she says, 'What's your name?'

'Marcello!' he beams, half-delirious at the attention.

'Marcello, you've made me very happy,' she coos, tucking a fifty euro note into his palm.

'No, no!' he protests her extravagance.

'No, you deserve it,' she is insistent.

She may not have any intention of getting it on with the waiters but she's certainly not going to let them know that.

'*Cin-Cin!*' I make a toast, raising my glass to Tiffany, slightly disappointed, but not surprised, to find that the Phantom has now moved on. 'Here's to love in Italy! *Oop!*' I give an over-zealous chink, slopping blonde bubbles all down my hand on account of the pair of human pincers upon my rear. '*Melvin*!' I exclaim, switching round to chastise him further, but he has already burrowed into the crowd.

I tsk as I shake my hand free of dribbles.

'Here, I have a tissue,' Tiffany sets down her glass to rummage in her purse. 'I tell you if I get matched with that little pervert I'm throwing myself in the canal.'

'Might be the best way to meet a gondolier!' I tease, setting my glass beside hers so I can clean up. 'But he wasn't wearing a mask so I think we're safe.'

'Safe but not spared – his is a face that could benefit from a mask . . .'

As we banter on, I again look around for Kier – where is he? – and when I turn back I see Tiffany's drinking my Prosecco by mistake.

I wait for the spray of disgust but instead she holds the flute up to the light and inspects it – the paler hue is a dead give-away. 'Oh, this is so much nicer than my champagne!' she enthuses, looking around for her waiter.

I don't think his eyes have left her since their last exchange because he's beside her in an instant.

'Marcello darling, can I have a glass of this?'

He looks confused. 'You want Prosecco?'

'Yes, it's divine!' she chimes.

He looks at the champagne. 'You don't want . . .'

She gives a dismissive wave of her hand. 'I love Prosecco! It's my new favourite thing!'

I smile to myself as she entwines glasses with a new mystery man, giggling as their foreheads bump. She's going to be one to watch this week.

I'm just deciding I should go looking for a shrouded figure of my very own when another non-Amore makes his approach.

'You alright?' he enquires, clearly a fellow Brit, probably in his early thirties with tufty brown hair, white linen shirt, darkest denim jeans and tan loafers – overall not an entirely dissimilar look to Joe. 'I saw the hit and run,' he says, motioning to my rear. 'You know, I think technically it was a *pizzicato*.'

'A what?'

He removes a small paperback from his jacket pocket. 'My dad got this book in the sixties, passed it on to me before I came here . . .'

'*How To Be Italian*!' I read the cover then look up at him. 'Are you telling me there's a section on bottom pinching?' I'm incredulous.

He nods, flicking through in search of the appropriate page. 'They name three specific techniques – the *pizzicato* which they describe as a quick nip with the thumb and middle finger, suggested for beginners.'

I roll my eyes. 'I very much doubt that was his first time.'

'The *vivace*,' he continues, 'which is a stronger pinch done many times in quick succession.'

'Oh no!' I wince at the mere thought.

'And the *sostenuto* which is prolonged, heavy-handed and rotating.'

We both look confused as we try to picture the move.

'They actually recommend having a small helium-filled balloon to hand to practise on!'

'Is this for real?' I peer over his shoulder at the illustration, enjoying a pleasant whiff of what I recognise to be Burberry cologne.

'It's all very tongue-in-cheek,' he confesses. 'Kept me amused on the plane ride over though.'

And you're doing a pretty good job of amusing me right now, I think to myself. He's rather nice, actually. I like the savvy look in his eyes and the stylish trim of his sideburns. I can't imagine why Tiffany is pulling faces and shaking her head so emphatically behind me. Alright so he's not one of the assigned Amores but a little genuine chemistry goes a long way, don't you think?

'You'll have to be careful not to confuse these tips with The

Love Academy manifesto!' I tell him. 'You could get yourself in a lot of trouble!'

'Isn't that the idea?' he winks cheekily, only to have the smile wiped off his face by Tiffany's frosty presence – she's stood right up in his face oozing 'why are you still here?' vibes.

'Well,' he sets down his bottle of Peroni beer. 'They'll probably be starting the matching soon and I need to pee so, see you later?'

'Yes, of course,' I wave him off before hissing, '*What?*' at Tiffany.

'Why are you wasting your time with him?' she scolds.

'Just because he wasn't dressed as some fifteenth-century Batman—'

'He's English isn't he?' She cuts in, eyes narrowed.

'Yes but—'

'You have to stay focused,' she growls. 'If English men were so wonderful you wouldn't be here in the first place.'

I open my mouth feeling I should be defending, if not my nation, at least Joe. And what of my brother?

What indeed? Where oh where *is* he?

Not wanting him to miss his match I chase back up to the room to check he's not hiding under his bed like he used to do as a kiddiwink. Nope.

Back down to the party, I move swiftly around the garden, weaving through the anticipatory guests realising just how many people I've yet to meet. One girl in particular looks more my brother's type – hair of a natural, unprocessed hue and kink, artsy sprinkling of freckles and a frock that's more running-barefoot-through-meadows than stiletto-through-the-heart – I just hope he gets to meet her.

Of course it would help if he were in the same place. I

hate to think of him alone with his misery when he could be sharing it with us.

'*No*!' I bark at Melvin aka the man with the amusement-arcade claws, sensing he's about to go for a *vivace*.

'But it felt so good before!' he protests.

'Oh gross!' I tut, stomping onwards, ignoring his cries of, 'Room three! I'll leave the door on the latch!' as I stick my head out of the garden gate into the street.

'Kier!' There he is, about to slip down the slimmest of alley-ways. 'Wait!' he doesn't turn back and his pace increases, perhaps recalling that I was the one hundred-metre sprint champ at school. 'Don't make me run in these heels!' I threaten, seconds before doing that very thing. 'Where are you going?' I call after him.

The alleyway is so narrow that attempting to pass someone practically constitutes a mugging so it takes no effort on my part to roughhouse him into the brick wall, causing the crumbling plaster to fall to the floor like crusty icing from a dry spongecake.

It's then two things happen:

1) I realise this man is not my brother
2) The package this stranger is carrying hits the paving emitting the unmistakable sound of breakage.

I leap back and then freeze, rigid with mortification.

The man looks at me, clearly hoping for some kind of explanation.

'I'm so sorry,' I suddenly come to life. 'I thought you were . . .' I halt myself. What's the point? The mistaken identity line won't glue his package back together.

He tilts his head, still strangely calm. '*Sono l'uomo sbagliato*?'

'Excuse me?'

'I am the wrong man?' he enquires.

I want to laugh out loud – *au contraire*! Now I've had the chance to fully take in his face I see he looks like the man every lovelorn girl visiting Italy might want to meet: lustrous dark hair, gleaming bronze skin hallmarked with a single beauty spot set high upon his right cheek, eyes that are the same perfect jade as the waters of the canals but instead of their milky-opal base, his sparkle clear. Never mind that his classy attire puts a person in mind of a more courteous era – I have caused the smashing of something that belongs to him but he's not yelling at me. In conclusion, he's so alluring that I've forgotten to answer his question.

He tries again. 'You have lost someone? *Perso*?'

My mouth falls open – his questions seem unnaturally profound. In a sense I have – my brother and I used to be so close . . .

'Are you unwell?' he frowns, looking increasingly concerned at my slack-jawed ways.

'I think it might be broken,' I finally form a sentence, pointing to the crumpled heap on the floor.

He gives a light shrug. 'I will simply have to make another one.'

'It was something you *made*?' I groan. 'I can't just buy a replacement?'

His mouth twists in consideration. 'I guess you can buy one from me!'

I can't understand why he's taking this so well! I look back at the package and tentatively begin, 'It sounded like glass . . .'

'*Si*,' he confirms. '*Vetro*.'

'So that would make you . . .' I want him to complete the sentence in case I'm getting carried away with Venetian clichés but instead he waits patiently for me to find the words. '. . . a glass-blower?'

'Yes.'

'And this is a . . . ?' I look at the package. '*Was* a . . .'

'*Cuore.*'

I don't get to the translation because my name is being hollered into the street: 'Signorina Kirsty!' It's Sabrina, beckoning me from the palazzo gate. 'It is time . . .' she chimes, looking somewhat intrigued by my situation.

'I'm coming!' I call back, trying to sound as casual as possible.

'You can bring your friend if you like,' she smiles mischievously.

'Oh no, no,' I bat away her suggestion.

'No?' he says, head cocked inquisitively as he tunes in to the sound of chatter and chinking glass.

'It's not exactly a normal party,' I cringe.

'I know what it is,' he says simply. 'Venice has just sixty-thousand residents. This is a very intimate city.'

'I thought it was supposed to be a city of secrets?' I challenge.

'Don't worry,' he smiles. 'Your secret is safe with me.'

I want to tell him, 'Look, I know what you're thinking but I'm really not that desperate. In fact I've got a boyfriend back home!' But then I realise I don't want to tell him that at all.

I look back; Sabrina is still waiting.

'I have to find my brother first,' I yelp.

'No need, he's right here, conversing with our gardener.'

Kier leans out the gate and gives a little wave, all the brighter for having spoken with a fellow green thumb.

'Same colour jacket,' my assailee notes, now understanding the mix-up.

A third head pops around the gate. Considerably lower down than the other two.

'If you're playing kiss-chase, can I join in?' Melvin puckers up his lips – as birdlike as George Bush's, adorned with a trace of bruschetta topping. Nice.

The man next to me coughs away his laughter. 'Of course, if you are already promised to another . . .'

I give him a remonstrative slap – oh hello! – even though there is fabric between my hand and his body, I sense his strength and tone and experience an impromptu thrill.

Maybe it wouldn't be a bad idea to have a back-up man? I think to myself. After all, I have no idea who they intend to fix me up with – there might be some Italian version of Melvin waiting in the wings.

'Come on then,' I concede, motioning towards the palazzo.

'You would like me to join you?' His eyes sparkle, as if awaiting a more formal invitation.

'I would be honoured if you would accompany me,' I try my best to be gracious. 'I'm Kirsty by the way,' I tell him as we proceed. 'Kirsty Bailey.'

'Dante Soranzo,' he responds.

'Dante?' I repeat wide-eyed. 'As in the inferno?' I get a sudden flare of foreboding and find myself stalling just before the entrance to The Love Academy.

'Well, *si*, but it could also be as in Dante Gabriel Rossetti.'

'I'm not familiar with—'

'He is one of your countrymen. A painter. A poet.' He looks up at the now dimmed sky and sighs, '"The sun was gone now; the curled moon was like a little feather fluttering far

down the gulf; and now she spoke through the still weather."'
His gaze falls to my mouth. '"Her voice was like the voice the stars had when they sang together."'

It is my turn to be slumped against a wall, quite weak from the proximity of his beautiful delivery. Is there anything more swoon-inducing than a green-eyed man with a husky Italian accent? Right now I can't imagine that there is.

'You have to try the liqueur chocolates,' I croak, as we enter. 'They're absolutely delicious.'

# 7

*'Open my heart and you will see graved inside of it "Italy".' – Robert Browning*

'Decided to do your own matchmaking, did you?' Kier eyes Dante as we assemble before a small platform swathed in white netting.

'I broke his *cuore*,' I attempt a justification of his presence.

'You broke his heart?' my brother looks astounded. '*When*?'

'What? No!' I fluster. I must have misheard him. 'It was glass. I broke something of his made of glass.'

'And this is how you choose to repay him – by making him your consort?' Kier snorts. 'Best stay away from Murano or you could find your dance card rather full.'

Again I find myself indignant in his presence. I thought he'd chilled out chatting to the gardener but apparently the prospect of potentially engaging his heart has turned him decidedly sour. The sooner we get him fixed up with that freckly femme, the better.

'*Benvenuti*! Welcome! Welcome!' Maria Luisa chants as she takes the stage.

With her waved blonde hair, sleek black dress and raised arms I totally get why my Brit pal quips, 'Look, it's *La Dolce Evita*!'

I turn around to give him a knowing smirk and see Tiffany beside him, draining another glass of Prosecco and then nonchalantly holding her glass out to be filled by her young waiter, who, it would seem, has now become her personal butler.

I quickly scan the room for Melvin, only to discover his googly eyes have already found me, so I dart my attention back to Maria Luisa.

'It is our pleasure to bring you pleasure,' she smiles graciously, with just the lightest hint of madam. 'Over the next nine days we wish your heart filled with romance, optimism and *energy*!' she enthuses. 'We want love to be a happy word again, not tragedy!' she tuts, surveying her audience. 'We know some of you are a little disillusioned, a little doubting, a lot *wanting*, *si*?'

'*Si*!' I confirm internally, alongside the audible cries.

'We make that go away,' she gives a cursory wave. 'Instead we show you the potential of real, everyday romance, the way Italians do it. No fairytales. This is true. Already you have a little hope that such a thing is possible or you would not be here. So now we build that hope into something you can touch.'

I see Dante's eyebrow raise and feel a little squirm of desire. She said *touch*!

'Many of you have asked questions about the itinerary but we do not reveal our plans for you in advance. Instead, each morning you will wake to find an envelope slid beneath your door, within you will find the personalised details for your day – this could be small group or single sex activities or one-on-one time with your Amore. We take this day-by-day approach because we want you to remain in the present, not always thinking about what comes next. This is very important. Be here with us. I think you will find we are very good company!' she beams.

I'm just casting a glance at Kier to see how he's responding when Sabrina creeps up behind Dante and asks me, 'May I just borrow your guest for a moment?'

'Of course,' I reply noticing the confidentiality agreement in her hand and quickly muttering to him: 'Please don't feel obliged. If you'd rather leave, I understand.'

He nods and follows her.

This really is a bizarre state of affairs. I wonder exactly how they assess his aptitude as an Amore? His physical charms are obvious but can they really induct a perfect stranger into The Love Academy in a matter of minutes? I mean, you'd think there'd be some kind of training or initiation, or is being Italian enough to qualify you? Perhaps it's just a given that natives know how to romance a woman within an inch of her life?

'So!' Maria Luisa claps her hands together, bringing me back into focus. 'To the matches!'

Here we go!

'Earlier this evening we observed who is drawn to whom, who was brave enough to approach another, who waited to be spoken to . . .' she winks at Freckles. 'Perhaps you have already formed an alliance?' Is she looking at me or the Brit? 'Or maybe you have assessed all your potential matches and decided none of them will put the chilli in your amatriciana,' she smiles in Tiffany's direction. 'Don't be too quick to judge!' she holds up a finger. 'We are not selling partnerships here – though of course we have had many successes – but instead we offer you *the experience of romance*.' She pauses before continuing: 'You may think you could only feel the leaping of the heart with someone of a particular physical type or personality but I am here to tell you that you are mistaken, or at best, naïve. We aim to show you some new possibilities!'

As she continues with her speech, I find her to be so confidence inspiring that I'm totally sold – to the point that I think it would be too easy to feel romantic around a looker like Dante. Maybe I need more of a challenge? Or am I just trying to convince myself of this because Sabrina has reappeared and Dante is nowhere to be seen. Not that I can blame him for leaving.

'Now Sabrina will announce the combinations.' Maria Luisa switches positions with her co-host, leaving us with an effusive cry of: 'Just remember to embrace the experience – and each other!'

As our applause subsides and the Academy's head girl steps forward there is a palpable sense of anticipation, not least because she has the power to unmask the Amores.

'As we announce your names we request that you and your partner take a seat just behind me in the garden area,' Sabrina is all business as she points to circular tables where the waiters are poised to serve coffee and petits fours. Jeez, are they trying to sober us up so soon? Don't they realise that is how British romance begins – with an excess of booze! Already I feel the rug being pulled from under me.

'Tonight is but a brief introduction,' she continues. 'Your real date begins tomorrow morning.'

Again I can't help but baulk. Isn't romance all moonlight and shadows not harsh, flaw-exposing daylight?

'*Iniziamo*,' she says as she straightens her prompt cards. 'I begin.'

Still no Dante. Ah well, it was fun while it lasted . . .

'Our first pairing is Amore Stefano and . . .' she pauses for dramatic effect, causing all the women in the room to hold their breath even though none of us have a clue who this Stefano fellow is. '. . . Signorina Megan.'

'Oh no!' I inadvertently cry out loud as Freckles makes her way through the crowd. There goes my brother's future wife.

'Anyone would think you wanted her for yourself!' the Brit gives me a quizzical look.

'Not for me, for *him*,' I discreetly tip my head in Kier's direction.

'Ahhhhh,' he nods. 'And who does he have in mind for you, I wonder?'

There's a playfulness to his tone that makes me feel suddenly shifty. What am I doing here? I have no business being matched with anyone. I already have an Amore named Joe. Suddenly I want to opt out altogether, but then I find my curiosity piqued as Sabrina tells Megan, 'You may unmask Stefano.'

She takes a hold of his enamelled beak and raises it to his hairline as he unties his cape. So embarrassed is she to be first up I can't judge whether she's squirming with delight or despair at the sight of him. I shuffle to my right to get a better look. Not a bad looking fella, a little fairer than your classic Italian prototype and certainly not as good a match as Kier would have been but these are just partners to practise on after all . . .

'Amore Marina and Signor Gerard,' Sabrina continues with her list.

Darting up on stage, Gerard is a little too eager to unclasp Marina's cape, clearly more interested in assessing her body than her face at this stage. I predict a little extra romance homework for him this week.

'Amore Roberto and Signora Cheryl.'

Another pair I have no vested interest in.

'Signorina Tiffany . . .'

Ah hah! Here we go! I turn around and mouth, 'Good luck!' to her.

'. . . we have you paired with Amore Lorenzo.'

Marcello the waiter curses animatedly under his breath as a slender figure appears from the crowd. As he raises his hands to help her with his mask she clocks his Rolex and her face lights up accordingly. I take in his poetic features – all cheekbones and sensual lips – but Tiffany continues to study his watch.

Two more matches and then Kier's up.

He manages to shoot me a final look of 'I despise you for putting me through this!' before they introduce him to 'Amore Valentina'.

'*Mamma mia*!' is how every red-blooded man in the place responds as she disrobes. With voluptuous curves and a winched-in waist, her bodice appears to echo the shape of bow-tie pasta. Her hair falls in luscious raven waves on to bare shoulders, her Bambi eyes are seductively lined, her lips provocatively crimson. In other words, total pin-up babe. Even the girls can't help but admire her, throwing their shoulders back in a vain attempt to improve their own womanly profile.

I turn to see the Brit's reaction and tease: 'Bet you're praying she's got a twin sister!'

'I can't deny it,' he grins, watching Kier awkwardly escort her to their garden seats, the only man in the room to avert his eyes from her alpine cleavage. 'Dear boy,' he sighs. 'He may never be the same again.'

I laugh along with him – let Kier complain about that! She's clearly the hottest woman in the room. He can teach those exquisitely pouty lips to pronounce 'rhododendron' and 'deciduous' and they'll have an absolute ball together!

'Signor Adam.'

'Oh, here we go!' The Brit clears his throat behind me.

So that's his name: Adam. Nice. I give him an encouraging smile.

'You sure you're not Italian?' he hangs back for just a second.

I shake my head as I nudge him on his way and clap enthusiastically as they announce his pairing with Amore Allegra.

He kisses her hand before he even goes for the mask. See that, Gerard! That's class!

Seconds later, a petite, pert brunette is unveiled. As she twirls for him I attempt to gauge his reaction with my raised brows. He gives me a look as if to say, 'Better than a poke in the eye with a gondola pole!'

She's certainly sufficiently attractive, I somewhat grudgingly concede as I take a slug of Prosecco, but is she a match for his distinctly British sense of humour?

'Signor Melvin.'

Now this name really gets everyone's attention. The matched pairs were starting to chat amongst themselves, but now everyone wants to know the identity of the unfortunate woman who has been assigned to the half-height man with the crab claws.

He looks desperately expectant. 'Yes?'

Sabrina consults her card, frowns, reshuffles the pack, shrugs and then reads, albeit in an unconvinced tone, 'Kirsty?'

What? *WHAT*?

I look around hoping to see my masked namesake heading for the stage but all eyes are on me. How can this be possible? Why do I get the runt of the litter? This is so not what the magazine had in mind.

'Wait!' Sabrina rifles through her notes.

'Try *no!*' I want to squeal. Is this my punishment for being a bogus single? Have they found out I'm undercover and hired him exclusively to torment me?

'Melvin, did you tamper with my cards?' Sabrina glares down at him.

He looks sheepish and is quick to confess, his only defence being: 'I know she's the one for me!'

I shake my head in disbelief. All these outrageously foxy Italian women and he's wasting his time on me! There really is no accounting for taste. Fortunately Maria Luisa rescues the situation with the original handwritten list and Sabrina tells Melvin that he is to be graced with the presence of an Amore named Filomena.

I want to cheer when I see her – she looks like the kind of woman who'd wear a horned helmet in an opera chorus; I know she'll be able to handle him.

Dolefully he responds, 'I'll try and give you my full attention but I can't make any promises.'

Which doesn't stop him eyeing her ample rear as they step off the stage.

As Sabrina celebrates the restored order, I give a quick assessment of the men still available to me – all I can see at a glance is some kind of wolverine type and a guy whose mask is more bedazzled than most of his female counterparts.

'Signorina Kirsty.' Sabrina summons me.

My heart starts thumping. I feel like I'm about to receive my exam results. This is ridiculous! It's not like this is for real. There's absolutely no need for me to feel so jittery and mouth-dry shy. All the same, I can't help wonder if I bolted now could I catch up with Dante and suggest we do something low-key and unmonitored? Like gluing his broken glass back together.

'We have you paired with . . .'

Enough with the drum roll! Just say it!

'Amore Dante.'

I look around. Was that just wishful thinking or did she really say his name?

'Dante?' she repeats.

I cringe to myself. She doesn't realise he's scarpered. How embarrassing! Like I need any more spotlight on me!

'I am here!' he leaps on to the stage, giving me the gentlest kiss on the cheek as he whispers, 'I apologise, I had to make a phonecall!'

Why do I immediately imagine he's calling his wife? 'Sorry, I'm going to be a bit late darling – managed to pick up a bit of work on the side. Don't wait up but *do* expect a little lipstick on my collar.'

Suddenly I don't know if I want this suspiciously elegant passer-by. Why can't I have a seedy escort like everyone else?

'You don't have a girlfriend or anyone who would mind you doing this?' I fret as we take our garden café seats.

'If I did I wouldn't be here,' he assures me, adding: 'Not all Venetians have the morals of Casanova.'

'Some have less,' Filomena mutters from an adjacent table.

Is that just a flip remark or does she know Dante personally?

Suddenly I'm so paranoid. I know that I've done nothing so far that constitutes cheating but the definitiveness of the pairing is sitting uneasily with me. Not least because, in a way, I did actually choose my Amore.

'Back in a moment!' I excuse myself, feeling the need to retreat and collect my thoughts before I lose touch with my more rational, respectable side.

I decide not to go up to the room or it'll be too big a deal for me to come down again. Instead I loiter just inside the vestibule, just out of view of everyone else. I'd like to call Joe, tell him what's going on to ease my conscience but I can't risk being overheard. And it's best I'm not gone too long – Tiffany has already slid up to Dante, presumably checking he's not the gondolier of her dreams, wrongly assigned to me. She seems to have lost all interest in Lorenzo. Was the Rolex a fake? Oh my god! I laugh out loud as I see Filomena's hand creep to Melvin's rear and embed her lacquered nails in his left buttock!

'You prefer to watch the world through a window?' Maria Luisa appears by my side, presumably wondering what I'm up to.

'Um, well, I don't know about that,' I reply, a little startled. 'I just came in search of a glass of water.'

'*Una momento*!' she catches the attention of a waiter, does a quick mime and seconds later he appears with a chilled tumbler.

'Th-thank you,' I stammer. 'I didn't mean to put you to any trouble.'

'I want my guests to have what they want,' she holds my gaze. 'You like your Amore?'

'Yes, I do,' I tell her. 'I hope it's alright that he's such a last-minute recruit.'

'Fate is a welcome guest at this palazzo,' she smiles enigmatically.

'Mmm,' is all I dare to respond. I really like Maria Luisa but her bountiful knowingness freaks me out a little. I decide the less I say, the less I will reveal.

'Perhaps you would like to return to him,' she looks at her

watch. 'Just five more minutes before we bid the Amores good-night.'

'Oh! Well! I'd better hurry then!' I leave her with an awkward wave and hurry across to where Dante has now joined Valentina and Kier.

'Everything okay?' I place a hand on my brother's shoulder as I approach their table.

He nods towards Dante. 'He's a good chap.'

'Why, thank you!' No sooner does a smile form upon my lips than he wipes it off with, 'Don't screw him over too royally.'

'What do you mean by that?' I gasp.

'He's just a plaything for your article, isn't he?' he accuses.

'Sshh!' I remonstrate, afraid he'll overhear. 'We'll talk about this later.'

'Don't frown,' Dante steps to my side and smoothes my brow. 'All is well.'

'Really?' I can't help but question the sentiment, even though it is delivered with such gentle authority.

He nods. 'All that is required of you tonight is that you allow the stars to sing you to sleep.'

As the tension in my shoulders subsides I sigh, feeling like he is kissing my eyelids with his words.

'We will meet again tomorrow morning,' he says with a gracious farewell bow.

Again my instinct is to say nothing but this time it's not in fear of revealing too much but because I simply don't want to ruin the moment.

As I watch his exiting feet on the flagstones, undisturbed by the hubbub around me, the cutting-short of the evening starts to make perfect sense: tomorrow there will be none of the awful embarrassed feeling that you said or flirted or drank too much. Instead us students will awake with the tantalising desire to know our Amore better.

Or not . . .

'Do you think we can switch?' Tiffany humphs alongside me. 'I'm not thrilled about Lorenzo.'

I'm still in a Dante-induced haze but tell her that I think Lorenzo seems perfectly lovely—

'He's broke.' She cuts me off.

'But the watch?' I frown.

'A present from ten years ago.'

'Well, this isn't really about a lifetime partnership, it's about romance, perhaps he's particularly—'

'I can't feel romantic about a carpenter,' she scoffs. 'There is nothing attractive to me about a man with sawdust in his wallet. Nothing. Oh and you'll never guess what he makes?'

'Not—'

'Yes! Gondolas!' She rolls her eyes. 'Oh the irony!'

'Are you sure he's broke? You know the Phantom said they cost about twenty-thousand euros a piece.'

'He's only an apprentice. One of those people who flit around from job to job, always reverting to entry-level pay.'

'What do you do, by the way?'

She gets a little pink. 'Well, nothing right at this very minute.'

Hence the requirement for a rich man, I suppose.

'Now, Dante looks fairly well to do . . .'

Oh no you don't! 'You know he's a glass-blower?' I blurt, keen to deter her.

'Christ! What's up with all these tradesmen?' She despairs, duly dissuaded.

I feel relief as she stomps off but I'm also a little thrown by just how possessive of Dante I felt in that moment. Surely it shouldn't matter to me who I'm paired with, this is just an experiment after all. Maybe I was just feeling protective of him seeing as I'm the one who got him into this situation. And to be fair, I wouldn't wish Tiffany on most men – look at her charging around, desperate to rustle up a professional before bedtime. She'll need to act fast – nearly everyone is headed to their rooms now, including my brother.

'I'll see you up there,' he announces gruffly in passing.

'You're welcome,' I mutter under my breath, realising he hasn't even made any grateful sounds regarding Valentina.

'Fancy a nightcap?' Adam gives me a peek of the Prosecco bottle he's stashed under his jacket.

I shake my head, not wanting to complicate things any further. 'I'm too pooped to party.'

'At least let me escort you to your room, you know, in case . . .' he looks around for Melvin.

'Actually I'm going to sit here a while,' I smile, wearily, suddenly devoid of all energy.

He nods in understanding. 'All this sexual tension can take it out of you, can't it?'

'Yes it can,' I concur.

He gives my hair the lightest rumple. 'Goodnight then.'

''Night.'

I stay out in the garden until everyone is gone, enjoying the cool air and the sensation of everything winding down. I want to cling to this feeling. This calm before the storm. Nothing bad can happen, as long as I remain here alone, perfectly still in the darkness.

When I do finally get up and walk inside I notice a familiar package jutting out of the bin under the reception desk. I can't believe Dante has abandoned one of his own creations like this! Yes it's broken but is it really bin-worthy?

I look around me – not a soul – so I reach down and pull the surprisingly weighty item from the wastebasket. As I manoeuvre it, it tinkles and crunches causing me to shush and cradle it like a baby as I steal swiftly upstairs.

Once inside our room I make straight for the light Kier has left on for me in the bathroom, lock the door behind me and set the package down on a towel upon the tile flooring. My heart is all thumpity as I start to unwrap layer upon layer of paper. As I untape the final cushion of bubble-wrap I catch my breath. It really is a glass heart. Albeit a shattered one.

Trying not to splinter myself, I re-form the major pieces. The outer layer is clear with ever deepening pinks to the core. At the most central point there seems to be some kind of squiggle or flaw. I peer closer. It looks almost like liquid lettering. Could it be Dante's signature? Perhaps he's such a master it adds to the value? My theory is ruined when I identify the first letter as an 'I'.

Grabbing my tweezers, and with Kier snoring in the other room, I work on fitting the corresponding shards together, feeling like I'm doing some kind of symbolic surgery – as futile as restoring Kier's own heart. Until . . .

'Isabella,' I breathe the name spelt out before me.

This seems terribly inauspicious for the woman concerned. Was Dante on his way to meet her, to give her his heart and I smashed it? I don't know how superstitious Venetians are but perhaps he took this as some kind of sign to abandon her and follow me instead? It's then I see a slip of paper with handwriting on.

I feel so guilty, as if I am prying but I can't stop myself

from reading it. But it's no love note, it's an invoice. For two-thousand euros.

I slide back on the tiled floor, hand clasped over my mouth. Oh my god. And to think I so cheerily offered to buy a replacement.

I sit for a while, leaning against the shower door, wondering how things managed to get so complicated so quickly and then decide I could just as easily be fretting in a comfy bed. Once I'm tucked in I decide to focus on sleep.

Let's face it, I need my rest – tomorrow I'm going on the most expensive date of my life.

# 8

*'Wherever you go, go with all your heart.'*
*– Confucius*

You've gotta love a woman who serves cake for breakfast.

Maria Luisa is looking lovingly at the three options taking centre stage on the positively resplendent buffet table – succulent plum, layered apple and marbled chocolate. Personally I like to start my day with a big dollop of sherry trifle but I suppose these will do.

As Kier helps himself to the more traditional European fare of deli meat slithers and waxy cheese and Adam reaches across me to get a boiled egg in lieu of the fry-up he really needs to absorb his bonus bottle of plonk, I notice the most unusual centrepiece – a white stone staircase, rising out of the table like a stepped wedding cake.

I peer upward. It appears to be leading to a room. I wonder if the occupant knows that when they descend they will be ankle-deep in fruit salad?

Here comes a foot now! I need only to see the signature red sole of a Christian Louboutin to know that it belongs to Tiffany.

'Oh!' she says, slightly surprised to find herself so much in the midst of things. 'None of this was here when I went to bed last night!' She reaches for a mini-box of cereal. 'Do you think they got these especially for Melvin?'

I giggle and invite her to join us, remembering too late Kier's particular aversion to her.

He watches with thinly veiled contempt as she unloads Ziploc bag after Ziploc bag on to the table, each containing twenty or so greyish-brown pills, each larger than the one before. She looks like she's setting up a stall at Glastonbury.

'Vitamins?' I say hopefully.

She nods. 'This is my Omega 3 Fish Oil and my Time Release Vitamin B-12,' she taps each pack. 'Selenium, Folic Acid, Colon Cleanser, Coral Calcium—'

'Wow. That's a lot,' I talk over her never-ending list. 'Do you think you'll have any room for actual food when you're done taking them?'

'You want some?' she jiggles a bag of horse-pills at me.

'No thanks, I feel fine.'

She makes a scoffing noise.

'What?' I ask, nonplussed.

'Well that's like saying your car is running fine because you've got the radio up so loud you can't hear the engine.'

*What?* I think to myself. 'Are you saying I'm sick but I just don't know it yet?'

She shrugs as she begins to glug down her succession of musty smelling oblongs.

'How do you feel?' I switch the attention to her.

'Terrible.' She paws at her throat. 'I think I might be getting a cold. And I've got a headache coming on. And I didn't *you know* yet this morning which is unusual because I'm very regular.'

'Oh!' I chew back a smile. Them pills are working a treat, then.

'So any luck switching Lorenzo?' I ask, giving a little wave to Adam who's passing to refresh his orange juice. I like his T-shirt.

'No,' she sighs, long-sufferingly. 'But I'm not giving up yet. He's supposed to be escorting me up the Campanile tower in St Mark's Square but I'm going to ask him to take me on a gondola ride instead. Don't they have oatmeal?' She's up on her feet now, surveying the spread.

'I don't think so. The muesli's really good though.'

She looks devastated. 'But I always have oatmeal for breakfast!'

'Try holidaying in Scotland next time,' Kier advises, clearly wishing he could spirit her to the Highlands right now.

'Is Marcello around?' she looks hopeful.

'Haven't seen him,' I shrug. 'Just a nice lady waitress and Maria Luisa.'

She sits back down, dejected and empty of plate. 'I'll just have hot water with lemon and honey.'

Did she just place her order with me?

'So what about you?' she pouts, distractedly. 'Where are you going with Dante?'

You mean, aside from the bank? I want to groan but decide to keep my monetary concerns to myself.

'I'm actually meeting him in Murano,' I chirrup. 'I got my instructions under the door this morning – it's a half-hour ride on a vaporetto and then I've got walking directions on to his studio – I feel like I'm going on a treasure hunt!'

'You mean he's not picking you up?' she sneers.

'Well, he has to work,' I say, feeling a little defensive, as if she's questioning his suitor-bility. 'You know this whole thing was rather sprung on him.'

'Mmm,' she muses. 'I suppose he's good-looking enough but aren't you curious who they had intended to fix you up with? I mean, what if they dumped some Italian count for him?'

'Well, I don't know if anyone actually got dumped,' I reason, 'there were definitely more Italians present than were matched. I think they probably allow a bit of room for manoeuvre to give chemistry a chance . . .'

'Well, I don't know what they were thinking with me because I didn't even speak to Lorenzo before they called our names.' With this she flounces off to the kitchen in search of tea, oatmeal and probably Marcello.

'That's because all the men she *did* speak to didn't want anything more to do with her!' Kier grizzles as he sets down his napkin. 'I'm going for a walk.'

'Oh wait!' I quickly swill back the last of my tea. 'I wondered if you wanted to show me your old workplace? We've got a bit of time before we have to be anywhere . . .'

'I can't right now,' he clips, softening just a tad to add, 'Maybe this evening?'

'Okay,' I sigh, watching him leave, again left wondering where he's going but feeling in no position to ask.

'Cheerful bugger, your brother,' Adam notes from the adjacent table.

'He's got a broken heart,' I explain.

'Haven't we all,' he shrugs.

'Yes, but his was inflicted by a *Venetian*!' I give him a knowing look.

'Sucker for punishment then, isn't he?'

I want to explain that Kier is here against his will but how can I without giving my game away? Again I feel a pang of guilt for bringing him on this trip. I can't even remember why it seemed a good idea any more.

'What's this?' Tiffany cuts into my regrets, bending down to retrieve something from the floor. 'Is this your brother's?' she enquires, holding up what is indeed his wallet.

I jump to my feet. 'I'd better get it to him!' I cry, still desperate to ingratiate myself to him any way possible.

'He'll be back within the hour,' she protests.

'But he might need it now!' I counter, haring out the door, determined that this time I'm going to jump the right man.

The figure ahead of me looks like Kier, walks like Kier and isn't carrying any potentially breakable packages but I want to be one hundred per cent certain before I make my move.

Oh typical!

Just as I'm about to make my move a multi-lingual tour group surges out of an alleyway obstructing my path, and my view. I nudge and writhe through them feeling as if I'm caught in a Tower of Babel twister, only breaking free in time to see him disappear into a building about a hundred metres ahead of me. Well, at least he's in a confined area, not lost in the never-ending labyrinth that is Venice.

I trot up to the appropriate entrance, catch my breath and then find myself hesitating at the door, suddenly feeling like a dreadful snoop. Maybe this isn't somewhere he wants me to know about. I step back and look for some kind of signage but the tiny inscription is in Italian and I'm none the wiser. Assessing the street I decide it is most likely residential. There's one tiny café bar further down but other than that it's all stone blocks and shutters. I listen for a moment for any giveaway noises. Silence.

Feeling torn between curiosity and nerves, I knock gently and turn the handle. It takes a moment for my eyes to adjust from the sunlight but I see I am in a small ante-room. To my left there is a closed door, much less grand than the exterior. To my right is a glassed-off office with a small cubby-hole at the counter like you might find at a ticket desk. Is this some kind of museum?

'*Buon giorno, posso aintala*?' a voice enquires

I turn and see a small wrinkled face not dissimilar to that of ET, looking up at me with gentle, milky-blue eyes. It's not the fact that this woman is in her late nineties standing no taller than four feet that throws me, but the nun's habit she's so neatly folded into.

'Oh!' I look around me for religious iconography, instantly deferential. 'Is this a convent? *Convento*?' I try a little guess-work Italian.

She babbles back to me something I can't understand but I nod and smile regardless, slowly retreating back out the door whispering, '*Scusi*!'

As I click the door closed behind me I take a breath – what is my brother doing in a nunnery? I wouldn't think men were even allowed inside. Unless they're members of the Von Trapp family hiding from the Nazis.

I try casting my mind back to *Sister Act*, attempting to recall the policy at Whoopi's convent hideout . . . Oh shame on me that all my points of reference come from movies! Hardly the most reliable of sources.

*Scccrrrp!*

There's movement from within so I decide to bolt back to the academy.

I'll just leave Kier's wallet back in the room, I decide as I sprint past an old wellhead and a recumbent cat. He'll notice it missing soon enough.

I rise up and over two bridges and then, feeling sufficiently ahead of the game, start to slow down. Will you look at me? I think as I take in my surroundings – I'm in Venice!

I stop mid-hump upon the third bridge to admire the white, marble-grid exterior of The Love Academy. There are of course many more elaborate buildings along the Grand Canal – the floridly gothic Ca' d'Oro and Moorish-arched Palazzo Bembo to name but two – but already I have a fondness for this simple structure with its slim dark ivy shutters and romantic three-window balcony. Ah, what's an Italian love story without a balcony? Hold on, is that a hand beckoning to me above the stone balustrade?

Oh lord, it's Melvin! Blowing me kisses now! I give him a terse wave back, grateful that I know where the nearest convent is, should the need arise.

Suddenly I stop in my tracks. *Could Cinzia be a nun?* Is that why their relationship was doomed to fail! Or, worse still, did she take a vow of chastity *after* they'd met?

I'm mulling assorted *Thornbirds*-like scenarios when I am confronted with the absolute antithesis of nun-dom – Valentina!

'Where is Kier?' she looks like a dejected puppy. In a canary-yellow tube dress and studded mules.

'I don't know,' I lie. 'I went looking for him to give him this,' I hold up his wallet. 'But I couldn't find him. When you see him—'

Her face lights up, 'I see him!'

As do I as I turn around, but I cannot look him in the eye. 'You left this at breakfast!' I explain before quickly excusing myself on the pretext of returning to the room to change my shoes.

What I actually do when I get there is call Joe.

'Well, what do you make of that?' I ask when I'm done relating the convent snoop.

'No idea,' he gives a verbal shrug. 'I think you're probably better off asking Kier than me, don't you?'

I sigh heavily – men can be so infuriatingly practical sometimes! Don't they know the fun that can be had with wild speculation?

'What do you want me to say, Kirsty?' Joe responds to my huffing. 'That your brother is going to be the world's first transsexual nun?'

'Now you're getting into the spirit of things!' I cheer.

'Anyway, I haven't got long. Tell me what's going on with you.'

'Well, they've fixed me up with this guy—'

'Hold on, babe!' I hear him muffle the receiver and say, 'Can you get copies made of those documents. Yes, all of them. Doesn't matter about the covers. Go on!' He's back with me now.

'This guy they've fixed me up with – his name's Dante. He's a glass-blower.'

'Of course he is.'

'No really, that's his actual job!' I laugh.

Joe gives a little snort. 'I bet he's a really hot kisser. Geddit?'

I nod into the receiver. 'We haven't got off to the best start – I broke one of his rather expensive pieces yesterday.'

'That's my girl. Well you have fun today and give me a bing later if you get the chance?'

'Oh. Okay.' I concede, feeling a little cut short. I can't believe he didn't even ask the cost of the piece I broke. Not that I should take it personally – he's got to work, after all.

'Love you!' he signs off, disconcertingly sing song.

'Love you too.' I respond, but the line is already burring.

I sit with my hand still on the phone, fighting the urge to call him back. But what for? He's clearly not in need of any extra assurance. In truth it would be me angling for some mush, but that doesn't fit with his current schedule. Once again I'm left feeling mildy unsatisfied. I try and get to the root of the feeling and realise that what I was really hoping for was some reason to turn Dante down. *Beg me not to go, Joe! I want you to be The One*. If only he could pay me a little more attention, I could be so happy.

But let's be realistic – I'm not going to get my wish today. So it's back to business.

While other girls are no doubt checking their bags for lipstick and Tic-Tacs, I'm loading in my notebook and my tape-recorder. I do hope Kier doesn't accidentally let slip any details of my work to Valentina. He is so absolutely unpractised at lying. Another thing we don't have in common.

'Bye then!' I give them a final wave – having got chatting to Maria Luisa, they are now exiting the Academy at the same time as me. As they're headed in the opposite direction I take a moment to watch Valentina sashay away, her bottom commanding its own drumbeat, with a little percussion from her clicking heels.

Perhaps Kier went to pray for the fortitude to resist her swervy-curvy charms, I decide as I turn, appropriately enough, on to Fondamenta Zen. Not that he'd have any real reason to resist, other than proving me wrong. But then again if there were any kind of prayer involved, he'd just go to a regular church, wouldn't he? Like this one here.

I come to a halt outside the looming great Gesuiti, noticing that one of the saint statues has a bright blue ball wedged beside its metal halo – Italy's answer to a basketball hoop? I look at my watch. If I had more time I would grind open the giant doors and peer into the dim, dusty light and take a moment before going to meet Dante.

You know, get a few confessions in ahead of time . . .

I shake my head as I continue on my way – I'm trying to be flip about this date but it just doesn't wash. Why couldn't they have hooked me up with some peroxide-maned Fabio? Why match me with such a class act? Why such temptation and why now?

# 9

*'Don't rely on others to show you the way, carry your own map.' – David Baird*

As the buildings crowded me, so did my thoughts. Mercifully things open out as I turn on to Fondamenta Nove – the lagoon extends as far as the eye can see and speedboats create carefree streaks of white upon the water's surface making me feel unexpectedly breezy and buoyant. I inhale the mixture of gelato-dripped sunshine and marine air and prepare for my debut on Venice's public transport.

First things first – my ticket. I pay five euros and thank the kiosk attendee for confirming that I am indeed at the appropriate stop for Murano. I simply walk the plank on to the prefab waiting room, perch on the bench and wait for the number 42 to come along. Whoa. I didn't realise this structure was also afloat! It's not in every city you can get seasick at the bus stop. Things get choppier still as the vaporetto announces its arrival with a vicious burring of water and an aggressive clanking as rusty metals collide. I watch with admiration as a petite woman in a powder-blue uniform works the chunky sailor's rope dragging the vaporetto into perfect alignment, tying some fancy knot and then sliding back the cattle gate to release the passengers. Once they have disembarked, the rest of us surge forward and I feel like I'm back on the London underground – bumped by a backpack, elbowed in the kidney, pushchair wheeled over my feet. In a place so elegant and sophisticated as Venice this does seem a little uncouth, especially after the white-leathered privilege of the water taxi. I find a nook and press myself against the industrial-bolted interior feeling like a stowaway on a merchant vessel. But then I see immaculately attired Venetians mingling with the slightly bewildered tourists. Well, if it's good enough for them . . . I think as we surge off, doing my best to stay upright and not suddenly grab at a dowager's sleeve or head-butt an American's camera.

All lenses are lifted as we approach our first stop – the cemetery island of San Michele (pronounced Mi-kaylee). I caught a glimpse of the pinky-beige brick crown encircling the island from the quayside, now I see it is studded with elegant white arches and tufted with cypress trees like a fairytale picnic park. Can this really be the island of the dead?

According to Kier, San Michele is on a par with Paris's Père Lachaise and the couple next to me further pique my curiosity reminiscing about their 'heavenly' visit. Perhaps on the way back I'll stop off and pay my respects?

Now there is a little more space I shuffle down the stairs, trading fresh air for a moulded plastic seat. Old habits die hard, so I take out my phone – anything new from Joe? Nope. I try to revive some feeling of connection with him by scrolling through previous texts and find comfort in a simple 'I love you so much.'

I'll say one thing for him, he's never shied away from saying those words. He began with sweet miss yous and then upgraded one night, somewhat tipsy, after his company work do.

'My boss loved you, Darren from accounts loved you, the cleaning lady loved you,' he slurred, 'I love you!'

There was a pause. I wasn't quite sure he meant to say it.

'Don't feel you have to say it back!' he blurted, suddenly self-conscious.

'Okay!' I was still holding my breath.

'I just wanted to let you know.'

'Thank you,' I smiled, maintaining my calm. 'Let's see if you feel the same way in the morning!' He was really, really drunk after all.

We went to bed, he was out in an instant but the next morning he rolled over and his very first words were, 'I love you!' and he pulled me into the most heartfelt embrace. I was beaming all over. Then he said, 'Do you love me? You don't have to say so. Don't feel pressured. But do you?'

'Yes,' I told him.

I sigh to myself. He wasn't always so distant. But am I going to spend the rest of my life trying to recreate that initial magic?

It's only when I have disembarked on Murano that I realise there are multiple stops on the island and I was due to have stayed on board for a further two. I look at my map, somewhat daunted but decide to persevere on foot. As I do so I pass countless glass vendors from dinky-chic duck-under-the-eaves boutiques to vast, airy emporiums, each with windows aflare with translucent colour. Seeing the wide-eyed ooh-ing and ahh-ing that's going on outside, they strike me as sweetie shops for the over-thirties: instead of bon-bons and jellybeans and sticky lollipops, there are vases and wineglasses and candelabra, all of an equally enticing candyesque palette.

It's hard not to get drawn into stalling and gaping at the

wares – in one store I see miniature figurines no bigger than your fingernail and in the next, chandeliers the size of playground roundabouts. Paperweights, picture frames, ashtrays, bottle-stoppers . . . if it can be fashioned from glass, it's here.

I cross a bridge, continue canalside, round a corner and find myself alone. No shops, no pedestrians, just one stray boat gliding off in the distance. I check my map – the area may be deserted but I'm right on track. Until now, Murano seemed to me like a toy town Venice but I'm leaving the clay-red and salmon-pink painted houses behind and instead find myself standing before a large brick factory, searching for the entrance. Ah, here it is around the side, marked SORANZO in elaborate metal lettering. Dante's family name.

As I push open the door, I half expect to find him perched on a stool blowing glass bubbles like others might work Hubba Bubba but instead there's a hip all-white reception area with a pony-tailed woman greeting me with a narrow, sheeny hand.

'I'm Bianca, can I help you?'

'Er, I've come to meet Dante?' I feel like a schoolgirl on a project. 'My name is Kirsty?'

'Ah yes, he's just finishing a piece,' she tells me. 'Perhaps you would like to see?'

'You mean watch while he's working?'

She nods.

'Oh I don't want to put him off . . .' I can't be responsible for any more breakages.

'Don't worry,' she smiles. 'It is a little hot in there but . . .' she shrugs and leads me down a series of corridors to a huge warehouse and a scene straight out of a Dickens novel.

A row of furnaces blaze yellow-orange heat, the floors are rough concrete, the workbenches primitive planks, the men swarthy and grimy. Aside from the expected clanking and chinking, there's also the sound of clashing sticks like someone is doing martial arts behind one of the heat-deflecting screens. The place is littered with instruments of torture and one man is wielding what looks like a blackened, flattened cricket bat. I wince as I look on at an actual blower – I for one would not want to put my lips on a thin metal tube leading into the fires of hell. The set-up is way more dangerous and dirty than I had envisioned and what with my pale pink frock I feel like a ballerina in a coalmine.

'Signor Soranzo is in the far corner,' Bianca points diagonally across the room and when I turn back to thank her, I find her gone.

For a minute I stand awkwardly, working up the nerve to tiptoe past the boxes of finished products, the metre-long red-hot pokers and the surly stares of the other men. Even though I have permission to be here, I feel like I'm trespassing on their trade secrets.

'Uh oh.' Dante places a protective hand over the piece he's working as he sees me approach.

'Oh don't!' I despair. 'Would you rather I waited back in reception?'

'Not at all,' he dismisses my offer. 'I am nearly complete.'

I peek at what he is making – something in a pale amber hue – and then peer around the workstation beside him. 'Have you already finished the replacement?'

He gives me a quizzical look.

'The heart?' I prompt him.

'Ah, of course, you do not know,' he notes before cheering, 'you have been spared!'

'How do you mean?'

'I called the man who placed the order – Signor Pozzini – and told him about the accident and he was so happy.'

'*Happy?*' I baulk.

'He and his Isabella had a very big argument last night and their relationship is no more. Don't look like that!'

'Like what?' I fret.

'Like it is your fault.'

'Well,' I puff. 'What time did the argument happen?'

'You think you caused it?' Dante looks amused. 'That they became angry and animated at the point at which the glass hit the ground?'

'I don't know, I—'

'No,' he shakes his head. 'This is not what occurred. I will spare for you the details but you should know this is a good thing.'

I sigh, unconvinced. 'I still broke something you made, whether Mr Pozzini is happy or not—'

'Kirsty,' he stops my waffling. 'Please forgive yourself! I have.'

I want to continue arguing, still feeling to blame, but he seems emphatic about dropping the subject.

'I wish you'd let me make some kind of contribution,' I plead. 'I can't get off this lightly for destroying something so beautiful.'

'How do you know?' He stops what he is doing.

'What?'

'That what I made was beautiful?'

My already flushed cheeks pinken another notch. 'Well, I saw the package in the bin and I was just curious . . .'

'It's okay,' he smiles. 'I'm flattered that you wanted to see my work.'

My toes scrunch in my pumps and not just from embarrassment . . .

Even though vocally Dante is still as deliciously smooth as the dapper chap I met in the alleyway, physically he's barely recognisable: the heat has curled his hair, his bare arms are tarnished with soot and instead of the polite bow he left me with last night, he looks more inclined to throw me over his shoulder and charge out the room.

As he takes a step towards me I'm on the verge of submission, but he's only reaching for some pincer-like tool behind me.

'What's that for?' I ask, trying to cover the disappointment that I don't now have black handprints all over my body.

'To make sure the measurements are exact.' He references the drawing by his side.

'You're making a chandelier?'

'*Si*, this is the central part,' he explains as he pulls another gadget along the toffee-like glass, making long, angular grooves.

As he works, an older man with a chunky gold chain dips in and out of the frame, knowing exactly how and when to assist Dante. Apparently glass-blowing is a team effort – Dante tells me that you have one master (a title that takes ten years to earn) then any number of helpers from one to six, depending on the scale and complexity of the piece.

'So you're the master?' I enquire, unable to keep the flirtation out of my voice.

He nods. 'You could be my helper if you pass me the *borselle*.' He holds his hand out to me.

'Er . . .'

'The tongs.'

I oblige and then ask the name of the iron rod the glass form is attached to.

'*Pontello*,' he smiles at my interest.

'*Borselle, pontello*,' I repeat as if I'm learning the names of his children. 'What about the blowing pipe?'

'*Canna da soffio*.'

I motion to his helper. 'I like that your man here was smoking before he blew into his *canna da soffio* . . .'

Dante chuckles. 'Generally people think you need a lot of breath to blow glass but if you use the right technique you don't need so much. The forces of nature help you.'

'How do you mean?' I frown.

'At the beginning you blow a little bit and then close the edge so the air inside becomes hot and that creates pressure . . .'

'Ahhh, gotcha.' He really does have a beautiful mouth. I watch it move as he describes how they use thick wedges of dampened newspaper to shape the glass as the fibres in any other kind of fabric would scratch the glass. As he goes on to explain the purpose of what looks like a denim leg-warmer on the left forearm of the workers, rivulets of sweat are wending their way down the backs of my legs. I try to wipe them off on each other before they stray below my hem and I suspect this is a move Dante has clocked before because he suggests I stand a few feet to my left, closer to the window. Ahhhh! It's a wondrous spot where the breeze comes dancing in, and I'm on the verge of feeling comfortable when I hear an alarming snap and tinkle behind me. Oh no, I freeze. Breakage.

'It's okay,' he assures me. 'It's just discarded glass cooling and cracking.'

I look behind me and see a series of bins containing just that. I just hope no shards are planning on making a leap for freedom. Frankly I'm surprised I didn't have to sign a disclaimer before I came in here – so many opportunities to get sliced and scorched. Naturally I have to ask if there are many injuries in this line of business . . .

'In the beginning you burn a little,' he concedes, oh-so-casually. 'Some of these ovens are heated to two thousand degrees Fahrenheit so you learn very fast what you can touch and what you cannot.'

'Right,' I gulp, deciding it's best I keep my hands to myself on so many levels.

Dante adjusts his footing. 'Now watch this – with just one drop of water we will create a thermical shock exactly at that point at which we want to break the piece from the pipe.'

'Wow!' I gasp as he does just that. I feel like I'm watching a magic trick!

'*Finito*!' He relinquishes the piece to Mr Gold Chain.

As we head back to reception he acknowledges his tarnished appearance, requesting five minutes for a quick *acquazzone* . . .

'Of course,' I smile, unable to prevent myself from revelling in the image of his toned nakedness streaming with water. There are no two ways about it – this man is head-rush sexy. With Joe it's more a case of, 'Oh you're so gorgeous!' announced with a contented sigh. I love the height of him, the straggles of hair on his chest, the way his boxer shorts gape obscenely when he's laid out watching TV on a Saturday morning. Joe is more casual in his sex appeal. With Dante, it's intense. So much so that when I return to the office and Bianca greets me with a glass of icy water, I feel the sensible thing to do is to ask her to throw it directly in my face.

But then I decide to really enjoy the sensation of this trippy, impulsive desire. We're just going to lunch after all. The most erotic thing that could happen is that we eat our spaghetti like Lady and The Tramp. This is a safe day. No harm can come of spending these spare moments thinking of his playful smile, his glittering eyes, his melodically rumbling voice . . . It's just a form of admiration really. One appreciates musicians and singers and painters for their talents. Dante's artistry just happens to extend beyond glass-blowing into the realms of physical attraction, that's all.

'So . . .' I try to engage Bianca. 'Are there any female glass-blowers on Murano?'

'Not that I know of. Of course there is the bead-making . . .' she muses. 'But mostly the women are involved with the sales and marketing aspect.'

'Uh-huh. So who mostly buys your products?'

'Women. And gay men!' she smiles. 'Actually many of the important collectors are straight men. But we don't sell so much to the lesbians.'

'No?' I wasn't expecting quite such a specific answer. I don't know what to say in response to that so I go back to thinking of the way Dante so masterfully manipulated the glass. I cross my legs. Uncross them. I smooth out my dress. I look at my watch. As the anticipation of seeing his freshly washed form continues to build, my eyes rove the room looking for something to engage me so I can reign in my giddiness before he arrives. But everything is blank white thus bouncing my lust right back to me.

'Perhaps you might like to view the showroom while you wait?' Bianca seems to sense my restlessness.

'Oh thank you, yes!' I gratefully step through the door she is holding open for me.

Wow.

The Soranzo products are clearly in a different league to the wares I saw in the tourist shops en route. Instead of looking appealing in the context of Murano and a garish fright at home on your mantelpiece, this collection wouldn't look out of place in the hippest design hotel.

Bianca explains that many of the pieces are one-offs as Dante spends one day a week in experimentation and then subsequently decides whether each particular piece will become a standard item for the catalogue, a limited edition or, if it closely resembles 'art', it will remain unique.

'So he does the designs too?'

'The contemporary designs, the more traditional pieces are from his father.'

She then tells me she must return to reception and hands me a leaflet from which I learn a few more glass-making terms – *aventurine* is the name for glass threaded with gold, *millefiori* is the multi-coloured glass and 'milk' glass is known as *lattimo*. It seems only the Italian language could do justice to such beauty. I mouth the words to myself, enchanted.

One vase has streaks of yellow like blurred car headlights on a motorway. I'm guessing that's Dante's work. This old Venetian mirror is most likely his father's, though I do remember Oasis using several of these in their stores – you know the ones with the etched panels? – so maybe it can also be considered contemporary?

As I tiptoe around, careful to not get too close, I marvel at the illusions created and the dreams spun. It makes me feel as though I am in a room filled with vessels best suited not to flowers or wine but *genies*. And with that thought, I conjure Dante.

Now in a rich blue shirt and ink-dark jeans, with damp hair

that I long to run my fingers through, he advances. I move towards him only to find one plinth-set piece standing in our path – an outsize bowl of glass spaghetti. Unable to meet his eyes after my recent lustings, I concentrate on the detailing, realising that each wiggly strand of glass contains intertwining black-and-white threads.

'We call that technique *incalmo*,' he informs me, softly. 'In connection.'

I look at him. He looks at me.

'Hungry?' he enquires.

'Ravenous,' I announce, surprised by the growl in my voice.

'*Buon*!' he laughs, offering me his arm. '*Mangiamo*!'

# 10

*'Love is friendship set on fire.' – Jeremy Taylor*

As we rejoin the world I feel self-conscious strolling with such a conspicuously attractive man. I even see one tourist surreptitiously snap Dante's picture, no doubt to be later labelled 'My Fantasy Holiday Romance'. I'm relieved he's not an official Amore or he would've probably been obliged to stop and hand over his card, informing her that he should have an opening in eight days or so.

We pass a range of restaurants, mercifully avoiding those with wipe-clean menus branded with German, English and Japanese flags.

'This pleases you?' Dante enquires as we stop instead beside a large open-fronted establishment facing the canal.

I peer inside – the buttermilk walls are decorated with what I previously would have described as rusty forceps and ye olde scrapbooking scissors, but now I know them as antique glass-blowing tools, including my old friend *borselle*. The overall look of the place is modern with slate floors, butcher's block side-tables and a shiny aluminium pipe running the length of the ceiling.

'Perfect!' I smile, slightly awed to discover the menu is less mama's pasta, more countessa's choice: Dante begins with a daring platter of shark carpaccio served with a mandarin sauce whereas I favour a more traditional caprese with tomato concassé. Our pasta dish is *bavette* – similar to tagliatelle I discover – with succulent lobster tinted the prettiest coral. Every bite creates a ding-a-ling sensation in the pinball machine that is my mouth. Then comes the baked sea bass (oh so soft and plump and white) and a collection of darling little rosemary potatoes.

Food appreciation has now surpassed my surge of amorous adrenalin. I'm amazed at how much I am enjoying this meal – typically with a new man I find eating an awkward, distracting chore and I can't wait to get it over with. (Flirting and digesting have always been a mismatch in my book.) But you can't rush a multi-coursed canalside lunch with an Italian. And nor would I want to.

As Dante tells me more about the art of glassmaking, I can't help but think how much better my school grades would have been if I'd had him as my teacher. All I remember about my chemistry class is the Bunsen burner and a lot of red pen marks on my homework but now I'm hanging off his every word learning that glass begins life as sand, and that whereas the aquamarine colour is created through the use of copper and cobalt compounds, a ruby glow requires a gold solution.

'So it's kind of like a recipe,' I note, spearing my last potato. 'Does each glass house have their own secret formula?'

Dante looks nostalgic. 'Once upon a time, yes. Glass-makers were even threatened with death if they took their secrets out of Murano, but today you can take a piece to a chemical lab, break it and they will tell you exactly all the different elements present.'

'End of an era,' I note, decrying modern technology as a spoilsport.

Dante takes heart. 'Today the secret is the way we work glass – my grandfather had a technique that other masters cannot even understand, let alone copy.'

'So your family business goes way back?' I lean closer as the waiter clears our plates.

'Six hundred years!'

'Wow!' And to think Hollywood makes a big deal if they offer up three generations of actors. 'That's a long line of Soranzos,' I coo. 'Did you feel obliged to follow the tradition?'

'No,' he shakes his head. 'My father was wise, he let me choose for myself. And when I did, it made him so much more proud to know it was what I really wanted.'

It's my history marks that are climbing now as I learn that the glass foundries were originally based in Venice but due to concerns for fire in a city made predominantly of wood, they all had to relocate to the island of Murano in 1291.

'Around the year you were born!' I tease.

'That's right,' he agrees with a twinkle. 'But I don't look bad for a man who is over seven hundred years old, do I?'

'Not bad at all,' I sigh.

Long after the bountiful cheese selection is reduced to stray crumbles, we linger chatting and sipping golden moscato. It's my favourite kind of conversation – a dozen tangents each embraced with vigour, however trivial the subject, all interspersed with banter. At one point we realise that though both of us did well at school, neither of us pursued an academic degree.

'I tried university for one year but it didn't like me,' he shrugs. 'I like to make my own discoveries.'

'Me too!' I concur. I'm dying to tell him how on one of the first magazines I worked on, the features editor took me aside and said, 'I just want to let you know that we don't think less of you because you don't have a degree.' The thought hadn't even entered my head! And the best part – her degree was in archaeology, of all things!

'I always want to be educating myself,' he tells me. 'Some Venetians concentrate very much on the exterior presentation but you must balance this with developing your cultural inside. For me, it is essential to continue to grow.'

I love how he speaks with such aspiration and assurance – especially since I feel so unfocused and unsure in my own life. It must be amazing to have a boyfriend like this – one who would challenge you to be your best. Talk about raising your game.

'Ah, would you excuse me for a moment?' Dante steps outside to have a word with a passing friend.

I sit back and think what a treat this all is. On the rare occasions Joe and I go out to dinner he practically requests the bill before they've pointed to the chalkboard of specials. No surrendering to the senses, no savouring the moment. His pacing policy is 'get-in, get-fed, get-home'. This is the middle of a working day for Dante and look how luxuriously leisurely he is!

I smile, all dreamy and happy of belly, then it dawns on me that I'm supposed to be working too.

'Damn!' I curse, scrambling for my bag, setting my tape recorder to voice activate and propping the open pouch on the empty seat, hoping it'll pick up our conversation.

Suddenly the whole scenario seems a tad less idyllic – this isn't a guy and a gal delighting in each other's company, this is a journalist and a paid escort doing business. I take the last sip from my tiny glass of nectar and shrug – ah well, nice work if you can get it.

'Please forgive me,' Dante returns to the table. 'I thought a simple handshake would suffice but my friend wanted to talk.'

'No problem,' I say, clearing my throat, ready for the interview to begin.

'He works at the Peggy Guggenheim art museum, perhaps you have an interest in visiting?'

'Yes, yes, absolutely!' I enthuse. 'I once—'

'You once?'

Oh god, I nearly slipped up and told him that I wrote an article on the flamboyant American art collector. Not for *Hot!*, obviously, but a friend's art mag.

'Um, I once read her autobiography,' I correct myself. 'So, er yes, that would be very interesting to me . . .' I trail off.

'*Bene*. What time do you become available tomorrow?'

I don't know about 'available' but I tell him that our morning class is over at half past twelve and we don't have to be back at the palazzo again until seven.

'Would you like to meet me there at one? You can give the tour to me because you are the expert,' he teases, 'and then after, do you have any preference for our activity?'

Keep it clean! I tell myself, and consequently come up with nothing.

'Perhaps some relaxation at the beach?' he suggests.

'The beach?'

'The Venice Lido,' he reminds me of the existence of the twelve-kilometre-long promontory that separates the Adriatic Sea from the lagoon. 'We can take a little holiday.'

I'm sold. 'Sounds like the perfect day!'

'So,' he tilts his head. 'You looked like you were going to ask me something. Before . . .'

'Oh yes.' Back on track. 'Well. I was just wondering, with The Love Academy—'

'Another glass of moscato?' The waiter nips in mid-sentence.

My yes is negated with Dante's order of an espresso. It's a disappointingly sobering choice. Is he afraid of what a loosened tongue might say? Or is it simply that he doesn't want his breath to catch fire once he's back at work?

'What do you want to know?' he enquires.

'Just, you know, what you think of it really?' I slightly overdo the nonchalance.

'So far I like it!' he gives me a winning smile.

'That's nice. But do you believe in their ethic, teaching the world to be more romantic?' Keep it conversational, Kirsty, not interrogational.

'I don't think it's going to hurt anyone.'

I decide to get more personal. 'Would you say you are romantic?'

'I am Venetian,' he utters, three of the sexiest words I ever did hear. 'Venice is romance itself. We are born with this idea of this unique city, this paradise, how can we not be romantic?'

Oh my god, he's too divine.

'Do women ever feel insecure around you?' I find myself voicing my own opinion. 'I mean, you're a very handsome man and as much of a bonus as that is for the girl, sometimes it can lead to a little insecurity.'

'I understand. And I have had that experience but in that case it becomes my crusade to change that. I think it is important for a woman to feel fully confident within herself and with her man.'

See! I knew it! He'd help! He'd rally round! He wouldn't do a Joe and tell me to 'Stop being ridiculous, you know I love you!'

'I wish English men could be more like Italians,' I sigh. 'I suppose in theory Kier and Adam and Melvin will be by the end of the course. What advice would you give them, I wonder, if you were teaching them?'

He gives me a quizzical look. Yes, I know that sounded like a total interview question.

'My advice?'

'A tip, you know, on how to be more romantic?'

He smiles. 'I have this idea that English men are very proper and that their idea of romance is to stoop and kiss a woman on the hand!'

Chance would be a fine thing, I think to myself.

'But I think a woman needs to be held,' he continues. 'So perhaps he should take her in his arms and allow her to feel his power.'

I swear I nearly pass out on the spot.

'Kirsty, are you well?'

So I did just whimper out loud. 'Mmm-hmmm,' is all I can manage.

'*Ciao* Dante!'

Mercifully another friend picks up the conversational baton for me.

This one bounds directly up to the table, an artsy forty-something speaking with great charisma, even though I don't understand a word he's saying.

'Kirsty, may I present to you the talented and fascinating glass-maker Lucio Bubacco!'

He shakes my hand warmly.

'We were just discussing romance,' Dante tells him, with a wink to me.

'Ahhh.'

'Are you romantic, Lucio?' I find myself being slightly impertinent, still not fully composed.

He laughs and mutters something dark in Italian.

'He says he's more of a dirty old man,' Dante translates. 'He wants us to go with him.'

What, so he can prove the fact?

'He wants us to visit his studio,' Dante expands. 'He's just finishing up a piece for Sir Elton John he wants me to see.'

My eyes widen. Did a certain high-paying celebrity tidbit just fall in my lap or is that a leftover piece of biscotti?

Lucio Bubacco's workshop couldn't be a more different set-up to Dante's inferno: his place is bright and airy with a big work surface running like a squared-off track around the room. This is where all the action takes place yet my eye is immediately drawn to the adjacent room where his work is displayed. Instead of solid, smooth chunks of glass inset with abstract designs, his work features clusters of intricate figurines, specific to the nth degree.

From a distance they look like a cross between molecular models and fairytales in miniature.

Up close I see tiny masked, wigged fellows in frock coats playing violins and trumpets, female dancers whose heads have morphed into long-necked swans and sirens amongst the wafting seaweed.

'These are exquisite!' I coo, inspecting his incarnation of Medusa. Suddenly my head jerks back. Is she wearing thigh-high PVC boots and no undergarments? Is that a whip in her hand? My eyes flit hither and thither taking in a sado-masochist's mask, a peeled banana, a Gene Simmonsesque tongue . . . Everywhere I look there seems to be something erotic occurring.

'His works do have a sensual nature,' Dante understates.

After all the cutesy clowns and goldfish in the tourist shops, I feel there really should be some kind of warning on the door: *And Now For Something Completely Different* . . . As I continue to take in the mythological perversions around me, I begin to understand his dirty old man comment.

'It all feels very voyeuristic,' I observe. 'Like we're catching them mid-action.'

'Movement of the figure is the central theme of his work,' Dante confirms. 'And of course, human anatomy is his speciality. If he had been born anywhere other than Murano he would have been a painter or a sculptor.'

I have to say the proportions of the bodies are flawless. Somehow he's managed to capture the flex of a foot and the flick of a wrist, even the way boobs fall when tilted forward. The miniscule detailing fills me with wonder. I cannot fathom how he can fashion a limb so precisely from something so fleetingly fluid as glass.

I'm about to ask him for an insight when I hear him mention Sir Elton and shuffle closer to surreptitiously eye the magnificent red and black devil chandelier he and Dante are discussing. As they talk, my hand finds my camera phone. I can feel Mitzi willing me on – one quick snap and it'll be with her in minutes! – but I can't do it. The exploitation would be too easily traceable back to me and thus blow my cover here at The Love Academy. I have to be resolute – my nosing must come ahead of Mitzi's nose job. Besides, I'm a writer not an informant.

As I squint at a horned devil holding a decanter of red wine that looks perfectly drinkable, I can't hold my question in any longer. 'How *do* you do it?'

Lucio smiles and turns to Dante. 'Why don't you show her?'

'You can do this too?' I gawp.

'Lucio is the master,' he defers my awe. 'He has exhibited all over the world. His designs have even been used on commemorative stamps for the Republic of San Marino. But yes I can show you the technique . . .'

We return to the workroom and Dante takes a seat in front of a torch flame and a small plinth. Above him there's a big contraption sucking all the hot air out of the room. He contemplates some narrow rods of glass that look like cocktail stirrers, selecting an ivory, pink and green.

After all I've just seen I'm a little trepidatious at what he might create but console myself that the colours he's chosen aren't exactly known for their raunch factor.

'This technique is called lampwork,' he explains as he works two of the rods, one in each hand, moving so swiftly and deftly dipping in and out of the flame, rolling, nudging, stretching the molten goo. From out of the opaque ivory rod I see the indented palm of a hand begin to form, and then, fingers extending one by one. This truly is magical. I can even see the fingernails! Next thing I know he's incorporating the translucent green, attaching the finest slither between the thumb and forefinger – is that a pen, because I am a writer? It's then I see the leaf. He reaches for the pink. Petals appear. It's a rosebud!

My toes scrunch in my pumps. He just made a rose for me!

He concludes by elongating the wrist into a candy-cane swirl of all three colours.

'That is just gorgeous! I can't believe it!'

'A Soranzo impersonating a Bubacco!' Dante again acknowledges his teacher.

'Quite a rarity,' Lucio tells me, proving he can indeed speak good English. 'You should find a special place for this one.'

He already has a special place, I think to myself. I don't think I've ever met anyone quite like Dante before.

When the hand is cooled sufficiently, he wraps it for me. Watching him be so gentle with this fragile object endears me to him even more. All puns aside, I feel in such good hands with this man.

Lucio looks at the clock; Dante and I follow. I know it is time for me to go now but it is with reluctance that I bid Lucio '*ciao*!' and amble with Dante to the nearest vaporetto stop.

'I am sorry to be apart from you but you understand that I must return to work.'

'I do. Understand,' I tell him, albeit a little sadly.

'Tomorrow I will see you at the Guggenheim Museum.'

'Yes,' I brighten. 'And thanks again for my beautiful gift!' I hold up the little bundle I am carrying as if it is a baby bird.

Here's the vaporetto now.

'Until tomorrow,' he says, giving me another of his self-contained bows.

I'm charmed but frustrated at the same time – I thought Italians were supposed to be all touchy-feely! Frankly I want one of those hugs he mentioned – the one that shows a woman the power of a man! I want to slam into his chest and be ever so lovingly crushed. I can't believe I'm feeling this way but in this moment I would risk everything for him. Joe seems so distant and secondary. My most primary instincts are crying out to embrace this beautiful man.

For a second I feel he reads the need in me and sense him about to step forward but the urgency and determination of everyone else to board carries me along, out of his reach.

Or is it that he is out of mine? Considering his affiliation with The Love Academy, he doesn't seem to be putting himself entirely on a plate for me. Is it possible that we *both* have some kind of double agenda?

One thing I know for sure is that this flick-flacking between enchantment and suspicion is messing with my serenity. As if I had any in the first place.

Ah, but I know just the place to get some . . .

# 11

*'Time passes, there is no way we can hold it back.*
*Why then do thoughts linger long after everything*
*else is gone?' – Ryökan*

As we pull up to the island of San Michele, I'm up and off the boat quicker than you can say ashes to ashes. There's nothing like spending time with dead people to give you a little perspective on your life.

I still can't believe the flurry of hormones I just experienced. It's a good thing these interactions with our Amores are intermittent – one night on Murano and I would truly be playing with fire.

But, it's okay, that insane craving is over now. No hot-heads here. Within half an hour my spasm of amorous avarice will surely calm to simple gratitude for being alive.

Curious . . . I pause to inspect a sign at the entrance showing a veiled woman in a black cocktail dress with a big red cross over the image. I'm not clear what the big 'NO' is – no widows? No weeping? No veils, rather like school kids are no longer allowed to wear their hoods up over their heads, gang-style? I peer closer. The dress has a somewhat plunging V. Could it be that exhibition of cleavage might be considered disrespectful to the deceased? I check my own. Hardly provocative but rather than conjure a scene from 'Thriller' and be chased out of the cemetery by a body-popping cadaver, I swathe my pashmina across my chest.

Two steps through the gateway, I stall in awe: this is truly one of the most beautiful places I've ever seen – rainbow bouquets, white marble and blue sky as far as the eye can see!

Stepping into the shade of a flourishing magnolia tree, I take in the display of splendour surrounding me: to my left are cloisters harking back to the days when this was a Franciscan monastery, to my right a sweep of columned arches putting me in mind of open-top carriages and plumed horses. In the far, far distance I see a tall diamond-grid gate opening out on to the now-turquoise lagoon. And in front of me, a million flower-festooned graves.

As I walk among them, crunching on gravel and sun-dried pine needles, the phrase 'Death in Venice' takes on a whole new meaning. I don't know if it's because it's such a gloriously sunny day but I've never seen a more vibrant place of rest. The brightness and lusciousness of the blooms adorning each grave seem to be a true celebration of the life that went before rather than a sad little posy of grief. Admittedly many of the flowers are silk, which I suppose accounts for the fact that so few have withered brown crinkles where once were petals. (That always seems so sad in a graveyard – who wants to be reminded of the decay and abandonment of death?) It may be an illusion but these people look as if they are being remembered daily.

And not just in name – nearly every headstone is personalised with an enamel photo plaque.

I smile back at Luigi Facchinnetti, Antoinetta Veronese, Gian Andrea de Candido and darling Guiseppe Limoncelli feeling like I am greeting them directly. It's the strangest sensation to see all these long gone faces and experience some sense of regret – as if these are people you might like to have known.

Many of their photos show them in swimwear (no problem with cleavage on the other side) as I suppose holiday photos are what dominate our albums. It's rare to be captured in everyday-life contentment – who takes out the camera to commemorate a satisfied belly after a good home-cooked meal, except perhaps at Christmas? Who is there to photograph an unexpected kiss from your beloved? A late-night sleepy sprawl with your cat?

I find myself pondering what picture I might put on my gravestone? What moment would you choose to immortalise for all eternity? You at your prettiest or happiest? What would count most in the final reckoning? I think how eagerly I've awaited the development of photos in the past, only to have the magic dissolve at the sight of my kinked hair or joyfully doubled-chin. Oh vanity. It's not enough to have had fun in the moment – for it to be a true success we have to be looking our best too. And don't think I don't know that it's magazines like mine that ram that message home.

For some reason the song, 'What Have You Done Today To Make Yourself Proud?' comes tauntingly to mind. And yet, career-wise I would say I *am* proud of what I've achieved, certainly how hard I've worked. And yet . . . More and more I question the value of what I'm contributing. Entertainment for entertainment's sake is cool. I'm all for that. But what about when it's at another's expense? Are the articles we run cruel or levelling? It's the 'We're only mean about them so you can feel better about yourself!' defence. I feel ashamed thinking of the disservice I may have done my brother – *Hot!* fuels aspirations for rich, famous footballer husbands, not shy, hard-up gardeners however loyal their hearts.

Coincidentally it's at this point that I notice certain designated areas of the cemetery are divided according to your calling – there is a section for priests, another for the military and one for concierges judging by all the men in grey suits and black ties. There's even one for gondoliers. I wonder if Tiffany one day might be buried alongside one? (With an extra grave for all the material possessions she'll be attempting to take with her . . .) Poor Lorenzo. I wonder what kind of day he's had?

And what of Freckles aka Megan? I'm hoping she's not falling too fast for Stefano. She seems so *ready* for romance. Adam and Allegra. Their names certainly go well together. Melvin and Filomena – for some reason I get an image of him sitting on her knee like a ventriloquist's dummy, jabbering away while she eats ice-cream. Kier and Valentina. She's probably taken him to see a doctor to find out why he's not palpitating like normal men do in her presence.

I place my hand over my own heart as I discover a freshly dug grave. It gives me chills to discover that the young man in question died just a matter of days ago. The sense of loss is palpable and the floral display wouldn't look out of place on a mardi gras float. You can feel the love in every petal that surrounds his picture. At twenty-three, I wonder if he passed away having known a true love? And then I wonder why that matters so much, why love from a lover is held in such high esteem, almost more so than the love of a friend or a relative which is often more enduring and unconditional.

But then look at the love I have for my brother – how much does that count for, really? Especially since it doesn't appear to be reciprocated at the present time. It's almost as if, having lost his love, he is somehow trying to punish others by withdrawing his affections. It's not just me that he's doing that to, but I do seem to be getting the brunt of his resentment and I have a theory about that – I think it's possible that he's mad at me because I got a second chance with Joe and he didn't with Cinzia. I could see how unfair that could seem – we both split up around the same time but with me and Joe it was temporary. Though none the less harrowing at the time . . .

Every morning I'd wake up swamped with a sickening panic at the thought of living without him. I seemed to be crying more often than not and longed for the day when I could simply breathe normally again. All the while he was feeling the same anguish. The ironic thing is that *I* actually broke up with *him* because I didn't think he was that into me. I knew what love looked and felt like to me, I knew what lengths I would go to, how doting I would be and when, after a year, he seemed only fleetingly present I had to conclude that the initial spark had dimmed and he was basically 'going off me'. I didn't want to stay around for further deterioration so I ended it.

For three months I struggled to get through the day. I found myself missing every darn thing about him, even the bad stuff. It was bizarre, I'd get sentimental about the way he sucked the air out of a freezer-bag with a straw to maximise the vacuum-packed effect. I heard he had a new girlfriend and even if he had been available I knew I couldn't go back to feeling like I had been, I had to just stick with it. Everyone assured me that I'd gradually start to feel better but it just wasn't happening. I suppose that's the stage Kier is at. I say stage but it's more of a lifestyle now.

Anyway, one day out of the blue, Joe rang me. My heart

leapt seeing his name on the display and it was so comforting hearing his voice again, I could feel the warmth down the line. We were on the phone for over an hour. Two days later he rang just to let me know that he and the girl had split up. She told him that he was 'emotionally unavailable' and that she thought he was still hung up on his last girlfriend. 'I thought you'd like to know that!' he teased. I did.

We began to email. One day we to'd and fro'd from 10 a.m. to 10 p.m. And then around midnight I got another call, this time telling me to look out of my window. And there he was, in the lamplight. He says he knew from my face that I still loved him and that I would be his again. He walked straight up to me and kissed me. Just like that, we were back together. He was so sweet and attentive those first few months, promised he'd never take me for granted again. I was so happy . . .

I get a sudden profound pang. How could I ever, *ever* think of hurting him much less deceiving him? It shocks me to think how susceptible I felt less than an hour ago. Until now I never understood those people who throw their whole lives away on a whim but I feel like I got a glimpse today. Wow. I'm really going to have to watch myself. No more drinking in Dante's presence for starters. I need to keep my wits about me. And my lips far from his.

I look around me at all the couples who honoured their union until death did them part and I realise that's what I want, the longevity, not some fling that leaves you alone and riddled with regret. I want my headstone to read, 'My Beloved Wife' not 'That Chick I Had a Fling With One Summer'.

I give a little internal cheer! This is the wake-up call I'd been hoping for! I have had commitment issues in the past but now I know I want to grow old with someone, I really do.

And Joe and I have already grown two years older in each other's presence so he's tried and tested, the practical choice. The most direct route to achieving that aim. We have a past, we have a future. Yes I'm having a few glitches with our present but they'll pass.

My new role models are Giovanni and Irma Zane Montesanto, I decide, studying their photo, her hand proudly on his lapel grinning delightedly, he looking attentively back at her. He died thirty-five years before her and yet here they are, buried together, man and wife for eternity. Now *that* is romantic.

But hardly a fit with current trends. These days everyone would insist you moved on and scold you for festering. 'It's been a year,' they would say, 'he'd want you to find someone new.' It seems almost laughable to me – so many of my friends have been single for three or four or five years and people don't stage interventions for them and they actually *do* want to meet someone new. But for those whose loves have been taken from them prematurely, they get hurried. Gotta get back out there! Can't have you being alone with your heartache! He's gone! On to the next!

What would it be with Joe, I wonder. Is that the kind of love we have for each other? Is it really that deep, that all-encompassing? So fulfilling that even after death it sustains you?

I wish I could be more certain. I bet Irma was the centre of Giovanni's world. And vice versa. What would it take for me to believe that I am Joe's number one priority? It's not like he's waiting for something better to come along. He's made it abundantly clear that I'll do. His search is over. I know he likes having me around, likes knowing that I'm puttering in the bathroom or wherever but it so rarely amounts to great passion. With the exception of when we were reunited after the split. He says he sometimes reads my break-up note to remind himself of how it felt to lose me in order to keep him on his best behaviour and while that is really touching to hear, it just doesn't seem to translate into actual action. I think we could be at something of an impasse there because he simply isn't going for ardour, he prefers comfort and steadiness. I seem to want more of the grand gesture. And a little more excitement.

I look at Irma, wondering how she did it. I suppose it helped that she had sons – Oscar and Lino. Giovanni lived on through them. Ah, the Italian family. Seemingly so indestructible and so vital. Why don't I feel the same way about creating that family unit? Have I spent too long involving myself in celebrity business that I've disconnected from my own bloodline? How did it happen that we got more interested in stars' activities than the real people in our lives? We gossip about them like they are extended family – judging them, envying them, offering advice they'll never hear. But you know what? They never once spare a thought for us.

So, ultimately, you can go to your grave with your Paris Hilton impersonation down to a T or you can be like this grandmother resting in peace here with fresh freesias from her daughter and crayon drawings from her adoring grandchild.

I look up and see a real-live seventy-something walking to a grave in the next row, bunch of flowers in one hand, bag of shopping in the other, like she's dropping by for a cuppa and a chat with a friend.

It all seems to boil down to people and the relationships that you have with them. And living a life you feel good about.

Which brings me right back to where I started. I was trying to trivialise the battle going on within me regarding Joe and Dante as purely hormonal. I thought I'd come here and it would seem ridiculous, that I would simply be glad to have my health. But I can see now that the choices I make over the next eight days could really impact the rest of my life.

No pressure then.

My phone bleeps the arrival of a text. If it's from Joe I'll take it as a sign that we'll endure and have matching Mr & Mrs graves. Nope. It's Sabrina instructing me to go directly to dinner instead of returning to The Love Academy – apparently when I step off the vaporetto back at Fondamenta Nove, I'll already be halfway to the restaurant. Really it's a tad too soon for me to be settling down to another major meal but I'm sure I could squeeze down a wee olive or two?

'Oh excuse me!' I bungle side-stepping some other tourists as we all inadvertently congregate at the back of a cremation area lined with what look like vast marble chests of drawers.

'Can't go any further – it's a dead end!' One of their party observes. And then laughs awkwardly at the accidental pun.

It's time for me to go.

# 12

*'No man was ever so much deceived by another as by himself.' – Fulke Greville, 1st Baron Brooke*

'So what's the deal?'

My phone rings just as I turn on to Calle Della Racchetta, back in Venice proper. It's Helena, the features editor, standing in for Ruth while she's in the Bahamas.

'The deal?' I'm still a little dazed from my trip to San Michele, not to mention disorientated – isn't there supposed to be a bridge coming up?

'With the love shack baby!' she sings. 'Have you been assigned an escort yet?'

'Well, yes and no.'

'Illuminate me.' I can just see her with her feet up on Ruth's desk, loving having the one private office to herself.

'Well, the guy I'm with,' I begin, 'he isn't exactly one of them.'

'What do you mean?' She sounds suitably bewildered.

'He basically got recruited the night I arrived.'

'Well that's no use,' she snorts. 'You'll have to switch.'

I decide to stop walking to have this conversation. I don't want to agree to anything in a state of distraction.

'Oh, I don't think that's necessary,' I breeze, once again defending my union with Dante.

'But what good is he if you can't pump him for all the juicy information? He's not going to have any history, is he?'

'No, but perhaps he won't be as loyal as some of the others,' I grasp figuratively at straws, and literally for his glass hand, as if it's some kind of good-luck charm. 'You see, because he's new he won't be as guarded,' I continue in earnest as I re-admire the dainty fingertips. 'And all the instructions they give him will be ultra-fresh in his mind.'

'I'm not so sure,' she resists. 'I think an old hand would be better. Someone who's done the rounds a bit.'

'Well that hardly sounds appealing!' I protest.

'It's not like you're doing this for real and it would make a better story.'

I think for a moment, ruing the fact that I'd told the truth. 'There is this guy Lorenzo . . .'

'Yes?' she sounds encouraged.

'I can easily talk to him without switching. I know the girl he's paired with would jump at the chance of a double date.'

Helena sighs at my resistance and then a hint of suspicion enters her voice as she asks, 'Why exactly are you so reluctant to be parted from your gigolo – what's his name?'

'Guiseppe,' I lie.

'Oh no, that won't do!' she hoots. 'He sounds like the uncle in *Pinocchio*.'

'That was Gepetto.'

'Whatever.'

I look back at San Michele, so honourable and respectful, at peace with itself.

'You know they're really very nice here,' I begin, somewhat tentatively. 'I hate to disappoint Ruth, but there is a chance The Love Academy could be for real.'

'God I hope not, where's the story in that?'

'Are you kidding?' I rally. 'Surely it's far more newsworthy for a place like this to be genuine?'

'Yes but you've got four pages to fill in the Scandal section!'

'Couldn't we re-allocate it to the Inspiration section?' I attempt a negotiation.

'Oh, that's been axed.'

'What?' I feel instantly faint. She can't mean it. The one redeeming section of the magazine, gone?

'Yup, Ruth decided yesterday. Phoned the decree in from the spa. She wants to dedicate more pages to paparazzi pics.'

I slump back against the plaster wall. 'Wow, that'll really set us apart from all the other magazines.'

'It's what the readers want.'

'Is it?' I'm not so sure.

'Sales figures don't lie,' Helena snips.

I can't argue with that. And I know those pictures provide a quick-fix kick but I don't see why they can't be balanced with something offering a little more sustenance for the soul.

Helena is still talking. 'Don't forget to get your brother to ask around his friends, see what they know of The Love Academy – someone's got to have some dirt on it.'

'Mmmnn,' I make the most non-committal sound I can.

'Oh and we want to do a side-bar on the tragics that have signed up for the course so make sure you get enough info on them to do mini-profiles.'

'I think "tragic" is a little harsh—'

'Defending them already? Good, that probably means they

like you too. All the more likely to confide in you. It's going to be a great piece.'

I stand in silent scream mode for a second and then shake myself out of it: 'Look, sorry to cut you off Helena but I've got to go – I'm meeting the "tragics" for dinner and I'm already late.'

'*Ciao ciao*!' she trills.

I simply click the phone to OFF.

I can't let this get to me now. I really am late but at least I've located the bridge, leading me to the appropriately named Fondamenta Misericordia.

I pace along it, pashmina pulled taut around my shoulders, the absolute antithesis of carefree romance. The only thing that cheers me up is passing a side-street called Larga Lezze. No Murano glass down there, then.

There are several restaurants along the canalside path, one with a cluster of dreadlocked scruffs and a dog on a tattered rope outside. Can this really be The Love Academy's dining choice? Again I regret having dressed like the Sugar Plum Fairy.

Ah, here it is now, a couple of doors up, *Paradiso Perduto*. Paradise Lost. As I enter I get the vibe of a bawdy Oliver Twist alehouse from the tightly packed trestle tables and swarthy accordion player within. There's my group, over at the back. Their eyes light up as they wave me over, eager to hear about my day and tell me all about theirs, oblivious to the fact that I am the mole and not to be trusted.

We dine on the plumpest spaghetti I've ever encountered – well, you have to at least have a taste, don't you? It's almost too wormlike to be palatable to me but the amatriciana sauce has a zesty intensity that goes great with bread and the rough wine from the fast-pouring carafes helps ease my pain. And Kier's, judging by the bleary look on his face. I even see him laugh once or twice though I'm not sure if it's with or at Melvin, who is seated beside him. After the elegant formalities of yesterday's matchmaking reception and today's assorted travails, this venue is definitely conducive to relaxation. Unless you are Tiffany who's already made one trip to the bathroom to inspect her cutlery in a brighter light.

'I like that it's so dark in here,' I shrug.

'Me too,' Adam concurs, his shoulder touching mine as he leans in to whisper, 'It's like being inside a confessional.'

For a second I think he's going to confide in me, and I don't want him to. Don't tell me anything I'll later feel compelled to use to make the story more salacious, please!

'Forgive me father . . .' I decide to speak instead, pressing back against him. ' . . . for I need to reach across you to get to the parmesan.'

'Oh.' He looks a tad disappointed as I settle back on to my section of the bench, quickly offering me more wine. 'So how was your date with Dante?' he asks. 'Oh that's weird, it almost sounds like "'date with destiny"'!'

I smirk back at him. 'It was good. Look, he made me this . . .' I reach for my little glass prop, hoping it will divert the attention from me.

'Oh wow!' Megan coos from across the table. 'Your Amore made that?'

'Right in front of me,' I tell her, handing it over for closer inspection.

'It's so delicate!' She holds it just millimetres from her face. 'He must have very good eyesight!'

'I know that's what I always look for in a partner,' Adam sniffs. 'Good eyesight.'

I give him a swat. 'You're just jealous cos you can't create mini-masterpieces in a matter of seconds.'

'You don't know that! I might be the most accomplished balloon-twister in all of Shepherd's Bush.'

'Are you?' I challenge him.

'No,' he concedes.

'What *do* you do for a living?' I ask him, curious aside from any side-bar profiles I might have to complete.

'Me? I, er—'

'Or have you forgotten?' I tease.

'No, it's just frankly too boring to even mention.'

'I know the feeling,' Megan groans.

Adam smiles benevolently at his fellow clock-puncher. 'How about we forget our "careers" tonight and simply call ourselves *lovers*?' he laughs. 'It's what we came here for after all.'

'I'll drink to that!' Megan gives a tipsy chink. 'I'm not a dental hygienist I'm a lover!'

'To the lover in all of us!' Adam cheers.

The toast rings around the table, yelped with extra zeal from Melvin. I feel his eyes upon me, trying to look intimate and suggestive from four seats down. All too soon he's by my side, taking Adam's place when he nips to the loo.

'Are you ready yet?'

'For what?' I ask, looking around me for a clue. 'Dessert?'

'If you want to call it that,' he leers, bathing me in his garlic breath.

'Oh Melvin!'

'You can't fight it forever, Kirsty.'

'Oh I think I can,' I assure him.

He gives me a pitying glance. 'I hate to see a woman so out of touch with her desire.'

I roll my eyes. If only he knew. I've had little flashes of Dante-desire all night. I'm just trying not to give those trouble-making feelings any credence on account of having so recently made a decision to grow old with Joe.

'Anyway I just want to let you know that though Filomena and I do have a strong physical connection, it's you I want ultimately,' Melvin concludes his pitch as Adam comes back into view.

'Right,' I grimace at the image of the two of them grappling with each other. 'Got it.'

No sooner is he up, than Tiffany sits down. 'You don't mind, do you Adam?' she says as he returns to find his seat taken.

'Well—'

'Good. So listen, I've got something to show you.' She reaches in her purse and pulls out three hand-scrawled phone numbers. 'Not bad for an afternoon's work!'

'Wow. All gondoliers?' I ask, trying to decipher their names.

'Two gondoliers and one seriously suave businessman.'

'I take it you didn't spend much time with Lorenzo.'

'Oh I got all these while I was with him,' she trills. 'I told them he was my translator.'

'And how did he feel about that?'

She shrugs as if the question is of no consequence. 'Sabrina says I just have to do tomorrow afternoon and the overnight with him and then I can switch to someone new, maybe someone of my own finding.'

'Is that allowed?'

'Well, you did it, as I reminded her when I asked.'

I feel a little guilty. What have I started? 'So what's this overnight you mentioned?'

'Oh you missed all that didn't you? Sabrina handed out sheets when we first got here. Hold on . . . Sabrina! Do you have the list of travel options for Kirsty?'

'You can have mine,' Megan offers. 'I've already decided to go to Verona with Stefano.'

'So we're all going to different places?'

'Yes.'

'Each with our Amore?'

'Yes.'

Oh cripes.

'Where are you going?' I ask Kier, who is standing behind Megan, apparently waiting for the waitress to finish serving the desserts.

'Back to the Academy.'

'I mean—'

'See you later!' He goes to move on.

'Wait! I'll walk with you!' I still want to ask Adam how his date went with Allegra but right now my priority is my brother.

'You don't want your tiramisu?' Tiffany queries as I fumble around on the ground trying to locate my bag. 'It's pretty good.'

'I thought you were detoxing?' I look up at her.

'I am,' she protests. 'Just not at this very second.'

'Okay, well, feel free to enjoy mine too. Oh!'

'What?' she asks as I get to my feet.

'I was wondering – you don't fancy double-dating tomorrow, do you?'

Her face brightens. '*Yes*!' she grins. 'Yes, yes, yes! Anything to break up the tedium that is Lorenzo.'

'Excellent! I'm meeting Dante at the Guggenheim Museum at one o'clock, will you get him to meet us there?'

'Absolutely! And we can double up on the overnight too,' she enthuses. 'I've picked the Prosecco Tour of the Veneto so I'll only have to be partially conscious.'

'Mmmm, that probably wouldn't work for me,' I decide – the last thing I want to be doing around Dante is sipping bubbly. I need to cling tight to my inhibitions.

'Well, whatever you decide, Sabrina needs your pick by breakfast.'

I give the head girl a little wave to let her know I've been informed and then wish the table at large a good night.

Just before I get to the door, I turn back – look at them chattering, singing along with the accordion player and ordering extra dessert! Anything but tragic. In fact, give me the choice between the evening I just had and lying in a spa in the Bahamas having every trace of ever having had an expression removed from my face, I know what I'd pick.

'Are you coming or what?'

'Yes, yes!' I hurry to catch up with Kier.

We stroll for a few minutes in silence, me in the vain hope that he'll actually volunteer some information. But no.

'So, how was it with Valentina today?'

'Fine. She's very sweet.'

'And very attractive,' I prompt.

He shrugs. 'If you like that kind of thing.'

I muffle a snort. What's not to like? The woman is a goddess.

'Was Cinzia attractive?'

I know I'm taking a chance asking this question but I'm wondering if his situation is akin to when someone dies and people are too afraid to mention the deceased for fear of setting off the griever, when in reality it would be a release for them to speak about the person they loved so much.

'You mean physically?' he stalls for time.

'Well, yes, I suppose I'm asking what she looked like – I never saw a picture or anything.'

He blinks rapidly as if flicking through an assortment of images of her. 'She was . . .' He shakes his head, seemingly unable to find the right adjectives.

'Her hair?' I try and get him started.

'Long. Shiny. She had these honey-coloured streaks . . .'

'Eyes?'

'Brown. Dark, dark brown,' he smiles to himself. 'She always wore a flower of some kind – behind her ear, pinned to her jacket, tucked in her handbag . . .'

'How sweet. Where did she get them?'

'I gave them to her. A new one every day.'

I look at Kier and then down at the pavement. It's just so sad. There's really no getting over a love like that – one that you really participated in rather than going through the motions. One you allowed to be really special. One you made the effort for.

Is it a choice that Kier lets himself get so involved emotionally whereas Joe keeps busy with other projects? Or is it that Cinzia was simply the right girl to inspire Kier that way? But then how right can she be if she dumped him? Joe thinks I'm the right girl for him, right enough to live with and be the mother of his child but he never romances me. Is it something I'm not doing, some way that I'm failing to bring out that side in him? Perhaps by the end of my session here I'll know.

In the meantime, I have an overnight location to decide upon . . .

'Lake Garda, Romeo and Juliet's Verona, the medieval hill

towns of the Veneto, the Ferrari Musuem in Maranello – bet Adam goes there . . .' I try to get the conversation back on to more practical ground. 'Have you picked one yet?'

'I'm not going anywhere.'

'Oh Kier—'

'I explained to Sabrina that Tonio needs me that night and she's cool with it.'

'Oh. Well, maybe she can switch you to another night?'

'We'll see.'

We're back in the room now. I'm still going over the list as Kier cleans his teeth.

'Bologna, Milan, the Dolomites . . .' I frown at the page. 'Trieste?'

He wipes his mouth on a towel. 'It's on the border of Slovenia.'

'Rimini?'

'Seaside town with a big marina.'

'Which would you say is the *least* romantic destination?'

Kier turns to face me. 'Why would you ask that? Are you having trouble keeping Dante at bay?'

'Not at all. He hasn't so much as pecked me on the cheek.'

'You sound disappointed.'

'No I don't!' I squeak.

He holds my gaze for a moment and then says, 'Bologna. I've never been but I can't see anyone feeling frisky after a great heaving plate of spaghetti Bolognese.'

'You're right.' I draw a big circle around the word. 'All these lakes and mountains sound way too idyllic. I'm going to leave my form at reception right now.'

'You do that,' he says, settling into bed with his book.

*

When I get downstairs, I can see a light on in the office behind the reception desk but there doesn't appear to be anyone around. Could this be my chance to make up for my pitiful lack of detective work so far today?

Gingerly I edge behind the desk, pretending to be looking for a pen – 'Just need to leave a little note for Sabrina . . .' I say out loud in case I'm being observed. 'If I could just find an envelope. Perhaps there's one in here . . .' I lean into the office. Empty. I quickly check the corners of the room for cameras. None visible. I creep in and scan the desks, noticing one book which seems to have a lot of numbers on the open page. I go to move closer only to spot something far worse than a security camera – a pair of human eyes.

'Oh! Oh!' I try not to panic. 'Hello!' I trill. 'Are you the night porter?'

He looks bewildered. *'Mi scusi, non la capisco . . .'*

'Um.' My Italian fails me. 'Er, *notte securite*?' I make up a new word as I point to him.

'*Sicurezza*?' he corrects me.

'Si!'

'Non.' He pats his chest. '*Io sono il ragioniere*.'

'Regional manager?' I try.

He looks confused.

'Never mind! Sorry to bother you!' I back out the office with him following me. 'I'm just leaving this for Sabrina . . .' I do an exaggerated mime as I pat the page on to the front desk. '*Grazie*!' I wave and tear back to the room.

'Oh, you're so lucky you speak the language,' I wail at Kier as I plomp on the bed beside him. 'That was excruciating.'

'What was?'

'Some guy down there, he said he was "*ragioniere*". For all I know he could have been telling me he was robbing the place.'

'Well it's possible,' Kier replies. '*Ragioniere* means accountant.'

My eyes widen. I can't believe it. I was so close to the man with the answer to my most crucial question – do the Amores get paid extra for extras? But even if I'd known his identity when I was down there, there's no discreetly throwing in a question to a man who doesn't understand a word you say – every syllable is under the spotlight. I cast a furtive look at Kier.

'No.'

'What do you mean, no?'

'No, I'm not going down there and interrogating the accountant for you.'

'It's hardly an interrogation, just a couple of questions.'

'No.'

I sigh and pace the room. With everyone still out to dinner it seems like a golden opportunity to find out what the deal is here.

'Do you really think he'd tell you anyway?' he says, setting down his book.

'What about if I distracted him and you snuck in and took a look at the books he's working on?'

'Kirsty, listen to yourself! Is this really what you do for work? I mean, I know you used to love watching *Magnum* but—'

'Don't you want to know about the authenticity of this place?' I whine.

'Not really. It doesn't make the slightest bit of difference to me either way.'

'You're not curious about whether Valentina could be a hooker?'

'If she was, which I very much doubt, she would have retired by now. There's not a man on the street that didn't turn and gawp as we walked by. If I so much as paused to tie my shoelace some guy would swoop in and offer her dinner, diamonds, whatever! But I've seen where she lives. She's not wealthy by any means.'

'You went back to her place?'

'She needed a sweater. Nothing happened.'

'Did she offer?'

'So now you're interrogating *me*?'

'I'm just trying to do my job!' I protest.

Kier gives me a withering look and reaches for the bedside lamp calling, 'Lights out!' I go to object but he continues, with not a little sarcasm, 'Sabrina says she wants us looking our best tomorrow. I need my beauty sleep.'

And with that he tugs the blanket over his head and turns to face the wall.

I look around the room, wondering what my next move should be. Already I'm losing impetus. But what if this is my only chance with the accountant? What if he only comes in once a week? Maybe every nine days to coincide with the new batch of students? It's now or never.

I open the door and find Adam on the other side.

'Oh good, you're still up!' he smiles.

'Kier's asleep,' I whisper, pulling the door to behind me.

'I just wanted to give you this,' he holds up my pashmina. 'You left it behind at the restaurant.'

'Oh, thank you very much.' I peer behind him. 'Is everyone back now?'

'On their way in dribs and drabs.'

Darn. I've totally blown it with the accountant. I can't have any witnesses around while I'm talking to him.

'Everything alright?' he looks concerned.

'Mmm-hmm.'

'You seem a little frazzled.'

'No, I'm fine. I really should be getting to bed.'

'Where were you going?'

'What?'

'When I came to the door, I didn't even knock – you looked like you were heading somewhere?'

'Um, do you know I can't even remember!' Oh I'm just so crap at this.

'Please don't tell me you were corridor-creeping to Melvin's?' his eyes narrow.

'You got me!' I laugh, all too heartily.

'Well. I've got a secret assignation with Gerard so if you'll excuse me . . .' he winks goodnight.

'Have fun!' I wave him off, chuckling at his faux mincing.

There's something so familiar about Adam that makes me feel like I know him far better than I actually do. As I retreat back into the room, all thoughts of snooping put to rest, I realise that not only is Adam physically and sartorially similar to Joe, but his playful interactions put me in mind of how we used to banter when we first met. That thought makes me feel a little sad on two accounts – one, I missed the besotted couple that Joe and I used to be. And two, I have to face the fact that there aren't enough Joe Clones in the world for me to keep reliving those halcyon days.

I sigh to myself as I climb into bed. Everyone else has come to The Love Academy to find a fresh new Love. I just want my old one to be new again. But am I the most delusional of all?

# 13

*'Was he attractive? She was too attracted to tell.'*
*– Audrey Beth Stein*

The next morning I awake from a disturbing dream in which Joe and Adam experienced some kind of facial merging and I couldn't tell them apart, other than the Adam persona seemed a hair more attentive. I then went to the mirror to check my own face and found Ruth's staring back at me. Chilling.

Kier is already off on one of his mystery walks and when I try calling Joe he's right up against it. 'They've brought all of tomorrow's events forward a day, can I call you this after-noon when everything's settled?'

'Of course,' I tell him, even though I'll probably be on Dante Time. Make that Dante, Lorenzo and Tiffany Time. How did that ever seem like a good idea? Ah yes, I'm doing it For The Magazine. I can't even imagine what it would be like to have an experience like this for its own sake, rather than attending with a pre-set agenda.

I try to limit my thoughts to putting together a less girlie ensemble than yesterday – going for khaki and white linen with a matching polka-dot headband – but the burden of seeing the dark side of the Academy weighs heavy on me as I walk down the staircase. It's only when my foot hits the salon floor that I see Sabrina studying me intently. Having her catch me even thinking about the article has me instantly on edge.

'You look very preoccupied,' she notes, unusually curt. 'Are you ready to be present with us?'

'Oh yes!' I say shaking off my assorted frettings and attempting a willing smile. 'I'm right here!'

'Please take a seat.' Her gaze switches to the staircase in the breakfast room where a wobbly impersonation of Andrea Bocelli announces Tiffany's arrival. As she approaches, she fluffs her hair and pouts at her reflection in the stained glass behind us.

'Is there a problem with the mirror in your room?' Sabrina asks, her words bone-dry.

Tiffany looks taken aback. 'No.'

Sabrina's eyes stray to the glass.

'I just wanted to check—' Tiffany begins.

'That your appearance hadn't undergone any radical transition between the bedroom and the entry hall?' Sabrina cuts in.

Now Tiffany's pout is authentic. 'You said we should take special care with our look today.'

'But ultimately you prefer looking at yourself rather than other people.'

Wow. This seems a little severe. I give a sympathetic wince as she slumps beside me, whispering, 'I think today is *Tough Love* Academy.'

Next up is Adam, sauntering down the main staircase with casual pep.

'Hey ladies!' he grins, noticing the line up but not the tension.

'You are being observed!' cautions Tiffany.

'You want me to put on a little show for you?' He takes the

last few steps high-kicking like he's in a Busby Berkeley musical.

Before Sabrina can comment Melvin appears. He can't get down the stairs quick enough. 'Kirsty, you look ravishing!' he says squeezing into the non-existent gap between myself and Adam.

'How do you think that makes the other women feel?' Sabrina turns on him.

'What?' His pointy little jaw goes slack.

'The fact that you singled out Kirsty and ignored us?'

'Can I help it if I only have eyes for this goddess?' I feel his clammy breath upon me.

The descent of Megan spares him any further beratings.

She's hurrying, concerned she's late and when she catches us all gawping at her she flushes raspberry and flusters, 'Sorry, have I kept you all waiting? I'm *so* sorry!'

We all look to Sabrina but she says nothing, apparently deciding Megan is already hard enough on herself.

Finally it's my brother's turn, tramping in from the garden shoulders scrunched, brow bunched, the picture of resistance.

'You seem like you don't want to be here,' Sabrina understates.

'Would you like me to leave?' he challenges her to give him a reason to go.

'No, but I would like you to take this opportunity to look at the kind of first impressions you make, simply from the way you enter a room.' She's addressing us all now. 'This is how you are presenting yourself to the world and to people who might have otherwise been destined to be your true love. Don't miss out because you are too busy studying your own reflection or lost in your own thoughts or worrying about what other people might think of you.'

She gives a brief smile of encouragement to Megan, which broadens to a beam as a slim woman with soulful eyes and dark, playfully flicked hair enters the room, visibly radiating goodwill and enthusiasm.

'This is Raeleen D'Agostino, author of *Living La Dolce Vita – Bring the Passion, Laughter and Serenity of Italy into your Daily Life*.'

'So delighted to meet you,' she shakes each of our hands, repeating our names and smiling directly into our eyes.

'Good cop to Sabrina's bad?' Adam suggests in an aside to me.

'What was that?' Sabrina catches him.

'I was just wondering whether that now you've broken us, Raeleen plans to rebuild us?'

'Something like that!' she laughs. 'This morning is all about *fare la bella figura . . .*'

'Making our best figure?' Melvin translates with a frown.

'Or less literally, putting your best foot forward,' Raeleen cheers. 'I want to send you out on today's dates feeling your absolute best so let's have you making your entrance once again. I want each of you to go up the left staircase as you would normally and come down Italian-style!'

'What exactly is *Italian-style*?' Megan wants to know.

'With the confidence of a movie star!' she whoops. 'You want your body language to be saying, I like myself and I'm ready to like you too!'

One-by-one we take our turn, in the order we first arrived. So me first.

'That's right – do you see how Kirsty has gone from one of those crazy ladies who's so busy in her own head she doesn't realise she's muttering out loud to—'

'Were you watching us before?' I switch back.

'Of course!' she tinkles.

'And I was talking out loud?'

'Not loud enough to hear what you were saying, if that's what you're worried about!' she winks.

'Oh ha ha ha!' I attempt a carefree laugh.

'Carry on. Don't forget to correct your posture. Here she comes now – a woman who is present and engaged.'

Everyone applauds.

She puts her arm around me. 'That's so much better – what a song and dance a man would have to do to get your attention before!'

Actually he'd just have to blow glass, I think to myself.

'It's a good point for all of you – try not to get too caught up in here,' she taps her head. 'You can't live in the past or the future, they haven't invented the time machine yet. Be in the moment.'

Next up, Tiffany.

'Before we saw only your vanity and insecurity, now here comes someone stylish and put-together with, yes!, a beautiful smile!'

Adam.

'What can I say – I loved the high-kicks but your natural saunter and open friendliness are the winning combination! Steady, no need to go too far!' she cautions as he starts acting like he's welcoming families to Disneyland. 'We want to see you not the caricature!' Raeleen urges. 'Next!'

Melvin slinks down the stairs so campily you'd think he was wearing a slit-to-the-navel gown. And yet he still manages to simultaneously eye each woman from head to toe.

'I think you may be overdoing the undressing motif,' Raeleen cautions.

'But at least he shared the sleaze this time,' Tiffany surprises me by coming to his defence.

'Let's just try and let the gaze linger on the face ultimately, Melvin, not your favourite body part.'

Now it's Megan's turn.

'I know it's very stressful being so scrutinised but just imagine everyone you are about to meet adores you and you adore them. Think warm thoughts. There is nothing to fear. Head up!'

'How am I going to look confident when I'm bright red?' Megan wails.

'Don't worry about that, the more you practise the less it will happen. Besides, many men find blushing fabulously enticing. They like to know they're having an affect on a woman, it makes them feel potent and powerful.'

'At the expense of me feeling so vulnerable and foolish?' she complains.

'Not at all, it's a powerful thing to have that effect on men, wouldn't you agree?'

'I hadn't thought of it like that,' she brightens.

'We're going to be talking more about male/female roles later tonight but for now, Kier, you're up!'

'Catwalk really isn't my thing,' he protests, though he knows it's in vain.

'Dead man walking,' teases Adam as he ascends the left flight.

His comment is oddly poignant. Kier's certainly not living as he is. We all hear his leaden sigh as he prepares to descend.

'Loosen up the shoulders, hands out of the pockets, release those fists, let your arms swing by your side,' Raeleen coaches. 'Smooth the brow, un-purse the lips, keep walking, try and look us in the eye, that's it – doesn't he look better?'

'I think I'm in love!' Adam teases.

Raeleen puts her arm around Kier, pulling him close to her side. I see him tense initially but she doesn't let go, seemingly sensing that this is a man who needs a hug but wouldn't ordinarily allow it. As she continues chatting about how we're going to take our act out on to the streets, the Strada Nova in particular, something in his face seems to soften, something is remembering how good the touch of another human being is when you can be sure that they are not planning to take anything from you or deceive you or ask anything in return.

When she finally claps her hands together and cheers, 'Follow me!' he looks almost forlorn to have lost contact with her. It makes me think of when Joe is squidging my feet as we watch TV and he gets up to get another beer, my feet always experience a mini sense of loss and exposure – they felt so safe and warm in his hands.

'I wasn't expecting this!' Tiffany confides as we step into the street.

'She wasn't here last session,' Melvin notes.

'Perhaps we're all such basket cases they've enlisted her in on an emergency mission – I can't believe we're actually being taught to walk, again!'

'I like her,' Megan smiles, practising her new sashay.

'Me too.' My brother's words are so quiet he was probably only intending to inform the dog community of Venice but I catch them and smile, just not so he can see.

Yesterday, when I followed Kier to the convent, the streets were mostly residential. Today we turn right instead of left, duck through the very alleyway where I assaulted Dante (my fingers graze the bricks, nostalgic after just two days) and then suddenly we are stepping out into a lively shopping street bustling with pedestrians.

'Oh!' I jump back to avoid having my toes mowed by a wheelie shopping cart, only to leap directly into a stranger's holiday snap. 'Sorry!' I apologise to the two be-shorted Germans, hurrying on to catch up with the group.

'As you know we are in the Cannaregio sestiere of Venice and this is the main street – Strada Nova. Remember your walk!' Raeleen coaches as she leads us past assorted shops and stalls selling rich brocade, petite glass ornaments and calendars featuring black-and-white photos of the twelve most handsome priests in Venice.

It's the food that really catches my eye – giant pastel-hued meringues, crazy colour candy displays and a gazillion varieties of pasta. I see a heart-shaped design (like mini cookie-cutters) and consider taking some home to create the ultimate romantic dinner for Joe.

'Talk about eat your heart out!' Adam quips, over my shoulder.

'How'd you like the one next to it, Kirsty?' Melvin enquires, standing all too close.

'Oh Melvin!' I tut as he points out the penis-shaped version. 'Don't!' I shush him before he makes any further comments. 'Just don't.'

Meanwhile Tiffany's more interested in the ebony-skinned men selling fake Louis Vuittons. 'Pitiful!' she sneers at the tourists stopping to inspect the bags and purses. 'If you can't afford the real thing then you have no business being seen with that label.'

The café Raeleen opts for is young and buzzy with paper-thin pizza and pavement seats facing a far more traditional version where we can observe authentic locals in action.

'I wanted you to see first-hand just how polished Italians look, how good they appear to feel about themselves and how graciously they interact with one another,' she nods to a group of silver-haired men and women, still dressing to the nines and clearly relishing the chance to socialise. Whatever their age, it does seem that Italians are incredibly comfortable with looking glamorous. 'They don't save themselves for Sunday Best – every day is best!' Raeleen observes.

'It's easy for them,' Megan looks despondent. 'They are just better looking to start with.'

Raeleen tuts. 'In Italy, learning to enhance the body and mind one is born with is more important than having been endowed with physical perfection.' She gets a conspiratorial look. 'You ladies have a Sophia Loren class coming up, I believe?'

'We do?' I'm thrilled to hear this sneak preview.

She nods. 'Well, I'm sure you know her famous quote: "*Sex appeal is fifty per cent what you've got and fifty per cent what people think you've got!*" You don't get sexier or more Italian than Sophia Loren so she should know!'

I want to tell Raeleen that I actually met the legendary beauty once but I have to keep my trap shut on account of the circumstances being, of course, magazine-related.

It was at a Damiani jewellery launch at the Four Seasons in Beverly Hills and when I say met, that is somewhat stretching it: I was in the same room with her for nearly three hours, waiting my turn to interview her but it was an utter fiasco – we were promised intimate chats, two or three journalists at individual tables, all very civilised, but instead a mob-like lunging ensued. The seventy-something goddess sat on a raised platform with flashbulbs popping, TV cameras rudely thrusting and tape-recorders jutting from every angle and despite having an aversion to crowds she withstood the chaos and answered questions about diamonds being a girl's best friend with aplomb until sixty seconds before I was due to take my turn, she up and left the ballroom. I had not a single quote to take back to *Hot!*, just a going-home present of a scented candle, which does not a one-page article make. Ruth was furious with me; she couldn't understand why I wasn't one of the journalists who had elbowed their way to the front. I wanted to tell her that I didn't want to be uncouth, that I respected this woman too much but that wouldn't have washed. Ruth actually threatened to send me on an assertiveness training course but then obviously thought better of it in case I came back and actually stood up to her. Still, I did see Ms Loren with my own eyes and she was everything you imagine her to be but with bigger boobs. Really! She was wearing this fitted black dress with a décolletage women half her age would kill for and—

'Kirsty?' Raeleen cuts into my reminiscences. 'Remember what we said about staying present?'

'Yes, yes, sorry!' I reach for my lemon soda.

'I want you to look at the people passing us by – the street is full of pretty girls, but who stands out?'

'The one in the blue,' we say in unison, pointing to a woman in her thirties, walking along laughing and talking animatedly to her friend.

'Don't you want to be around someone joyous?' Raeleen asks rhetorically. 'So much of what makes you attractive is in your energy, your attitude.'

'But what if you don't feel like laughing?' Kier asks.

'Let me tell you a secret,' she huddles up. 'Behaviours change thoughts and thoughts change behaviours. It doesn't matter which comes first.'

'Fake it till you make it?' Tiffany suggests.

'Exactly. Positive body language promotes positive thoughts which in turn elevates your self-esteem.' She leans over to Megan and whispers in her ear.

'Really?' She hesitates for a second but then seems eager to accept the challenge, trotting off down the street.

We look at each other wondering what she's going to do next. Finally she turns back in our direction and throws off her timid exterior to walk with absolute panache, smiling at everyone in her path.

It's a beautiful thing to see – heads turn, mouths return her smile, one low voice even coos, '*Bella bella*!'

Megan returns to the table breathless with exhilaration. 'That was crazy!' she gasps. 'I've *never* had men look at me that way before!'

'Did you like it?'

'Do you really need to ask?' She squeaks giddily.

'The point is that you don't have to wait until you are reincarnated as a supermodel, you can start living *la dolce vita* right now!' Raeleen insists. '*Bella figura* beauty requires only that we learn to appreciate what we have and emphasise our best features. Besides, trying to perfect yourself for the opposite sex is an exercise in futility. The research on male-female attraction tells us that in reality neither males nor females find physical perfection a turn-on. It's the slightly tousled hair or imperceptibly loosened tie, the little flaws that attract us to someone because we perceive them as human and thus more like ourselves.'

'Do you know, it's funny – there was this guy I met once who was absurdly out of my league good looking and a group of us went out to eat and I noticed that throughout the meal various items would fly off his fork or spatter into his lap and I can't tell you how attractive this made him to me!' I laugh. 'Before he was just like some flawless model but his dining mishaps made him seem so endearing, like he probably wasn't as confident as I presumed he was!'

Raeleen nods in understanding. 'And speaking of eating, another reason Italians mostly look so trim is that they tend to eat dinners cooked from fresh, unprocessed ingredients, rarely snack between meals and, most importantly of all, their attitude to food is not adversarial.'

I sit back in my chair. Now that's big. Are you getting this Ms Tiffany Detox?

'It is as if Italians resist internalising the media message that puts pressure on them to be thin. My own research on body image found that it isn't so much mere exposure to mass media that determines how bad we feel about our appearance but how much we take that message to heart. There is a difference between admiring a swimwear model's physique and actually berating ourselves for not having the same shape ourselves!'

'What about working out?' Tiffany asks. 'I haven't noticed any gyms here.'

'The Italian way is more about keeping your body in natural motion than an hour of pre-programmed torture!' she laughs. 'They are generally out in the world more – moving, walking, cycling, pulling up weeds in the garden!' She winks at Kier and then something occurs to her. 'It's ironic, here's the man with what would be considered by many as the ideal physique,' she says laying a hand on my brother's bicep. 'Tall and strong and lean but instead of doing the *bella figura* thing and highlighting this, he walks hunched over as if he's trying to enclose himself in a shell.' She gives him a gentle smile. 'Now why is that?'

He shrugs. 'Sometimes you just want time to think and you don't want to be interrupted.'

'Okay,' she concedes. 'But you need to be aware that you are shutting out the good things as well as the bad. I mean really, if you met someone's eyes, what's the worse that could happen?'

He gives her question due consideration, answering quietly. 'That they will see me. That they will try and engage me.'

'Isn't that what you want?'

'And then what?' he gets a little testy. 'You talk, you decide to meet for drinks, you like each other, you go on a second date, you get that feeling, for a while you're so happy and then,' he puffs a breath, 'something happens and it's all over and you're left feeling way worse than when you walked down that street that day and you know what, you're still alone.'

Raeleen reaches out and touches his chin, looking intently into his glossy eyes. 'Kier, I want you to know, you are not destined to be alone.'

I see him swallow hard and then reach for his coffee as a distracting prop. She looks up at the rest of us. 'None of you are.'

For a moment we all just breathe – could that be true, that our darkest fear isn't real?

Apparently 'you had your chance and you blew it' is a very un-Italian way of thinking. For them there is this absolute belief that 'love will always find you again'. It doesn't mean that Italians don't feel the agony of a break-up, they just don't go into doom-panic mode, choosing instead to prioritise keeping their dignity and moving on.

That's got to be a healthy thing.

'I'll tell you something else,' Raeleen adds, rallying us. 'I love the fact that you are all here rather than sitting at home lamenting that your phone isn't ringing! You have to put yourself in the running or you can't win. You have to be open to love!'

'But I am open,' Tiffany complains. 'Really. Wide. Open. But nothing.'

'If you go hunting for love with a shotgun, I guarantee you will only scare it away. You have to be open without obsessing. How many of you think your life is meaningless without a partner?'

The hands may be tentative but everyone except Adam is raising theirs.

'What an ominous burden it is for someone to feel that he or she is required to give your life meaning.'

Gosh. I've never thought of it that way before. Joe certainly doesn't ask that of me. He's doing his thing and I'm a bonus. Is that how it's actually supposed to be?

'So how are you supposed to go about being open without frightening people?' Tiffany wants to know.

'Do things that put you in contact with other available people but make sure they are things you like to do anyway.'

'But all the men that work at the spas and designer shops are gay,' she pouts.

'Then you might need to expand your interests,' Raeleen says with a wry smile. 'Aren't you going to an art gallery today?'

She nods, still less than enthused.

'That's a wonderful place to start! When it comes to romance the arts can be such an inspiration – sculptures, paintings, especially of the human form, classical concertos, romantic poetry . . . the more exposure you have to the human expression of romance, the more you will feel like opening your own heart up for passion.'

'I know I always feel more like I want a boyfriend after I've watched a romantic comedy,' Megan admits, prompting a debate on our all-time favourites. She chooses *While You Were Sleeping*. *Pretty Woman* for Tiffany. Raeleen *Under the Tuscan Sun*.

'What about you Kirsty?'

'Oh gosh, how can you choose?'

'That's easy – which one have you watched the most times?'

I think for a moment and then smile cautiously. 'This may just be cos I always seem to catch it on TV and then can never tear myself away . . .'

'What?'

'*Overboard*!' I cringe mildly at myself.

Adam bursts out laughing. 'Goldie Hawn and Kurt Russell?'

'She just cracks me up!' I shrug. 'And I don't know if it's because they're a couple in real life but it always makes me cry!'

'I don't think I've seen it,' Melvin frowns.

'It's the one where she's all spoilt and rich and falls off her yacht and gets amnesia and basically finds redemption acting as the mum to the poor carpenter guy's kids,' Megan explains.

Gosh. Is that my most profound romantic wish – to be made to do housework and bring up someone else's children? I think back to the film and realise none of the romance was about being flown to the opera in a private jet. It was all down-home, day-to-day, intimacy-between-the-chores. Hardly very me. Or is it?

Kier picks *Before Sunrise*, fitting of his current unfulfilled ending. And Adam surprises us all with *His Girl Friday*.

'I don't know that,' Megan frowns.

'It's an old black-and-white with Cary Grant, isn't it?' I say, feeling all the more foolish for picking *Overboard*.

'It's great,' he raves. 'Rosalind Russell is this feisty reporter and—'

I don't hear the rest of what he says, I'm so thrown that he picked a movie in which the leading lady basically does what I do. When I tune back in, Melvin is explaining his choice of *As Good As It Gets*.

'Two reasons. One, Helen Hunt in a wet T-shirt.'

We all groan.

'Two, the obvious comparison with Jack Nicholson.'

We blink blankly at him.

'Do you want to see my impression?'

Mercifully Sabrina's arrival spares us.

She tells us that the class is over. For now at least. 'Raeleen will be joining us for dinner to talk about . . .' she cues her.

'The unabashed joy of romance!' Raeleen finishes her sentence.

'And we have a copy of the book for each of you,' she duly hands out six pristine tomes.

'Sounds well worth reading,' I turn to Kier, who's already scanning chapter one.

'Can you sign mine?' Megan eagerly relays hers to the author.

'My pleasure,' Raeleen beams before waving the rest of us off. '*Vi auguro una romantica giornata!* Have a romantic day!'

'She wants to try spending the day with Lorenzo and see how romantic she feels,' Tiffany grizzles as we separate from the crowd.

'I'm sure he can't be that bad!'

'Live it and then let me know. Wait a sec!' Tiffany yanks me back from the Ca' d'Oro vaporetto stop. 'Can we just take a quick peek at the knock-off bags?'

'I thought you said—'

'Yeah but these look pretty convincing,' she decides as she kneels to inspect the grain and stitching.

I've got to attempt to curb the eye-rolling she brings out in me or I'll be seeing no works of art today, just ceilings and a lot of sky.

# 14

*'To become rich is easy. Much harder is to solve the riddles of the heart.' – Cao Xuequin*

Now that's what I call a *bella figura*,' I growl to myself as I spot Dante taking long, lean strides towards me in dark mocha trousers and a retro-style short-sleeve shirt. I give him a little wave, toe-tinglingly happy to see him.

'So your prince has come, where's my pauper?' Tiffany looks impatiently around for Lorenzo.

'It's not even one o'clock yet, he'll be here,' I assure her.

'I just need him to be one minute late and I'm calling for back up,' she says, fanning out her gondolier numbers. 'All of them said they could be available at short notice.'

I want to ask why she's here – if it's that easy for her to get a date, why leave Florida? Did a hurricane blow her across the Atlantic? But Dante is now by my side and I'd rather talk to him.

'*Buon giorno!*' I try out my minimal Italian. '*Come stai?*'

'Ah, *bene*, *grazie*!' he replies looking suitably impressed.

'You remember Tiffany?' I prompt.

'She is not easily forgotten,' he understates.

'That's it, I'm calling Luigi!' Her eyes are still trained on her watch.

'Lorenzo! How wonderful to see you!' I throw my arms out in welcome as he appears from an alleyway, just in the nick of time.

'Oh. You're here,' is Tiffany's heartfelt greeting.

'These are for you, typical Burano biscuits,' he hands her a small bag of rusk-like yellow squiggles.

'Well. That's sweet I suppose,' she says as she accepts them, only to mutter, 'Not quite sure what I'm supposed to do with them . . .'

'You could put them in your new bag,' I say, chirpily.

She catches my eye, seeming to understand my message – be nice or I tell the boys you bought a knock-off.

'Shall we?' Dante motions for us to enter the museum annexe, informing us that he already has the tickets so we can go straight in.

'I will get the coffees after we've had a look around,' Lorenzo volunteers. 'There is, I hear, a charming café overlooking the sculpture garden.'

I can think of at least three girls back home who would simply adore Lorenzo. Girls who find machismo a big turn-off and prefer a *gentle* gentleman. Girls who like to take picnics in parks and strolls in the woods and believe that the best things in life are free. I don't know what they were thinking pairing him with Tiffany. Couldn't they tell she'd just stomp all over him? I wonder why they're holding her to two more days with him? Perhaps they know something we don't about the overnight visit. Perhaps as the clock strikes midnight he starts channelling Casanova and she'll return to the Academy with crazy, sex-bouffed hair, converted to his hitherto hidden charms?

For now at least she'd rather link arms with me, marching

us ahead as we enter the atypically single-story Palazzo Venier dei Leoni. (Venier being the original family name and Leoni on account of the stone-sculpted lion heads decorating the waterfront façade.)

I've been to many a London gallery with my artist friend Annabel and though it's always a kick to see a genuine Picasso or Miro or Magritte, the true thrill for me today is knowing that this building was once Peggy Guggenheim's home. The white leather sofa being used to admire the Rothko in comfort was actually one she used to sit on – it's right here in the black-and-white photo of her old lounge. Even before it became a gallery it was starkly modern in décor, complete with the current statement trend of a zebra-skin rug.

Moving on to her former bedroom, I notice from another biographical photo that she used to display all her jewellery like art itself on a wall beside her bed. I comment out loud how I covet her chic sixties wardrobe, with the possible exception of her Dame Edna star-frame sunglasses, to which Tiffany concedes, 'A trend-setter perhaps, but not exactly a great beauty, was she?'

'She actually had a nose job but the surgeon bungled it,' I explain.

'Why didn't she get it fixed?'

'Well, having had one hideous experience I think she decided to go the *bella figura* way and make the most of what she had.'

'Yeah, like a lot of money,' Tiffany coos as she moves on to the Dali. 'Can you imagine how much this whole collection is worth!'

'Are you an art fan, Lorenzo?' I try to include her abandoned beau.

'Oh yes,' he nods vigorously. 'Before I became a carpenter I restored paintings. I can really appreciate each brushstroke,' he says, peering close to the canvas.

'Tiffany tells me you've had many careers?' I continue with my dainty inquisition.

'Jobs,' she corrects me from across the room. 'He's had many jobs.'

'I want to experience many different aspects of life,' he defends himself. 'It is hard for me to pick one thing, I have so many interests.'

'I quite envy you. I've always done the same thing.'

'You write, yes?'

'Mmm-hmm,' I say wanting to get off the subject no sooner are we on it. 'Nothing of any importance.'

'She's very modest,' Dante winks as he joins us.

'To say that I'm modest is to imply that I'm good at what I do but unwilling to brag,' I get pedantic. 'For all you know I could be dreadful at what I do.'

He raises an eyebrow.

'I could be! Or maybe I'm genuinely ashamed of my work!' I persist.

'Ashamed of writing children's stories?' He laughs. 'How is that possible?'

I wish I could tell him the truth! But it's not just him, there are three pairs of eyes upon me now. 'Well I'm no JK Rowling, put it that way.' I back down.

'Yes, but I'm sure you make a very good Kirsty Bailey.'

I don't know what it is about him saying my name but it slays me! 'Say it again!' I beg.

'Oh god, is that absolutely necessary?'

For a second I think Tiffany is referring to our sweet talking but I see she has stumbled upon the infamous blackened bronze statue on Peggy's wonderful canal-front terrace.

'Now this piece has a certain notoriety,' I say as we gather beside the primitive rendition of a horse with a naked man astride it, arms flung wide, face to the sky.

'This part,' I address what could easily be mistaken for a policeman's truncheon, 'actually comes off. Apparently she would use it to get the attention of a prospective lover.'

Tiffany looks confused. 'What, did she bludgeon them into submission?'

'I think it was more of a playful jab. As if to say "You're it!"'

'At least you knew where you were with her,' Tiffany decides.

'According to Venetian gossip she had her own gondolier too so she could cruise the canals after dark looking for a little company . . .'

'Really?' Tiffany wanders over to the balustrade and gazes down the Grand Canal. 'Did she ever marry?'

'She was actually married twice before she moved here,' I tell her. 'Her first husband was a Dada sculptor named Laurence Vail.' An amused smile plays upon my lips.

'What?' asks Dante.

'There's just the funniest quote in her autobiography about her losing what she called her "burdensome" virginity. I remember it quite clearly, she said she had a collection of photographs of Pompeii frescoes showing people making love in various positions and was very curious and wanted to try them all out herself; and it occurred to her that she could make use of Laurence for this purpose!'

Everyone chuckles. 'And did she?'

I nod. 'She says she reckons Laurence had a pretty tough

time of it because on their very first night together she demanded *everything* she had seen on those frescoes!'

'Go Peggy!' Tiffany laughs.

I start to tell them how Laurence introduced her to many avant-garde artists in Paris during their life there in the thirties but Tiffany interrupts to ask, 'Any children?' clearly far more interested in her personal life than how she became an art collector.

'Two. Pegeen and Sindbad—'

'Sindbad?' Dante queries.

'Sindbad,' I confirm. 'But Peggy divorced their father following his affair with actress Kay Boyle.'

'Bastard.'

'Apparently she didn't think so, Peggy was Matron of Honour at their subsequent wedding.'

'What?' Tiffany splutters.

'Well they had a very unconventional relationship to start with and besides which by this time she'd met the love of her life so I suppose she didn't mind so much.'

'Who was that?' Lorenzo's now sucked in.

'John Holmes, an English intellectual. Unfortunately, after just six years together he died.'

'Oh no!' Tiffany gasps.

'That is tragic,' Dante looks pained and turns away.

'What happened next?' Lorenzo queries.

'Well I seem to recall she then had a long affair with a friend of his and then, when World War Two began she returned to New York, opened another gallery then married the German-French painter Max Ernst.'

'So she found love again!' Tiffany marvels.

'Love will *always* find you again!' Lorenzo reiterates Raeleen's earlier statement.

'Yes, well, they divorced four years later.' I feel like I'm being a downer but Tiffany is now resilient.

'It's okay! I just know she finds love again!'

'She certainly did,' I confirm. 'She had a thirty-year love affair with Venice!'

Though my affair has only just begun I predict a passionate longevity. The vantage point from this expansive terrace is amazing – you can see from the Accademia bridge all the way down to St Mark's Square. Then again, this really is a city that looks enticing from any angle.

'She's actually buried here in the Sculpture Garden beside her beloved dogs,' I tell the others. 'Shall we go and have a look?'

We stroll back across the large central courtyard, complete with marble throne, and continue on to the prettier brickwork garden, pausing to study a large geometric structure made of Perspex, glass and subtly mirrored surfaces. Depending on where you stand, you can see yourself and/or another person reflected back at an angle or clean through. It plays tricks on your eye though I do rather enjoy the image of myself layered with Dante.

'Ready for refreshments?' Lorenzo motions to the gallery café.

'I've got a better idea!' Tiffany pips. 'Why don't we go to the Cipriani for cocktails instead?'

I shrivel my nose.

'It's where all the celebs go!' she tries to tempt me.

Precisely why I'd rather not, I have enough moral dilemmas without catching some A-lister skinny-dipping in the hotel pool.

Fortunately Dante steps in. 'You two are more than welcome

to do as you wish with your afternoon,' he addresses both Tiffany and Lorenzo. 'But I promised to show Kirsty the Lido.'

Smooth! And I like the neat segue into us leaving.

'Are there any five star hotels there?' Tiffany halts us.

'One, the Westin Excelsior,' Dante turns back.

Her brain does a little clickety-clicking. 'Isn't that where all the A-listers stay during the Venice Film Festival?'

He nods, knowing all too well this will seal the deal.

'Good enough for me,' she says, now linking arms with Dante. 'Have you ever been to any of the movie parties?'

She's about to sweep him off when he holds up a finger. '*Momento*!' He looks back at me. With a nod I let him know it's fine that they join us. It may not be the ideal romantic situation but it will at least offer me the opportunity to speak with Lorenzo alone. I've got to get busy or I won't have any work to feel ashamed of.

On the six stops from Salute to the Lido, Tiffany and I become The Floating Inquisition. As I overhear her ask Dante such questions as, 'Who is your richest client?' and 'Which of these gondoliers do you think is the most eligible?' I mentally start compiling Lorenzo's profile.

'So, how did you get to become an Amore?' I begin.

He gives me an awkward look. 'The Academy prefers we don't talk too much about the process. They want us to maintain our mystique.'

'Fair enough,' I concede, a little peeved with myself that I've managed to get his guard up with my first question. 'We can talk about something else.'

We sit in silence for a second.

'So do your friends think it's cool or do they tease you about it?'

He gives me a look as if to say, 'I thought we were changing the topic!' but he decides to answer anyway, with just one word: 'Both.'

'What about your mother?' I'm really curious about this, seeing as Italian men are supposedly such mama's boys.

'My mother is happy if I am happy.'

'And are you?' I cast a glance at Tiffany. 'Not necessarily today but in general. Or is Tiffany your first?'

'You ask a lot of questions!'

'Nothing you haven't been asked before, I'm sure,' I shrug.

'Sometimes people don't want to know,' he says quietly.

'But you would, wouldn't you? If the situation was reversed.'

'I don't know,' he looks out of the window. 'What does it achieve, to peek behind the curtain during a performance?'

'Is that what this is to you, a performance?' It's a fairly logical analogy. I'm sure an acting background would be of benefit in this situation, especially experience with improvisation and love scenes. Could The Love Academy essentially be a theatre troupe, assigning certain personas to each Amore?

Lorenzo sighs. 'It is easy to criticise, easy to poke fun. I'm sure a lot of people don't understand what we do, or why we do it. But I consider it a special honour, to bestow the gift of romance upon someone.' He looks at me with earnest eyes. 'To see a heart blossom in your care and become open to all the possibilities of love, can you imagine how wonderful that feels?'

For a second I buy it, but then my devil's advocate kicks in. 'But isn't it just an illusion?'

'Why must it be? Why can't these feelings be for real?' He sounds exasperated.

'Honestly? I think it's the fact that money is changing hands . . .'

'People pay for spiritual enlightenment,' he reasons. 'Personal trainers. Dating agencies. Life coaches. All of those things you could do for yourself – you can work out a regime at the gym, you can come up with a plan for your life, you can ask out every available man sipping wine in the *bacaro* – but sometimes people feel they want expert guidance.'

'So you really do consider yourself an expert in romance?' I'm on a roll now.

'Well that would depend on your definition of the word.'

'So how do you define it?'

He takes a moment to collect his thoughts, then speaks soft and slow.

'Romance to me is paying very close attention to someone, taking discreet note of what brings them joy and then engineering subtle ways to deliver those moments to them. Romance is sneaking up behind someone and resting your head on their shoulder and placing your hand over their heart to show them that it is safe with you. Romance is stopping in a busy moment to say, "Do you know how much I love you?"' He takes a breath. 'If you want an actual definition I would say it is a combination of attentiveness, thoughtfulness, little surprises and a fearlessness when it comes to expressing your feelings.'

I take a moment to marvel at how Italian men are so bold when it comes to discussing emotions and then counter, 'But so much of what you describe comes from intimacy,' I note. 'How can you truly be romantic with strangers?'

He smiles in the face of my cynicism. 'If a man you'd never met before took you dancing under the stars, are you saying that couldn't feel romantic?'

I heave a sigh. 'You've got me. It would be heaven.'

'You'd like that?' Lorenzo brightens at my first sign of being human.

'I'd love it! What girl wouldn't? But don't you go saying anything to Dante!' I warn him. That would push me over the edge. I couldn't be responsible for myself pressed against his tango-ing torso in the starlight.

'I can see you're romantic,' Lorenzo gives me a knowing look. 'You are just out of practice.'

'Well, a lot of British men don't go in for that kind of thing. They think it's cheesy.'

'Cheesy?'

'I don't know, they don't seem to think it's very masculine.'

'What could be more manly than being able to please your woman?'

'Try telling Joe that!' I accidentally blurt.

'Joe?' he frowns. 'Who's Joe?'

Jeez! I mentally kick myself. 'My ex!' I tell him. 'Last guy I dated. He was a good chap, solid, fun sometimes but he lacked that tender touch, you know that little thing that made you skip down the street cos you felt so adored!'

Lorenzo nods. 'I think a lot of men sneer at romance because they fear if they tried to be romantic they would get it wrong and be laughed at. They can't see any of the romance in themselves so they'd rather not try at all.'

'That sounds about right.'

'Well I feel sorry for Joe,' Lorenzo decides. 'For it is he who is truly missing out.'

'Not me?' Why doesn't he feel sorry for me?

'Because you're here. And every day you will feel it a little bit more and when you leave you will never be without romance again because your heart will demand it. It simply won't be able to settle for anything less.'

Wow.

Finally Lorenzo has found a way to shut me up.

# 15

*'As I gaze upon the sea, all the romantic legends,*
*all my dreams, come back to me.'*
*– Henry Wadsworth Longfellow*

For some reason I pictured the Lido as a flat band of sand set with boxy apartment blocks, all too modern and characterless after Venice. I'm way off. I should have trusted that when Dante with his artist's eye calls something picturesque, he means it.

Whereas in Venice the greenery is secreted away, here it is flourishing visibly. The leafy boulevards that greet us as we step from the vaporetto put me in mind of France, with big bountiful trees and infinite pavement cafés each with more vibrant table-cloths than the last. One has a buttercup yellow swingseat that makes me want to put my hair in pigtails and order a knickerbocker glory.

'It really does feel as if we're on holiday,' I marvel.

'How far to the beach?' Tiffany enquires, plucking a flower seemingly made from pink silk crepe and tucking it behind her ear.

'Well, it's walkable – straight down the Gran Viale Santa Maria Elisabetta here,' he motions double-handed like an air steward. 'But I have a better idea.'

Lorenzo chuckles to himself, apparently knowing what is coming next.

Tiffany and I exchange a look. A horse and carriage perhaps?

'Oh no! Oh no, no, no!' Tiffany shakes her head as a tandem bike whirrs past us.

'Are you serious?' I gasp, looking at Dante.

'It will be fun!'

'In these?' Tiffany extends a high-heeled mule.

'You might have to go barefoot,' I decide.

'Next you'll be suggesting I wear lycra,' she tuts. 'I'm not rocking up to the Westin Excelsior looking like Lance Armstrong, it's all too absurd.'

'How about the surrey-with-the-fringe-on-top ones?' I point to a contraption with two bikes attached side-by-side with a canopy and a front basket. 'They are kind of cute.'

'Well, maybe . . .'

I'm surprised she's actually wavering and suddenly wonder if I'm up to it. I reach for the steering wheel and give it a twirl.

'That steering wheel on the passenger side, is just for show,' Dante informs me. 'Do you want to drive or shall I?'

So, we are actually doing this.

'You. Please.' I'm going to have enough going on trying to keep my skirt from flaring up as I pedal without worrying about which side of the road I should be on.

'Well, I'm driving ours,' Tiffany informs Lorenzo, surprising me again as I would have thought she would have preferred to have been chauffeured.

'As you wish,' he obliges.

'Everyone ready?' Dante enquires, having made the necessary arrangements.

And we're off, with very little need for the dringing bell on account of my squealing.

I'm amazed at the pace we pick up and try desperately to coordinate my rotations with Dante as we veer off the main high street down a slanty side street, faster still.

'Okay?' he checks.

'Just!' I yelp, closing my eyes every time a car passes us.

'You're quite safe,' he assures me.

'Mmm-hmm.'

I calm down a little as we pass through a park-like scene and decide to reach for my camera to do a mini-movie of the sun-dappled greenery. I try to hold the camera steady but it's all a bit of a blur so I leave it hanging off my wrist by its cord, ready to take a few snaps when we stop. It's then I realise Dante is laughing at me.

'What?'

'You turn your steering wheel every time we go around the corner!'

'I know it doesn't do anything!' I pout. 'I just want to feel I'm participating!'

'You want to help? Stick out your arm and signal right, please.'

'Right you are!' As I do so my camera swings out violently, whacking straight into the windscreen of a parked car.

'Oh god!' I cry aghast. 'Stop the buggy!'

Dante screeches to a halt causing Tiffany to bumpercar right into the back of us.

I look anxiously at Dante. 'Did we get insurance?'

He hops down, inspects the damage and calls over to me, 'Not a dent.'

'Really?' I get out and look for myself, most concerned about the windscreen, gently pressing the glass, half tempting it to crumble beneath my fingertips but it remains intact.

'What's the hold up?' Tiffany calls.

'Nothing! False alarm,' I call back.

'We're overtaking,' she tells us. 'You guys are a hazard.'

Off she goes, bowling straight ahead, Lorenzo with a look of mild panic on his face.

'*Right!*' I call after her. 'You're supposed to go right!'

'They have a map,' Dante waves them off. 'They'll work it out.'

As we climb back on board, I feel the pace changing.

'Let's take it easy, shall we?' he suggests as we resume pedalling. 'Slowly,' he places his hand on my thigh to try and decelerate my manic mousewheel manoeuvres.

I feel incredibly aware of my muscles flexing beneath his palm and grip the steering wheel tighter than ever. It's only when the sea comes into view that I truly relax.

'Oh my gosh, look at it!' I marvel at its glittering majesty, filling my lungs with daintily salted air. 'This place is just beautiful!'

Even the wide street running parallel to the beach – Lungomare Marconi – is lined either side with elegant trees. No bucket and spade shops, no Kiss-Me-Quick hats, just the occasional kiosk café, beachfront nightclub and the grand old belle époque hotel, the Des Bains.

'A measly four stars?' I feign disgust. 'Drive on!'

This really couldn't be any more lovely – I feel a freedom and a contentment I haven't felt for ages. Who'd have thought cycling could be such a lark? The location and the company don't hurt any, of course. Suddenly I can see the appeal of being an Amore. It's like you get all the good aspects of dating without having to work out any long-term glitches. Unless you're paired with Tiffany in which case it's more of an endurance test. But at least the end is always in sight. I've stayed in dodgy relationships a lot longer than ten days. Months I've spent with men who I knew I had no future with just because of the awkwardness of extracting myself. I sneak a peek at Dante realising I have yet to see his flaws. What might they be? Unable to commit, hence his single status? Too easy going? He barely batted an eyelid when I broke the glass heart. I'm sure there must be more, but for now that's the best I can come up with.

As we draw level with the film festival building we see Tiffany and Lorenzo ahead of us mid-squabble. English couples might bicker with bodies tense and lips pursed but put an American drama queen with an animated Italian and you get a mime-show you can interpret from two hundred metres away.

'Ah, young love!' Dante smiles as we pull up beside them.

'Five star,' I point ahead to the positively palatial Westin Excelsior in a bid to cheer up Tiffany. 'Oh dear god!'

'What?' she grumps.

'My legs!' I exclaim as I attempt to stand upright. 'Is it just me or are your thighs in knots?'

'Spin classes twice a week,' she shrugs. 'I'm good.'

'Can you walk?' Dante offers me his arm, chuckling lightly.

I grimace as I take it and turn to Lorenzo, 'About that coffee break . . . ?'

Dante guides us through the pink marble reception to a brilliantly sunlit and spacious lobby dominated by Moorish arches and lanterns, past the sixties sci-fi tunnel that leads to the spa, into the bar with black-and-white holiday snapshots of the rich and famous and finally out on to the vast terrace. This is the picture of glamour. We're overlooking white cabanas, golden sand and glinting cobalt sea. Suddenly I feel like some idle rich heiress from the thirties, out with her pals.

There's certainly plenty of money around us though none of it eligible – the three other men on the terrace are an octogenarian with a wrinkly-glitzy wife, a workaholic who doesn't once look up from his palm pilot and a spoilt child of three.

'Let's have some fizz!' Tiffany holds the drinks menu across for me to read alongside her.

'I'm happy with coffee,' Lorenzo nods his order to the attendant waitress.

'Hot chocolate,' I sit back in my chair. I need the sugar rush.

'*Un bicchiere di vino rosso del casa, per favore*,' Dante orders a glass of house red.

'Well, thank goodness for Dante or I'd be the only one drinking.' She addresses the waitress. 'Do you have any really good champagne?'

'And by good, I think she means expensive,' Dante observes, dryly.

'I thought you were converted to the Prosecco?' I frown.

'Westin is an American hotelier,' she tuts me, adding, 'When in Rome . . .'

Her logic confounds me. Aside from the fact that champagne is French not American, we're in Venice not Rome. Why can't she have a bellini like every other tourist in the place?

'We have a Grand Année Bollinger,' the waitress informs her, kindly not going too overboard. 'But we only serve that by the bottle.'

'That's fine,' she trills.

'You're going to drink a whole bottle?' I double-check.

She shrugs as if that's neither here nor there as she rummages in her bag. 'Oh damn, I've forgotten my cellphone. Lorenzo can I use yours?'

He dutifully places his phone in her outstretched palm.

I expect her to either step away from the table or leave the quickest message but instead Tiffany appears to have called one of her mates back home for a chat. Even when the waitress returns with the drinks she continues yapping, so loudly that the rest of us can't carry on a conversation and have to listen instead to her asking her velvet-rope friend who was at the Delano hotel bar last night and telling her to make a reservation at Argo for when she gets back and no, she hasn't done any real shopping here because it's all creepy carnival masks and lurid glass.

'No offence,' she shoots a quick glance at Dante, the first acknowledgement that we're still here.

All the while I feel a rising annoyance in my chest. How can she take such blatant liberties? Knowing how much international calls cost from a mobile, I start to feel sick and anxious on Lorenzo's behalf and stare fixedly at her, hoping my disapproval will bore through her beef jerky-like hide but no.

'Not yet,' she says. 'I'm beginning to think it's a myth.'

'Would you excuse me?' Lorenzo gets to his feet, gesturing to the bathroom.

'*Un momento*,' Dante follows after him.

'What?' she pouts as I jab at her leg. 'Oh well, say hi to him. I'll call you back later.'

Unbelievable! She's only getting off the phone now because her friend has someone else she'd rather talk to.

'How can you make an international call on his mobile when you know he's totally broke?' I hiss as she closes the phone.

'It couldn't have been more than twenty bucks,' she shrugs, tilting her face to the sun.

'Which is nothing to you but is probably a couple of meals to him.'

She huffs indignantly. 'It's not my fault he's poor.'

'But you are to blame for making him poorer!'

'Oh don't be so ridiculous!' Her face sours. 'Try looking at things from my point of view – I'm paying a man I'm not attracted to, to go on a date with me! The least he can do in return is let me use his phone for two minutes!'

'More like twenty,' I grumble.

I can't seem to get through to her with words so I do the thing I suspect will annoy her most – I tell the waitress that we'll be taking the still half-full bottle of champagne to finish later.

'That's so tacky!' she shudders as I reach for it.

'You would know,' I clip.

'Are you ready to leave?' For a moment I think Lorenzo has returned to the table with renewed authority but then I discover that Tiffany informed him earlier that she wants to squeeze in a mini-date with one of her gondolier suitors before dinner tonight.

I give him a hug to convey my sympathy but realise Tiffany does have a point – at least Lorenzo is being paid to suffer her prima donna ways, Dante and I are not.

Nevertheless I can't help feeling bad for him. 'Do you think we should call Sabrina and have her arrange a replacement before she bankrupts him?' I ask Dante as he leads me down to the beach where we find a sheltered nook beside a cabana and kick off our shoes and burrow our feet into the hot, spangly sand.

'As contrary as it sounds,' he replies, 'he won't want to lose the income.'

'But he won't have any if she carries on like this!'

Dante sighs, leaning back on his arms. 'I shouldn't really say this . . .'

My ears alert.

'. . . but they have a policy for clients like her.'

'Go on,' my journalistic nerve-endings are tingling.

'Provided that he presents them with a receipt, or in this case the phone bill, they charge any excess back to her at the end of the week under *incidentals*.'

'Well, that's a relief!' I reach for the champagne bottle and take a swig to celebrate Lorenzo's salvaged solvency before handing it to Dante. 'So if Lorenzo's in this for the money, what's your excuse?'

He gives me a slow, affectionate smile and says, 'I think you can probably guess,' before taking a slug himself.

I look at his lips and think that if we kissed now, we would both taste the same.

'So, does this feel romantic to you?'

He startles me with his directness – was that some kind of proposition?

'I heard you asking Lorenzo many questions on the subject earlier,' he explains.

'Ohhh!' I nod. 'Well, I'm just trying to get to the bottom of what romance is.'

'Why?'

'I just want to understand the concept better,' I say vaguely.

He thinks for a moment and then says, 'Technically I think we should be at the beach at sunset for it to qualify.'

I laugh. 'But then it would become a cliché.'

'And that in turn would rule out the possibility of romance for you?'

'Well, it might just make me feel a bit unoriginal. Maybe even a bit of a sucker.'

'A sucker?'

'I don't know.' I attempt an explanation, 'It's like when you see a movie and the heart-wrenching music starts building and you know the film-maker is trying to make you cry and you want to but you feel a little manipulated?'

He nods. 'I understand.'

'Not that it's like that with you at all,' I hurriedly add. 'You are very natural, nothing seems staged with you.'

'*Grazie*.'

'Of course, some people like the big, highly prepared gesture. They like to know someone has gone to a lot of trouble for them. Others would find that overwhelming, they'd prefer something simple and more spontaneous. I suppose it very much depends on the individual.'

'And what do you prefer?'

I think for a moment and then confess, 'I don't know that I've had enough experience of either to decide!'

Although I do remember saying to Joe really early on in the relationship, 'I wish we could spend the whole weekend in bed and not even have to get up for food.' And the next time I went over he'd brought in the side table from his lounge and laid it out with enough snacks and goodies to survive a month's hibernation.

It was such a lovely gesture but I remember feeling extremely self-conscious and suddenly neither in the mood for cuddling or eating. We got undressed and into bed and it was basically: 'Cheese puff?'

'Er, thank you. Could you pass the onion dip?'

We got over the initial awkwardness eventually but he never tried anything like it again. Was my reaction to blame?

'Personally, I think you have to have a romantic sensibility in the first place,' Dante decides. 'People always talk about romance as if it is something bestowed upon them by another but I think it is possible to feel romantic by yourself.'

I raise an eyebrow.

He sits up and dusts off his hands. 'Think of this beach at sunset. If you were here alone, would it still be a cliché? Or would it take on a different meaning? Could you look up at the sky and all its magnificent free-form art and feel, how you say, *dreamy*?'

I smile and nod a yes. I know exactly what he means.

'A true romantic feels romance all around him. He does not need candlelight or firelight or starlight to feel it.'

'Isn't it interesting how romance typically requires low-lighting?' I note. 'I do like that though.'

He leans across and shields my eyes from the sun. 'How's that?'

'Perfect!' I grin at him. 'Suddenly I feel very romantic!'

I also feel rather bold. As if I might take a step that perhaps I shouldn't.

And then his phone bleeps.

'This,' he says removing it from his pocket. 'Is the enemy of romance!'

'Aren't you going to see who it is?'

'I know it is my father,' he shrugs. 'We have dinner tonight with a very important collector. When he gets anxious he likes to text. He used to pace the room but now,' he mimics his father's thumb making staccato movements over the keys.

'How long do we have?'

He sighs as he looks at his watch, seemingly equally dismayed that our time together is drawing to a close. 'Twenty minutes?'

I nod and recline, propping my head on my bag so I can still see the frilly edge of the sea. 'Do you want to lean on it too?'

He rests his head directly beside mine. I feel my hair touching his. I take a deep, slow breath and my eyes involuntarily close. He's so close to me. Closer than he's ever been. All it would take is for one of us to roll over. But we both lie still, trying to keep our breathing steady, saying nothing.

I listen to the sound of the sea and the children playing ball and I think of all the romantic words I've longed to hear, all the things I thought it would take for my heart to leap like a springbok and I realise that I'm already there, no speech required. Who knew silence could be so sexy?

With Joe, when he's not talking to me, it generally means his mind is elsewhere, preoccupied, distracted. It's a wonderful feeling to be right next to someone and know you are both thinking about the same thing – each other.

And then his phone bleeps again. Our time is up.

But it's okay. Tomorrow we'll have all night. Though that thought in turn brings with it certain concerns. In the fifteen or so hours until we meet again, my conscience will reboot and the simple pleasure I'm feeling right now will be reduced to muddled guilt and confusion.

'Come on then!' I say, first to get to my feet, even if I am still a little twanging of tendon.

'This time we get a taxi!' Dante shows mercy on my thighs.

The return journey takes just a matter of minutes and I feel strangely sentimental as we flash past all that we pedalled.

'I love it here,' I sigh, leaning out of the wound-down window.

'I'm glad you had a good day.'

I turn to face him. 'Did you?'

'You know I did,' he confirms.

The driver says something in Italian, motioning to the approaching vaporetto. 'Is this you?' I ask.

'I will wait for you to leave first, it is polite.'

'Not to your father it's not,' I contest. 'I've still got plenty of time to get back, you haven't. Please go!'

He gives me an admiring look. 'You are very gracious.'

'And you,' I begin but then realise this is not the time to tell him how I feel. 'You I will see tomorrow.'

'Bologna,' he smiles quirkily, giving me a little wave. 'And please send my regards to Kier!'

Fuzzy and emboldened from the bubbly, I decide to reach for him – just a friendly hug in mind – but in lunging forward I inadvertently slip my hand through a disembarking woman's shopping bags. As we tangle plastic and entwine, Dante continues boarding, oblivious, and ultimately I am left holding someone else's groceries instead of him.

'Sorry, sorry!' I apologise to the now quite agitated woman, 'I'm such a nelly.'

She huffs on her way muttering something I'm glad I can't translate and when I look back for Dante, I see the vaporetto has already pulled away from the jetty. I stand watching the boat shrink from view until I become aware of another woman, equally laden with shopping, staring at me.

Does she have me pegged as a shopping snatcher? Is she challenging me to try to make off with hers?

'I'm English!' I call to her, hoping my nationality will explain my ineptitude.

'Forgive me for staring,' she says as she approaches. 'Your face . . .'

'My face?' My hand instinctively raises to my cheek. Have I come up in some kind of boozy lust rash?

'That gentleman,' she nods to where Dante had been standing. 'He said the name Kier . . .' I'm still missing the connection until she tentatively enquires, 'Are you . . . ? Could you be Kier's sister?'

I'm just registering her honey-coloured hair as she adds these two heart-stopping words: 'I'm Cinzia.'

# 16

*'Belladonna, noun: In Italian a beautiful lady. In English a deadly poison. A striking example of the essential identity of the two tongues.' – Ambrose Bierce*

Now I'm the one who's staring. I can't believe I'm actually face to face with the cause of my brother's abject misery. She looks so nice, so harmless in person.

Cinzia looks down at her shopping bags. 'I have gelato, it will melt, I live just . . .' she motions to an apartment building down the street. 'Will you come for an aperitivo?'

'To your home?' I gawp.

'Yes,' she looks surprised by my surprise. 'Do you feel this would somehow be disloyal to Kier?'

'Um. Gosh. Honestly I don't know what I'm feeling.' I'm still in shock.

'Just today I was looking at a picture of you and Kier and now I see you in reality . . .'

She's got me now. I'm a sucker for anything that can be branded 'synchronicity'. Besides, I really can't pass up this opportunity – what if she says something that will ultimately help my brother?

'Okay. Thank you,' I tell her. 'May I help you with your bags?'

'*Sei molto gentile*,' she smiles, accepting my offer.

'I think Kier is under the impression that you moved from here,' I tell her as we proceed down the street.

'Yes, that was the plan at one time. But then, well, my circumstances changed and I was able to stay.'

'I had no idea how beautiful the Lido was, I always thought it was such an afterthought.'

'Well, you understand we don't have the uniqueness of the city but we have our own charms.'

I nod in agreement. She certainly seems to have a few charms herself – all soft and golden and seemingly very caring. I can see why Kier went so ga-ga. She also didn't run a mile when she made the connection between me and him. So what went wrong?

'This is me,' she halts outside her building, reaching for her keys. 'Three flights of staircase, I apologise.'

My thighs can't believe what I'm putting them through. I wince at every step.

'You went on cycling today?'

'Is my pain that obvious?' I laugh.

'Either that or you really don't like the décor,' she jokes.

It is a little musty and old-fashioned, and thus all the more of a shock when she opens the door to her apartment: all three of her rooms – bedroom, kitchen-diner-lounge and bathroom – are stark white and lilac. Lilac walls, white marble table, lilac Perspex chairs, white bed linen, lilac throw, you get the picture.

'Wow! I take it this is your favourite colour?' my hand touches the petal of a lilac blossom in a glossy white vase.

'For now,' she shrugs. 'I change the colour of my apartment like other women change their hairstyle.'

'Really? Was your flat a different colour when you were

with Kier?' I hope I'm not being impolite, the question popped out before I realised it could be taken as a dig.

She seems unfazed. 'Yes. Back then it was a soft green colour, you know sage? Very calming. There was always a lot of flowers in the house in those days.' She looks wistful.

'So you keep the basics in white but change the paint on the walls and the details . . .'

'The towels in the bathroom, the cushions on the bed . . .'

'Nice idea. Like having a fresh start without actually having to move.'

She nods as she puts away her shopping, the immaculate units hiding a multitude of oils and spices.

'Rose petal jam,' I say as one little pot catches my eye. 'That sounds nice.'

'It is hand made by the Armenian monks on the island of San Lazzaro,' she tells me. 'Just a few minutes on the vaporetto from here.'

As I inspect the jar I tell her that I actually thought at one point she might live in a convent.

She gives me a quizzical look.

'Well, when we first got here, I saw Kier go to this nunnery and—'

'You thought I had become a nun?' she laughs.

'For a moment.'

'Did he explain why he was there?'

'No. Actually I didn't ask. I didn't want to pry. Just in case.'

'It is no great mystery. When he lived here he would take care of the convent gardens – the sisters cannot afford to pay a gardener, but he would go every week. He made it so pretty for them, found flowers to match all their favourite colours, even planted a little orchard and a small corner for vegetables so they could have fresh aubergine and peas and figs and pomegranates.'

And what did he get in return? I shake my head. Surely he's due some kind of mini-miracle as recompense! I might have to have a word with the nuns – they're clearly not praying hard enough.

'As you can imagine, they loved him.'

So why didn't you? I want to ask. Instead I merely mumble, 'That's such a lovely thing to do.'

She nods in agreement. 'He is a wonderful man.'

I almost want to correct her – *was* a wonderful man, before you crushed him.

'I suppose you are wondering why I broke us apart?' Unpacking now complete, she turns to face me.

I am slightly thrown by her directness. 'Well, it's none of my business really, but yes. I mean, I know I'm biased but even by your own admission he's this big-hearted, great guy – you know when he loves, he loves forever.'

She nods. 'It's true.' She sighs and seems to ponder for a moment. Then she draws a deep breath and gravely announces, 'I think we need some gelato.'

'Is that like the Italian version of a stiff drink?'

'Actually, the way I prepare it, you get both,' she giggles.

'Really?'

'It is a little speciality of mine, you have to try.'

'Okay,' I agree, intrigued.

She opens the cupboard, takes out two bowls, unwraps the ice cream which comes so beautifully packaged I want to move here tomorrow so I can come back from food shopping with items that look like actual gifts.

'Oooh, it's so deliciously smooshy!' I enthuse as she dollops a generous spoonful in each bowl. 'Can you believe this is my third day in Italy and I haven't had any gelato yet!'

'Shame on you!'

'I know.' Again I catch myself feeling too relaxed. I have to remember who I am dealing with here.

'So now for the good bit – instead of sauce I use nocino.' She takes a glass bottle from the shelf and splashes liberally. 'It is similar to amaretto, you know?'

'The almond liqueur?'

'Si, but this one is made from green walnuts gathered on Midsummer Night.'

I smile at the mystical connotations and take an expectant mouthful. 'Mmm, that's amazing!' The flavours tease my tongue. 'Am I detecting some kind of spice?'

'Cinnamon and clove,' she confirms.

'I love that!' I enthuse.

'I like it with frangelico too. That has the taste of hazelnuts.'

'So, you and Kier . . .' I switch back to the key topic – I can see how an hour could pass and all we'd be on to was sambuca floats and I really can only stay thirty minutes at the most.

'He has been greatly on my mind for the past few days – a friend of mine said they thought they had seen him at the airport . . .'

'On Monday?'

'Yes,' she confirms. 'And then today I was clearing out the desk drawers and I found this.'

She reaches over and hands me a photo of Kier and myself from our Dad's seventieth birthday party. Kier in the suit he has packed for the wedding. 'It was the only photo he had of him looking smart enough for an Italian woman, he said!'

I feel nostalgic as I look at the picture. That was a really good day. We put together a retrospective of Dad's life so far, Kier doing all the research for the first thirty-five years, even going back to the old chemist's shop he used to live above as a child and taking pictures for the slide show, me having the easier task of taking us up to present day. I thought we made a really good team.

'You are very close, yes?'

I want to answer a simple affirmative but find myself revealing that there is a little distance between us of late.

'My friend said he was with a woman at the airport. I hoped that perhaps he had met someone new?' She looks at me, waiting for me to confirm or deny the fact, perhaps wondering if that is what has made him less accessible to me of late.

I shrug non-committally. 'It was just li'l ol' me.'

She takes another spoonful of gelato. 'So has he?'

'What?' I continue to be evasive.

'Met someone new?'

'Does it make any difference to you?' I challenge, remembering my role as protector and indignant sibling.

She sighs. 'I don't know if "difference" is the right word. I would certainly love to hear that he is happy. That he has found a better caretaker for his heart than I could ever be. That would give me a little peace, I suppose.'

'So,' I clear my throat in preparation for my boldest question yet. 'You don't want him back?'

She looks at me directly, seemingly imploring me to have a little mercy.

'I'm sorry,' I apologise. 'He's my brother. I hate to see him hurt. I can't help wishing . . .'

She lays her hand on mine. 'I understand.'

She seems so sympathetic, I wonder out loud if there is anything she can tell me that could help Kier understand how things went awry – something he did that perhaps he could avoid doing the next time, something he could take from the experience, to learn from?

'He did nothing wrong,' she says simply. 'Nothing.'

'You just didn't feel the same way about him?' I venture.

She sits forward in her chair and contemplates me for a moment. 'Kirsty,' she says my name earnestly. 'I didn't tell him the truth. I wonder now if that was a mistake.'

'Well, it's very hard for me to comment without knowing exactly . . .' I trail off.

She nods then takes a deep breath. 'If I tell you, it is important that you listen until I am complete so that you understand fully.'

'Okay,' I agree, feeling a little quaky on Kier's behalf.

For several minutes we sit in silence as she searches for the right words to begin. Then she shrugs and says, 'A few months after I began to be with Kier I was diagnosed with breast cancer.'

My jaw falls open.

'It's okay, I'm fine now,' she assures me.

I shake my head in disbelief. 'Kier never said—'

'He didn't know. I never told him.'

'What? Something so huge? You couldn't tell him?'

'It's not that I couldn't, it was what could happen if I did . . .'

'What do you mean?' I just can't believe this.

'Even though I knew him less than a year, I could see that Kier would be the man who would stay with you through any kind of crisis.'

'And that's a bad thing?' I can't help but interject.

'Of course not, it's admirable. I know he would have done anything – *everything!* – for me. But I didn't want that. I didn't want him feeling beholden—'

'Oh Cinzia!' I gasp. 'He would have been happy to—'

She holds up a finger. 'I need to remind you to let me finish.'

I bite my tongue. 'Go on.'

'I was having a very nice time with Kier. He was sweet, romantic, so intelligent, so interested in everything around him . . .'

This is making less sense to me by the minute. *'But?'* I ask, almost impatiently.

'When I knew that my life could end . . . I thought of everything that I wanted if I survived and I realised that my feelings for Kier were not equal to his. I was enjoying his devotion but I knew that if we endured this test together we would be bonded in a way that could not easily be broken. How can you reject a man who holds your hand through such an ordeal?'

'So you did it by yourself?' The most scandalous thing to me right now is her bravery.

'I had my family,' she acknowledges.

'But you broke up with him at the time when you *most* needed someone to hold your hand.'

'It wouldn't have been fair.' Her eyes mist up now as she relives the break-up in her mind. 'It was so hard. I was so scared and so much of me just wanted to be held and when I saw his face . . .' She looks away and the tears start to stream.

'Wait there!' I leap up and grab a handful of lilac tissues from the bathroom.

She mops her eyes, continuing through the tears and little snatched breaths. 'To be that cruel, to hurt someone that much when all they have done is love you—'

My heart aches for her. And for Kier.

'If I was going to die, I probably could have gone through with it. Spend my last few months with someone who loved me. There are worse things, right?'

I nod understanding.

'But I wanted to live, Kirsty. And to live meant looking beyond Kier. It was almost like I made a pact with myself. I had to break up with him in order to promise myself a different kind of future. At the time the kindest thing seemed to spare him all knowledge of this.'

Of course he doesn't know he was spared anything – not the treatment, nor the sickness, nor the spectre of death.

I inhale deeply, barely able to process all this. It seems hard to imagine he could have been in more pain.

'You look so well,' I comment finally.

She smiles broadly. 'Thank you. I have been very fortunate. Compared to how so many women suffer . . .' She gets up and pours us both a purifying glass of water, her hands shaking a little. 'When I first received the diagnosis, I thought I was going to have to move back with my parents. That's why Kier thought I was leaving. It was all part of the lie – I told him I wanted to move back to my hometown. That I had tired of Venice.'

'I would imagine he offered to move with you.'

'Yes. So then,' she takes a breath. 'I told another lie. I said my first boyfriend had got in touch and that I was very sorry to do this to him but I was going back to him.'

'Oh no!' I cry.

'It was my mother's idea. She said he would never accept the split if I didn't put another man in his place.'

'You really couldn't tell him the truth?'

'You think he would have let me go that easily if I had?'

I think for a moment. 'He would have been determined to help you through it, even as a friend.'

'Exactly. And we both know that wouldn't have been possible.'

'You had to do what was right for you,' I concede. 'You were in survival mode.'

She nods. 'It was my life, my disease.'

'You did what you had to do,' I conclude.

'So you don't despise me?' She looks anxiously at me.

My own eyes bulge with tears. I shake my head, fighting back the sobs. 'I think you're amazing!' And with that I reach out and wrap my arms around the woman I have been cursing for the past year.

# 17

*'If you have a garden and a library, you have everything you need.' – Cicero*

The church bells peal, telling me in the most charming manner that it is time for me to start heading back to the Academy.

'Which vaporetto stop do you go to?' Cinzia enquires as I reluctantly gather myself together. Were it not for the fact that I was late for dinner last night, I'd be tempted to linger longer.

'Ca' d'Oro,' I reply.

Her face brightens. 'Well, if you like, we can travel part of the way together – I have an evening tour leaving from San Marco.'

'You're a guide?'

'We are four women in our company – you can look at the website while I quickly change. Small groups, private tours,' she says as she places her laptop on the table before me and clicks on walksinsidevenice.com.

On the 'Who We Are' page I see a photo and mini-profile of Cinzia, Sara, Cristina and Roberta. They are an impressive quartet with multiple PhDs, languages and published books between them. From what I can see, their itinerary options are accordingly high-brow – 'An Architectural Tour: from

Renaissance to Neoclassicism', 'Ca' Rezzonico and the Eighteenth Century', 'Bellini, Titan and Tintoretto: The Venetian School of Colour.'

'Do you have to be a graduate to go on these tours?' I laugh as Cinzia returns from the bedroom looking pretty in a peach sundress with matching tote bag.

'We sound smart, huh?' She winks. 'We also show people how to marbleise paper!'

'I haven't even heard of Cicheti,' I say pointing at the screen. 'What kind of paintings did he do?'

Cinzia leans over me and clicks on the link.

'Oh!' I cover my face with my hands. Cicheti is the Italian term for fingerfood!

'It's a gourmet tour of the local bacari,' she explains, 'which are basically wine bars that also serve food. Not recommended for teetotallers!'

'Sounds like fun!'

'We take turns with that one so we don't spend the entire week drunk!' she laughs then looks a little sentimental. 'That's actually how we met – Kier and I.'

'On a tour?'

'Well, I was with this English couple and he was at the bar . . . The couple had a very strong accent and I could not understand what they were asking me – he overheard the confusion between us and kindly translated their Newcastle English into something I could understand!'

'That is a tough accent,' I concede. 'I do love it though.'

'After a few drinks it started to make more sense to me!' she laughs.

'So did you two carry on talking long after the tour was finished?'

She nods and smiles. 'I think we were the last to leave the bacaro!'

I smile too. I love hearing about how people got together. Joe and I were a bit of a near-miss seeing as our mutual friend Matt seemed hell-bent on fixing him up with anyone *but* me. Initially he suggested a girl named Natalie on account of them both supporting the same football team. But the only picture Matt had of Nat happened to have me in it too and when he saw it, Joe said, 'I think I prefer her!' Naturally that got back to me but he made no move. Next time we were out as a group, his dad happened to be in town and he said, 'Why don't you go out with Kirsty? She's a good-looking girl.' Thank you, Mr Simmons! Ever dear to my heart on account of that comment. Still Joe made no move. He hadn't long since broken up with someone so I could see why he wasn't in any rush. I thought I had all the time in the world too but then came Matt's girlfriend's birthday drinks. I couldn't take my eyes off Joe and halfway through the evening Matt nudged me and said, 'I've got it! I know who'd be perfect for him!' and I thought finally my turn had come but he pointed across to a mouthy redhead I barely knew, and as he went to make his way over to introduce them I thought, 'Oh no you don't!' and scooted ahead and that was it! Joe and I had our first proper sit-down conversation and later he said he knew he was really into me because for the next two hours he wasn't even aware that he didn't have a beer in his hand. He'd also told everyone else that he couldn't stay late because he had an extremely early start the next day but in the end, like Kier and Cinzia, we were the last to leave.

'Okay! I am ready!' Cinzia smiles as she completes the stocking of her bag with relevant reference books for her tour.

We're nearly out the door when her eye happens upon a memoir. 'Have you read this – *A Thousand Days in Venice*? Marlena de Blasi?'

I shake my head, though I do have a faint recollection of it on our reviews page a couple of years ago, back when we actually acknowledged the existence of books.

'I am always asked to recommend stories set in Venice and when a woman is asking the question I have to choose this. Her language is so evocative, so enticing and she lived here on Lido Island so now you have visited us you must read.'

She hands me her copy.

'Oh, I couldn't take yours.'

'I have many copies, it is the nicest gift I can think to give.' She urges me to take it from her.

'Thank you very much,' I say, adding it to the bijou library in my bag.

'It's about a foreigner falling in love with a Venetian,' she continues as we head down the stairs. 'Or the "blueberry-eyed stranger" as she calls him in the book.'

'Does it have a happy ending?' I can't help but ask.

'Is real life ever that simple?' she queries enigmatically.

Once settled aboard the vaporetto, I ask Cinzia which tour she is hosting tonight.

'Literary Venice,' she replies. 'We will sit at Florian where so many writers have sat before and I will quote them passages from Wordsworth, Goethe, Byron etcetera, and then take them to such places they describe.'

'Sounds wonderful,' I enthuse.

'Well, if you are free sometime, I could take you.'

I give a regretful frown. 'I'd love to but I'm on a pretty tight schedule this trip.'

'You are with a group?'

'Kind of,' I say, not wanting to get into the whole Love Academy scenario.

'Where do you stay?'

'In Cannaregio,' I tell her, averting my eyes.

'But which hotel?'

'Palazzo Abadessa,' I muffle into my cuff.

Her eyes widen. 'You are with The Love Academy?'

I open my mouth wishing I could say something that makes it sound like I'm there for any reason other than the one she's thinking but all I can manage is 'Yup!'

'So the man I saw you with earlier . . .?'

I nod. 'He's my Amore.' Wow, how easily those words slip off the tongue.

'And Kier?' she looks confused.

'Well, he's really here as a favour, first of all to me, to keep me company and second for his friend Tonio—'

'Ah, si, si. I know Tonio.'

'He needs his help with something so . . .'

She nods vigorously. 'So who is his Amore?'

'Well,' I gulp. This is almost funny. I don't know how over your ex you have to be *not* to find Lady V a threat. 'I don't know if you know her but, um, Valentina Sciarpa?'

Her eyes become saucers and she laughs out loud. 'Not his type exactly but I'm sure he is the envy of all the other men.'

'Indeed.'

'Valentina,' she smiles, shaking her head.

'How well do you know her?'

'More by reputation than anything else.'

'She has a reputation?' I gawk.

Cinzia shrugs. 'All female beauty in Venice is compared to hers. She looks like a movie star, no?'

'Like the sister Salma Hayek and Penelope Cruz never had!' I acknowledge.

'It is true,' Cinzia laughs. 'But she is too shy for stardom. All the staring people do – it has made her self-conscious. I can see why they put Kier with her . . .'

'Have you ever thought of becoming an Amore?' I find myself asking.

'Oh no, I couldn't do that!' she scoffs.

'Why not? Is it considered shameful in some way?'

'Not to me, I am simply more comfortable teaching classes there.'

I gulp nervously. 'You teach there?'

She nods. 'Occasionally.'

'Are you teaching any classes this week?'

She looks at me, realisation dawning. 'Yes. Italian love poetry on Friday evening. Gruppo Bellini.'

'That's us,' I tell her aghast. 'We're Group Bellini.'

She shakes her head ruefully. 'Fate is indeed cruel if she intends for us to meet there. You know that is where he proposed?'

'*Kier proposed to you at the Palazzo Abadessa?*' I can't believe how little I know about my brother! How can he keep these things bottled up? It's just not natural!

'This was before it was The Love Academy. We were attending a friend's wedding reception. It was so beautiful, in the garden . . .'

'I can imagine,' I say, picturing the scene all too vividly.

'At the end of the night, when everyone was gone and it was

just us and the moonlight, he took me to a secret corner where he had spelled out the words "Marry me!" in white rose petals.'

'What did you say?' I gasp.

She looks sad. 'It was then that I told him we had to end.'

'It was that night? At the Abadessa?'

My mind is reeling. How has Kier endured these past few days? And to think I complained that he's showing me no love right now. I can't believe what he has put up with for my stupid article. His grouchiness is entirely understandable. In fact, I'm surprised he's coped as well as he has, I know I would be a wailing wreck.

'It would seem we have come full circle,' Cinzia sighs.

'I suppose I should forewarn him – I mean, listening to you reading love poetry . . .' I roll my eyes despairingly.

'Yes, yes,' she nods.

'Vallaresso!' calls the captain. 'San Marco.'

'I have to go!' she jumps to her feet, apologising profusely.

'Don't worry; we'll sort something out. Somehow.'

'Will you tell him that we met?' she turns back just before she disembarks.

'Y-yes,' I falter, a little overwhelmed by all the information she has given me. 'Not the . . .' I mime breast cancer by tapping my boob. The man next to me looks bemused.

'Tell him what you feel is right.'

'Okay!' I call as we pull away, all the more dismayed to have things left to my discretion.

I look at my map. Just nine stops to come up with a concise, coherent account of all that just occurred. And then be prepared for the inevitable questions: How did she look? What did she say? Who was she with?

It's then I realise I never asked her romantic status. I'm

guessing she's living alone on account of the girlish hue of her paintwork, but I don't know for sure.

For a second I think it would just be easier to get Kier to skip the poetry class on some pretext and keep my mouth shut about seeing her but that wouldn't be fair. Apparently Kier and Cinzia's paths are meant to cross, at least one more time.

# 18

*'The man who can keep a secret may be wise, but he is not half as wise as the man with no secrets to keep.' – Edgar Watson Howe*

'Kier, are you here?' I'm roaming the Academy, anxious to get my news out of the way.

It seems fitting that I should be burdened with this incendiary information since it was my ingenious plan for closure that brought Kier here in the first place. This is what I get for meddling in his own private heartache – even more of it for myself.

'Sabrina!' I latch on to the woman who always seems in the know. 'Have you seen my brother?'

'Ah yes, he is meeting us at the restaurant.'

Darnit! He's skedaddled again.

'Everything is okay?' she looks concerned.

'Yes. Well there is one thing . . .' I toy with broaching the subject of Friday night's poetry class but decide I really need to speak to Kier first and besides I'm supposed to be working on a new policy to stop making decisions for him. 'Actually everything's fine,' I assure her.

'Everything?' She eyes my outfit. 'You know we leave in twenty minutes . . .'

'I know! I need to change! I'm going right now!' And with that I hare up the stairs and burst into the room.

Got to focus. Posh restaurant. *Bella figura*. Can't wear that cos I'm saving it for the wedding. Already done the pink and the wraparound. I could wear the Zara sundress with the Grecian blue print and some chunky jewellery. It is summer after all, don't need to be so formal. That's it. Commit to it. Move on to hair and make-up. My hair is a little bit starchy from the sea-air so I decide to sweep it up. I re-do my face and go bold with the eyeshadow – electric blue on the lids and a liquid liner tick at the outer edges. Sheeny coral lips to finish. Done with one minute to spare. A minute in which I could go back to Kier anxiety but instead decide to reach for my perfume. Clinique Happy. Ever the optimist.

'Wow! Look at you, blue!' Adam is there at the top of the stairs and offers me his arm to walk down.

'Oh look, we match,' I say, noticing the sky-blue stripe in his sheeny tie.

'Yes, we do,' he smiles.

As we make our descent, I feel like we are about to be presented to all our family and friends for the first time as newly-weds. And yet I'm still smiling. It is strangely comfortable being on his arm. But like I say, it's probably just because of his Joe-ness.

'Oh!' I stop suddenly, grappling for my phone. I look at the display. He's called, Joe's called and I didn't even realise. 'Could you hold on for thirty seconds?'

Adam nods and adopts a statue-like pose. Meanwhile I bolt back to the room and listen to his message. He called while I was on the beach with Dante. Oh the guilt! He'll be out of his dinner around ten and will try me again then. If not, tomorrow morning. I sigh. He's so good. If the situation was reversed and I hadn't been able to get hold of him I'd be frantic. I send him a quick text and return to Adam.

'Everything alright?' he enquires.

'Yup, all is well.'

'Allow me to get the door,' he scoots ahead of me.

I smile and tease, 'Allegra teach you that?' as I walk through.

'I have a few moves of my own,' he tells me.

'Like . . . ?' I push for an example.

He thinks for a moment as he eyes me up and down. 'Well, for starters I want to be the first to offer you a piggy-back on the way home.'

'A piggy-back?' I hoot. 'A gondola ride too much of a cliché for you?'

'Hey, those shoes, four hours from now?'

I look down at my toes, triangulated into the tip of my stilettos. 'You know I might just hold you to that!'

'Ready to take your first official *passeggiata*?' Sabrina greets us in the courtyard.

Everyone looks excited, dressed to impress with Tiffany unsurprisingly the glitziest in a low-cut black cocktail dress, jet-beaded around the hem. Even Megan is in romantic ruffley silk the colour of vintage claret. I look down at my flimsy cotton number and decide I should pack a personal picnic and forgo the restaurant to sit beside the canal, using my own dress as a tablecloth.

Just to make me feel more of an outcast, Tiffany links arms with Megan, sending a very clear message that she has a new best friend and I am now *persona non grata*. It's actually a relief. And this way I get to chat a little more with Adam.

'I can't believe how well-behaved Melvin is tonight,' I cast a furtive glance at him, attentively escorting Sabrina.

'He's playing hard to get.'

'Is that what it is?' I titter.

'Seriously. It's his strategy. He told me that Filomena had advised him to give you a chance to miss his attentions.'

'Gosh!' I blink. 'Well, I certainly like him better at a distance, so I guess it's working.'

I look around me at our fellow early evening strollers and decide that this is a very nice tradition. In London everyone is scurrying at top-speed trying to get from A to B as quickly as possible; it's so rare to see people other than tourists ambling down the Mall, just walking for walking's sake. It gives a nice sense of community – a sense of being part of the human race, without any competition to get to the finishing line. But would it fly on Holloway Road?

Just thinking about my life back home gives me a little slump. If I want a job to go back to I'm going to have to start employing my supposedly enquiring mind . . . Mind you, there are worse things in life than probing Adam.

'So,' I ask him, 'do you have any amorous feelings for your Amore?'

'Is that your idea of small talk?' he chuckles.

'Is that rude?' I question, faux naive. 'I'm just curious. I mean, people come here with high expectations. I just wondered if yours are getting fulfilled?' I frown to myself. 'That sounded like an innuendo, didn't it?'

'Somewhat!' he grins.

'Okay, let me re-phrase that. Does Allegra appeal to you as a romantic partner?'

'As in a proper relationship?'

'Well, they do have certain statistics to maintain – at least one proposal every month, isn't it?'

'Honestly, if I'm going to get my hopes up I'd rather it be

with someone who lives in the same country as me. Weekends in Venice is a nice concept but a little impractical. Especially since I work weekends.'

'Ah yes, the job that shall not be named.'

He pauses. 'Can you keep a secret?'

'Me?' Oh god. 'No,' I tell him.

He laughs as if I'm just jesting and lowers his voice as he makes this disclosure: 'I'm a travel agent.'

'Is that something to be hush-hush about?' I'm confused.

'My boss made me come here. We've had so many enquiries about The Love Academy he said we should experience it first hand in order to best advise others.'

'How very thorough.'

'Basically he wanted to be sure it was legit. There was a recurring concern that it may be a form of prostitution!'

'Really?' I cough.

'Well, you can see their point . . . You pay money, you get paired with a girl, or a boy. There's "romance" . . .' he pulls a face. 'Anyway, all the women in the office are married, so here I am.'

'Does Sabrina know that's why you're here?'

'No. I wanted to be treated like a regular punter so I said I was an event planner. Which I am in a way, because holidays are big events in people's lives, aren't they?'

'Yes they are.' I can't believe we have so much in common – both here on false pretences.

'So what's your story?' he turns to me.

'Hmmm?' That's the trouble with asking questions, there's always a chance that they'll get asked of you.

'I wouldn't have pegged you for the type – not that there's anything wrong with . . . It's actually great but . . . You know . . .'

I smile at his stumbling. 'I guess I'm here for the same reason as you – I heard a lot about it and I wanted to know if the hype was for real.'

'It's a fairly high price to pay for curiosity,' he eyes me. 'I don't know if I would have stumped up my own cash.'

I shrug. 'They were doing a special offer for brothers and sisters.'

'Really?'

'No!' I groan. 'I just . . . I just wanted to know what romance felt like. I wanted to know if having it in my life would make me happier. I wanted to know if that was the name for what I feel is missing.' How did that happen? That all sounds true.

'And is it?'

'You know, it actually might be.' I give my mouth a ponderous twist then ask. 'What do you think?'

'I think all men should come here, just so they can catch up, you know, get on the same page as the women in their lives. You ladies have got all this stuff inside your head, all these wishes, all these little fantasies and it seems to me that a guy can really benefit if he taps into those.'

I look at him and grin. 'You're smart!'

'Well,' he shrugs. 'If it's that important to you, then it should be important to us too.'

I feel a little twang of understanding. Why can't Joe be more like this? Why can't he see how much better our relationship would be if *both of us* are getting what we want.

'Here we are,' Sabrina heralds our arrival.

And there, as promised, is Kier, leaning on the wall beside the entrance like he owns the place.

I let the others go on ahead, angling for a moment alone before dinner, reluctant as I am to spoil his appetite . . .

'This is it,' he says as I sidle up. 'This is where I used to work.'

'What?' I step backwards to take in the sign above the door, just a few inches shy of backing into the canal. 'Hotel Boscolo Dei Dogi,' I read and then gawp. 'Five stars? *This* was your garden?'

He nods, exhibiting a certain pride.

'Finally I get to see it!' I cheer.

'You understand why I had to come on ahead,' Kier shrugs himself off the wall, motioning for me to enter. 'I couldn't walk in here with The Love Academy posse without first explaining—'

'You didn't tell them—' I fret, foot frozen on the doorstep.

'I said I was keeping you company as a favour.'

'Which is true,' I note.

'And that it seemed like a wonderful opportunity for me to come back and see my old friends.'

'Also true.'

'To a degree – I would never have come back here were it not for the fact we were booked for dinner.'

'Really?' I don't understand him at all. 'Why not?'

He grimaces. 'They all knew what happened and I didn't want their pity.'

'But . . . ?' I tilt my head, sensing there is something more hopeful to come.

His face lights up. 'As soon as I saw everyone – Fillippe and Fabrizio and Alessandro the barman – it felt like I was home.'

Now I'm equally illuminated. I did a good thing! He's happier than I've seen him in months and it's because I interfered! I'm not a bad person. I am triumphant!

'Just wait till you see the cocktails Alessandro has prepared,' he says, leading me through the first set of doors, only to stop suddenly before the second. 'Oh – was there something you wanted to say?'

'What?' I blink.

'When you first arrived, I felt like you were hanging back from the others, did you need a word?'

The setting seems oddly significant – here we are in the transitional ante-room between fondamenta and foyer, panels of coloured bottle-bottom glass all around us. Outside he was happy, what I say now in our little multi-hued booth will determine how he feels on the inside. Naturally I can't bring myself to ruin his mood.

'Nope, no words!' I chirrup. 'Just wanted to walk in with you.'

He deserves at least one night of joy. What harm can it do to wait until tomorrow? It'll have to be first thing though because I'm leaving for Bologna – not entirely ideal to drop the bomb and disappear for two days but then again he'll be with Tonio so that'll bolster him. Everything's going to work out fine, I'm sure of it.

# 19

*'Your task is not to seek for love, but merely to seek and find all the barriers within yourself that you have built against it.' – Rumi*

You would think the evening was being held in Kier's honour, all the fuss that's being made of him. I feel pretty special myself being sister of the most celebrated man in the room – the staff are clearly delighted to see him and are a delight in themselves, not a sniff of snoot amongst them despite this being a sumptuous establishment with dramatic marble flooring, hand-stencilled ceiling beams and of course the requisite Murano chandeliers dominating the lobby – a pair of glass merry-go-rounds this time, elaborate as ever with cute little rosettes in fondant green and orange.

And then there's the cocktails. The Doge Orseolo Bar is abuzz not so much with what Alessandro puts in the drinks but on them – the crushed peach bellinis come in a sugar-rimmed martini glass with a blackberry-raspberry-blueberry skewer and a pristine fan of apple slices. The spritz has two shiny strawberries, a triangle of juicy pineapple nipping the glass and shoelace spirals of orange rind draped on the bobbing ice. True Alcoholic Art.

'What exactly is in a spritz?' I ask, wincing at the bitterness of the clear red concoction I opted for.

'Well, you have two kinds,' Alessandro tells me, 'Both feature white wine but one is with campari the other with aperol. You may prefer the sweeter aperol.' He offers me the alternative.

Ah, that's better! I raise my highly decorated glass in cheers to him, studying him as I sip. He's a petite package with laser-blue eyes, a fabulous Roman nose and something of a Speedy Gonzales sensibility in his fast-forward execution and enthusiasm. Though he's looking sharp in a white tux, you'd think he was wearing a suit made entirely of one hundred dollar bills the way Tiffany is looking at him.

'This is the best spritz I have ever tasted! *Ever!*' she raves, googly-eyed.

'Have you had one before?' Sabrina enquires, intrigued.

'Yes,' she nods vigorously, holding up her glass, 'This is my second!'

She's equally enchanted by his selection of bar snacks, laid out on the pretty rose-pink glass bar top, eyeing them as if he had set out trays of jewels before her. Most strange.

'So Kier,' Sabrina turns to my brother. 'Perhaps you would like to give us a tour of the grounds before dinner?'

He looks a little surprised but quickly locates his inner Italian. 'It would be my pleasure,' he says, with a subtle bow, adding, 'You mean now?'

Sabrina nods.

He gets to his feet. 'If you would like to bring your drinks and follow me!'

'Top-up!' Alessandro swiftly ensures everyone is brimming over with bonhomie before we leave his bar.

'Tiffany!' Sabrina calls back to the one person still attached to her bar stool.

'I'm fine here,' she dismisses her.

'I think some fresh air would do you good,' Sabrina insists, not one to be fobbed off.

She huffs and rolls off her stool like a sulky schoolgirl being prised away from her biker boyfriend.

'You're here all night, right?' She checks with Alessandro before she leaves.

He nods emphatically. I don't know what it is with her and bar staff. Already he looks like he's gone the way of Marcello.

'Good,' she says. 'I need more of you.'

'This is where we'll be dining tonight.' Kier guides us outside to an elegant votive-lit table in the canopied courtyard.

'Oooh, pretty!' Megan inspects the white infinity petalled bloom taking centre stage in a spherical glass vase. 'From the garden?' she enquires.

'Of course!' my brother smiles winningly.

Was that their first interaction? Could this be where it all begins for them? I have such a good feeling about tonight; my heart is racing.

While everyone else moves on, I take a moment to peer closer at the flower, observing its nest of green grasses, floating above a handful of blue glass pebbles, the same opulent hue as the napkins. Nice touch.

'Do you want to see the garden or would you rather move on to inspecting the cruets?' Adam calls back to me.

'I'm coming!' I chime, catching up as the group turn the corner and enter a surprisingly dense cluster of ewe and laurel trees. 'Wow, it's like an enchanted forest!' I gasp as Kier points out assorted hidey-holes and layering within. There's even a wooden hump-back bridge, probably the only one in Venice not traversing a canal.

'The Palazzo Rizzo Patarol was built back in the seventeeth century and this area – known as the Madonna dell'Orto quarter – was the only district of Venice that was cultivated for crops, hence the unusually large and historic garden,' Kier informs us. 'Two thousand square metres to be precise.'

I'm so proud of him! I love a man with facts and figures!

'It used to be the French embassy,' he continues as he leads us past a lovers' nook complete with marble loveseat and then up a windy side-path, under an arched remnant of a folly and out on to a sheltered woodland terrace fittingly appointed with furniture hewn from tree-trunks.

'This is where the squirrels and chipmunks come on their dates,' Adam decides.

It's a great spot, rustic and earthy yet, by contrast, overlooks the manicured lawn and vibrantly thriving flowerbeds that lie ahead of us in a neoclassical design, Kier tells us.

'What's this?' Melvin is staring into what I took in passing to be some kind of well.

'Can you see down it?' Kier asks, placing a foot on the wrought iron daisy-petal lid.

We crowd around looking down a vertical tunnel into what looks like a bricked cave – yet another location for a secret assignation? Trust Melvin to find the closest thing to a peep hole.

'That's actually an underground ice house, used more recently for cooling the wines,' Kier informs us as we backtrack to its entrance and then practise various vocal exercises in the echoey interior, Sabrina being the hottest contender for Italian Idol.

'Cool place to propose,' Adam observes. 'You know, lay some ice on a chick in the ice house.'

As the others groan, I chuckle to myself. He's so adorable when he's tipsy.

'Did you know the word "casino" originated in Venice?' Sabrina asks as we exit.

For a second we wonder at the connection but then she explains that back in the day, adulterous husbands had a designated spot to meet their mistresses away from the main palazzo and the eyes of the servants, and this small building at the furthest point in the grounds became known as the *casino*.

'*Casa*!' Megan blurts, making a linguistic connection.

'Yes, but *casino* is a very vulgar expression in Italian,' Sabrina purses her lips. 'It means, and I say this politely, "House of Prostitution".'

'So it's appropriate to Vegas in more ways than they even knew!' Adam chortles.

Continuing down the gravel path, along a carpet runner no less, Kier speaks of the honeysuckle, jasmine, acacia and paper mulberry that abound in Venetian gardens and then presents a further surprise at the end of the lawn – two bonus buildings.

'Casinos?' Melvin enquires hopefully, peering at the dinky cottages.

'These are actually hotel suites.'

'They're *so* cute!' Tiffany coos as we reach to bury our noses in the white roses entwined upon the wooden pergola fronting the building.

'They look very English country garden but if you look at the design of the brickwork along the top . . .'

We all take a step backwards and crane our necks.

'. . . you will see the crucifix motif in the crenellations.'

'You don't have to be Catholic to stay here, but it helps,' quips Adam, on a roll now.

'Nuns.' I find myself saying out loud.

'Monks, actually,' Kier corrects me. 'Though the nuns do love their roses.' He strokes the velvety petal of one lipstick-pink bud. 'It's the symbol of Mary to them. And passionflower, they love those too because the purple spikes resemble Jesus's crown of thorns.'

I'm dying to tell everyone that Kier also tended the gardens at the local convent – resist that if you can Megan! – but I can't risk revealing the source of my information so I button my lip.

'Oh, I'd be so happy if I lived here!' Tiffany sighs, wistfully, attempting to peer in one of the windows.

I can't help but smile – typical that her fantasy of a quaint little cottage just happens to be built on the grounds of a five-star hotel. Mind you, it's not a bad proposition, especially when we discover that the walkway through the open-air lobby of the second building (housing the Presidential suite) leads directly to the lagoon. And when I say directly, you could literally walk the wooden planks of the jetty, take one extra step and plop into the water. And then have an eye infection for the rest of your life like Katherine Hepburn, on account of her authentic fall in the movie *Summertime*.

There are two raffia armchairs invitingly positioned at the end of the jetty and Sabrina insists my brother takes the second to thank him for his tour. The rest of us sit at their feet like dutiful children.

The sun is setting to our left, a blaze of tangerine making a wavy silhouette of the distant mountains. The sky above is drifted with clouds of misty mauve and apricot blush creating a two-tone reflection in the rippled water – it looks to me like swathes of shot silk, pinched at intervals with peg-like tripods of timber bound a-top with low-glowing lanterns which in turn bounce stepping stones of soft yellow light on the water's surface.

'Now this is romantic!' Adam croons, taking a swig of his beer and then leaning back to rest his head in my lap. 'Mind if I . . .?'

How can I object? I feel like we're a cast of Shakespearean nymphs. As I smile down at him I notice that his skin, all our skin, has become a burnished peach in this golden hour. Megan's hair is now shimmering copper and Kier's hazel eyes have taken on a warm gleam. I sigh. It's nigh on impossible to feel discontented in this gilded light. There's even the subtlest wisp of breeze, creating the perfect combination of comfort and serenity.

So quiet.

Even with seven bodies a-breathing all we hear is the light slap of water on the jetty and the burr of a distant boat. I follow its path. Is that Murano over yonder? Dante's Island! And further to my right, San Michele? Yes it is! Gosh. It's only day three and already the scenery is imbued with such significance to me.

I don't seem to be alone in this – everyone appears to be taking a moment, a mental snapshot of this feeling. It's as if the world has slowed right down and would like us to do the same, to take time to pause and reflect.

'I'm thinking of trying out a new hairstyle,' Tiffany consults Megan. 'How do you think I would look with asymmetrical bangs?'

Yes, it's moments like these that offer you the potential to re-route your very destiny.

'Melvin, stop that!' It's now my turn to ruin the vibe. Despite the fact that Adam is still in my lap, he's shuffled up behind me and is fondling my hair in such a way that I feel he could at any moment give a vicious tug and pull out a clump as a keepsake.

'Bastards!' Adam is suddenly on his feet swatting at a pair of mosquitoes.

So much for serenity.

'Well, don't send them in my direction!' Now Tiffany is in motion. Despite the fact that she has lined her stomach with infinite nibbles, the booze seems to have hit home because she stumbles as she gets to her feet, sending her sunglasses slipping from her head, straight into the lagoon.

'Oh my god, *no*!' She looks despairingly around – isn't anyone going to dive in and retrieve them for her?

Er, no. We're in Venice, not Tahiti.

'They're Chanel!' she protests as if the lagoon might spew them back, realising their worth.

'I could try—' Kier starts rolling up his sleeves.

Sabrina stops him from doing anything gallant. 'It is not advisable to touch the lagoon water.'

'Yeah, there's some things antibiotics can't cure,' Melvin notes, sounding like he's speaking from experience.

'I can get you a lovely copy cat pair down Brixton market for a fiver!' Adam offers.

'That's hardly the same,' she sneers.

'Oh no, trust me, they're identical. All the girls at work have them and I promise you, they haven't stumped up a couple of hundred quid for them.'

Before Tiffany can get any more testy, Sabrina cuts in. 'Perhaps it's timely that we discuss letting go of baggage?' She then gets to her feet to welcome Raeleen, excusing herself, saying she needs to cue the waiters.

'*Buona sera*!' Raeleen acknowledges each of us before she takes her seat. 'Are we all ready to begin?'

Tiffany humphs back to a seated position with the most almighty pout of dissatisfaction. Melvin attempts to console her but she sees his creeping hand for what it is – an excuse for an attempted grope – and swats him off. Megan offers Kier the rest of her drink confessing she'll be in the canal next if she drinks another drop and Adam decides to sit with his back propping up my own. Now we're ready.

'I want to talk about how handing the burden of your past over to your lover for them to fix is the quickest way to drain a relationship,' Raeleen gets straight to it. 'My friend Luana from Piacenza uses the analogy of money in the bank. She says: "If you don't have anything in your account, you can only give loans to the person you are trying to love. On the surface it looks like you are loving them back but before long you become deeply indebted and start to become needy."'

There's a hum of recognition in the audience. I loathe being accused of being needy and I hate feeling it even more, it just leaves me so vulnerable and on edge. That's really no way to live – waiting for someone else to do something in order for you to feel alright. I tut myself – essentially I am giving someone else control of my happiness. How ludicrous is that? It's just that at the time I feel so deprived, so neglected, so orphan-like tragic . . .

'Do you know what neediness does to romance?' Raeleen continues. 'Kills it.'

Whoa. That's a slap in the face. Is that why Joe isn't

romantic? Because I'm too needy? I step forward with outstretched arms and instead of pulling me into an embrace, he recoils. I still don't understand why – what does he think I'm going to take from him in that moment? It seems a total Catch 22 – if he was more romantic then I wouldn't be so needy! Oh this is so confusing!

Tiffany raises her hand.

'Yes?'

'This emotional bank account of ours, how do we fill it up?'

Six pairs of ears perk up.

'Well I'll first tell you the primary thing that prevents you from making deposits – unresolved negativity. That's what puts you at risk of becoming stingy or lacking in the abundance your heart needs in order to be generous in romance.'

Hmm. That's interesting phrasing. I think I'm pretty loving to Joe but I don't know if I would exactly describe myself as generous. Especially when I don't feel he deserves to be lavished with affection on account of me not getting enough myself. I've always thought of him as the stingy one but is it me doing the withholding?

'Recovering from past hurts is what makes you whole and psychologically ready to love. Rather than calling this process "healing" I call it "wholeing" because you are taking the fragments of your past and piecing them together so that you can feel complete and start to like yourself.'

It seems really key, this liking yourself. I remember Oprah saying, 'Liking who you are comes through in everything you do'.

It seems Raeleen would agree: 'Once you like yourself you can love joyfully and without diminishing your own self-reserves. You will be ready to open your arms wide and let romance in. You will also be able to say no to experiences that don't feed into your positive self-image.'

Now that's a good one. I must remember that.

Funnily enough, the thing I don't like most about myself right now is that I'm deceiving these people for the sake of a magazine article. I can't help but wonder if my lack of integrity is having more of a knock-on effect in my life than I even realise?

'As an old Italian proverb says, *Chi vuol farsi amare, amabile deve diventare*. If you want to be loved, you have to make yourself lovable,' Raeleen urges us. 'You must start with you!'

'So how exactly do we start putting our broken pieces back together?' Megan asks, looking slightly daunted.

'Number one – you have to stop dwelling on past hurts.'

I see Kier take a deep breath then concentrate hard as Raeleen talks about journaling as a way of learning and responding to your own needs and issues. 'It's a form of self-education,' she says. 'You ask yourself pertinent questions. The answers may not come instantly but most of the things we need to know are right inside us the whole time.'

I wonder what question Kier would be asking himself? Is *Why didn't Cinzia love me back?* still top of his list?

How about, *Why am I finding it so hard to move on?* Or, *Why do I feel so angry all the time?*

Mentally I jot down the three questions I would like to answer before my time at The Love Academy is up:

*Do I want children?*

*Do I want children with Joe?*

*Do I want Joe?*

And then there may be a query or two about Dante. I can't believe we're spending the night together tomorrow. I feel a whisk of nerves and excitement at the prospect. Do I like myself for feeling that? No. It makes me feel guilty. But it's still there.

No doubt all these things will be addressed in due course. Right now my most pressing question is this: *What are we having for dinner?*

# 20

*'In the bel paese, romance is as natural an expression as eating a spaghetti dinner, and one approaches it with the same gusto and frequency!'*
*– Raeleen D'Agostino*

'Tonight the Giardino di Luca Ristorante has prepared a very special menu for us to celebrate the best of Venetian cuisine,' Sabrina announces as we take our seats.

Kier gives me a sympathetic look from across the table.

'What?' I mouth back at him.

'Seafood!' he grimaces.

While the others salivate and gleefully rub their hands, I gulp quietly to myself. I've never been a great fan of food bearing tentacles and suction cups.

'Could you pass the bread?' I ask Adam, preferring to twist my body in his direction as Melvin is on my other side.

'Don't fill up too much,' Sabrina cautions. 'There are many, many courses! Ah, here is the first. The raw fish.'

I blanch as the waiter points out, 'Oysters, tuna, sea bass and prawns.'

Raw prawn? Are you kidding me? I assess my selection of slime and tentatively dip my fork prong into the finely diced tuna topped with chives as it looks akin to dark pink candy. That's actually not bad. You wouldn't even know it was fish. As for the rest, I simply can't.

It's then I notice a black cat weaving among the legs of the other outside diners. I drop my hand to my side and twiddle my fingers, trying to entice it. No luck. Surreptitiously I pluck a prawn, still with its beady black eyes and whiskers, and repeat the motion. There she is. Youch! Chomping a little too hard with her spiked fangs.

I manage to dispense with a good portion of sea bass before I have a sudden fear that the cat might throw up. Do cats eat raw fish? I mean, obviously they eat it, but is it good for them? Oh please don't let her start yakking mid-meal! My anxiety is compounded as the waiter heads in my direction. I look frantically between him and the cat – stop licking your chops for god's sake, you'll give the game away! He's getting closer, she's still extending her pink tongue, switching it around her mouth.

'Signorina?' He hesitates before giving me my next plate, as if to say, 'Shall I just set it on the floor?'

I look down pretending to notice the cat for the first time, 'Oooh hello kitty! What have you got there?' I coo.

Perfectly professional, he simply whisks away the raw plate and now sets down – I can't believe it! – a plate of octopus carpaccio. I have never seen the eight-legged beastie served in this form before – it looks like a cross between thinly-sliced turkey and a lacy doily, complete with decorative purple circles.

'It almost looks too pretty to eat!' I only half-jest.

'We also have sardines prepared with onions and pinenuts and raisins according to a fifteenth-century recipe.'

I feel quite overwhelmed, like I'm in a highly sophisticated version of the Bushtucker Trial. Well it's too late to say I'm vegetarian now, and the staff are so proud to present their finest delicacies, I'm just going to have to do the best I can. Separating the pinenuts and raisins from the melange I create my own marinated version of trail mix. Mmm, that's quite tasty.

'Are you going to try the octopus?'

I can hear the dare in Adam's enquiry. Before I lose my nerve I cut a slither and pop it in my mouth. I can tell he's waiting for the comedy grimace but none is forthcoming.

'I can't understand this, it actually tastes good,' I chuckle, going on to polish off the entire doily.

'So!' Raeleen gets our attention as we take a short break before the next course. (I'm predicting a big pile of lagoon monster blubber.) 'Here we are in Italy – the country where men sing shamelessly about the emotional torture of unrequited love and where women smile flirtatiously, fully aware of their elevated status in the hearts of Italian men!'

All the women quickly raise their glasses to salute that, though the men seem a little more hesitant about endorsing the singing element.

'Let's talk about being male and being female,' she continues in earnest. 'Italians believe that their god-given masculine/feminine differences have a right to co-exist and be openly cherished.' She glances around the table. 'How many of you men open the door for a woman?' I sneak a smirk at Adam who did that very thing just this evening. 'Here in Italy men carry bags for their women, help them with their coats, gaze into their eyes over dinner.' Hmm, Melvin definitely has the edge in the last category. 'In turn, the women are unapologetic about letting their sensuality shine through in their gestures, in their dress and in their receptivity of the male overture. They smile sweetly and move with grace as if they deserve to be treasured.'

I must confess I'd love to nail that – the deserving-to-be-treasured thing, without becoming Paris Hilton or Tiffany. Maybe the reason Joe doesn't appear to treasure me is because I don't believe the sentiment myself. As Raeleen would say, it has to start with me. Well I'm starting right now! Hello, my name is Kirsty and I deserve to be treasured!

'Italian men and women appreciate the inherent sexual prowess of the other and they are also proud of their own natural sensuality. That's the key – be proud of who you are and act like it!'

I discreetly reach into my bag and click on my tape recorder. I need to be getting this.

'It may sound old-fashioned, but women really do love men who are strong and men love women who are gentle. Those qualities represent the nature and essence of men and women and they are what make us attractive to the opposite sex.'

'But there are plenty of men who like strong women . . .' I find myself protesting.

'Of course! I'm not saying you can't be strong too. It's not either or. But don't deny your gentleness.'

It's a fair point so why am I resisting? Is it because gentle sounds a bit namby-pamby to me? A bit too mild-mannered for an independent career woman? But then, I suppose gentle also means tender. That's a nice quality. That's sexy. In a man too. As far as strength goes, I'd take strong over weak but I do want a fair quota of sensitivity too. Not exactly Joe's forte.

Megan raises her hand. 'Is there such a thing as being too gentle?'

'I think you mean shy,' Tiffany opines. 'You just need to be more confident, flaunt yourself a bit!'

Megan looks uncomfortable. 'No offence,' she says, eyeing Tiffany's provocative neckline, 'but don't you think there's something a little demeaning about presenting yourself in such an, um, *obvious* fashion?'

'Let me tell you about Guilia,' Raeleen steps in before further offence is given or taken. 'I was once in a café, quietly sipping my latte when the whole place came to a standstill at the sight of this gorgeous Venetian woman in a form-fitting leather skirt and high-heeled boots with blonde hair reminiscent of the metallic tint used by her Renaissance predecessors.'

Melvin makes a strange gurgling sound. I shift my chair a little closer to Adam.

'Some men whistled out loud, others found their mouths hanging open, all of them stared but she neither quickened her pace nor called the police. Instead she looked directly into the eyes of her admirers, gave them what looked like a subtle smile of acknowledgement and sashayed past them as if she were on a catwalk in Milan.'

'Like Megan today on the Strada Nova!' Adam teases.

'That was out in the open,' Megan differentiates. 'If it had been in confined space like a bar I would have just died.'

'I would probably have just turned around and walked out,' I admit.

'Why not just enjoy it?' Tiffany shrugs. 'I know for damn sure she didn't buy her own biscotti!'

'Most of us can't imagine perceiving such a sexually charged scene as innocuous but she reacted as graciously as a theatre performer might respond to applause.'

Now that's an interesting take on the situation. 'I suppose it is a form of appreciation,' I muse.

'Anyway, my point is this,' Raeleen says, continuing. 'A few days later I met Guilia again when I went to the emergency room of the local hospital with a sprained ankle—'

'What was she in there for?' Adam cuts in. 'I would have thought it was all the men she left in her wake with whiplash!'

'She wasn't a patient,' Raeleen corrects. 'She was the doctor who examined me!'

Our eyes widen.

'This to me was the quintessential unity of brains, beauty, professionalism and femininity. She was like an Italian romantic work of art!'

Now that is admirable. And rare. More than ever it seems that you're either some self-confessed dollybird aspiring to be on the cover of *FHM* or you have some class and thus feel obliged to tone things down so as not to send out the wrong message. But in doing so you relinquish the kick of being described as 'hot'. Mind you, you don't see Angelina Jolie downplaying her sexuality. And yet it is absolutely not what defines her. She's so much more than a sex-bomb. Hmmm, food for thought.

Speaking of food . . . Now we have baby gnocchi with king lagoon crab, shortly followed by spaghetti with langoustine 'busera style', taking its name from the red ceramic pan in which it is prepared. Brazenly tucking in now, I find it deliciously spicy. In fact I'm just about full when the main course arrives. Yup, the previous *four* were just little samplers. Now we have cooked sea bass folded with capers and olives and my old friend the potato, never to be taken for granted again. This is accompanied with giant platters of lightly battered calamari, shrimp and vegetables. My ultimate favourite of the night is the deep-fried courgette. Next time I'll just hold out for that, it's so salty and crispy and goes so well with the Sauvignon Blanc. Don't mind if I do have another glass . . .

All the while Raeleen continues to educate us on romance,

Italian style. I really hope Kier is taking on board what she's saying about banishing self-punishing talk and the importance of being positive – 'because romance is attracted to energy similar to its own'.

'What about when you do have a partner?' Melvin asks, ever the optimist.

My ears prick up but I try to look like I'm not listening too intently, seeing as I'm officially single.

'The thing is to know how to recognise, appreciate and acknowledge your lover's romantic gestures. Remember, no two people are identical in romance. You might like to say *I love you* a hundred times a day, whereas your partner may prefer not to say it at all but he will massage your feet every night while you are watching TV.'

There's a murmur of acknowledgement from the group.

'Differences in romantic expression are what keeps things interesting. You can't simply demand that someone relate to you in the precise way you relate to him or her. That is not only unrealistic, it's boring and meaningless,' she insists. 'Think about it – if I demand you tell me a certain number of times a day that you love me, how much depth would those words carry? Instead, if I could interpret those foot massages as *I love you*s then romance would thrive on its own terms.'

I feel a little shamed. Am I dismissing all the ways Joe shows me that he loves me because they are not an exact match for the passionate show-stoppers I have in my mind? Have I become blind to the nuances, focusing on the lack and missing all the divine subtleties? Have I, in a nutshell, become ungrateful? I get the urge to run to him and beg his forgiveness for my callous ways but then I think of how he left me at the station and decide his secret love code must be pretty darn subtle. I mean, I totally get Raeleen's point. I absolutely agree with her. And yet there are certain triggers within me that Joe is just not triggering. Am I really supposed to just let those feelings go?

Perhaps there's some kind of compromise we could come to – I try to become more attuned to the ways he's showing me that he loves me and in return he promises not to suck the romance out of situations that otherwise could be quite dreamy. Like that gorgeous B&B suite in Doughty Cottage in Richmond. I remember at the time thinking I would have had a more romantic experience if I were by myself but now I think that if he'd just kept his mouth shut, it could have been a night I looked back on fondly.

But here I am again, wishing for him to change when perhaps I'm the one who needs changing the most. After all, he's happy – what motivation is there for him to change? I'm dissatisfied, so in a way it falls to me to do something about it. Blaming him isn't getting me the required results. So, if I reassigned romantic feelings to the things he *does* do for me, as opposed to the Hollywood movie things he doesn't do, wouldn't I be better off?

'Romance doesn't have to be logical, it just has to be enjoyed,' Raeleen confirms.

Okay, that's my new plan. Let's just hope Dante doesn't do anything too romantic in Bologna and spoil my resolve.

I turn my attention back to Raeleen.

'What I would like to say to you in conclusion is this: romance is the dessert,' she asserts with a smile. 'If you are hungry, you need to be working on the main meal – *yourself*. That means learning how to fulfil yourself first, and once you have achieved that, then you will be ready for dessert!'

Right on cue the waiters appear at the table, taking down requests for either ginger mousse with amaretto sponge, fresh berries or gelato.

'The mousse,' says Melvin.

'Gelato for me,' I chirp. 'Oh and could I get nocino with mine?'

Kier's face darkens. 'What did you say?'

Oh god, oh god, please don't say Cinzia invented this combo. 'I just thought I'd try mine with a splash of liqueur,' I gulp, seeing if I can get away with it.

'There's only one person I know who makes that combination,' he continues to glare. 'You went to see her, didn't you?'

All other conversations peter out as everyone awaits my response.

'I didn't *go* to see her,' I clarify, 'but yes, I did see her.'

'And you ate gelato with her?'

Oh, it sounds so pally. As if we were gaily trivialising everything.

Before I can reply he gets up and throws down his napkin. 'That's it, I'm done.'

'Wait!' Here I go, running after him again. 'I was going to tell you—' I call after him as he charges through the lobby and out the front door.

'When?' he stops suddenly, turning on me. 'When were you going to tell me?'

'Tonight, when we arrived – it only happened this afternoon – but you were so happy, I didn't want to ruin your mood.'

He continues pacing, glowering, 'It's just not fair.'

'What's not fair?' I ask, part-exasperated.

'*Everything!*' he despairs, looking stricken.

'For starters . . . ?' I stand before him, blocking his path –

I've got to get him to talk, get him to start getting these bitter irks off his chest.

He looks pained as he says, 'That you got to see her and I didn't.'

My heart goes out to him. I know that feeling. 'You know,' I tell him softly, 'if you want to, you still can.'

He looks at me like I'm mad.

'I mean it's a real option – the day we get back from our overnight, she's teaching a poetry class at The Love Academy.'

'What?' he looks panicked.

'Of course you don't have to go,' I bluster, no clue whether I'm making things worse. 'Look, I know how excruciating this is, when I was split up from Joe—'

'That was temporary,' he almost spits. 'You got to go back. You had a choice. You dismissed him—'

'Not exactly dismissed,' I begin to reason.

'You broke his heart and he still took you back. I don't have that luxury.'

Well, there it is, the root of his resentment, just as I suspected.

'It's all the wrong way round,' he wails.

'You mean you should be back with Cinzia but I should not be back with Joe?'

'No,' he looks at me with haunted eyes. 'I should have been born first.'

'What?' I splutter. Where the hell is this coming from?

'The man should lead the way for the woman. That's what Imogen said.'

'Imogen?' I frown. For a second I just can't think who he means. Then it dawns on me. 'Imogen who just had the baby?'

He nods, confirming that he is referring to his old university pal who just had her second child. 'I went to see her before we left and she said she was glad that she had Blake first, that that's the right way round.'

I can't help but scoff. Is he actually saying that all brothers should be born ahead of their sisters? Is this really why he's been so mad at me since we got here? Some throwaway pap psychology remark from a smug, new mother and suddenly the blame for all the ills in his life is laid at my feet?

'Let me get this straight,' I bristle. 'You're angry with me because I was born first?'

'I'm not angry with you so much as the sequence of events—'

'That's rubbish,' I beg to differ. 'I can feel your hostility towards me, *I can feel it!*' My voice chokes.

I can't believe this. I thought my brother was an unconditional ally, a person I could always rely upon and trust implicitly. It's chilling to discover that someone who you thought was so close to you resents you so.

Until this moment I thought he blamed our parents' divorce and the absence of a strong father figure in his life. But apparently that is old news now. I'm the new scapegoat. And it sickens me to hear it – I've always been on his team. Even through the inevitable brother-sister kiddy conflict years. Even when he said he hated me every day, even when he hit me in the same place on my arm and wrote spiteful notes about me and left them for me to find, I loved him unconditionally with utter devotion, waiting patiently for him to grow out of that phase and like me again, and now this?

I never once complained that I didn't have the protective older brother. Maybe I'd have liked to have had someone to watch over me instead of always the other way around. But my mind never went there because he always was enough of a hero to me. I've admired him for so long, always prided myself on our close adult relationship and all this time it would seem he felt patronised by me and diminished, simply by my presence?

I feel cold towards him now as I say, 'We're only a year apart. I can't see that it would even make that much difference.'

'But you were the successful one.'

'Success isn't either or!' I debate. 'I didn't steal all the success and leave none of it for you! Besides you've made a great career out of gardening. I don't see the problem.'

'Maybe I ended up being a gardener by default, maybe I wanted to be a writer!'

I don't know who the hell I am speaking to right now. This is all so random.

'So if you had been born first . . .' My brow is furrowed.

'At least I would have stood a chance! At least I could have tried without feeling second best all the time. Maybe then I would have liked myself more.'

Raeleen's words have obviously hit a nerve. But I'm still not convinced of his argument.

'I've never been competitive with you about anything. I was doing my thing, you were doing yours. And can I just say, we both know you are way more intelligent than me academically. You could have done anything you put your mind to. My great advantage was that I only wanted to do one thing. You were spoilt for choice.'

He shakes his head as if I just don't get it. And frankly I don't. In this moment I despise him – it seems like the worst kind of transference, a shunning of all personal responsibility.

When he turns away from me, shoulders hunched and skulks down the fondamenta into the shadows, I let him go. No more running after him.

I stand there in the now chill night feeling betrayed, feeling like I'm being punished for a crime I didn't commit. I lean against the wall but I don't cry. I'm still smarting too much. Joe kept telling me to leave him to it, to stop pandering and indulging and trying to fix everything with him. Well, I guess my time to step back and let go has finally come.

He's done, is he? Me too.

# 21

*'Amato no sarai, se à te solo penserai.' ('You will not be loved if you think yourself alone.')*
*– Italian Proverb*

'Oh perfect!' On my way back to the Abadessa it starts to rain. I couldn't face going back into the Dei Dogi after 'the scene' so I decided to call it a night but now I find myself ducking into a late-night café-bar waiting for the shower to pass. I end up staying for an hour, just people-watching and reflecting on how one minute your life seems to be ticking over and the next it turns into a time-bomb.

When I do finally return to the Abadessa, all is quiet, except for a strange noise coming from the back of the garden.

'Tiffany!' I gasp, identifying its origin. 'What are you doing?'

She looks up at me all sodden and sobbing, 'I've been gypped!'

'What do you mean?' I fear she means mugged or worse but then she whimpers the name Alessandro. 'What did he do?' I gasp.

'He's just so lovely!' she wails. 'He walked me the whole way back under his umbrella and he didn't even try anything!'

'And you're disappointed?'

'*Nooo*!' She wails. 'He's got a girlfriend! He loves his girlfriend!

He'd never cheat on her, never!' she splutters a little more. 'That's why I'm crying.'

'You really liked him that much!'

'*Noooo*!' she's howling with impatience at me. 'All this time, I never knew men like him existed and they DO! They do!'

'Isn't that a good thing?' I venture, oh-so-gently.

'Not when you've spent the last fifteen years confirming to yourself that they are all bastards!' she howls into the night.

'Look, I think I'd better get you inside,' I try to coax her to her feet.

'I want to be in the rain!' she resists. 'I belong in the rain!'

'Well how about I stick you under the shower and we can talk there.'

Finally she concurs and we sit in her room, wrapped in an assortment of towels, toes tucked under the gold counterpane of her bed.

'Do you know what word he used when he was talking about his girlfriend? Wonder. Both the wonder *of* her and wondering *at* her, like he is so very fascinated and enchanted by the sheer uniqueness of her . . . Can you imagine how special that must make her feel?' Her eyes implore me. 'And you should have heard him describing their first date – they went to the lake to count the falling stars!' She blinks, reliving her amazement. 'He said that when a star is falling you can express a desire and that night he saw many stars fall but already his number one desire was a reality because he was with his girl and ultimately that was all he could wish for!'

I can see how such stories could drive a woman to tears.

'I told him he had an unfair advantage living somewhere so beautiful but he said it is the person who is by your side that can make the situation perfect. Obviously the lake and the stars help, but they acquire a higher meaning when you are with someone you care about.' She throws her hands up in despair. 'And he's right! I live right on Miami beach, for god's sake, I've walked along the sand under the moonlight a hundred times but I've never felt what he describes – that total feeling of satisfaction and elation!' She turns on her side. 'I even asked him – why when I'm surrounded by men all the time am I still single?'

'And what did he say?'

'He said that it could be raining men and it does not necessarily mean you will find someone because there is no probability in love. He said that if I continue to say "I can't find love!" then the right person could be standing in front of me but because I am thinking all these bad thoughts, I can't see him.'

'Confirming Raeleen's theory that you have to be relentlessly optimistic.'

'Though even Alessandro admits that the heart and logic don't run on the same rail.' She looks wistful. 'Do you think there are more like him out there? Or is he the only one?'

I smile at her. 'I think he has some friends. I do know what you mean though – I've certainly had some horrors in my time.'

'And I've found exactly what I was told was out there,' she sighs gazing up at the ceiling. 'My mum said men aren't to be trusted; my dad said they're only after one thing. It doesn't exactly make you want to run out into the world with an open heart.' She looks back at me a little shyly but can't stop her loosened tongue. 'One day I read that men are powerless in the presence of beauty and I thought that would be the way to get the upper hand. I can't tell you how much money I've spent at salons and spas getting my hair blown out, my cellulite pummelled, my face slathered in some miracle elixir – I thought if I was this paragon of beauty I couldn't get hurt.'

'But it didn't work?'

She shakes her head. 'They still had the control! Still they came and they went – took what they wanted and left a few trinkets behind on the dresser. It started to feel like trade.'

So basically she decided that if all relationships were going to end in tears, she might as well come out of them with some goodies – a new car, the latest mobile phone, a necklace from her namesake store . . .

'And I needed to know upfront that they had the money to pay for these things because then I could justify taking the risk of getting emotionally devastated. I can't believe all the people who do it for free!' she exclaims. 'There's got to be some kind of compensation, hasn't there? Something you can tell yourself when you're left in a heap. "Well, at least I had a nice holiday in St Lucia!" or "He did pay my mortgage for a year."'

'Sounds good in theory!' I admit.

'So why am I feeling like this now?' she despairs.

'Because you've seen that there is an alternative,' I scoot down beside her. 'You know now that the thing you convinced yourself didn't even exist – love for love's sake – does.'

For the first time since she arrived Tiffany looks vulnerable, and infinitely more human than her gold-digging caricature would allow.

'You know, deep down you must never have given up hope or you wouldn't be here,' I decide.

'But when I think of all the time I've wasted!' she cries getting vexed again. 'I'm so mad at my parents – the lies they told me!'

'That's all in the past now,' I soothe her. 'Let Alessandro

be your new template,' I urge her. 'Instead of looking for the bastard in a man, look for the Alessandro in him. Look for the sweetness!'

She lays back on her pillow, clearly emotionally exhausted, not to mention sozzled.

'You should probably try to get some sleep now,' I note. 'When you wake up in the morning you can start anew.'

She nods, her eyes already closing.

'Sweet dreams,' I say as I tiptoe out of the room.

Now that was interesting, I think as I fumble for my key. I wonder if Lorenzo is going to experience a whole new Tiffany tomorrow on their Prosecco tour? Now the dollar signs have fallen from her eyes will she be able to see *his* sweetness? Or will this insight only last as long as Alessandro's magic cocktails remain in her system? Only time will tell . . .

When I get back to the room I check my phone and find a message from Joe. I smile gratefully – he may not have the star-gazing sensibilities of Alessandro but at least he's there for me. I dial him with a cosy feeling in my heart, only to catch sight of the clock just as he answers – it's 1 a.m. in England!

'I didn't wake you, did I?' I wince.

'No such luck,' he says, clearing his throat. 'I'm just going over the last-minute schedule changes.'

'Ah yes, tomorrow's the big day,' I tell him something he already knows. 'How are you feeling about it all?'

'Borderline panic mixed with eagerness to get started,' he replies. 'Big Boss Man announced today that he'll be attending after all, just to pile on the pressure.'

'How nice of him.'

'I'm attempting to rise to the challenge, as opposed to cry like a little girl.'

'Good for you,' I tell him.

'So, what's up?' he enquires. 'You sound a bit deflated.'

'I'm just wrung out,' I sigh. 'One of the girls just had a meltdown and Kier and I had a big argument at dinner and,' I pause, deciding the last thing I want to do is re-live it all. 'Let's talk about something else . . .'

Joe sighs. 'Sometimes I think it might be healthier if you two took a little break from each other.'

'Funny you should say that . . .'

'What do you mean?'

'He stormed off into the night and I doubt very much that he's coming back.'

'Well, presumably all his stuff is still in the room?' Joe remains ever-practical.

'Yes, but I bet you anything it's gone by the time I get back.'

'Get back from where?' Joe queries.

'Bologna.'

'*Bologna?*' he repeats.' Why on earth are you going there?'

'It's part of The Love Academy programme, we all have to do one overnight with our Amore.'

Silence.

'Joe? Are you there?'

'Yes,' his voice sounds a little strained.

I gasp – could this be the jealousy I've been holding out for? I've come to think of Joe as so immune to such feelings I didn't think twice about telling him about this.

'Well, that'll be fun,' he recovers, though somewhat dryly. 'What hotel are you at?'

'Hotel Corona D'Oro. I'll text you the number when I get there. You don't mind do you? They do give us separate rooms.'

Joe laughs.

'What?' I ask him.

'I'm just thinking that this is probably the one occasion where it's actually cheaper *not* to share – I wonder how much these escorts charge for a full overnight session?'

'Oh Joe! I really don't think this place is like that. Everyone seems to be genuinely here in the name of romance.'

'Well, maybe you'll be in luck then and he'll give you a freebie.'

I feel uneasy. On second thoughts, this jealousy lark is nothing but a drag.

'I better get back to my papers.'

'Oh don't sign off just yet,' I plead.

'I really need to finish up. I'll only get four hours sleep as it is.'

I feel the stab of panic I always experience when he shuts me out. Not that he's being unreasonable; I'm just feeling needy. And then I remember Raeleen's words: neediness kills romance! so I quickly switch to chirpy mode and sing, 'Okay, well, good luck with it all and give me a call to let me know how it all went!'

Was that still needy, asking for a call at all?

'Thanks,' Joe is already back to his papers, I can tell. 'Night babe.'

'Night.'

Click.

And there it is, the biggest disappointment about romantic relationships – they are no real cure for loneliness.

# 22

*'I never travel without my diary. One should always have something sensational to read in the train.'*
*– Oscar Wilde*

I sleep fitfully, waking every hour or so to check Kier's bed – still empty at 7 a.m.

How could an evening that began with an idyllic lagoon sunset go so awry? I feel at odds with the world, as if I have seen too clearly that us non-Italians are all doomed to live lives of insufficient love and understanding.

I wonder where Kier is now, what he's thinking? Surely he's got to be feeling some remorse for the things he said? Surely he too would have spent the night soul-searching? I'm willing to acknowledge that I may have tampered with his independence by trying to help him too much, but there was certainly no malice intended.

It's a good thing we don't live in America or he would no doubt be suing me now for emasculation.

I decide to get up and pack for Bologna so that if Kier does re-appear I'll be able to give him my full attention rather than quizzing him on what outfit goes best with Bolognese sauce.

I'm kneeling over my suitcase when the room phone rings.

'Kier?' I gasp, ever hopeful.

'It's Mitzi. I need you to grab your suitcase and get packing!'

'I'm one step ahead of you!'

'Who told you?' she gasps.

'Told me what?'

'That you're going to Lake Como?'

'No one,' I frown. 'Mostly because I'm going to Bologna.' She isn't making any sense.

'Como, you're going to Como,' she insists. 'There's a train that leaves at 11 a.m. that will get you there with plenty of time to beautify yourself.'

'Beautify myself? For what?' I'm still in the dark.

'The Midsummer Gala Dinner at Villa d'Este!'

'Well it sounds very nice but I'm—'

'We've got a tip-off that George Clooney is attending! We need you to go and snoop for us! No doubt the paparazzi will be swarming but they'll never get in. You will, especially in the designer dress that Anya is couriering over for you.'

I roll my eyes. 'Look I'd love to help you out, but I'm already booked on an overnight with my Amore. You don't want me to mess up The Love Academy story do you?'

'Overnight in Como instead of Bologna,' she says with a verbal shrug.

'It's supposed to be romantic,' I complain. Spending all night with my eyes on another man just doesn't seem right.

She clears her throat and reads, 'Cocktails and hors d'oeuvres on the lake terrace with piano serenade, five-course gala dinner, dancing to a big band, fireworks at midnight. I think that probably trumps whatever you had in mind.'

Not a lot I can say to that.

'We booked you a room at a relais nearby. Do you want me to get an extra room for Lorenzo?'

'Lorenzo?'

'Please tell me you're not still with Gepetto!'

Silence.

'Tell you what, I'll just go ahead and do it. Just make sure you take someone, you'll look less conspicuous if you have a date, especially an Italian one. You could even pass for honeymooners, so much easier to take discreet photographs when you appear to be capturing the image of your beloved . . .'

I sit back on the floor in a daze, wondering what it might be like to feel like you have one iota of control over your own life. Mitzi has made such a convincing case, the question is not whether or not I should go but whether I call Dante or Sabrina first. I decide on Dante. Ever since yesterday's critiquing, Sabrina makes me nervous.

'How do you feel about Lake Como?' I ask, wasting no time with small talk.

'Well,' he replies. 'I feel like I am going there next Thursday. I have a delivery for a client there.'

'How do you feel about making that delivery today?'

'Today?' he baulks.

'It's just there's an amazing Midsummer gala event on the lake and there's fireworks and—'

'If it would make you happy, I will gladly go.'

'Really?' I can't believe how accommodating he's being. 'Will you be able to make your delivery while we're there?'

'What time do we leave?'

'There's a train at 11 a.m.'

'If we can go two hours later, the vase will be complete.'

'Deal!' I'll just have to beautify at double-speed.

'So I see you at Santa Lucia just before one o'clock?'

'Santa Lucia?' I query.

'The train station. But don't let me confuse you – the vaporetto stop is named Ferrovia.'

'Got it,' I confirm, jotting the name down. 'I'll see you there.'

'I'm in your hands.' He signs off.

I take a breath and dial Sabrina. As I tell her about the change of plan I play up how convenient it is for Dante to be able to make his delivery and how much fireworks make me swoon and she seems utterly unfazed by the switch.

'Just be back by tomorrow night, you may miss dinner if you wish as you are going a little farther than most, but we need you here first thing the following morning.'

'No problem,' I confirm. 'Um, I don't suppose you've heard anything from Kier?'

'He didn't come back last night?' she sounds surprised.

'No, he didn't,' I sigh. 'But he does know people here in Venice so maybe he stayed with one of his friends . . .'

'I'm sure that is the case. Don't worry, he will return. Especially as he knows everyone will be away from the city tonight.'

'But if he doesn't? What about Valentina?'

Sabrina laughs. 'You know she won't be alone for long! We have some new arrivals due so if he doesn't return today we can re-match her.'

'Okay. Well, I should finish packing but thank you so much for being so great about all this.'

'My pleasure.'

'And if Kier returns . . .'

'I'll call you straight away!'

'Thank you!' I sigh.

I put down the phone and take a moment to re-set my head. Bologna and Bolognese are out, Como and Clooney are in.

* * *

I've actually met George Clooney once before, way back in 1998 when he was promoting his first great movie role after leaving *ER* – Jack Foley, the cool-cat bank robber in *Out of Sight*. I flew to Los Angeles for the junket held in a utilitarian soundstage with black drapes dividing up the action. Typically there may be five or six other journalists at the table, all keen to project their questions to the fore, but this time there was a mob-like ten of us. All women. He handled the group so expertly I don't recall asking a single question, I just sat back in awe at how gracious an actor could be. George was totally present and engaged. Not to mention cheeky, quick-witted, savvy, opinionated, wry, disarmingly honest and humble. He also laughs a lot. You'd truly think he was having a good time. I can't tell you how frequently I've felt like apologising for seemingly bugging whichever celebrity with the inevitable questions, but not him. You actually start to feel classy by association.

It's therefore all the more distasteful to be sent on this spy mission. He already gives so much more than so many stars, that shouldn't be an invitation to take more. But there's no saying no to *Hot!* You are so disposable as a magazine writer. You say no, there are a hundred others willing to say yes. When I first began interviewing celebrities my motivation was to make the reader feel like they too were in the room, sharing the same experience as me, having an intimate audience with the celeb in question. Now I'm led to believe that people would rather see a picture of them stumbling drunk from a nightclub, making them as much the same as us as they can be, rather than finding out what makes them unique.

I step off the vaporetto at Ferrovia as Dante instructed and bump my case up the narrow steps and into the busy station terminal.

It's strange to think of Venice connected to the rest of Italy via something so accessible and earthbound as train tracks. Until now I was enjoying the sensation of being cut off, as if the lagoon was acting as a giant protective moat around us.

'*Buon giorno* Kirsty!' Dante greets me, immediately taking control of my suitcase. 'Are you ready for our adventure?'

'Yes!' I grin hopefully, trying to disguise the unease I feel at using him as a cover for my celebrity spying. 'Thanks for being flexible about the location. Did you manage to get everything finished in time?'

'The piece is all safely wrapped in my bag,' he confirms. 'No, no!' He prevents me from stepping aboard the earliest carriage I come to. 'We travel first class.'

'How decadent!' I coo.

He looks confused for a second and then nods sagely. 'Ah yes, I remember the price of British first class,' he winces. 'It is quite a different story here.' He hands me my ticket as proof.

It's the euro equivalent of £42 for a return trip, four hours each way, the same distance as my last trip from London to Edinburgh which would have cost £300 for First Class. I paid £94 for the standard fare, which was bad enough.

'Isn't that just mind-boggling?' I frown as Dante helps me aboard.

'Some would call it extortion,' he notes.

'How come the rest of Europe is so reasonable?' I ask as I settle into my window seat.

'Well, I know in Italy so many of the population travel far to work but they want to come home to their family so the government makes it a policy to keep the transport affordable so they can do this.'

'That's so considerate,' I sigh. 'I don't suppose you have to pay extra for buying the ticket on the day?'

'Of course not. But you do pay more to travel on the faster trains.'

'Well at least you have options,' I shake my head thinking of the outrageous National Rail walk-up fares. 'I just hate that feeling of being ripped off when they know there is no alternative.'

'I haven't seen this side of you before,' Dante teases. 'This fire!'

I roll my eyes. 'Just don't get me started on call centres. Or bank charges! Or the fact that British Airways now charge you fifteen pounds if you want to book your airline ticket over the phone. Fifteen pounds! Imagine if you're a little old lady without an internet connection! These days you're actually financially penalised for not having internet access 24/7.'

He shares my dismay and as the train starts rolling along a causeway with an infinity of baby blue water either side, we rant about all the things that make our blood simmer. Dante is describing his frustration at the influx of 'Murano glass' which is actually made in China as we make our first stop on the mainland – Mestre.

After the decaying splendour of Venice it's a shock to see modern towerblocks and council-style living, not to mention the newfound oddity of four-wheel vehicles zipping by on the adjacent flyover. As we continue on, passing by flat fields, low-rise warehouses and an abundance of grafitti, I feel like I have lost my rainbow-tinted glasses but then a steward enquires which lunch seating we would like in the restaurant car and suddenly the world seems a civilised place again.

Over a plate of tangy tomato spaghetti, Dante and I talk food

– I still can't get my head around the Venetian speciality of ink-spurting cuttlefish – which leads to the inevitable question about whether his mother's home cooking is superior to all others – 'Of course, do you really need to ask?' – and thus we transition on to the subject of family.

'Do you want to be a father?' I find myself asking, quite bluntly. 'That's if you don't have children already . . .'

'I do have one child,' he surprises me. 'A daughter. Chiara.' He smiles admiringly as he says her name.

I try not to look too shocked. 'She doesn't live with you?' I ask casually.

'She is away at university.'

'What is she, some kind of child genius?' I picture a ten-year-old in campus plaid and pigtails.

'She is eighteen. I married very young.'

'Oh.' I did know Dante was a couple of years older than me so it's really not that far-fetched. 'And your wife?'

He shakes his head. 'Gone.'

He looked a lot happier when he was talking about his daughter so I ask him how highly he rates parenthood, seeing as its one of my current quandaries.

'It is vital,' he says simply.

'Vital?' I question.

He leans forward to explain. 'When you arrive at fifty years old and you look back and see what you have done under the job aspect, under the money aspect, you might feel proud but the family is the only thing that rests on this earth when you leave.' He looks at me intently as he continues, 'For this reason the family is the most important thing a person can do. To combine with another person, this experience is a unique thing that God gives us.'

I blink back at him, amazed. He really should be in sales. I can't quite remember Joe's pitch to me but I think it went something like, 'Imagine little Bobby in his Man U shirt.'

'And you? Are you ready to become a mother?'

I sigh. I almost don't want to tell him the truth and risk putting him off me. But I just can't seem to pull off a gleeful, 'Oh yes! I've already stocked up on nappies!' So I tell him that the issue has somewhat snuck upon me. That I am still having trouble picturing it vividly; that it remains a somewhat abstract concept to me. That I'm sure it must be worth all the agonies but the horror stories do scare me. I leave out the bit about not being one hundred per cent sure of Joe, and then think secretly to myself what an amazing blessing Dante's genes would be to any child.

'Wave to Megan and Stefano,' I instruct as we pass through Verona.

As I look out the window I see the scenery has become far more appealing – undulating hills and snow-crested mountains in the distance and then, quite suddenly in the foreground, the vast expanse of emerald water that is Lake Garda.

'I didn't think Italy had things like that!' I laugh as I point to a cartoony billboard for 'Gardaland' complete with Disney-esque skunk and bear. 'I thought you people were too stylish for theme parks.'

Dante cocks his head. 'You think our children would prefer Pradaland?' he quips.

'Exactly!' I laugh. 'Fashion shows instead of rides, cigarettes instead of ice-cream!'

We spend the remainder of the journey talking about our childhoods, from best and worst holiday memories to our biggest arguments with our parents. (Oddly the thing that seemed to rile my mother the most was my penchant for boys who wore black lipstick.) Dante admits that he has a whole new take on things now he knows what it is like to be a father as well as a son, and he is glad both his parents are still alive so he can apologise to them daily.

'You can't have been that bad!' I titter. 'Besides, I'm sure you've more than made it up to them with Chiara.'

'That is true,' he concedes.

I take a breath and lean back in my seat. Suddenly Joe seems way more evolved than me. Why don't I feel his urgency to procreate? If it is indeed 'vital', what am I waiting for?

'*Lago di Como!*' Dante cheers as we catch a flash of sun-sparkled water.

It's all the incentive I need to dismiss my concerns – I'm not going to let them intrude on my time spent here. I'm going to have a holiday from my life for just one day.

And one night . . .

# 23

*'When you write of two happy lovers, let the story be set on the banks of Lake Como.' – Franz Liszt*

If you picture the lake of Como as a pair of legs, the small but pristine station of Como San Giovanni lies on the sole of the left foot. Alighting there just after 5 p.m., we dip straight into a taxi with one of those drivers who behaves like you just yelped, 'Follow that car!' even though we're the only vehicle hurtling along the leafy road. Something of a blessing, I feel.

Racing onwards, I get further glittering glimpses of the expansive lake and it seems so inviting: a body of water that you could dive into and not need medical attention as you emerge. How nice!

'Is that a swimming pool jutting out into the water?' I gasp, stubbing my finger on the window as I point ahead.

'That belong to Villa d'Este,' the driver names our evening destination with suitable awe.

The hotel estate is way more imposing than I had anticipated, dominating the waterfront with its majestic buildings, elegant terraces and private marina, all set in twenty-five acres, our driver informs us, of luxuriant parkland.

That's quite some meandering to be done, glass of Prosecco

in hand, just two hours from now. Feeling a little overwhelmed, I wind down my window so I can breathe in the rushing air as we pass the quaint map-dot villages en route. My suspicion that everyone will know I am here for celebrity stalking isn't helped as the driver points out 'Villa Clooney' to our right. All I see is a blur of stone wall and iron gate but I quickly tuck myself back deep into my seat to avoid the glare of the locals sat outside an insalubrious bar as we pull over to let another vehicle pass.

Despite building work to create some trendy new units and one particularly tempting pavement ristorante, I get the feeling this village isn't the swishest locale on the lake. Dante tells me that honour goes to Bellagio – but this town certainly does feel *real*, as if people actually live their lives here as opposed to dropping by to shop at Tod's and air-kiss fellow jet-setters.

Suddenly I am put in mind of a story George Clooney told on a recent *Oprah* show about the appeal of Italian life: he said he was sitting in his room overlooking the street watching all these construction workers walking home at 6 p.m. and along with their loaves of bread, they were carrying wine and flowers. And it hit home – Italians really know how to celebrate their day-to-day life!

It makes me want to ask Dante what his day-to-day dating is like, when he's not on extravagant trips like this, but it would seem we've arrived. At least there's the promise of accommodation behind the solid-metal automated gate.

The driver requests the code then proceeds down the driveway to our villa, comprising two main buildings, one of mottled apricot, the other terracotta, both trimmed with grey-blue shutters and fronted with a courtyard bursting with pink oleander. In this moment it really does feel like the Regina

Teodolinda is all ours – there's not another guest around and when we are shown to our rooms the overall vibe is so 'private residence' I feel as though we are being welcomed home by our loyal housekeeper.

'You have good taste,' Dante notes as the lounge area of my suite is revealed: a pair of lake-view windows are set either side of a grey marble fireplace and an outsized, calico-covered armchair begs me to sink into its nest of cushions and read *A Month By The Lake* by the light of a five-foot paper lantern.

'Actually a friend recommended it,' I tell him, enjoying the Peggy Guggenheim-like detail of the zebra print rug splayed on the floor.

The mix of styles works well as the colour palette is hushed and oh so calming, to the point that I almost wish we weren't going out at all tonight. But we are. And soon.

'Shall we reconvene in an hour?' Dante asks as he is beckoned to his room next door. 'At the water's edge?'

'At the water's edge,' I repeat, unable to curb a dreamy sigh as I head for the window, leaning on its frame as I look down at the tiered garden with its narrow pool and S-shaped raffia sunloungers. There's even a grassy verge with a small desk and bench overlooking the lake. What an office that would be for a novelist! I can't recall ever being anywhere so still and quiet, you can really hear yourself breathe.

For ten minutes I stand transfixed by the view allowing all my concerns to ease to nothingness. I can't believe anything bad could happen in a place like this, it's simply too full of grace.

It's then I notice a note on the mantelpiece. *Mitzi says look in the wardrobe!*

I walk through to the bedroom, take in the gorgeous ivory-swathed bed accented with amethyst shot-silk cushions and then turn and contemplate the wardrobe. It's one of those old-fashioned free-standing pieces that duly creaks as I open the doors and discover an extra-long garment bag within. I can't deny this is a little bit thrilling.

Reaching to un-sheath the contents, I feel like I'm in a movie. Is this really happening? Am I really here? Does Anya really think I can carry off a dress like this? I gnaw my lip as I inspect the jewel-encrusted plunge of the neckline and the entirely absent back. I know they filmed selected scenes from *Casino Royale* in Lake Como and this certainly looks like it's been purloined from a Bond Girl but unless the perfect body is awaiting me in the bathroom I could be in trouble . . . I have a quick check – nope, just a selection of the hippest fixtures and most aromatic toiletries. Well, I can but try.

I take the quickest shower and then set my giant tongs to heat up while I do my make-up. One of my eyeshadow sets has an iridescent aquamarine colour that I've never used before but it's the exact match for the dress so I decide to give it a go, gently blending it up to the shimmering pearl on my brow bone. Dior Show mascara for maximum lash volume, gold-flecked bronzer and my most shimmery peach lipgloss and I'm complete. On to the hair. I can feel my heart starting to rattle with excitement as I methodically roll each section in turn around the barrel – *I'm going to a gala dinner on the arm of a stunning Venetian, possibly getting within a shrimp's whisker of George Clooney, all the while serenaded by a live orchestra!* I can't help but emit a shrill whinny of anticipation and I have to set down the tongs for a moment so I can pace the room and shake off some of my excess energy.

Just ten minutes to go! I finish my hair and then it's time to attempt the dress. As I pull it on I get the unusual sensation of something being made for me, contouring my curves so snugly that all my fears of wardrobe malfunctions are allayed. One shoe, two . . . I step back to contemplate my reflection and then baulk as I see a contestant from *Strictly Come Dancing* staring back at me. Oh no! What with the intense colour on the eyes, the overly styled hair and blinding sparkles on my dress, the look is just too ballroom! I've got just one minute to tone myself down so I hurry back to the bathroom, dip my eyeshadow brush in face powder to soften my butterfly wing eyes, then hold my head upside down and rumple my curls to loosen them but when I stand back upright I look like a Dream Girl. In a desperate bid to reduce the volume I ease my widest-tooth comb through the nest, slick it with a little serum and add two daintily appointed clips behind my ears. Now we're in the Roaring Twenties, but at least I'm less likely to get critiqued on the dancefloor.

Diamante earrings, silver clutch, cashmere shrug. All set! As I descend the staircase, I marvel at the way the silk of the skirt ripples around my pointy silver toes – suddenly I feel undeniably feminine and slinky. I have to slow my pace as I cross the gravel courtyard, so by the time I reach Dante I'm feeling almost serene.

Initially he says nothing, just gazes.

I might feel self-conscious but I am too preoccupied with the vision of him in a sleek tuxedo.

'You look—' we both begin at the same time.

He smiles and then steps forward and gently raises my hand to his lips.

'I thought you didn't rate that move!' I tease.

'There are some moments when only something so genteel and worshipful will do.'

'Well, in that case,' I return the gesture, leaving a shimmer of peach on his knuckles.

'*Sei bellissima,*' he sighs, looking at me in such a way that makes me feel I just drank a glass of champagne.

I could happily dwell in this moment for all eternity but I am aware that we need to get going and when I suggest this to Dante he steps aside to reveal the vessel awaiting us at the water's edge.

'This is how we're getting there?' After Venice I was expecting a sleek motor launch but this is basically a wooden rowboat with an engine. With the emphasis on basic. 'Do you know how to work this?' I eye the toggle dangling from the engine and, worse yet, the oars.

Dante gives me a withering look, 'I'm Venetian. It's a boat. You need only be afraid if you ask me to drive a car!'

Despite my concerns, I can't help but chuckle as I accept the hand he is offering to help me in.

'Whoa!' I'm instantly unsteady and there's nothing to grip on to at a standing height so I stretch out my arms like I'm surfing until the boat settles to a gentle rock.

'Okay?' he enquires.

'Okay,' I reply, regaining my composure but wondering if perhaps I should have waited to put on my lustrous frock until we got there.

'Can I pass you this?' Dante holds the packaged vase out to me.

'Are you crazy?' I recoil. 'After what happened last time!'

'Ah, but now I know you will be extra careful!' he winks, full of misplaced faith.

I brace myself and reach out my arms. The way he's been toting it around in his bag you'd think it was made from spun sugar but it is of course way heavier and I very nearly topple right back off the boat as the full weight of it falls into my arms.

'Whoa!' I cry again, doing an even more precarious dance, concentrating furiously on finding my centre of gravity. It doesn't help that Dante then jumps aboard in a bid to steady me – now there's two pairs of hands upon the bubblewrap and we look like we're doing some kind of sixties dance while wrestling a bongo. Finally our disjointed jig settles.

'You can let go now . . .' he soothes me.

'I didn't break it!' I cheer, triumphant.

'I know. I'm glad.'

'It's still in one piece!' I can't quite believe it.

'Yes,' he continues to humour me. 'We can set it down now . . .'

'Are you sure you've got it?'

'I've got it.'

'You sure?'

'Kirsty.'

'Yes?'

'Let go.'

He sets it casually down beside the main bench. I'm quick to strap a lifejacket around it, just to be extra sure.

'That's actually for you,' he observes.

'I'm alright, I can swim, which is more than can be said of your friend here,' I tap the vase. 'Besides, the fluorescent orange doesn't go with my outfit.'

He shrugs and takes up the oars. 'Please, take a seat.' He motions to the bench behind me, which he has kindly covered with a blanket so I don't snag my dress.

I go to step back but find my heel is caught in the wooden panelling.

'Let me help you,' he reaches for my ankle about to yank it free when I screech, 'Wait!'

He looks up at me, so very patient. 'What?'

'Well,' I puff. 'What if my heel's made a hole in the boat and when you remove it we start filling up with water and sink?'

'You want the lifejacket now?' he deadpans, removing my heel with a swift tug.

No fountain erupts.

'Okay, okay, no more drama. I'm sitting down,' I do just that.

Dante reaches forward and then pulls back hard on the oars surging us free from the jetty.

'Are you really going to row us all the way there?' I think of the distance in the car and calculate we'll arrive just in time for coffee and petit-fours.

He shakes his head. 'I'm going to row us as far as Mr Doug's. It's very near. And so much more peaceful than the motor.'

I've never seen a man in a tux row a boat before, but it's a beautiful blend of sophistication and simplicity. And he's right. It's a much gentler pace. Gradually I find myself relaxing and my eyes stray beyond our craft.

The water around us is deep green, reflecting the verdant folds of the surrounding mountains and I squint in delight as the slippery surface dances with blinding white flares sent down by the sun. In this moment I couldn't imagine wanting to be anywhere else in the world. This seems to be the definition of idyllic. What must it be like to live here and contemplate this sparkling view daily? I look up at the little cubed clusters of dusty mustard, rust-red and powdery peach buildings pinned to the mountainside and wonder if breathing in such clean air everyday gives you a clearer perspective?

'This is Mr Doug!' Dante points ahead to one of the grandest waterfront villas we've swished past.

I get a curious sense of familiarity as I take in the large buttercream building with its dark ivy shutters set amidst a generous sprawl of grounds featuring towering poplars and a row of prettily-trained floral arches. As we pass the grey stone arm of a sea wall creating a little inlet for local boats (and a nice place to sit, feet dangling, to admire the sunset) and continue on to the villa's private jetty, even the previously moored motor launch gives me déjà vu. Was I here in a previous life, I wonder?

Dante secures our vessel and jumps up on to the jetty, motioning for me to hand over our precious cargo.

'You've definitely got it?' Once again my fingers ooze superglue.

He gives me a stern look and I release it.

'I'll just wait here.'

'Oh no,' he shakes his head. 'Some pirate might come by and steal you.'

He extends his free hand. I take it. It feels good to be wanted.

'Okay, now we unwrap.' He sets the package on the ground and starts to peel away the layers.

'Really?' This seems unconventional – opening someone's gift before you give it to them.

'It's not like I am ruining the surprise at Christmas,' Dante tuts. 'The customer needs to check the quality and the design and this is the best possible light for that,' he winks at the sun.

'Whatever you say,' I join in the peeling process until . . .

'Oh Dante,' I gasp, admiring the sensual curves and the shimmers of palest ice-green. 'It's stunning!'

We cast the wrapping back in the boat and make our way along the jetty to the gate, Dante allowing me to carry the vase despite his initial concern that I make an unlikely porter. It may be heavy and of such a proportion that I have to look through it in order to see my way, but I want to feel like I'm serving a purpose, rather than just standing there twiddling my curls and besides, as I told Dante, I can use my cashmere wrap to avoid any fingerprint smudges.

He presses the buzzer, says something in Italian and receives the appropriate response. Two minutes later I see a man approaching us through the distorted glass. Even though his form is blurred and warped, there is something distinctly recognisable about his easy gait and the crop of his grey hair. As he gets closer I identify those crinkly brown eyes and the particular curve of his upper lip.

It's a good thing the glass has a green tint to cancel out the raging red blush I'm experiencing.

The man is George Clooney.

# 24

*'Fame does not always light at random: sometimes she chooses her man.' – Seneca*

As George Clooney runs his tanned hands over the lines of the vase I feel like he's stroking my very cheek. This is beyond surreal. Can he see me looking directly at him? Apparently so!

'*Ciao*!' he smiles that wonderful smile of his as he peers around the glass to me. '*Come sta*?'

'*Molto bene, grazie*!' I bleat, praying I pass as Italian so he won't see me for the spy that I am.

As the two men continue talking I avert my eyes as though I am thinking of something else entirely. Though I don't understand the words, Mr Clooney seems extremely pleased with Dante's workmanship, but then his face falls and he sighs, 'Oh no, not again!'

I turn around and see a speedboat approaching bearing a small man with a giant lens. *Paparazzi!*

'Do you mind if we step inside?' George beckons us into his sanctuary.

Dante obliges but I remain rooted to the spot.

'What are you doing?' Dante ducks back to retrieve me.

'I'll just wait here,' I tell him.

I can't go in! I'm just as bad as the man in the speedboat; I just carry a tape-recorder instead of a camera.

Dante frowns at me as if to say, 'You *are* female, aren't you? Surely this would be considered by most to be a huge treat?'

'Honestly, I'll be fine, you go ahead.' I turn back to check on the paparazzi and then realise to my horror that he's now taking pictures of me. Oh no! 'Actually, I will join you after all!' I scuttle in, eyes averted from everything but my own silver toes, mentally blocking my ears though I do hear George say that he's in the middle of an interview and would we mind waiting a couple of minutes while he finishes up?

Naturally Dante says that's fine. All I'm thinking now is, 'Oh god, please don't let it be anyone I know!' I'm fairly confident he'd only let the likes of *Vanity Fair* within these hallowed gates not one of my 'Twenty Questions: *If you were a scoop of gelato, what flavour would you be?*' compadres. I just hope whoever it is can't smell the journalist in me.

'You're very quiet . . .' Dante observes, seemingly trying to weigh up whether I'm starstruck or experiencing some kind of reverse seasickness that hits when you step on dry land.

'I'm just hungry,' I shrug, mumbling an addendum of 'low blood sugar . . .' though I'm not sure that concept is known in Italy.

'Beautiful gardens,' Dante notes, looking around.

'Mmm-hmm,' I remain staring at the paving beneath my feet.

'We'll get you some food soon, I promise,' he looks concerned.

'Oh, no rush, really.' I squirm. Next he'll be asking if George can rustle me up a few slices of bruschetta.

Coincidentally the man himself starts talking about fine dining when the interviewer asks him to describe a typical day at his villa . . .

The itinerary goes something like this: morning boating and duck-feeding, afternoons spent script-reading and dipping in the pool interspersed with lively debates about what food to eat and what wine to drink and concluding with lavish lake view dinner parties with friends visiting from America. And by friends I think we know he means fellow movie stars.

Wow. I mean, WOW!

He goes on to say how much he enjoys the atmosphere of being in a small town and describes the people as respectful and kind, clearly chuffed at being treated like a local.

'So no trouble with people following you?' she checks.

Only people on vacation, apparently. I cringe guiltily as he explains that the roads are just too cramped for looky-loos though the local merchants and café owners seem happy enough with the extra business. At least he hopes so, explaining that he doesn't want to become *persona non grata*. Especially since he feels so at home here.

Though facially I look like I'm daydreaming, I'm hanging off his every word as he talks about his passion for motor-cycle-riding in Europe and how pleasant it is to live a completely different lifestyle for a few months at a time. She asks about romancing Italian women (tricky with the language barrier) and whether he'd like to give up Hollywood completely for this (no need, he can do both) and suddenly I have a question of my own – for Dante . . .

'Why did you call him Mr Doug?' I ask, wishing he'd been upfront ahead of time and I could have been a little more prepared.

He shrugs. 'That's how I think of him – Dr Doug Ross from *ER*!'

I can't help but smile. I wouldn't have even thought Dante was the type to watch TV.

'Do you like him?' I whisper, keen to get the native opinion.

Dante nods. 'I think he makes a very good Italian.'

I grin, thinking how high a compliment that is. He's certainly taken Raeleen's *dolce vita* concept at its word, really embracing the sweet life. I believe him when he says that buying this villa was the most romantic thing he's ever done. I wonder if he is going to the gala tonight – hard to tell because he always looks so Cary Grant impeccable.

Here he is again, apologising for keeping us waiting, again complimenting Dante on his work and now saying goodbye.

'I trust you have a good stay in Como,' he says, looking directly into my eyes.

I gulp – his choice of words may be pure coincidence but he looked so knowing as he said 'I trust you' . . .

All I can do is nod and say, '*Grazie*.'

I can just imagine Mitzi and in fact the entire staff throwing up their arms in despair as I turn and walk away – *You didn't utter one word of English to him? You were right there, in the grounds of his villa and you didn't even ask to use his loo?* Ruth would fire me on the spot if she knew.

I can't get back to our scrappy little boat quick enough. As I settle in I realise why the moored white vessel looked so familiar – last time I saw it, it was on the pages of our magazine, whisking through the water with Brad and Jen and Matt Damon and Lisa Snowdon aboard with Captain Clooney at the helm. What a summer fantasy that presented. No wonder people want to come and peek.

Mind you, based on the temperament of our taxi driver it's probably best to sail by at a respectful distance – I would not want to be holding up any local vehicles on the skinny, cliff-hewn roads.

'Now I use the motor,' Dante announces, charging it up with one vigorous pull of the toggle.

The engine has something of a lawnmower quality to it but nevertheless I appreciate the extra speed it provides. My hairdo is less enthused. I try to use my shrug to protect the delicate styling but can't quite seem to judge the breeze right and end up with my face covered like one of Michael Jackson's children.

'That's one way to foil the paparazzi,' Dante teases.

'Can you imagine living like that?' I peer out, referring back to our recent encounter with Hollywood Royalty.

He shakes his head. 'Already in Murano everybody knows my business but I can go anywhere else in the world and be invisible.'

'Hardly,' I mutter.

'What is that you say?' he frowns as the engine burrs ever more fiercely.

'You're just not the invisible type,' I call back to him with a smile.

We travel the rest of the way in relative silence passing assorted yachts and hydrofoils with their passengers clearly enjoying the breezy tousling, leaving me wondering how I'm ever going to return to travelling on the airless London underground. I even find myself pondering the price of those George Clooney adjacent apartments.

# 25

*'The loveliest faces are to be seen by moonlight, when one sees half with the eye and half with the fancy.'*
*– Persian Proverb*

Puttering into the marina at Villa d'Este, we receive a few bemused looks, but Dante is so dashing we could frankly arrive on a pedalo and still pull it off.

'I hope this evening is all that you wish for,' he husks as he helps me ashore.

'Mmm,' I mumble, feeling a little deceitful leading him to believe that it was my heart's desire that lured us here, as opposed to an instruction from the magazine. But then I look up at the regal splendour that awaits us and the notion becomes entirely believable – what girl doesn't yearn to play princess, at least once in her life?

I take a breath, inhaling an exquisite blend of jasmine and rose. My fingers brush upon a petal as soft as velour and some sentimental part of me wishes that Kier was here to correct me on my naming of the surrounding azaleas or camellias.

According to Dante, the hotel grounds are a tourist attraction in their own right, but he wisely prioritises booze and nibbles ahead of a languorous stroll around the gardens.

Passing the open-air, yellow-canopied restaurant, we proceed to the terrace set with a white-skirted champagne bar and several linen-clad tables of food. There's also a man positioned at a Yamaha home organ. Not quite what I had in mind when Mitzi mentioned a piano serenade, but I'm sure after a couple of slugs of quality fizz he'll seem like Harry Connick Jnr to me.

'*Cin-cin*!' I say, chinking glasses with Dante and then getting him to talk me through the silver trays of hors d'oeuvres beside me.

'You must try the zucchini flowers,' he recommends, pointing to the crispy yellow crinkles.

I lay down my shrug beside my purse so I don't get crumbs on either, only to get viciously scolded by a skeletal woman in a turquoise pantsuit and the thousand pound version of Christmas Cracker earrings. She has something of the look of Celine Dion, with none of the poise. To think she's scolding me for bad table manners when she is literally grabbing passing waiters by the sleeve and then helping herself two-handed to their wares, shovelling whole pizza slices down her throat like a sea lion devouring a fish.

'My guess is that she's been coming here for forty years and thinks she owns the place,' Dante notes, somewhat diplomatically.

As I look around at the other guests I begin to think that Mitzi may have been misinformed about George's proposed attendance. He may well dine here with friends on occasion but tonight, other than a self-conscious dollybird on the arm of a waxy-looking spiv and the children of one picture-perfect family, Dante and I are the youngest people here. This is not a *Hot!* crowd. Unless George has been invited to judge the 'fullest head of hair in the over seventies' category, I'm guessing he'll be a no show. Perhaps it was a deliberate decoy? I hope so. I hope wherever he is tonight it goes undocumented. Which is more than I can say for my time with Dante.

We're down to the crunch now – this is where I discover if he's just playing at being an Amore or if, come midnight, he lets me know that his physical services are available, for a price . . .

'Shall we visit the Nymphaeum?' he offers me his arm.

Hmmm – maybe we don't have to wait until midnight. Maybe he senses that two glasses of champagne in and I'm mentally totting the change in my bank account.

I ask if we can walk through the hotel itself, rather than circumnavigate it, just to have a nose. It doesn't disappoint. We enter through a grand pillared ballroom, pass the bridge room with freshly brushed suede tabletops, pause at the window of the jewellery boutique to gawp at a pair of earrings that exactly resemble lion's head doorknockers and continue down the *Alice In Wonderland*-like corridor, marvelling at the liberal use of marble statues indoors.

'I wonder how much it costs to stay here?' I whisper, hoping my question is not too crass.

Dante diverts us to reception where a quick interaction informs me that a standard garden view is €650, with suites available at €2,000.

'A night?' I try to sound breezy and not at all shocked that even the most basic room here costs the equivalent of two weeks' mortgage to me.

'You look like you need some fresh air!' Dante teases, fanning me with the hotel brochure as he escorts me out to the topiary-trimmed main entrance. 'Do you know this place was once owned by a former Princess of Wales?' he asks as we edge around the sweeping circular driveway. 'Caroline of Brunswick circa 1815.'

I frown. 'I've never heard of her!'

'She married the man who became King George IV but he repudiated her shortly after the wedding, which was arranged purely to give him a legitimate heir.' He reads to me. 'They appeared separately in public, both becoming involved in affairs with other lovers. She was a tragic figure with many slanderous things written about her. Her death was untimely and shrouded in some mystery.'

'Sounds woefully familiar.'

'The good news is that the happiest times of her life were spent here.'

'I can see why!' I gasp, stalling beside Villa d'Este's idea of a jogging trail – 126 steps leading up to a distant statue of Hercules and Lydia.

Running parallel both to the steps and a green première carpet of grass, are an equal number of shallow granite troughs trickling water from top to moss-slicked bottom. There is a curious frothing to the water adding a urinal quality so I quickly move on to the ethereal ivory cameos that have caught my eye. These turn out to be part of the Nymphaeum itself – a freestanding structure with a grotto-like aspect covered in a flinty mosaic of grey-green and black marble, flecked with gold.

'This is considered to be one of the most photographed monuments in Italy,' Dante notes. 'It dates back to the sixteenth century.'

Peering at the features of the gargoyles on the inner walls, we amuse ourselves comparing them to celebrity faces. The only snag is I don't know any of the names Dante references and he doesn't know just how uncanny the resemblances are to Rowan Atkinson, Kenneth Branagh and Mick Hucknall. For a split-second I wish Joe was here. He'd find this hilarious.

We conclude our tour at a pretty seating area beside the waterfront, beneath the oldest plane tree in Lombardy.

'Six hundred years old,' he coos looking up at it. 'Six hundred Midsummer Nights it has stood here.'

'I wish Kier could see this,' I sigh, mournfully placing a palm on its hefty, flakey-barked trunk.

'You look very sad but I don't think it's going anywhere,' Dante consoles me.

I sigh. 'We had an argument last night,' I confide. 'A big one.'

Dante sighs sympathetically. 'That is one of the penalties we pay for being close with our family – when you are mixing with the same blood, sometimes you have to fight for your identity.'

'I think I might be guilty of being over-protective and interfering,' I confess.

He shrugs. 'It is natural to want to spare those you love pain, especially when they are younger than you. But you step in front of them too much, how can they see where they are going?'

My eyes widen as he makes all too much sense. 'Point taken.' And then I blink remembering my earlier pact with myself. 'You are very wise and I am very bad company!'

'Not at all,' he smiles, indulgently. 'But perhaps another glass of champagne will restore your bubbles?'

'It's worth a try!' I grin, getting a sudden flutter as it once again strikes me how glorious my date is.

'Please take a seat,' he ushers me to an available cocktail table. 'I will return.'

No sooner does he leave than a waiter presents me with a glass. Oh well, you can never have too much champagne.

I'm sitting quietly contented in near darkness when a distinctive voice says, 'Here's a candle for your table. A pretty girl like you shouldn't be in the dark.'

I look up. Grey hair, elegantly receding, a downward pointing arrow of a nose. My jaw drops – it's Len Goodman from *Strictly Come Dancing*!

As he walks away I gawp after him, strangely thrilled. I love that show! I want to tell him how it stirs me up and spirits me away but Dante has returned.

'See that gentleman there, the one with the distinguished features?' I whisper.

'Yes . . .' Dante looks curious.

'He's a judge on this ballroom dance show on British TV!'

Dante tilts his head. 'You are a very interesting girl, Kirsty,' he smirks. 'You meet a famous movie star and you are more interested in looking at your shoes but this man,' he wafts a hand at Len, 'has you all a-glow.'

'It's a good thing Bruno Tonioli isn't here,' I hoot. 'I'd probably have passed out with excitement! He's amazing – he makes these fantastically witty puns and it's not even his first language. Oh my gosh, he's Italian! Do you know him?'

Dante laughs as he shakes his head, prompting me to ask, 'Am I drunk?'

'I think it is more a case of, how you say it? *Tipsy*?'

'What about you?' I dip my chin coquettishly. 'Are you feeling it yet?'

'Well, I was just about to invite your twin sister to join us for dinner,' he jokes.

'Is it time?' I look eagerly toward the restaurant.

'It's time.'

Dante opens with a selection of seafood and summer fruits whereas I favour the divinely refreshing cucumber gazpacho garnished with smoked salmon and yoghurt. Our main course is a saucy veal dish and dessert an exquisite Grand Marnier and poppy parfait with peach and lavender honey. Peach and lavender – I mean, what a heavenly combination! Good food is such an uplifting experience! Add to that the fact that a summer rainstorm is now pattering down on the canopy and it somehow conspires to make the whole experience even more intimate and magical.

I smile contentedly – look at us: Dante and I sitting outside in the rain with a collection of golden oldies. Hold on, I take that back – there appears to be some fresh blood in our midst, honeymooners if I'm not very much mistaken. I watch them with interest as they make their coffee selection. They look so fresh and optimistic. Some would dismiss that as naivety but these two seem like straightforward people who like each other as well as love each other. Just watching how easily they interact, I can't see a huge amount of complication in their future. I wonder what I would see if the exact copy of Joe and I walked in now . . . A guy who's perfectly content and a girl who's fidgety and unsure and her own worst enemy? And what of me and Dante? I'd love to know what kind of couple we project to the world. Is it obvious he's way more sophisticated than me? Do I look transparently in awe? Or would they say we compliment each other like the rich, intense espresso and the frilly lacework of the brandysnap by its side?

'You often have conversations with yourself in your head, don't you?'

For a second I feel defensive. If Joe had made the same comment it would have been accompanied with a roll of the eyes but Dante is simply looking intrigued.

'Yes, I do.' I don't deny it.

'You know there is one place you can go where those voices become less than a whisper . . .'

'Where's that?' I croak, feeling a little nervous and susceptible. Is he going to say *the bedroom*?

'The dance floor,' he replies.

Minutes later I'm in his arms, swaying to 'Fly Me To The Moon'. It couldn't be a more appropriate tune – I am truly having an out-of-this-world experience. I've waited so long to feel his arms around me that the sensation is making me quite light-headed. It's a good thing his torso is so strong and his hold so masterful, I know he can support me no matter how giddy I get. When the singer implores 'Darling, kiss me!' I'm ready to submit. Slowly I raise my face to his, dancing for a moment just with his eyes and then the unthinkable happens – the band break into 'YMCA'!

I look around with a mixture of horror and amazement as everyone, including the woman in the turquoise pant-suit, shapes their bodies into the requisite letters. Y-M-C-A. All the romance in the room is zapped as the Villa d'Este becomes Butlins for billionaires.

We should probably leave before they start playing 'The Birdie Song' but I suggest one last drink at the bar.

'Perhaps we take our liqueur al fresco?' Dante motions to

the terrace. 'The rain has ceased and the fireworks will soon begin.'

All is not lost! Perhaps the romance can be recaptured? 'Yes, that would be lovely,' I concur.

And so we stand, glass globes in hand, beside a potted lime, gazing into the black night at the white lights across the lake.

'You are cold?' Dante enquires, running his hand down my shivery forearm.

'A little,' I confess.

'Allow me,' he says before enveloping me in his tuxedo jacket, with him still in it! 'Body heat,' he explains with a twinkle.

He's not kidding. I feel like I should go back and trade my Baileys for one of those flaming sambucas just to be in keeping with the current sensation. It's the weirdest feeling being hot yet shivering, tipsy yet hyper-aware of all that is going on around me. Not to mention the tug-of-war that has me fervently drawn to Dante and yet dig-your-heels-in determined to remain loyal to Joe. I'm just about to extricate myself on the pretext of visiting the ladies when the inky sky erupts with colour, scattering electric confetti as far as the eye can see.

'Oh wow!' I breathe, instantly enraptured.

Dante holds me tighter as fluorescent jets of green and purple whizz into orbit with a frazzling pop. We gasp in unison as a celestial glitterball shatters into a zillion diamonds. What is it about fireworks that send your senses soaring? Even the most cynical adult can't help but find these neon constellations inspirational! Look at these faces around me, illuminated with childlike wonder. As my spangled vision returns to the sky, I see something I've never seen before – a heart-shaped firework! Thirty or so pink beams flashing the outline of a heart! I can't believe it's even possible. I'd think I imagined it yet it seems to hang there just to be absolutely sure I get the message. I turn to Dante but before I can even speak, his lips are upon mine, melting their warmth into my own. His kiss has an ardent tenderness that makes my stomach flip with excitement. How can I not reciprocate when Cupid surprises me like this?

I hear cheering and for a moment I think the other guests are celebrating our embrace but through my closed lids I see patterns of light and we part at the peak of the crackling crescendo, just in time to see the wonder of the finale reflected in the lake. How can I possibly knock The Love Academy after this?

I turn back to Dante who is gently tracing my curls and then bury my head in his chest, trying to stop all the questions that are suddenly rushing at me.

'We need to keep dancing,' I tell him, though the music has long ceased.

He smiles understanding and in lieu of the band softly hums a Sinatra medley, caressing my ears with his Italian-lilted versions of 'I've Got You Under My Skin' and 'Strangers In The Night' – dancing me all the way back to our villa . . .

# 26

*'He travels best that knows when to return.'*
*– Thomas More*

After the pleasure comes the pain.

I wake up bamboozled and parched of tongue with sunlight glaring in through the window at me like an interrogation lamp.

*What did you do last night?* my conscience demands.

I squeeze my eyes tight shut trying to block out everything – the light, the memories, the headache that's compressing my temples like a car-crusher . . . I want to go back to sleep where I don't have to take responsibility for anything I may have said or done but I can't because my phone is ringing. And ringing. I don't even look to see who it is until the third successive sequence. 'Please don't let it be Joe, please don't let it be Joe!' I chant as I reach for it and flick to missed calls. Thank god, it's just Mitzi. Here she is again now. This time I answer.

'Finally!' she shrieks. 'Tell me everything. *Everything*!'

My god – has word got to London already? Was someone spying on *me* at Villa d'Este? And then I realise she's not talking about me and Dante at all . . .

'I hate to disappoint you Mitzi, but the only silver-haired celeb at the gala was Len Goodman.'

'I'm not talking about the gala!' she hoots. 'I'm talking about you at gorgeous George's lakeside villa! *Unbelievable!* So what's it like up close?'

How does she even know about that?

'I really couldn't say,' I croak. 'It was just the briefest meeting on the jetty—'

'Ha! You can't tease me – we have pictorial proof of you going inside the gates!'

It's then I remember the paparazzi.

'Ruth is just delirious!' Mitzi continues to babble. 'Of course all the papers are saying, "*Who is the mystery brunette?*" and we know cos you're ours, all ours!' She emits a maniacal gurgle. 'Ruth's even scrapping Fenton's piece on his night out with Paris Hilton to run this! You've got a drop-in shot on the cover and everything!'

'What? Just how big is this going to be?' I gulp.

'At least six pages, so Ruth wants as much detail as possible.'

I want to laugh. Finally she wants details instead of bitchy captions. It would be over this.

I hoik myself upright in bed. 'Look Mitzi, you have to get everyone to calm down. There's really nothing to tell.'

'You're kidding, aren't you? Anya says you rocked the dress by the way!'

'Thank you,' I stumble.

'Anyway. You've got until midnight tomorrow to meet the deadline for the next issue.'

'The next issue?' I blurt. 'But that's published while I'm still here! What about The Love Academy story? It could screw the whole thing up!'

'Ruth says she's willing to forfeit it for this. This is *huge* – an exclusive insider report on George Clooney.'

'So you'd take a few words on him over a whole piece on the Academy?'

'Yup.'

'And as a result, I wouldn't have to write about anyone here?'

'I suppose so.'

Oh god, what a dilemma. Sell Clooney down the swanny and save The Love Academy. Not that I have anything bad to say about either but *Hot!* has a way of skewing stories and making you look far bitchier than you ever intended to be. One total prat I interviewed did such a brilliant job at stitching himself up I literally had to quote him verbatim and it was plain what an arrogant, twisted piece of work he was. But then, on the last proof, Ruth added in all this commentary that ultimately made me look like I had it in for him. It was so completely unnecessary. And unfair – it wasn't her face and name branded on the page. I was the one who came off looking spiteful. Besides, the big snag with giving them the George Clooney story is that I would land Dante in it. No more A-list movie star commissions for him – he brought the spy to the door. Inadvertently yes, but they'd never trust him again.

'You're taking the train back to Venice today, right?' Mitzi is talking again.

'Yes,' I reply, absently.

'How perfect is that? You can bash the piece out on the journey and then send it over when you get back. We'll be a day ahead of the game.'

'I don't know, Mitzi.' I sigh. 'I can hardly get out my laptop in front of Dante.'

'Who's Dante?'

'Oh, just the guy I brought with me as cover . . .' I lie, experiencing a small flip of nausea.

'Tell him you've got a sudden idea for a new children's story and you have to get it down before you forget.'

'Trust me, nothing that happened last night is appropriate for a children's story.'

'Oh my god! More scandal! Tell me, tell me!'

'Nothing!' I bark. 'Nothing happened. I'm just joking.'

'I can't believe you met George Clooney.' Mitzi gets misty. 'This is all too awesome.'

I scrunch my brow. 'Is there another bonus tied in with this?'

'No,' she tuts, her voice suddenly getting sincere as she confides, 'He's the one, Kirsty. He's my dream guy.'

'Really?'

'Really.'

'Well, running a story that totally invades his privacy is sure to endear you to him greatly.' I can't help but snort. 'He'll probably call you for a date the second it hits the news-stands.'

Silence. Then a forlorn voice enquires, 'I'm never going to marry a movie star, am I?'

'Are you serious?'

I hear her sigh. 'This seemed like the perfect job to get into – going on photoshoots with the stars, being around them with a purpose not just googling at them from a distance. I thought it would put us on a level playing field but now, now I've become the enemy.'

I've never heard Mitzi like this. She's always so relentlessly peppy.

'Gregory Peck married a reporter from a celebrity magazine,' I volunteer, trying to make her feel better. 'She interviewed him for *Paris Match* and they were together forty-eight years.'

'But look how long ago that was! Got any more recent examples? And I don't just mean random snogs or flirtations, *actual relationships . . .*'

'You might want to think about becoming an actress,' is the best advice I can give. 'Casting is just one big dating agency, that's probably the way to go.'

She heaves another sigh and then it's like a switch is flicked. No more introspection, back to the dirt. 'So, dish! Dish! You've kept me waiting long enough!'

I pause for a second and then enquire, 'Hello? Mitzi?'

'I'm right here, all ears.'

'Can you hear me? I can't hear you,' I fib. 'The reception here is dreadful. I'll try and call you back.' And with that I shut the phone. And then switch it off.

I've got some serious thinking to do before I give away a single morsel of what I saw.

Two seconds later the room phone rings. Of course she knows where I'm staying. I roll my eyes and ignore it. Next there's a knock at the door. Has she sent a messenger? Will she never leave me in peace? I roll out of bed and stagger over, a little dizzy from getting upright too quickly.

'Hello?' I grumble at the closed door.

'Kirsty?'

Oh my god, it's Dante.

'Er, hang on,' I run back to get my robe and peek the door open a tiny crack so he doesn't get the full horror of my crazy-lady hair.

'There is a phone call for you, in my room.'

What? Surely she didn't?

'Someone called Mitzi?' he continues. 'Something urgent about a cat?'

Yes, I think to myself, it's in terrible danger – curiosity is about to kill it.

'You have to excuse the state of me, I'm not really up yet,' I apologise as I reveal my dishevelled form.

'Me also,' he says rumpling his bed hair. 'I was just about to get in the shower.'

Hence the towel around his waist. I try not to look at his bare torso but it's so smooth and brown my eyes glide all too easily over its surface. It doesn't help any that as I sit down to answer the phone beside the bed, the sheets are still warm.

'Hello? Kirsty?'

'I'm here,' I murmur, envisioning lying here, skin-on-skin, my hand running the length of his bicep.

'Can you hear me? What is up with the phones in Italy?'

I hear the water start running and pinch myself back to reality.

'I can't talk now Mitzi. We'll have to catch up later.'

'Are you seeing him again today? Is that why you have to go?'

'Seeing who?'

'George of course.'

'No,' I groan. 'Why would I be? Look, I really can't talk any more.'

'Suit yourself – I guess I'll just have to wait to read about it in the magazine like everyone else!'

And with that she puts down the phone.

Lying back on the pillow, I find myself inhaling Dante's delectable scent. I close my eyes and part of me wants to pull the covers over me and just revel in this feeling but the hungover part just wants to run away. And she's the one who gets the final say.

I leave a 'See you at breakfast!' note for Dante and return to my room standing under my own shower for far too long, on the offchance that the water will wash my worries away.

On the way down to breakfast I tentatively switch on my phone to see if there are any other messages, namely from Sabrina or Kier but there are none. So my brother is still AWOL, and still angry no doubt. I consider calling Joe seeing as Dante and I will be together pretty much from now until we get back to Venice but I can't bring myself to press call. The guilt is really kicking in now that I'm out in reality-bright daylight.

*It was just a kiss, that's all*, I reason with myself.

And yet in my current unhinged state it almost seems worse than if we'd slept together. If that had happened I'd feel so disgusted with myself it would make me hate Dante for bringing out the adulterer in me and I'd shun him and return wholeheartedly to Joe. But that's not what happened. Though my memory isn't crystal clear, it all seemed very romantic. He serenaded me, he clasped me to him but he didn't try to lure me into his room. Even though we have just four nights left together you'd think we had the rest of our lives. There was no rush, certainly no mention of money, just a savouring of the moment – maximising the thrill of the first kiss by not muddling it with any other physicality. Not that the desire wasn't there. Not that it isn't here right now as I think of his towel-clad form.

I feel so confused. These feelings are real, they are what they are. But the key thing is not to act on them. And that means no more kisses. I scold myself – here I am congratulating myself on stopping short of sex, trying to barter back some credit for the things I *didn't* do but I can't ignore what I did. I kissed another man. And it makes me feel sick as I look at Joe's name on my phone. If he'd done the same thing . . .

'Colazione?' Dante appears by my side bearing pastries and orange juice.

'I – I was on my way to breakfast – I just promised I'd get back to Mitzi!' I blurt, holding up my phone. I don't want him to think I'm avoiding him. 'I have better reception out here.'

'Is her cat alright?'

'Cat? Oh yes, yes. She just got her own claw stuck in her paw.'

'Ouch!'

'She'll be fine. Is this all for me?'

He nods. 'I thought you might want to eat out here so you can make the most of the lake before we leave.'

I sigh heavily. I'm really not ready for the long journey back.

'Unless you'd like to get a later train?' Dante proposes.

I give him an 'if only' look.

We really should be getting back. I should be going to see Sabrina along with Tiffany and asking to change Amores. The thought saddens me, but it's what I have to do. The temptation is just too great with this man. What a different story this would be if I were single. Oh to have the freedom to reach out and touch him now. To pull him on to the seat beside me, swing my legs over his thighs and kiss in the sunshine, not just after dark. He must think I'm being so cold this morning.

'I leave you to make your call,' he bows out.

'Thanks,' I smile. 'I'll be ready to leave in twenty minutes.'

All the years I had no one, why this clash and overlap now? It's too cruel. Now I'm feeling testy and annoyed instead of guilty. A good time to make my call . . .

'Kirsty?' Joe sounds instantly shifty. Weird. Isn't that my role?

'Are you okay?'

'Um, yes, can you hold on?'

I hear a woman's voice. I'm straining to hear what she's saying but only grasp a flirtatious sounding, 'Sir!'

'Sorry about that – Rich just needed me to sign-off on something.'

That wasn't Rich. What's going on? I open my mouth to accuse him but realise I'm in no position.

'What can I do for you?' he asks.

'Do for me?' I frown. 'I'm just ringing to say I'm about to check-out of the villa. I'll try and call you from the train if I get a chance—'

'Actually I'm going to be incommunicado for a few hours,' he hurriedly announces. 'I'll call you later, shall I?'

'Okay.'

'Okay, bye.'

Huh. He couldn't get off the phone quick enough. You don't think – No . . .

Of course, there was a big conference dinner last night, lots of free booze, not unlike my do. Then the inevitable surge of relief that all the work is over. Maybe an attractive woman from marketing caught Joe's eye. Maybe there was dancing . . . your room or mine? I get to my feet. No. I'm just projecting. Joe would never do that. Would he? I don't know anything anymore. I certainly didn't think I'd ever be unfaithful. I shake my head at the absurdity of the situation – here I am on location in Lake Como with another man and I'm calling it work. Well, this is where it ends. Today is my last day with Dante.

I take a deep breath, committing to that notion. I can't put my long-term relationship in jeopardy for a holiday romance. It's such a cliché to believe it's any more than that, isn't it? Of course it feels intense in these surroundings, but it's just a fantasy.

I look at my watch. Hmmm. I shouldn't really be having this thought but Sabrina did say we could miss dinner tonight, seeing as we travelled that little bit further . . .

Back up in my room I scramble for the train timetable. There's one at 7 p.m. that would get us in around 11 p.m. It does seem a terrible waste of the lake not to explore a bit more. And I don't want to be rude to Dante and cut him off after he's been so charming, he's only doing his job after all. Wouldn't it be nicer to end things after a pleasant day?

I knock on Dante's door.

'Yes?' he responds.

'How do you feel about having lunch in Bellagio?'

It feels so good to be back on the water, this time on the ferry.

As we glide along I comment that the rich velvet covering the surrounding mountains seems even more luxuriously green than yesterday, if such a thing were possible.

'And those trees there look like a cluster of cheerleaders,' I say, drawing attention to their pom-pom-like foliage.

Dante laughs and challenges me to come up with a colour match for the houses nestled around them. I suggest 'latte macchiato', 'curried apricot', and 'crème caramel'.

'Are you ready for lunch already?' he enquires with a twinkle.

'Almost!' I confess before pointing to a tangle of yellow

plastic ribbons strewn over a speedboat, making it look like a cross between a crime scene and a wedding vehicle. 'What's all that for?'

'To keep the birds away,' he explains.

'Oh,' I say, gazing skyward just as a falcon swoops over us.

Continuing on, we pass Villa del Balbianello where they filmed Daniel Craig's recuperation scenes as James Bond, but my favourite sight comes when we disembark at Bellagio and discover a church offering 'Religious Messes' instead of masses.

This little town, known as 'the pearl' of Lake Como, does indeed have the promised air of supreme elegance and relaxation. We take a stroll past the lively cafés and boutiques along the front promenade and then choose a spot for lunch in a sheltered walkway by the quayside.

The dessert is one of the most unusual of the trip, presented in a Japanese-style black lacquered box – I lift the lid to discover half a crinkly passion fruit, a bauble of vanilla ice-cream, two slices of starfruit and three puffs of deep-fried ravioli! It sounds so wrong but in reality it's crispy and delicious – the hint of grease offset perfectly by the tartness of the fruit.

'Mmmm!' I rave, grabbing Dante's thigh to convey my rapture, forgetting for a second who I'm with, and quickly withdrawing my hand on the pretext of reaching for my water.

Dante eyes me, never missing a trick. 'Is it a problem for you, this kiss between us?' he asks, no doubt wondering why I've been so twitchy about touching him ever since.

For a second I am too embarrassed to speak, but I feel I owe him some kind of explanation, without going too near the truth, of course.

'The thing is,' I begin. 'I came on this course because I had just broken up with someone and I'm not entirely over him. When we kissed last night, I felt as if I was being disloyal to him in some way. I know it's ridiculous—'

'Not ridiculous. A feeling is a feeling.'

I look up at him. 'I am very attracted to you.'

'Very?' he smiles.

'Very,' I confirm with a little whimper of frustration. 'Of course, there is the other element that you are being paid to make overtures in my direction.'

'No, I'm not.'

I look up. 'It's alright, it is what it is.'

'I am not being paid. That was my one condition when I agreed to this. Which is not to say that I think that the other Amores are wrong to take the money, Lorenzo for example is certainly earning his. But it is not for me. At least not with you.'

'How do you mean?' Can this be true?

'I didn't want there to be that element between us, at least in my mind, I know you had accepted it, or at the very least expected it so I knew it wasn't a problem for you.'

'Well—'

'I am not judging anyone here,' he assures me. 'I just wanted you to know that I am here because I want to be. Because I want to be with you.'

Oh god! Just when I thought this couldn't get any harder.

'You don't have to say anything,' Dante soothes. 'I just wanted you to know. Would you like to take a little walk to the harbour before we leave?'

I nod, in something of a daze. It was a stupid idea to spend more time with him, *stupid*. He just keeps getting better.

We wander down a series of high-walled backstreets leading to an area well away from the throng of sightseers. To look at him you'd think Dante's favourite thing would be to shop at Coach or Gucci but I love that this is his preferred spot. The cobblestones and ivy-clad walls and small wooden rowboats give the harbour a cosy, locals feel. We sit on the bench and close our eyes, letting the sunshine warm our faces as we listen to the slappy-lappy sound of the water wet-kissing the bobbing boats. I really would love to immerse myself in the cool of the lake right now. I'm imagining the sensation of the water enveloping my bare skin when a rushing sound reminds me of when I push off from the side of a swimming pool – opening my eyes, I see a cluster of ducks surging for a scrap of bread.

'He's a funny-looking fella,' I point at a larger white bird sporting what looks like a red rubber carnival mask.

'You're not the only one whose curiosity has been captured,' Dante nods over to a cream cat with a smoky grey tale and Wedgewood blue eyes stalking stealthily towards our feathered friend, oblivious to the fact that she herself is being eyed by a shaggy black dog. She creeps closer, body low, focus intense. Then all of a sudden the dog starts at his lead, startling the cat and in turn alerting the now-flapping bird! It's a comically chaotic moment that briefly disturbs the peace and we share a laugh with the couple who own the dog before giving up our bench to them. It is time for us to leave.

Reluctant as I am, I have to concede that this has been the perfect end to a perfect day.

We enjoy the last of the sunlight on the ferry back to Como and then doze off on the train as the dark night slips by, emerging at Santa Lucia station in a sleepy-haze.

I feel no resistance as Dante hugs me goodbye, kissing the top of my head, keeping the vibe friendly not suggestive.

'*Grazie mille*,' I tell him. 'That was . . .' I'm lost for words.

'Yes, it was. Thank you also.'

I wonder if I should tell him now that we're going to have to separate? Probably, but I can't bring myself to. I feel so close to him in this moment, the thought of bidding farewell, other than for the night, seems alien and unacceptable.

'Goodnight,' I say, bestowing the lightest of kisses on his lips as we part.

He smiles and touches his lip as if to acknowledge how precious that kiss was.

I sigh as I take my seat on the vaporetto, and then take out my notebook and write a note to Sabrina requesting a new Amore. I have to do it now. One more day with that man and I'll be hooked forever. I know that for a fact because a teardrop splashes on the page as I write.

When I get back to the Abadessa I leave the note on the front desk for Sabrina, drag my weary frame and bumpity suitcase up the stairs and let myself into the room. I'm just reaching for the light switch when I hear a snuffling sound . . .

Kier's back! *He's back!*

I heave a sigh of relief. That's my reward for doing the right thing with Dante!

I change into my pyjamas in the bathroom and tiptoe into the bedroom only to find that the snoring is coming from my bed. Has he decided to claim the queen in my absence? Oh well, I'm happy in the single.

'Shit!' I stub my toe on the nightstand as I fumble for it.

There's movement from the other bed and a dream-dredged voice says, 'Kirsty?'

I freeze. It's not Kier.

More fumbling and the light comes on.

'JOE!' I gape, stunned. 'Wha—*What the hell are you doing here?*'

# 27

*'All who would win joy must share it; happiness was born a twin.' – Lord Byron*

'Surprise!'

He's not kidding.

He's reaching for me, trying to pull me in bed beside him but I'm immovable.

'This isn't quite the reaction I was going for!' he frowns.

'How did you get in? Did anyone see?'

'Sit down and I'll tell you everything.'

My knees concede to bend but my spine remains stiff.

He pulls himself into a sitting position to address me. 'As you know my conference finished early, so I thought what could be more romantic than to surprise my darling in Venice!'

'But I'm working, you know this is—'

'A secret mission!' he grins. 'I know, I'm incognito too.'

*'In my room?'* I despair.

'Don't worry, I haven't blown your cover – I've got my own room but I switched with Kier for tonight so I could be with you. Four nights I've been without your lovely Stella-scented skin . . .' he begins to nuzzle me.

'Wait!' I pull away. 'So Kier's back?'

'Mmm-hmm.' He reaches for me again.

'And he's still doing the course?'

He nods. 'I'd like to take all the credit for persuading him to stay but I think it was mostly Raeleen.'

I have a million more questions but one is rather more pressing than the others: 'How exactly have you got your own room here?' I ask Joe. 'You surely didn't sign up?'

'As a matter of fact I did!' he looks very pleased with himself.

My jaw drops. 'I can't believe you paid money to come here.' This really is amazing to me.

'Well actually I didn't go that far.'

'What do you mean?' I don't like the sound of this.

'Well I rang Helena to get all the details and she got on the phone to Ruth who thought this could be a brilliant new dimension for the article to have a couple's perspective, so guess what?'

'What?' I whimper.

'I got my first writing commission!'

Suddenly I feel horribly claustrophobic.

'I was all for surprising you but she said she was going to call and warn you in case you had to make any preparatory lies. Didn't you get her message?'

I think of my phone, still switched off and fib, 'No, the service has been really hit and miss of late.'

He studies me for a second and then observes, 'You don't exactly look ecstatic that I'm here.'

I force a smile. 'I'm just surprised they let you come on board mid-course, or are you a different cycle to us?'

'No, I'm the same – it was a fluke really, apparently one of the guys in your group dropped out and they said it wasn't standard practice to slot in a replacement but seeing as I was friends with Kier . . .'

'You told them you knew him?' I'm aghast. 'That means you know me too!'

'Not necessarily. And don't worry, when I filled out the form I put Rich's address so they wouldn't connect us.'

I finally twist my body around and lie flat on the bed, still trying to process this sudden turn of events. Kier is still here. That's something, I suppose. The Love Academy have accepted Joe because they think it'll help Kier, I can see them doing that – they don't want a failure on their books, especially if they've already got one registered drop-out. And if someone is willing to pay for half a course and it'll help keep their group balanced, why wouldn't they agree? But who is it that has dropped out? Melvin or Adam? I get a sudden pang at the thought of Adam leaving, like when you're at a party and you've been working up to chatting to the guy in the far corner and you keep putting it off, having another drink and another and then you find out he left and you missed your chance.

But chance for what exactly?

I turn to face Joe and kiss him emphatically on the lips.

'Finally!' he chuckles, pulling me close.

Gradually the warmth of his body eases my tension and I relax into him.

'So what do you think of this place?' I ask, only now getting my head around asking some normal, civilised questions.

Silence.

'Joe?'

He rustles up some kind of guttural grunt.

'Are you asleep?'

'Mmmf.'

That'll be a yes.

* * *

When I wake up the next morning, he's gone.

For a moment I wonder if I dreamt the whole encounter but then I hear the shower running and realise he's still very much here. I suppose I'm going to have to be all pleased to see him now, seeing as I didn't quite pull that off last night. As I hear the water squeak to a stop I prepare my face with a cheery 'Hi honey!' countenance only to be surprised again.

'Kier!' I gasp as my brother emerges from the bathroom.

'Kirsty!' he faux-gasps back, before breaking into a smile.

Now I'm really thrown. Considering how we parted, I hardly expected to be greeted with a grin.

'You'd better get a move on,' he tells me as he shuffles his feet into his sandals. 'Sabrina wants to have a word with us all before breakfast.'

I want to ask him what happened to lure him back to The Love Academy but daren't risk ruining his breezy mood so instead I enquire after Joe, principally his whereabouts.

'He's back in his own room. Bastard woke me up at 6 a.m. to trade places.'

'This is all so surreal,' I shake my head.

'Twenty minutes and counting,' Kier taps his watch, uncharacteristically eager to get to class.

What have I missed?

Hold on, did he say twenty minutes? I groan as I stagger to the bathroom. I'm just going to have to get clean now and then get groomed after breakfast. So much for *bella figura*.

When Kier and I enter the lobby, our group is fully assembled, bar Adam.

'So he's the one who's gone?' I ask Kier, wilting a little.

'Yes,' Sabrina answers me. 'He left yesterday. Quite suddenly.'

That sounds a little worrying, I hope he's okay.

'Fortunately we have a replacement,' Sabrina brusques onward. 'I believe you are the last one to be introduced to Joe?'

'I am?'

'The others met him over cocktails last night,' she explains.

'Oh,' I reach to shake his hand. 'I'd say pleased to meet you but I'm sure I've seen you before at one of Kier's barbeques.'

'I'm flattered that you remember me,' he toys with me.

'Mmm,' I look away, embarrassed. This is actually more awkward to me than the George Clooney vase-stroking incident.

'Okay,' Sabrina claps her hands. 'We have many changes of Amores to announce today!'

'Oh no!' Megan and Melvin cry out in unison.

'Not you two,' Sabrina soothes. 'Megan you will continue with Stefano and Melvin you remain together with Filomena.'

'You couldn't keep us apart if you wanted to,' Melvin announces with a valiant jut of his jaw.

Who'd have thought he would make such a strong match? It really is true that there's someone for everyone. Maybe even two someones, I think to myself as I eye Joe, wishing I knew how I really felt about him. When did it all get so foggy between us? When we first met I didn't question anything about him . . .

'Tiffany and Kirsty,' Sabrina continues with her list. 'As requested, you will switch Amores – Kirsty, you are now with Lorenzo. Tiffany, you have Dante.'

My jaw drops.

'Oh thank you!' Tiffany claps her hands together before giving me a look of simpering sympathy. 'I'm so sorry.'

'Don't be,' I tell her. I'm sure Dante's going to be sorry

enough for everyone. I shake my head. I can't believe I've inadvertently subjected him to Tiffany. I didn't realise the Academy were into recycling, I thought they'd simply draft in some fresh flesh.

'Kirsty, you don't look happy,' Sabrina looks concerned. 'This is what you wanted, yes?'

'I . . . Yes. Lorenzo is lovely, thank you,' I smile meekly. 'My mind just went elsewhere.' What else can I say?

'Kier?'

'Yes?' he looks at her clear-eyed and direct.

'Since you defaulted on Valentina, we give you Allegra.'

Also known as Adam's former Amore. This is beginning to feel like a wife-swap party.

'Which leaves Valentina for—'

Oh no. *OH NO!*

'Joe.'

'Ohhhhh, you're going to love her!' Melvin gurgles.

'Actually we met last night,' Joe tells him. 'Maria Luisa felt that as we were not seeing the Amores today—'

'We're not?' Megan looks particularly disappointed.

Sabrina shakes her head and smiles, 'Absence makes the heart grow fonder' before turning back to Joe. 'Continue.'

'Well, she felt like I had some catching up to do so we went to dinner together at Centrale.'

'Trendiest place in town,' Melvin announces. 'Did you like how the bar keeps changing colour? Purple, green, blue . . . '

'Totally hypnotising!' Joe agrees. 'We were there for hours.'

I can't believe my ears. Not only did Joe turn up in Venice uninvited but he went on a date with an Italian siren and *lingered* over dinner. This atypical act irks me more than the fact that he was sat oppposite a woman whose cleavage probably obscured her plate of gnocchi.

'So what *are* we doing today?' Megan huffs, still lamenting the lack of Stefano in her immediate future.

'Today the men will take their Casanova Adventure,' Sabrina winks at Melvin.

'Oooh, this is great!' he rubs his hands together.

'And the women have their Sophia Loren Experience. Now this movie icon may not be quite so synonymous with Venice as Casanova, but as a representative for Italian womanhood there can be no more legendary role model!'

Ordinarily I'd be thrilled at this prospect but today I feel at odds with the world and I'm not sure how learning to maximise the sway of my hips is going to help with my mood.

'Well, that is everything for now,' Sabrina concludes her business. 'Please enjoy your breakfast.'

'Can you believe they serve cake alongside the cornflakes?' Joe chuckles as we help ourselves to the ever-abundant goodies.

I narrow my eyes at him and hiss, 'How come you didn't tell me about your date with Valentina? Oh, that looks delicious, could you pass me a slice?' I raise my voice as Melvin sidles past.

'I didn't exactly get a chance, you were too busy being annoyed at what was supposed to be a romantic gesture.'

'I wasn't annoyed!' I protest.

'Well you are now.'

I can't deny that.

'Kirsty, come and sit with me,' Tiffany shanghais me by the orange juice, oblivious to any tension between me and this new guest I supposedly barely know. 'I want you to tell me all about the divine Dante.'

Joe raises an eyebrow.

'We'll talk later,' I mutter as I'm hustled over to the far corner.

'Welcome back,' Megan toasts me as I pass. 'We missed you last night at the Italian Poetry Class, it was just lovely.'

'Mmm,' I pause beside her, hoping Kier didn't hear that reference. 'How's Stefano?'

'Oh, just too delicious!' she raves. 'Last night we snuck out and he took me to this place that serves thirty-six flavours of hot chocolate – pistachio, pear, rose petal . . . there's even one flavoured with chilli pepper!'

'Kirsty!' Tiffany is getting impatient.

'We'll talk more later,' I promise Megan as I move on to my assigned seat.

'So how was your overnight with Lorenzo?' I ask Tiffany – anything to stay off the subject of Dante.

'Same old, same old,' she rolls her eyes as she tucks into a sinful mix of wheat and dairy – i.e., a slice of buttered toast. 'The only blessing was that he was so chummy with everyone at the vineyard I didn't get lumbered with hours of solo time with him. But I did get a crate of bubbly at a really good rate . . .'

'But what about seeing the Alessandro in him?' I fail to keep the disappointment out of my voice.

'Oh god! Can you believe I went so ga-ga over a barman? So embarrassing!'

'No it's not!' I protest. 'It was the person you were responding to, not the job.'

Her lips purse. 'Well, put it this way, his type could hardly keep me in the manner to which I've become accustomed!'

'What about if you took care of that element of your life yourself?' I make a rather daring suggestion. 'What if you paid for your own extravagances and just let the man concentrate on loving you?'

She looks a little piqued and then reveals, 'I don't work,' in a terse voice. 'I tried it a couple of times and it didn't pan out. And don't tell me it's never too late to try again.'

I can't help but feel deflated. I really thought she'd had a revelation the other night. What a shame those seen-the-light feelings didn't last.

'So, Dante,' she gets back on track. 'Everywhere I go I see Soranzo glass so I'm guessing he's making a pretty decent living. I even heard whisper that he has some celebrity clients!'

'Really?' I say, not welcoming the reminder that I only have until midnight to give in my George Clooney story. I've done a remarkable job of blocking out that little fact.

'What's the matter now?' Tiffany huffs, eyes narrowing: 'You're in a weird mood today, aren't you?'

'Yes,' I confess, buckling all the more. 'My book publisher has brought a deadline forward and I just don't know when I'll have time to meet it.'

'Well, we have the evening free tonight, there's a table booked at Do Forni but Sabrina said that we are at liberty to go off and explore on our own if we want to.'

'Well, that's the time sorted out,' I give a weak smile. 'It's just the inclination I need now.'

'Oh, you'll be fine. These kids you write for are like six aren't they? Like they'll know the difference between literary genius and something you dashed off in an hour.'

And I wonder why Tiffany wasn't a wow in the workplace.

'So can we please talk about Dante now?' she persists. 'I was too busy despairing of Lorenzo on our day at the Lido to really check him out but I did catch him staring at me a few times.'

Yeah, in disbelief, I think to myself.

'So what can you tell me about him that I can use to my advantage?' she enquires.

'Actually my Rice Krispies have gone soggy,' I find another excuse to avoid the issue. 'Let me get a new box.'

'I'll get it for you!' Melvin volunteers, eavesdropping as ever.

Before I can protest he's handing me the little package, dragging his chair over and launching into a tale of his overnight with Filomena in the dinky hill town of Marostico, famous for the life-size chessboard in the town square dating back to 1454 when, rather than having two knights duelling to the death for the hand of his daughter, the lord of Marostico proposed that the rivals played a game of human chess, with townspeople as assorted pawns. Are you listening, world leaders?

As he talks I look over at Joe and Kier – the two men I'm supposed to be closest to in the world – and I feel like I don't know them at all. How come they get to be all cheery and jokey when I'm feeling so stressed and wretched?

With Melvin still talking, I excuse myself from the table and go up to the room fighting back some unexpected tears and an overwhelming desire to run to Dante. I end up calling Mitzi to distract myself and check to see what is the latest *latest* deadline for the George Clooney piece, as I obviously want to put off doing the deed to the absolute last moment.

'Midnight for real,' she tells me. 'It's all designed, we'll just paste your words as soon as you send them. Can you believe you're going to be on the cover?'

'It's just a little drop-in,' I try to play it down.

'Oh no, they're using it as the main shot now. You're a covergirl!'

'But I haven't got anything significant to reveal,' I despair. 'It was all so brief, *nothing happened*.'

'So?' Mitzi scoffs. 'When has that ever stopped us before? We can make a story out of someone walking from their house to their car, you know that.'

I switch off my phone and place the pillow over my face wondering if I can muffle myself to oblivion.

'Need a little help with that?' Kier enquires before pressing down playfully on the corners and then flumping on to his bed groaning, 'I think that third round of toast soldiers may have been a battalion too far.'

I turn and survey him. He seems so much bouncier than when I left. He catches me looking and, mirroring my pose back to me, says, 'I'm sorry about what I said before. My being born second has got nothing to do with my issues.' I go to tell him it's okay, not to fret it but he seems keen to continue. 'After you left I went to see Tonio and he told me straight off that I was being an idiot. He has an older sister and it's never stopped him doing anything. And then he gave me about ten examples of friends of his in the same position.' He rolls his eyes. 'I felt such a fool. It's like I'm always looking for a reason – or an excuse, more to the point – for why I am the way I am and that latest theory sounded plausible to me for a brief moment. *It wasn't my fault! I was just born in the wrong sequence!*' he mocks himself. 'I didn't mean it to come off as blaming you but I know from the look on your face that it seemed that way. I felt awful about that.' He looks genuinely contrite and then he shakes his head. 'You carry around this chip on your shoulder for so long you don't even notice that it's getting bigger and bigger. The easiest option seems to be to blame other people but it's also fatal because then you are living a lie and not taking responsibility for yourself. And it actually doesn't make you feel any better anyway – if anything you feel more helpless. Raeleen helped me see that.'

'Raeleen?' So Joe was right, he has seen her.

'I had a one-to-one session with her while the others were in the poetry class,' he explains. 'Traded her dinner in return for a little more of her *dolce vita* wisdom. She's really wonderful you know.'

'I know,' I tell him, delighted to see the warmth return to his face. 'So are you.' And with that I get up and give him a big 'all's forgiven' hug. It's amazing how much quicker arguments are resolved with Kier than with Joe. We're terrible for stringing out our irks.

He cocks his head. 'So what was with the pillow, when I came in?'

'Oh, it's nothing. Magazine nonsense.'

'Tell me. You never know, I might be able to help.'

What have I got to lose? I take a deep breath and explain my sorry situation. Kier listens diligently and then says, 'You know I said I might be able to help?'

'Yes?' Is that a glimmer of hope I see on the horizon?

'I think I may have spoken too soon.'

My shoulders slump.

'Come on,' he pulls me to my feet. 'For the next six hours you are not Kirsty Bailey, frazzled magazine journalist, you are the poised and goddess-like Sophia Loren.'

'Yeah yeah, and you're Casanova.'

'You don't think I could pull a nun?' he faux challenges.

'The nuns you know are seventy plus.' I give him a withering look.

'So what's your point?'

I laugh out loud – my first real smile of the day. We're back! Brother and sister, back in business!

# 28

*'Everything you see, I owe to spaghetti!'*
*– Sophia Loren*

Aside from Megan and Tiffany I count six other women as I enter the re-configured breakfast room. This should be a good chance for me to find out whether any of them made any physical or financial transactions with their Amores while away on their overnights. I know Megan's virtue remains intact, not least because she just confessed that she is now ready to get steamy with Stefano. Obviously Tiffany didn't do anything more than scowl at Lorenzo, and Dante went one step further and forwent all payment altogether. I wonder if his morals will change when it comes to 'dating' Tiffany. This new set-up is so very strange to me. I'm surprised Dante went along with it. I would have thought he would simply politely decline. Then again, I don't know what Sabrina had him sign on that first night . . .

I have two minutes before class is due to begin and decide to dip out to get some water, only to collide with our tutor.

'Cinzia!' I gasp.

'Kirsty!' she beams. 'You're still here!' She gives me a hug. 'I missed you at the love poetry class yesterday – I wondered if you and Kier had left.'

'Well,' I grimace. 'He did temporarily . . . '

'Because you told him we had met?' she looks concerned.

'It wasn't just that,' I assure her. 'But he's come a long way since then, you mustn't worry.' I smile suddenly. It's really nice to see her. And she certainly puts my own problems in perspective.

Cinzia takes a rousing breath. 'I suppose we should get started – you have to wish me luck,' she says as she guides me back into the room, 'this is my first time with this subject.'

'*Buona fortuna*!' I find myself singing as I forgo the water and take my seat.

Cinzia takes her position in front of the canal-side window and then faces us with a smile. 'Today I would like to welcome you to the wonderful world of Sophia Loren!' she begins, striking a suitably sassy pose. 'You will all know this woman as a most glamorous and voluptuous international movie star, but it is her spirit and grounded wisdom that elevates her and can inspire us.' She surveys her students. 'I am clearly in the presence of nine natural beauties but who doesn't want to learn an extra trick or two? This morning we will take advice from the goddess Sophia on hair and make-up, fashion and style as well as the inner beauties of charm and tranquillity. At one o'clock we will cook one of Ms Loren's very own recipies for our lunch – spaghetti with lemon and cream. Delicious!' she enthuses. 'In the afternoon we will turn to the subject of men and love! But for now it's just us girls!'

I smile in relief – I am glad to be in all-female company right now. So much less complicated. Of course, it doesn't hurt to know that Joe is with an all-male group as opposed to the vamp that is Valentina.

As Cinzia gives us a biographical overview of our subject, I'm surprised to learn of certain hardships she has had to overcome – to begin with she was an illegitimate baby, brought up in poverty in Naples. She may have found the love of her life – producer Carlo Ponti – early on when she was just 16 (he was judging a beauty contest she had entered to try and rustle up a few lire) but their romance was no smooth ride – initially he was married to another woman and there was no divorce in Italy so they were forced to live apart and ultimately had to become French citizens for their marriage to be considered legal. Cinzia tells us how Sophia always longed to be a mother and, having suffered two devastating miscarriages, had to remain in bed for the entire term of her first pregnancy. But the bed-rest worked and she gave birth to Carlo Junior and then four years later gave him a brother, Edoardo. I get a warm feeling when I recall that these two sons were with Sophia at the Damiani jewellery launch I attended – it's gratifying to know that over thirty years on, they are still mama's boys, in the nicest sense of the phrase.

'Sophia says that motherhood is the greatest role of her life and not even winning an Oscar can compare to the pleasure and sense of accomplishment it has given her,' Cinzia tells us.

Again I smile. Is that the faintest ticking I hear within me?

After we have mastered the art of the liquid liner flick and learned that cider vinegar removes the smell of onion from your hands after cooking, we retire to the garden, the group dividing into sun-worshippers and those who are more comfortable in the shade.

'Now we come to the subject most relevant to your stay here at The Love Academy – *men*!' Cinzia grins, adding, 'And this information from a woman who was proposed to by Cary Grant, so she knows a thing or two!'

A number of us look confused. 'Are you saying she turned him down?' a woman with a blonde bob voices our disbelief.

'Yes, because she was already with Carlo Ponti, who sadly died in January 2007 age ninety-four. They were together for fifty years you know!'

'Fifty Years! That's older than me!' The dame of the group exclaims.

'Impressive isn't it?'

'Wow,' I murmur, thinking again of my visit to San Michele – she's one of them! One of those love-you-for-life couples. I sit forward, ever more eager to hear what she has to say.

'As you can imagine, living the life of a movie star, Sophia mingled with some of Hollywood's greatest leading men and she has confessed that she often playfully imagined creating an ideal man from their most appealing aspects! This is her check-list: Marlon Brando's mouth, Paul Newman's eyes, Gregory Peck's nose, Richard Burton's voice, Jean Gabin's magnetism, Cary Grant's elegance and Marcello Mastroianni's charm.'

'Who is Jean Gabin?' Tiffany frowns, going back a step.

'A rather controversial French actor and war hero who had a torrid romance with Marlene Dietrich,' Cinzia replies.

'Oh. And Marcello Minestrone?'

Cinzia looks the tiniest bit miffed. 'Mastroianni,' she corrects. 'He is one of our country's finest actors. You have not seen *La Dolce Vita*?'

'No, just read Raeleen's book,' Tiffany shrugs.

'Perhaps his other famous Fellini film – *8½*?' Cinzia persists.

Nothing.

'What about *Pret A Porter*?' I suggest, suspecting her passion for fashion could be the connection we need.

'The grey-haired guy with the accent? He was really hot!' Tiffany praises.

'Wasn't Sophia Loren in that movie too?' Megan enquires. 'In a really big brimmed hat?'

'*Esattamente!*' Cinzia smiles. 'The two of them actually made thirteen films together.' She takes a sip of tea. 'Interestingly, when Marcello escaped from a Nazi prison during World War Two, he hid out here in Venice.'

'The perfect place for hide and seek,' I note, looking beyond the gate to the narrow, secretive streets.

'You know, he too had a very long marriage – forty-eight years to a woman named Flora Carabella,' Cinzia continues. 'But there was also an enduring affair with Catherine Deneuve and, when he died of pancreatic cancer in 1996, both women were at his bedside.'

'Wow, he must have been *really* charming to manage that!' Tiffany coos.

'Anyway, I'm getting distracted!' Cinzia scolds herself. 'The point is that having created a composite of the highest virtues of an elite collection of much-admired men, Sophia then pronounces him a *failure*!'

'But why?' Megan gasps.

Cinzia reaches for her notes. 'She said a man with these qualities would be terrible because he would be perfect and who could live with a man who is so handsome, charming and saint-like?'

'I wouldn't mind giving it a try!' The blonde bob opines.

We all laugh.

'It is her theory that grace and good looks alone cannot satisfy a mature woman. Imperfections are the real challenge of love.'

She takes a moment to let the sentiment sink in.

'You see, Sophia doesn't believe in judging a man against ideals decided by a common vote. You should find the man who is ideal for you, no matter how strange that choice might appear to another woman's taste.'

Well, Joe wins that contest. Not everyone gets our union. Whereas Dante is a blatant ideal by any woman's standards. But does that necessarily make him wrong for me? Not that I'm even thinking these thoughts any more. I promised myself I was done. Besides, he is no longer my Amore.

'Now this next notion may seem at odds with the aims of The Love Academy, but I think it is vital to consider,' Cinzia clears her throat. 'Have we become preoccupied with the idea of romantic love and its place in our lives to an extent that is unhealthy and counterproductive?'

'Yes,' we chorus as one, quick to admit our weakness.

'You are not entirely to blame,' Cinzia concedes. 'It is as if we are being set up for this. Sometimes I wonder if we've been fed a line about love being so transformative and unique that no other life experience can compare. I love Sophia's biting insight that for people who put love on such a pedestal and worship it so, we can't seem to stay *in* love for very long!'

I don't think I'm alone in feeling a little smart. Was I really considering giving up on Joe that easily?

'I think Sophia suspects that most of us prefer the fantasy of love to the day-in, day-out version.'

Is that what Dante represents to me – a fantasy of love? I already have a real live boyfriend in Joe, but here is Dante all fresh and sparkly and extra-attentive. I sigh in frustration – how am I supposed to distinguish between infatuation and a more profound attraction? And if I already have one imperfect love – and it sounds like Sophia's saying all love is imperfect and purposefully so – then why would I trade that? Is Dante my Cary Grant temptation and Joe my enduring Carlo Ponti?

I'm just berating myself – once again – for always questioning my relationship choices when Cinzia slaps me with another insightful comment from the woman who is fast becoming my relationship guru.

'Sophia is against this constant pulse-taking in relationships, the microscopic inspections, the endless judgements – she believes that is what diminishes our love until it disappears. And she's got a point – how often have you taken a compatibility quiz in a women's magazine or compared your relationship to another couple's and felt better for it?'

That is so me. So horribly me. I'm always looking at other couples. Wishing Joe could be more sensitive like our friend Ben, conveniently overlooking the fact that I wouldn't in any way want him to be as pally with all his lady exes like Ben.

'So what's the answer?' I wail.

'Sophia suggests that perhaps it would do us all good to forget for a week, a month, a year about the vigour of our relationships.'

I heave a sigh. 'I wouldn't even know how to stop obsessing. They say men think about sex every fifty-two seconds don't they? I know I think about my relationship all day long!'

Tiffany narrows her eyes at me.

'You know, when I'm in one,' I quickly add. 'Every day I wonder – is this the guy for me?'

The only respite I seemed to have was when we first moved in together. Prior to that I'd always had one foot out the door but initially when he did something 'displeasing' I was more accepting because I'd think – what am I gonna do, move out?

'Well this may seem harsh but the best lessons often are . . .' Cinzia pats me on the hand before stepping across the grass and plucking nine flowers, one for each of us.

As she hands them to us she asks, 'Do you remember dissecting items in your biology class at school?'

We shudder in recognition, wondering where she is going with this.

'Well, Sophia makes the point that to dissect something we must kill it. We scrutinise love so closely and yet is it really a subject meant for a science lab? In many ways it is indefinable, certainly unpredictable and maybe even a little unkempt. Love is not groomed and manicured. Sophia says it is closer in nature to a wildflower than a long-stemmed rose and I have to agree.'

I look down at the delicate bloom in my hand and realise that the quickest way to destroy its fragile beauty would be to start pinching the petals or stripping the stem of its furry fibres or trying to transplant the bud or thorn from another flower. When you look at a flower you don't see its short comings, only its beauty. We don't say, well you're a nice-looking buttercups but I'd like you better if you were purple like a violet or had an abundance of petals like a peony. Look at this bloom – it doesn't need changing at all. It's perfect just as it is. Why is it so hard to think the same of our fellow human beings?

I look up at the blue sky and think, I don't need a long-stemmed rose like Dante, I want my very own wildflower.

Now the class is over, we all applaud fervently, causing Cinzia to blush happily as she wishes us a good evening and reminds us that we have the option of dinner with the group at Do

Forni or something more private. 'Whatever your heart desires,' she shrugs.

Megan immediately reaches for her phone, no doubt dialling Stefano. I hear the other women a-buzz, keen to do the same. Naturally my thoughts turn to Dante. I should at least call him. Apologise for Tiffany. And try to offer some kind of explanation for my decision . . .

'Did you enjoy the class?' Cinzia steps in to my deliberation.

'More than you can imagine – who would have guessed that a flower from a woman could hold so much more meaning,' I say, twirling the pale peachy petals under my nose.

Cinzia is chuckling along with me when her expression suddenly changes.

'What is it?' I ask, but before she can reply I turn and see my brother, stalled in the entranceway of the palazzo . . .

# 29

*'I always willingly acknowledge my own self as the principal cause of every good and of every evil which may befall me; therefore I have always found myself capable of being my own pupil, and ready to love my teacher.' – Giacomo Casanova*

I immediately freeze – I can't believe I've been caught being pally with Cinzia again!

As the ex-lovers take a step closer to each other, Joe and I remain a pace behind our respective charges like awkward chaperones.

'Hello,' Kier begins, clearly dazed.

Cinzia smiles, stretching up to kiss each of his cheeks. '*Come stai*?'

Suddenly I feel Joe removing the room key from my hand to place it in Kier's palm. 'In case you need somewhere private to talk,' he says before reaching for my arm and pulling me out through the gate.

'Wait!' I protest. 'Where are we going?'

'I have some things I want to show you.'

'But I can't leave Kier!'

'Yes, you can,' Joe asserts. 'He needs this time alone with Cinzia.'

'But—'

'Aren't you supposed to be meddling less?' he tsks.

'I can't desert him in his hour of need!'

'In this particular hour I think he needs to be with Cinzia,' he assures me. 'And then, most likely, he needs to be with himself. And if not, if he wants some company, he can call us.' He waggles his mobile phone at me. 'We're only going to be twenty minutes' walk away.'

I remain rooted to the spot.

'Come on, Kirsty. I want to tell you all about the crazy Casanova stuff I learnt today. It's really cool.'

'Wouldn't you rather be with Valentina?' I pout, still resisting.

'No,' he smiles. 'I would rather be with you. I would rather share the secrets of the world's most notorious lover with you.'

I feel an unexpected tingle. Maybe it wouldn't be so bad after all. 'Go on then,' I encourage him as we set off.

'Well, did you know Casanova nearly married his own daughter without realising it?'

Oh. This isn't quite what I had in mind. 'I did not,' I cringe as we begin weaving down the wiggly streets beyond Strada Nova.

'Or that, in lieu of a condom, he used a reusable sheep gut sheath tied on with a ribbon?'

'I thought this was supposed to be a romantic take on the man?' I complain.

'Well, they gave us an overview of his libertine lifestyle to get started,' he explains as we briefly come up for air in the large shopping square of Campo San Bartolomeo. 'Ready for the next round?' he reaches for my hand as we face a particularly chockablock alley.

'We can't!' I reject his hand. 'Someone might see.'

'I just don't want us to get separated.'

'I'll hold on to your jacket,' I tell him, trying not to dwell on the poignancy of his words. 'Don't worry, I won't lose you.'

'Okay,' he groans. 'Clandestine it is. I suppose it's appropriate considering the subject matter.'

It feels strange being led down the tangle of backstreets by Joe, who until yesterday was a stranger here. How'd he get so cocky after just one day?

'Wait a minute!' he frowns, reaching for his map and wedging us into a doorway so we have enough room to open it out.

I guess I spoke too soon. I wait while he readjusts his internal compass. And then we're off again, squeezing down seemingly narrower and more congested alleys.

'Now I know how the meat feels in a sausage factory!' I grizzle. 'Where *are* you taking me?'

'One more turning . . .' Joe surges on, giving me a final tug before we emerge in to . . .

'St Mark's Square!' he cheers.

Six days I've been in Venice and this is the first time I'm seeing the most famed scene in the city. I swirl around in utter awe. It really is *vast*. And strikingly monochrome – arch upon arch of tear-stained grey, pillars of charcoal-smudged marble and, it would appear, a pigeon for every person.

'Look how plump they are!' I gasp at the birds' puffa-jacket chests and then spot the reason – bags of feed being sold for one euro a piece, all you need for that classic holiday snap of you looking like a human scarecrow with a pigeon on your head. And a further seventeen along your shoulders and outstretched arms. 'Urgh!' I shudder, turning my attention to the statues atop the back perimeter – a dozen or so men each with one arm extended in gesticulation, one beckoning in a 'Come on if you think you're hard enough!' way. 'They look like they're demonstrating dance moves!' I giggle.

'It's the Venetian macarena!' Joe agrees, mimicking their poses.

We laugh together and then I gasp again as I notice another iconic image. 'The clock with the winged lion!'

'Glad you came now?' Joe looks chuffed. Like he arranged the whole scene, just for me.

I nod, still trying to absorb all the sights.

'Melvin said you hadn't been yet,' Joe smiles. 'He's quite a fan of yours, that chap.'

I chuckle. 'He's actually grown on me. At first he was such a pest but now . . . Oh! We've got to get you a pair of these!' I'm distracted by a tourist-tat stand with a pair of men's undies printed with the Statue of David's sculpted genitalia.

'All of this magnificence and you want to go shopping,' Joe groans.

'I even quite like these *Ciao Bella* shirts,' I wind him up further. 'The ones written in the Coca-Cola logo . . .'

'And to our left we have the Doge's Palace,' he ahems. I turn and give him my full attention once more. 'This is where Casanova was jailed, in the rooftop cells known as the leads,' he says, with all the expert knowledge of a man that heard the information for the first time just six hours ago. 'He is the only prisoner to have ever escaped!'

'What was he charged with in the first place?' I ask.

'Impiety, imposture and licentiousness, I believe,' Joe tries to sound casual. 'The thing I didn't get was why he was sleeping with prostitutes – it seems rather unnecessary given the general willingness of all the other women in Venice.' Joe stops abruptly. 'I tell you something strange that was going on in the world of prostitution a couple of hundred years prior to Casanova – in the fifteenth century there was a very high proportion of homosexuals here, and the local prostitutes were facing economical difficulties so they started dressing up as men to attract more clients!'

'Are you serious?'

'Yes! The only snag was they got a whipping if they were discovered and the men themselves were condemned to death if they were found out so they took to dressing up as women to attract other men!'

'Oh good lord! How confusing!'

'And we complain about today's sexual politics!' Joe shakes his head.

We are now standing before the red-bricked Campanile bell tower, a seagull stronghold in a world of pigeons.

As Joe watches me gaze up a hundred metres to its pyramidial peak, a smile creeps over his face. 'This is like Venice's answer to the Empire State Building, isn't it? You want to go up, don't you?'

I shrug, not entirely sure that I do.

'But you must, that's what the hero and heroine always do in the movies you love, isn't it – arrange to meet at some picturesque vantage point overlooking the whole city? Only in this case we'll be going up together so there won't be any awful tension about whether the other person is going to show up!'

'Alright, let's do it!' I decide to give in before Joe bursts with good intentions.

We shuffle in with the queue, pay our entry fee and squeeze into the lift where Joe makes the most of the enforced proximity, pressing himself close to me. My eyes narrow at him.

'What?' he protests. 'It's very crowded in here!'

'This is a watch tower,' I hiss at him. 'As in you never know who's watching . . .'

Seconds later the doors open and suddenly I'm nothing but grateful to Joe, for the amazing view he has bestowed upon me.

'This is great!' I marvel as I see a Venice made-up almost entirely of terracotta tiled roofs.

'Do you notice what's missing?' Joe looks expectantly at me.

I study the vista, gradually managing to place The Love Academy and Dei Dogi hotel in Cannaregio, the Dorsoduro district that is home to Peggy Guggenheim's art collection, the distant Lido, Murano and San Michele cemetery island – everything seems to be accounted for in my book.

'What?' I ask Joe, mystified.

'You can't see a single Venetian canal from here. Not even the main artery – the Grand Canal!'

'Surely . . .' I hurry to the side where it should be visible and he's right – nothing. I can recognise certain key palazzos but none of the lattice of waterways, only the lagoon waters surrounding us and the distant sea. 'Isn't that bizarre?'

Suddenly I feel Joe's arms around me and his lips avariciously kissing my neck.

'Joe!' I jump away from him, checking no one has seen. 'I already told you twice – no public hanky panky!'

'Oh come on, you can't blame me for trying! I've spent all day in the company of a sex maniac. You're lucky I didn't come back wearing velvet bloomers and ravage you right there in the garden. How was your day, by the way?' he asks as we make our descent.

'Really great,' I tell him, surreptitiously tweaking his bottom so he doesn't think I'm getting too school ma'am-ish. 'Aside from being a goddess, that Sophia Loren is one savvy signora.' Unfortunately thinking of her makes me think of Cinzia and thus Kier . . .

Joe reads my mind. 'He'll be fine,' he tells me as we step back into the main piazza.

'Oh Joe!' I stop short of the crowds. 'You don't know the half of it – what that poor girl has been through!'

Instead of telling me – once again – to stay out of their business, he steps closer and says, 'So, tell me.'

'What?'

'You're right, I don't know. And if it's going to prey on your mind and you'd feel better talking about it, talk to me.'

'Really?' This is unusual. Is it possible that Valentina has had an impact on his sensibilities in one night?

And then he reveals that one of the most alluring aspects to Casanova was 'his sympathetic ear'.

'Well, that explains a lot,' I note.

'Now I was going to take you to Do Spade where us chaps had lunch today but it might be a bit noisy in the evening and it's over in San Polo . . . I know, why don't we have drinks and a little nibble here at Florian—'

'Florian the literary café?' I remember Cinzia mentioning it as the place she was meeting her tour group.

'Well, I don't know about that but I do know it as a former haunt of Casanova,' he grins, adding, 'they say that on the morning he escaped his prison cell, he stopped in for a quick coffee – how bold is that?'

'Positively audacious,' I agree.

Joe side-steps a tour group led by a man in a three-storey-high felt hat refusing to let the crowds interfere with his images of the past. 'Doesn't it blow your mind that Casanova was a real person and we can actually walk where he walked? Eat where he ate?'

'Indeed,' I agree. I'm actually more intrigued at Joe's enthusiasm than anything. He's the last person I thought would embrace all this history and romance.

'Anyway,' he continues. 'We'll get comfortable and then you can start at the beginning – there's so much I haven't heard about your time at the Academy.'

'Well, I mean, you get the idea . . .' I bumble. There are some things I'm not so keen on going into minute detail over. 'Besides, you haven't told me about the grand finale of the conference. Which reminds me, when I called you yesterday morning you said you were talking to Rich but I heard a woman's voice in the background . . .'

Joe grins broadly. 'Girl on the check-in desk at BA. I wondered if you'd caught that. Right, here we are . . .'

I smile with relief – both that he had a legitimate answer and that the suspicion was not bounced back to me.

Caffe Florian is located in the colonnade on the left-hand side if you are standing with St Mark's basilica and its Eastern domes and spiky spires behind you. An impeccably-dressed waiter shows us to a heavy marble table and a velvet-covered bench seat with absolutely no spring in the cushion.

'Well, this place has been around since 1720,' Joe says as he hands me a menu. My eye keeps straying from the list of tremezzini and tisanes to the tobacco-smoked décor in the sequence of salons. Each wall features hand-painted panels and exotic portraits set behind glass. I feel we should all be assigned period costume upon entry as our modern dress looks so crass set against such finery. And as for the person using their mobile phone – straight to Casanova's former cell!

Once our drinks have arrived on a silver platter befitting the exorbitant prices, I bring Joe up to speed on Kier and Cinzia.

He listens sympathetically, which in turn eases my anguish, and then, taking a fortifying sip of wine he blusters, 'So. This Dante,' looking almost nervous as he says his name.

I too take a sip, equally in need of fortification to answer.

'Melvin says he's quite a looker,' he prompts me.

'Did you ask about him?' I throw the ball back at Joe.

Joe shrugs.

'Did you?' I smile, for a second almost more flattered than nervous.

'Well, I just want to know what my competition is. I mean, if he's the male version of Valentina . . .'

I raise an eyebrow. 'Meaning . . .'

'What?' he looks suddenly boxed into a corner.

I strum my fingers on the table expectantly.

'I just mean—' he splutters.

'It's okay!' I laugh. 'I know she's a total fox.'

Joe looks relieved. 'Well. Was *he*?'

'If you like that kind of thing,' I give the classic get-out clause shrug. 'Anyway, he's not my Amore any more. As you know. I'm with Lorenzo now.'

'So why did you switch?' Joe leans back to allow the waiter to place our dessert in front of us.

'Oooh, doesn't this look lovely . . .' I fawn over the delicacy of the chocolate squiggles.

'Did he try it on with you?'

'No!' I bat away his concern.

'Why then?'

'He . . . he wasn't right for the piece. He isn't really an official Amore. I just happened to bump into him on the street on the first night and they recruited him on the spot. I needed someone more established, someone I could pump for information.'

'I see. Why wait six days to switch then?'

Oh god. My eyes roam the room, looking for a legitimate excuse. And then I remember I actually have one. 'They have a policy at the Academy that you have to stay with your assigned Amore until at least the overnight. Only then can you trade.'

'So what happened on the overnight?'

My stomach knots. Terrific. I'm now totally incapable of eating my dessert.

'We went to a Midsummer gala in Lake Como,' I glance at my watch. 'Oh god – I've only got two more hours!' I wail.

'Until what? You turn into a cannoli?'

I rub my forehead fretfully. 'I haven't had a chance to tell you yet – I've got myself in a bit of a predicament with George Clooney.'

Joe's eyes widen. 'You're kidding, right?' Suddenly Dante is the least of his concerns.

I blurt out everything. Including the scheduled horror of being splashed across *Hot!*'s front cover.

'You actually went inside his villa?' he gawps in response.

'No!' I roll my eyes. 'Just into the garden. I didn't see anything of the interior. And even if I did I just wouldn't feel right about revealing anything. Honestly, I just can't do this any more.'

Joe sets down his spoon and smiles proudly. 'This is your defining moment. This is where you draw the line.'

I look up at him, confused. 'How do you mean?'

'You tell them straight – I'm sorry, but I am not writing anything on this subject. I don't feel right about the invasion of privacy.'

'They'll just laugh in my face!' I scoff.

'Let them. What's the worst they can do?'

'Fire me,' I reply in a small voice.

'Isn't that what you want? A way out? At least this way you wouldn't have to work your notice.'

I blink back at him. He's right. 'I'd be free!' I gasp. And then I feel a flutter of panic. 'What if I couldn't get another job? It wouldn't take long to get around that I can't follow through on a story.'

'There are still plenty of magazines that just want honest descriptions of legitimate encounters.' He hesitates. 'Aren't there?'

'I do quite like the idea of working on an interiors magazine,' I offer.

'Right,' he nods approvingly. 'That sounds sensible – considerably less call for paparazzi pictures of architects and wallpaper designers,' he acknowledges. 'And I can tide you over financially until you get a job.'

'You'd do that?'

'Of course! You'd do the same for me, wouldn't you?'

I nod dumbly. So we really are a proper couple. In it together. I didn't think it was possible, but I'm starting to feel like I really have got options.

'Or you could write a children's book for real,' Joe adds, taking things a step further. 'That's what you put on your application for the Academy, wasn't it?'

Again with the mute nodding.

'Isn't that something you'd actually like to do?'

I can't believe he's being so patient and understanding with me, so genuinely concerned about my well-being. Is he always this sweet and am I really too hung up on all the ways he doesn't meet my fantasy standards that I've stopped noticing all the good?

I ponder his question for a moment. 'Well, I've always liked the idea but I don't feel qualified – in a way I think you should probably be a mother first, to really know the minds of children, you know, how to talk to them . . .'

His face looks warmer. 'You know, that's something we could work on.'

My uneasiness returns. We're back here. I was hoping to have some kind of epiphany about having a bambino while I was away from home but I'm still uncertain. Not least because the night before last Mummy was kissing a man that isn't Daddy.

'We'll talk more about this later, here comes Kier,' Joe gets to his feet to pull out a chair for my brother.

I look around, surprised to see him at the door.

'He called while you were in the loo,' Joe explains. 'I told him to come and have coffee with us.'

Again Joe's kindness warms the cockles of my heart.

'I really appreciate that,' I tell him. 'This being our romantic night out in Venice . . .'

'No probs, I knew you'd want to see him ASAP. Here you go, mate,' Joe welcomes Kier. 'Looks like you get Kirsty's uneaten dessert into the bargain.'

'Really?'

He actually looks like he wants to eat it. That's got to be a good sign!

I take a deep breath as I contemplate him. 'So . . .?'

He lets out an elongated sigh.

I reach for his hand. 'That can't have been easy.'

'It wasn't. But I tell you something – when you start telling the truth about yourself to yourself, it's a lot easier to hear the truth from other people.'

'She told you—' I stop myself, afraid of saying too much.

'She told me everything – the cancer, the lie about the ex-boyfriend coming back into her life, the fact that ultimately in her eyes I wasn't The One.'

'And you're okay with that?' I am simply marvelling now.

He takes a deep breath. 'It just felt such a huge relief to be able to talk to her again. And what she said made sense. I can't argue with what she told me. She's entitled to her feelings. It's her life.' Kier studies me for a second. 'You really liked her, didn't you?'

I nod ruefully.

'Well at least you know my taste in women is improving!' he manages a joke. 'Of course, I wish things could be different but I have to say I've walked away with a new kind of peace – almost as if I knew she was hiding something from me and, now I know what it was, I don't have to go over and over things, always wondering, never accepting . . .' He gives me a lop-sided smile. 'That's what you wanted for me all along, isn't it? Some closure.'

I give a shy nod. 'But I promise I'm not going to meddle any more.'

'Meddle all you like,' he laughs. 'God knows how long I would have stayed stuck if you hadn't brought me here.' He leans across the table and kisses my cheek. 'I couldn't ask for a better sister.'

I blink back the tears and gulp, 'Do you mean that?'

He nods an affirmative. 'I just hope I get the chance to return the favour. In fact I was thinking about your problem with the magazine and I remember you saying that Sir Elton trumps everything and what with him having a house over on the Guidecca and Tonio having a friend who's rather good with sticky locks—'

'You're not suggesting we break in!' I splutter.

'Well, not exactly but—'

'There's no need,' I stop him before he initiates a felonious activity. 'I've decided what I'm going to do. With Joe's help.' I give him a wink then turn back to Kier. 'I'm giving them nothing – nada! And if they don't like it they can fire me! Please god!' I waggle my crossed fingers at the sky.

We sit and chat for a second round of coffees, even ordering two more desserts to share, before we wend our way back to Cannaregio.

As we reach the peak of a hump-back bridge, I see another ahead of us creating a perfect circle as it reflects in the tranquil, moonlit water and I reach for Joe's hand.

'Nuh-uh.' He un-entwines my fingers and reprimands me, 'We might be seen!'

As he walks on, I realise that the want has come back. I want to touch Joe and have him walk with his arm comfortingly around me. I want to crawl into bed with him tonight.

I just hope it's not because I'm being denied his affection. Emotions can be so contrary, after all.

Turning onto Calle Priuli, the two men stride ahead chatting and I wonder if I should hang back and take this opportunity to call Dante? But then it hits me – he's no longer a part of my life. These two men ahead of me – my brother and my boyfriend – belong to me. Dante belongs to Venice.

# 30

*'The Creator made Italy from designs by Michelangelo.' – Mark Twain*

'Was that you or me?' I ask Kier the next morning.

'I think it was both of us,' he grips at his stomach. 'I am *starving*! Let's go straight down to breakfast . . .'

We throw back our respective covers and jump to our feet. But then my phone rings and the name on the display stops me in my tracks. *Hot!* magazine.

'You go ahead,' I tell him. 'I have a little something to attend to before I deserve my morning cake!'

I take a deep breath – if Kier can face Cinzia and survive, I can certainly face my celebrity editor.

'Hey, Mitz.'

'It's Ruth.'

Oh god. My face scrunches in horror.

'Hello,' I say in the most microscopically small voice.

'Well, it's over,' she breezes. 'You can pack up and call it a day.'

Gosh, I gawp. It's really happened. I can't quite believe it. I am no longer employed by *Hot!* magazine.

'Oh, and you were right about the Clooney piece, it works far better this way.'

'What way?' I'm bewildered. 'I didn't send you anything.'

'And Mitzi explained why. Smart move. Everyone loves how it's turned out.'

'You ran it?' I'm incredulous.

'Of course!'

'With no words?'

'Well obviously Mitzi wrote on behalf of the magazine, just as you suggested.' Ruth's voice takes on an amused tone. 'You've just woken up, haven't you?'

'Yes, actually.'

'Thought so. I'll read it to you if you like, "*These pictures show our jet-set reporter Kirsty Bailey vacationing with George Clooney at his Lake Como villa.*"'

'Vacationing?!' I splutter. 'That's stretching it a bit isn't it?'

'Well, you weren't at work in the office and you were abroad and that sounds like a vacation to me.'

'Go on.'

'"*We'd love to tell you what she saw and heard when she swanned into the private grounds of his villa in a slinky Scott Henshall gown but as George is such a good friend of the magazine we wish to respect both his and Kirsty's privacy!*" Brilliant!' she cheers. 'It makes us look even more in with the celebs than we actually are. Love it.'

Now I'm really foxed. 'So if you're okay with that, why are you firing me?'

'Who said anything about firing you?' she snorts.

'You said to pack up—'

'Oh that,' she groans. 'Bloody tabloids have beaten us to the punch with their Love Academy exposé, haven't they?'

'What?'

'It was in the *Daily News* this morning – some Amore by

the name of Allegra was revealed to be a former call girl, so it's all over.'

'Allegra?' I baulk. 'There's an Allegra in my group – she went out with my brother last night.'

'Ah yes, "brother and sister Kevin and Krista,"' she reads. 'There's a whole paragraph on you two, at least they had the decency to slightly moderate your names—'

'You mean we're in the article?' I'm aghast.

'Don't worry, you get off pretty lightly. It's poor Trixie that got the worst shredding.'

'Tiffany . . .' I mumble.

'It's a bit of a hack job. I certainly won't be head-hunting Adam Barrows anytime soon.'

'Adam?' The blood drains from my face. 'He was a journalist?'

I'm reeling. Is anything as it seems? Anything at all? I am seriously considering relocating to a farm in Devon. Sheep don't lie.

'Must go,' Ruth clips. 'Got a meeting.'

I'm still sitting on the bed in a daze when Joe and Kier return to the room.

'There's my girl,' Joe bounds up to me. 'I brought you cake and . . .' he rummages in his pockets. 'A couple of boiled eggs.' He sits down beside me. 'Kier said *Hot!* rang. Are you unemployed? Am I now your rich benefactor?'

'Actually, I still have a job.'

'Oh. That's a shame,' his shoulders slump.

'Yes it is,' I agree with a sigh. 'What I *don't* have is a story.' I look up at Kier. 'Adam was an undercover newspaper reporter. His big exposé ran today.'

'Exposé?' Joe hoots. 'What is there to expose? This place seems totally legit to me.'

'Allegra was a former hooker,' I announce.

'That was years ago,' Kier dismisses the charge.

Joe and I do a doubletake. 'You knew?'

'She's pretty upfront about it. She got in with a bad crowd in her teens. It was just one night but, luckily really, she got arrested before she did the deed. That was enough of a wake-up call for her to re-think where her life was going.'

We continue to gawp at him.

'It just came up because we were talking about the distinct crossroads in your life and the choices you make when you reach them . . . anyway,' he shrugs, 'it seems a bit mean to make such a big thing about something that happened twenty years ago.'

'Well, either way, it means it's all over for us.' I get to my feet. 'We can leave today.' There is something of an advantage to this for me – at least I don't have to face Dante again after so rudely dismissing him via the note to Sabrina.

As I pull out my suitcase from under the bed I catch the men exchanging a look.

'What?' I frown. 'I thought you'd be pleased.'

'Do we *have* to go?' Kier surprises me further. 'I mean, everything's already paid for here, isn't it?'

'Yes,' I confirm. 'But is there any point—'

'We can't leave,' Joe scoffs. 'I just got here!'

'It is just two more nights,' Kier reasons. 'Don't you want to complete the course?'

I can't believe this – they actually want to stay!

'You know it's the wedding today?' Kier ventures.

'Sabrina just announced it at breakfast – it's in Florence!' Joe coos.

'Firenze!' Kier sighs.

I can't help but smile. The romance in this room is palpable!

I think for a moment. Perhaps I am supposed to have some kind of closure with Dante. After all, I was so insistent about such things with Kier. I tilt my head. 'This may be the only time I ever get to wear my purple and gold dress . . .'

'Well then,' Joe claps his hands together. 'It's decided. We're staying!' He gets to his feet. 'Now if you'll excuse me, I just have to go and slip on something dashing for Valentina.'

'Oi!' I squeal, swatting him as he darts for the door. 'That boy,' I shake my head.

'You'd better get in the bathroom,' Kier urges me on. 'We haven't got long.'

'Are you sure you want to do this?' I hesitate.

'You mean go to a wedding so soon after seeing Cinzia?'

I nod.

He gives a philosophical shrug. 'Much as I might like to, I can't hide from love.' He forces a brave smile. 'Apparently it's all around.'

I'm stepping towards him to give him a bolstering hug when there's a knock at the door. Did Joe forget something? Nope. It's Sabrina, looking somewhat fretful.

'I am so very sorry,' she intones. 'We have lost both your Amores.'

'Well, that's very careless!' I joke, not minding at all.

'Allegra has resigned,' she looks rueful. 'And Lorenzo, his father died last night.'

'Oh no!' That wiped the glee off my face. 'Poor, poor Lorenzo.'

A curious expression passes over Sabrina's face.

'What is it?' I ask.

'Just your choice of word – "poor" . . .'

'Yes?'

'His father left him a vast inheritance in the form of the family's Prosecco vineyard.'

'The one he went to with Tiffany?' Now I come to think of it she did mention he was extremely familiar with the staff there . . .

Sabrina nods. 'Nevertheless, he is in mourning . . .'

'Oh I quite understand. Perhaps I can send some flowers or something?'

'I will arrange that directly but I am afraid it is too late to arrange new Amores for you – the cars leave from the Piazzale Roma in less than an hour.'

'We quite understand,' Kier assures her. 'We will be more than happy to escort each other, right sis?'

'Right bro,' I confirm.

'You are most gracious,' Sabrina looks relieved. 'I will see you downstairs shortly?'

'Just finishing packing now,' I tell her, though I have yet to begin.

'Don't forget to add something sporty for the day after the wedding.'

'Sporty, got it.'

I shut the door and lean on it for a second. 'Better not tell Tiffany about Lorenzo's upturn in fortune, she'll be all over him.'

'Will you just get in the shower?' Kier rolls his eyes.

'Yes, yes, I'm going now!' I hurry on my way.

After traversing the canals of Venice and gliding the lake of Como, it jars me to be travelling again by car. The little cubicles of metal seem so clunky and crude, dirtily parping exhaust into the already hot, dusty air. I'm relieved when the congested traffic gives way to tree-shaded roads winding up and up a particularly scenic Tuscan hill, seemingly following a path laid out by a gymnastic ribbon twirler.

'We seem to be getting closer to heaven with every tyre rotation . . .' Megan sighs, resting her head on Stefano's shoulder, where it's been on and off for the past couple of hours.

Mercifully I have been spared any of my feared awkwardness sitting between Dante and Joe, as my former Amore is in the other vehicle with Tiffany, Melvin and Filomena. Not that my current situation is entirely stress-free.

'Such a beautiful setting for a wedding!' Valentina concurs, nuzzling closer to Joe.

I'd find her repeated attempts to canoodle with my boyfriend unbearable were it not for the fact that Joe has extricated himself each time on account of being 'too hot' (that old chestnut!) and yet keeps finding excuses to lean across me or brush my hand in a reassuring way.

'Are they locals, the bride and groom?' I ask as I catch my first glimpse of the distinctive dome of the Uffizi below us, only now fully registering that I am in Florence.

'Actually no,' Sabrina replies. 'She is Welsh and he is from Southern Italy – Capri. But this venue – the Villa San Michele – brought them together, or should I say, reunited them.'

'They were apart for a while?' Kier enquires.

'Over four years. But their hearts were strong.'

'What happened?' I ask, intrigued.

'Well, I don't know the couple personally but I can tell you as much as I have been told,' Sabrina confides. 'For private reasons, when they first met they could not be together. For a year they kept in touch but then they decided it was too painful to be constantly reminded of something they wanted so much but could not have, so they ceased communication. It was only when the bride's best friend, Cleo, came to a cookery course here at Villa San Michele that she discovered the man – Luca – was finally available for her friend to love.'

'He was on the cookery course too?' Megan searches for clarity.

'Actually it was his son, Nino, who was in attendance. He was only eleven at the time but he is something of a culinary prodigy I am told. Ah. We arrive.'

Although the facade of the main building was designed by Michelangelo himself, it is the balcony that draws all the attention as we disembark. The glorious elevation affords us the sensation of being suspended in perfect peace above the extravagantly thriving greenery that gives way to the terracotta rooftops of the bustling city below. In awe, we all take a moment to breathe in the panorama.

'Isn't it stunning?' I turn to look at Joe but find he has moved on to the reception, and Dante is standing in his place.

'Oh, hello,' I bleat.

'Hello Kirsty.'

'Um, I'm sorry about, um, switching Amores without telling you to your face.' I get my apology out as quickly as I can.

'I understand,' he hushes me. 'Everyone comes to the Academy for different reasons. I know you have your own.'

'Yes,' I confirm, grateful he is being so understanding. I look back at the landscape and try to sound casual as I continue: 'I was surprised that you agreed to team up with Tiffany.'

He shrugs. 'I have friends in the wedding party. It is not so much hardship in a large group. Besides, tomorrow is the last day – I wanted to see you before you left.'

'Kirsty! Are you coming?' It's my brother calling. Trying to keep me out of mischief no doubt.

'Are you a fan of weddings?' I ask as we make our way to reception.

'Of course,' he smiles. 'Do you know that in Venice when a local marries, it is a tradition for every gondolier in the city to parade the couple down the Grand Canal?'

'Really? That must be quite a spectacle!' I stall at the doorway. 'Did you have that with your wife?'

He nods, his eyes instantly misty.

'I'm sorry if I—'

'No. It was a beautiful day. The most beautiful . . .'

Though I'm reluctant to leave him in a potentially depressing nostalgic haze, Sabrina moves me on, introducing myself and Kier to Maritza – an effortlessly elegant ash-blonde from Peru who will be showing us to our rooms.

I look around for Joe but evidently he has already gone ahead to his suite. Tiffany too is chomping at the bit. 'This place has got to be at least six star!' she trills as she heads off, already high from the exclusivity of this former monastery turned movie-star retreat. 'I think I just saw Cate Blanchett!'

'See you later,' I gently touch Dante's arm as I pass him.

I can't help but respect that man. On top of being so debonair and charming, he's also so reasonable. I always thought romance went hand-in-hand with a little hot-headedness but he always seems remarkably calm. Maybe it comes of handling fire on a daily basis?

'Kirsty, are you taking all this in?' Kier nudges me as we walk the length of the Loggia restaurant with its soft cream arches offering an outlook of even greater magnificence.

'An amazing vantage point during a storm,' Maritza tells

us. 'You barely need the candles on the tables, the lightning illuminates the entire vista.'

I can't help but flash to the summer rainstorm at Villa d'Este but quickly pinch myself – I really need to curb my sentimentality as it gets me into all manner of trouble. It's partly why I went back to Joe after we split up the first time. I wonder, is that why I have the greater pull toward him now, because we simply have more memories for me to get sentimental about? Whatever the reason, there is something about Joe that my heart refuses to let go of. Even when presented with an option as enticing as Dante . . .

'We have many wonderful rooms within the main building but as honoured guests we have placed you in one of our suites.' Maritza motions to what look like mini villas nestled in the vertiginous hillside. I can't quite believe my eyes.

She nods for us to proceed through a dinky gate and cross the bijou patio to a glass panel door, set beneath an arch of what could best be described as bridal foliage – fluttery white petals and heart-shaped green leaves.

'Go ahead,' she encourages us to step inside.

There I behold a cream dream of a bed topped with tonged black curls of wrought iron. Even more artful is the positioning of said bed – I hurry across the shiny bricked floor so I can turn around and take in the view from this aspect – the heavy draped curtains add a theatrical quality so that the Florentine countryside appears to be the most lavish stage set ever conceived. What scenes might play out before us tonight I wonder?

'Are you sure this isn't the bridal suite?' I tease, noticing the chilled Prosecco and array of prime-time fruits – some succulent, some heavily seeded, some strokeable, all begging to be hand-fed to you by a lover.

'Oh no, the newly-weds will sleep in the chapel tonight,' she replies.

'Is that a tradition here?' I frown.

'No, no,' she laughs, shaking her head. 'The chapel is a room conversion. Small, but very romantic, yes?'

'Unspeakably so,' I concur.

'You have to see the bathroom,' she encourages us onward. 'Please . . .' she ushers Kier over to the door to the right of the bed, me to the left. We are both greeted on the other side by our own sink in almond-coloured marble, a giant walk-in multi-jet shower and tub you could do laps in. But the grooviest aspect is the inset wardrobe with a waist-height ledge to accommodate suitcases for those guests on the run who prefer to fumble and yank rather than go to the trouble of unpacking.

'Well, I suppose it'll do,' I say, feigning apathy as I take in the stylish ginger robes and Bulgari toiletries.

Waving off Maritza with profuse thanks, I notice a bowl of olives the size of quail's eggs and bite into the salty green sheen while eyeing the Prosecco. Is it too early to be opening the fizz? I look up to consult Kier but find he's moved out on to the patio. Surreptitiously I edge up behind him, following his gaze down to the grassy bank below where the finishing touches are being made to the seating arrangements for the wedding. I feel a spear in my heart just imagining how heartbreaking it must have been for him to think he'd found the woman he wanted to marry in Cinzia, only to have her vanish from his life. Such a loss, of both the present and the future.

I've never really had that vision myself, and marriage has never been of great concern to Joe – he sees it as a lot of unnecessary expense. The same could be said of children, of course, I think to myself as I watch a young brother and sister refusing to be corralled by their despairing mother. Just when it looks like the two are submitting to her will the little boy, who can't be more than four, suddenly throws off his shirt, drops his trousers and announces to the world, 'I'm naked!' with such celebratory glee I can't help but laugh out loud.

'American,' Kier observes, as if that explains his exhibitionist tendencies.

'Are they part of the wedding party?'

He shakes his head. 'I don't think so. They're probably hotel guests, which is why the mother is trying to get their sticky fingers away from the perfectly arranged furniture.'

'They seem to be heading this way,' I watch as they approach, the young boy, still naked, assuming the character of assorted superheroes as he pogos along the path.

'Probably going to the pool,' Kier notes as they continue on to the next level.

'I hold up the bottle of Prosecco. 'Ready for a bit of bubbly?'

Having changed into our party duds, and not a little tipsy, we skip down to the wedding terrace passing century-old wisteria and a divine intermingling of rosemary and lavender.

I was concerned my outfit might be a little gaudy in such a natural, outdoorsy setting but it turns out the mother of the bride used to be in the fashion industry, formerly owning a boutique in Capri, and many of the guests have gone for just-stepped-off-a-yacht trash-glitz, so I fit right in.

'Hey foxy lady,' Joe sneaks up behind me. 'You look a vision.'

'Why thank you,' I say, casting a quick glance around to see who might be watching us before I fix his tie.

'I thought this would go with your outfit . . .' he surreptitiously hands me a small purple bloom – a wildflower if I'm not mistaken. 'I thought maybe you could tuck it behind your ear. Or not. I don't really know, I just wanted to give you some little token—'

I take a chance and give him a dainty kiss on the cheek. He really seems to be warming to this romance thing, I don't want him to go unrewarded.

'Remember the last wedding we were at?' he asks, unaware that he's undoing all the good work he just achieved. 'Jared and Sasha's?'

'Mmm,' I say looking away.

'What's the matter?' he enquires.

'It just makes me sad, thinking about it.'

'What do you mean? Why?' he looks confused.

'You didn't dance with me.'

His brow furrows. 'You know I hate to dance. I never do.'

'But you promised. You said the one exception you'd make was a slow dance at a wedding and when the time came you weren't even in the room.' I sigh to myself. 'I was the only one left sitting at our table. Jared and Sasha, Tim and Greta, Greg and Kate, Pete and Lori, all our friends were up there, swirling around, smiling, loving each other and I was sat there feeling completely abandoned and alone.'

The situation just seemed to scream: 'We all love each other more. We're close and attentive to our partners. We want to be with them in these significant moments. Your chap obviously just can't be bothered.' I know I sound like I'm whimpering on but it really was a horrible moment. Even in *My Best Friend's Wedding* Julia got to dance with Rupert Everett at the end. I had no one.

'I didn't realise it was such a big deal to you,' Joe looks fretful.

'It shouldn't be,' I admit, regretting having my second glass of emotion-enhancing Prosecco. 'But it was.'

It was the first wedding I'd ever been to with a man on my arm and I thought for once it would be different and I wouldn't be the wallflower. I can't help but feel a pang as I catch sight of Dante. I know what it feels like to be dancing in his arms. I know that if he'd been at the reception we would have been first on the dancefloor, and last off.

'I'm going to check on Kier . . .' I excuse myself from Joe.

'Wait! Don't go feeling like this.' He attempts a winning look. 'I'll make it up to you tonight.'

'It's probably not the most appropriate setting,' I tell him before moving on, keen to change the topic and my mood.

'You alright?' Kier enquires as I sidle up to him, resting my head on his shoulder in a plea for sympathy.

'Just having a maudlin moment,' I confess.

'Perfectly normal at a wedding,' the girl next to him assures me.

'This is Cleo,' Kier introduces me. 'She's the bride's best friend, remember Sabrina telling us about her?'

'Oh yes!' I enthuse, reaching to shake her hand. 'You're the culinary cupid who brought Luca and—'

'Kim!' she fills in the blank.

'Luca and Kim back together. Nice work! How was the cooking school here, by the way? It seems an idyllic setting.'

'Oh, it's just incredible. You're in this little greenhouse-like room overlooking all this,' she extends her arm. 'And right outside there's this chef's garden where we'd pick fresh herbs . . .' She looks rapturous. 'That is my ideal. A bit of parsley in a window box in Cardiff just isn't the same.'

'Have you thought about an allotment?' Kier enquires.

'No,' she shakes her head looking intrigued.

'You might be on the waiting list for six months but somewhere like Cardiff you'd probably only pay about five pounds a year for a plot the size of a tennis court and, provided you keep it in good condition, it can be yours for life!'

'Really?' she gasps. 'I never would have even known—'

'He's a gardener,' I announce proudly adding, 'And my brother.' Just in case she thinks we're together.

Her face brightens even more at the second sentiment, giving me the cue I need to move on to Sabrina. No sooner have I chinked glasses with her than we are told to assemble for the ceremony.

'Cleo seems nice,' I whisper to Kier as he takes his place beside me.

'Yes,' he says, hesitating slightly.

'Oh. Is she weird? What is it?'

'Nothing to do with her. Just something she said—'

*'Signore e signori, il matrimonio sta' per cominciare!'*

'I'll tell you later,' he hisses as we all turn to marvel at the bride.

# 31

*'La fanciulle pensano al matrimonio, le maritate pensano all'amore.' ('Young girls dream of marriage, married women dream of love.') – Italian saying*

'Uh oh!'

While the majority of the congregation are taking in the bride's glorious gown of sinuous white chiffon fronted with a large tumbling bouquet, another figure has caught my eye – it's the little boy we saw disrobe and morph into a superhero earlier. My first thought is, there's going to be a streaker at the wedding but then, as he starts hurtling towards the al fresco altar, I clock his day-glo orange water pistol . . . his target? Naturally the bride.

As she squeals with shock and does a spasmodic dance trying to protect her hair and eyeliner, hands clasp to the mouths of every woman in the place imagining their own make-up so violently spritzed, not to mention the horror of sporting a dress freshly customised with clingy see-through patches.

'Not again!' Kim wails, somewhat intriguingly.

'Do you suppose this happens every time she gets married?' Kier asks me as the child's mother tears past, leaving a trail of apologies and curses in her wake.

Before I can reply I feel Dante yank me down the aisle, the wrong way, propelling me forward with the mission, 'You get the boy!'

'Signora! Wait!' he calls after the mother

'*Ethan!*' She howls oblivious. 'Don't make me lasso you!'

I sprint past her, retrieving the human hose from the hedge he's about to burrow into, and wrestle the now empty weapon from his hands feeling like the true definition of *Kindergarten Cop*. Meanwhile Dante calms the mortified mama.

'It's okay,' he insists, panting lightly. 'A wet bride is a lucky bride.'

The mother and I exchange a look – we've heard Italians finesse many subjects but this?

'What?' We frown in unison.

'I don't lie, it's an Italian proverb – *Sposa bagnata, sposa fortunata!*' he insists. 'Technically it means that if it rains on your wedding day you will have good luck in your marriage. Today is sunshine but here we have the next best thing . . .' He motions to the water pistol.

Ethan's hopeful cornflower-blue eyes flit between us – could he be on the verge of forgiveness?

The mother huffs, torn between an obligation to punish and not wanting to create any more of a scene. Besides which, without his weapon he's the picture of vulnerability – entirely naked with pale peachy-soft skin and a blond Oliver Twist mop top. I can feel his little heart going like the clappers under my restraining hand and I'm overjoyed that Dante has spared him a spanking. Thus far at least . . .

'Why would you shoot the nice lady?' the mum enquires despairingly, crouching beside her son.

'I was watering the flowers,' he replies plaintively, holding out his hands as if to say, 'Isn't it obvious?'

We all look altar-ward, at Kim and her outsize bouquet, now happily resuming the ceremony (apparently recently apprised of the proverb herself).

The mum sighs and shakes her head, unable to stay mad at her little tyke. 'Will you apologise on our behalf?' she asks of Dante. 'I'd offer to do it in person but I've seen the beautiful wedding cake and I just couldn't bear—'

'Of course, consider it done,' Dante cuts in, graciously accepting the charge just as a cheer goes up for the bride and groom's first kiss.

We all pause to admire the intensity of the embrace – his dark Mediterranean locks falling forward to brush upon her pale Celtic skin as their lips meet and merge in celebration of their long-awaited unification. It's a beautiful sight, giving me a flashback to the smooching couple Kier and I saw at Victoria station the day we left for Italy. Back then my brother and I were resentful and disapproving at such an exhibition of bountiful love, now he's staring longingly at Cleo – currently doing a celebratory jig with Kim's mother and Nino – and my eyes are lovingly upon Joe, who appears to be surveying the guests, possibly looking for me. I watch as he absently pats the hand of his Amore Valentina who, if she nuzzled his shoulder any closer, could be mistaken for an epaulette. Now that is going to have to stop!

'Andiamo?' Dante enquires, offering me his arm.

'Um,' I hesitate. With the ranks now disassembling and reclustering for photographs, I decide I won't be missed right away and tell Dante, 'I'll catch you up,' adding my warmest smile so he won't feel slighted.

He nods his acceptance, winks at Ethan, and returns to the party.

'You don't like weddings?' The mum gives me a wry look.

'I just want to keep a safe distance from the bouquet,' I jest.

The truth is that I can't bring myself to let go of Ethan's hand. He placed his tiny, soft fingers in my palm while the grown-ups were concluding business and the silent bond made me feel so valued and full of purpose I can't bear to lose the feeling.

'You wanna watch me make waves in the pool?' he jiggles my arm, gazing up at me with wide-eyed enticement.

'I'm not sure you should be going near any more water today,' Mum tuts.

His expression flicks instantly to near tears.

'Oh no,' she mutters, looking nervously at the congregation. I'm guessing he's not a silent sobber.

'Just for five minutes?' he pleads.

She rolls her eyes knowing she's going to pay for these indulgences down the line. 'Alright, but no more water pistol.'

I smile enviously. 'A swim sounds heavenly right now.'

'Well, you're welcome to join us,' she offers. 'We have Factor 50 for whities such as yourself!'

'Really?' I muse, genuinely tempted.

'And we've got a yacht!' Ethan proclaims.

'Toy one,' Mum adds, under her breath.

'Well, that's settled then. I'll get my cozzie and meet you up there.'

I feel naughty yet strangely liberated escaping the wedding party. Apparently there is a limit to how much non-stop romance a person can take. Besides, I've got an entire evening of awkwardness ricocheting between Joe and Dante, is there really any rush to begin that rally?

Throwing my dress on the bed, I slip on my costume and a gauzy tunic, then chase up the steps to the highest terrace, happy to be in flip-flops once again.

'I'm Kirsty by the way,' I introduce myself formally to the family upon my arrival.

'Shari,' the mum beams back. 'You've obviously met Ethan . . .'

'Watch me make waves, watch me make waves!' he teeters on the edge of the pool, ready to create a toddler-size tidal wave.

'I'll be right there!' I call to him.

'And this is my daughter, Mackenzie.'

Ethan's older sister prises an eye from her industrious colouring to survey me.

'Hello,' I nod over at her drawing. 'That looks like quite a work of art.'

She gives me a disdainful look.

'You probably think I talk funny,' I begin apologetically.

'I am familiar with the English accent,' she tells me archly. 'I watch *Doctor Who*.'

'Oh right.' That told me.

As she goes back to her drawing, Ethan is on the verge of implosion, so very excited to be getting back in the pool. 'Ready?'

I give him the go ahead.

He sploshes into the shallow end, flapping his yellow water-wings. 'See? See?'

I watch the tranquil waters churn and race.

'Okay, now my turn!' I shrug off my flip-flops.

'Are you getting in?' He sounds like he can't believe his luck.

As I take two steps back to get a good run-up, I feel something press into my back. It's the water pistol, passed to me by Shari, with a wicked glint. Instead of jumping, I now approach the steps with stealth, lowering myself into the pool so the water can glug into the pistol behind my back. I wait until it feels full and then launch my attack, feeling all very Lara Croft.

'Hey!' Ethan protests scrambling for the second gun.

He's such a good aim that I have to swim into the deep end to get away from him.

'I can't go any further than this line,' he says forlornly from the shallow end.

I torment him by floating on my back and whistling chirpily and then out of the corner of my eye I see him running around the edge of the pool towards me. Little tyke! He's going to zap me from dry land! But then I see he's not carrying a water pistol. And, before I can even register his intention, he's thrown himself gleefully into my arms with total disregard for the fact that I am in the forbidden deep end. I feel myself sink beneath the surface with the weight of him and scrabble my feet like crazy to give myself a boost up to get his head above the water. As I surface I gasp for breath and then propel myself to the side of the pool where Shari has rushed to help him out. Naturally he's still giggling, oblivious.

I take a moment to pant and marvel at what just occurred – he had no fear! He'd only just met me and he knew instinctively that I'd catch him. A little boy named Ethan trusted me with his life! I feel on the verge of euphoria – this is the moment I've been waiting for! All this time, deep down, I think I'd been worrying that I wouldn't make a good mother and all of a sudden I feel like I've been given a seal of approval!

As I swim to the steps and then climb out of the pool, something Angelina Jolie once said about her first encounter with her soon-to-be adopted baby Maddox resonates with me. She said that the fact that a child could fall asleep in her arms and thus seem at ease with her gave her the courage to feel that she could make him happy.

Suddenly I know how she feels!

I feel like grabbing Joe and working on a little conception right here and now! I suppose I'd have to call her Florence if she were a girl. Perhaps Florian for a boy?

'Are you alright?' Shari asks me.

I nod vigorously, confiding, 'Lately I've been in something of a quandary about having children but now I look at yours and I think—'

'Oh no.'

'No!' I laugh. 'Quite the opposite!'

Shari studies me for a second and says. 'It's every bit as hard as people say. Maybe even harder. But I will say that I can be having the worst day and I guarantee one of these two will do something to make me smile . . .'

We look over as Ethan babbles ecstatically about the yacht he is now whizzing around the pool.

'You know, he barely spoke initially, to the point where we were quite worried, but now . . . he hardly pauses for breath!'

Everything with him is 'awesome!' and 'delicious!' His *joie de vivre* is an infectious, energising delight making me feel for the first time as if I might be capable of pushing through the invisible force field separating me and motherhood.

'Awesome kick!' Ethan compliments me as I return the ball he has just lobbed at me.

This is what I hadn't anticipated – the brimming over of the heart. As we play football and then dinosaurs, I understand that these simple interactions can fill you up in the way shopping trips can leave you feeling drained and empty. Who was it that said when you try to attach meaning to meaningless things it just leaves you feeling even more forlorn? I get the same way when I look at all the pap pictures in our magazine. I feel compelled to view them like a guilty pleasure but it never leaves me feeling anything other than slightly tawdry or as if my own life is somehow lacking.

Right now, instead of looking at a picture showcasing Lindsay Lohan's latest hair colour, I'm watching Mackenzie create her own original image. She looks to me and then back to the picture and, realising she is drawing my portrait, I feel ridiculously honoured.

'Do you want your hair to be chocolate brown or golden-brown?' she asks, coincidentally tapping in to my ongoing dyeing dilemma.

'You decide,' I tell her.

She opts for golden to go with the metallic stars she is sticking on the navy sky above me.

'I'm making it night-time,' she tells me as she etches a moon surrounding it with a series of short, stubby lines.

'What are those for?' I ask.

She looks at me like I'm an utter imbecile and pronounces, 'It's a Van Gogh moon.'

'Oh!' I bite back a smile of amazement. 'Wow! That's . . .

impressive.' I sit back in the chair wondering how I'd feel if this was my own daughter astounding me so casually. I'd forgotten all about the wedding until a whoop goes up down below – the bouquet has finally been thrown.

That'll be my cue to return.

'Where are you going?' Ethan quizzes me as I get to my feet.

'I have to go and eat dinner with the rabble down below, if that's okay with you?'

'Yes, it's okay,' he concedes.

'I'll save you some wedding cake though.'

'Here!' Mackenzie presents me with her portrait.

'That's brilliant!' I rave. 'You have to sign it for me.'

Naturally she doesn't settle for a simple squiggle of her initials, instead she scribes, 'Farewell Miss Kirsty. It was a pleasure to meet you!'

'I've got something for you too . . .' Ethan gets in on the act.

'What's that?' I enquire, looking at his empty hands.

'A hug!' He says, gripping my knees with such gusto I nearly buckle.

'Thank you,' I stammer, so touched.

'Think you might give it a go?' Shari raises a knowing brow at me.

I nod. 'My only concern now is how horribly disappointed I'd feel if I didn't get children as awesome as yours. You're doing a really good job.'

She smiles gratefully with just the teensiest smudge of pride. 'Thank you.'

I feel my eyes well up as I walk away.

It's finally happened – my body-clock has started ticking . . . I can hear it, loud and clear!

# 32

*'A sudden, bold, and unexpected question doth many times surprise a man and lay him open.'*
*– Francis Bacon*

'You look different,' Joe comments when I rejoin the party.

'It's my hair,' I tell him. 'I went for a sneaky dip in the pool and it got all messed up.'

'I like it,' he smiles. 'You look pretty.'

I wonder if some part of him is unconsciously responding to the fact that I've had an inner shift, bringing me a little more in sync with his desires?

I'm about to tell him that I'm finally ready to make him a dad when he cheers, 'Ay up! Grub's up!' and returns to Valentina's side to take their seats at one of the two tables assigned to The Love Academy.

Oh well. I'll tell him after dinner. It's not the kind of revelation to be squeezed in between courses.

'Do you know Cleo made the wedding cake?' Kier comments as we find our place cards on the next table. 'She and Luca's son Nino were in the kitchen from eight o'clock this morning, right up until an hour before we arrived helping prepare everything. In fact this appetiser,' he nods to the Pecorino tortino set before us, 'is entirely the work of a twelve-year-old chef!'

'What a lovely idea,' I grin. Truly prepared with love.

The whole meal is exquisite but I'm barely present for the accompanying conversation, mostly revolving around Megan's idea of a dream wedding. (Are you getting the hint, Stefano?) Instead my mind drifts to all the ways my life would change if I really do embrace my new-found motherly instincts. I always thought it would be so limiting becoming slave to a small person's needs but now I can see the pleasure that might be hidden in those actions. I certainly loved the sense of focus and surrender I experienced with Ethan and Mackenzie. Of course, it does seem that the children don't necessarily have to be your own to feel the benefit – further proof of this comes as I look over at the bride, interacting delightedly with her now official stepson, who for some reason she addresses as Ringo instead of Nino. They even pretend to take the first dance together before Luca takes up his rightful place in Kim's arms.

Is that a hint of a tattoo peeking out of Luca's suit? I am completely intrigued by this Anglo-Italian pairing. I wonder how they first met? Was it a holiday romance? A chance meeting in the Blue Grotto? I don't have the answers, but from the expression on Luca's face you'd think he'd been waiting his whole life for Kim to be his bride.

As their song concludes and Dean Martin's 'Return to Me' strikes up, various family members join them on the dance-floor and then two-by-two more familiar couples form – Megan and Stefano, Melvin and Filomena, Tiffany and Dante, even if he is looking very distant. Where's Joe? I look to his table but find his seat empty. I was sort of hoping that he would defy protocol and ask me to dance anyway but he's nowhere to be seen.

'You dancing?' Kier turns to me.

'You asking?' I smile back at him.

He is and we are.

For a while we sway along to the music, lost in our own thoughts and then I say, 'I meant to ask you at dinner – what were you going to say to me earlier, you know before the ceremony?'

He frowns as he remembers. 'It was just something Cleo said—'

'Speaking of which,' I cut him off.

'What?'

I nod behind him.

'Is it too soon to cut in?' she asks nervously, looking a little bemused by her own daring.

Kier seeks my blessing, which is swiftly given.

I'm about to take my all-too familiar seat alone, observing all the other couples dancing, when I feel a gentle tap on my shoulder and a man's voice husks, 'Dance with me?'

I turn to find Dante holding out his hand. It's the strangest sensation but I'm almost disappointed. I really did want it to be Joe this time.

'What about Tiffany?' I ask. Like I'm really concerned about hurting her feelings.

'She got a better offer!' he points to where she is perched on the knee of some presumably fantastically rich wrinkly.

'Oh perfect!' I scoff.

'Well?' he raises an eyebrow.

I smile. 'I'd love to.'

This is the first time I've been in his arms since the Villa d'Este gala. Last time we were this close it led to a kiss. So much has changed since then. Instead of feeling giddy with lust I find myself wondering if I might ever meet his daughter Chiara, and how we'd get on.

I'm just telling him about my further dealings with Ethan and his water pistol when we are interrupted by the sound of someone clearing their throat noisily beside us. It's Melvin.

'May I cut in?'

Dante and I exchange a look.

'This is our last night all together,' Melvin pleads.

'Is it?' I look back at Dante. That fact has rather snuck up on me.

He nods confirmation. 'Tomorrow night you are free to go your own way.'

'Well?' Melvin persists.

'Why not,' I concede, as Dante bows out gracefully.

Melvin and I shuffle around for a couple of minutes, me finding arm strength I never knew I had in order to keep his frame locked at a palatable distance from my own. And then I sense the presence of another man by our side – my fourth dance partner in half as many songs. This time it's the one that I want – Joe.

'My turn!' he cheers, skilfully swapping places with Melvin before he's even had a chance to register what happened.

'It's alright,' Melvin composes himself with a little tug at his jacket cuffs. 'I just wanted to have the experience of having you in my arms, at least once.'

Surprised by the sweetness of this sentiment, I give him a little peck on the cheek, and then send him back to Filomena.

'Sorry I'm late, I was in the loo,' Joe announces and then frowns, 'That's not the opening line of a great seducer, is it?' He shakes his head then pulls me closer whispering, 'I want to make amends, Kirsty.'

'For Jared and Sasha's wedding?' I presume.

'For all the times I haven't romanced you,' he sighs.

'Really?' I question, though he definitely sounds sincere.

I listen closely as he tells me: 'I had a revelation earlier – when you used to complain that I wasn't romantic, I actually think I took it as a compliment!'

'What?' I scrunch my brow.

'I know it sounds ridiculous but I think to me, the word romantic had all these namby-pamby, wet connotations so when you said I *wasn't* that, it made me feel . . .' he struggles to find the words.

'More of a man?' I suggest.

'More of a bloke, specifically. But what I've seen over the past few days . . . I get that there's nothing sappy about making your woman swoon. I mean really it's something very cool. And under-valued.' He tilts back so he can look me in the eye. 'You really are the most important thing in my life, Kirsty.'

My heart swells. There is just such a depth of warmth and comfort with this man. The moment has come to tell him my news.

'Alright you two, break it up!' Kier jokes as he prises us apart.

'Wait!' I protest.

'I'm not giving her up,' Joe clings tighter, a blissful smile on his face.

'Just for a minute, Joe, there's something I need to talk to her about,' Kier is insistent. Apparently the little thing he wanted to mention to me has become more of an urgent concern.

'Hold on to that feeling!' I instruct Joe as I submit to Kier's will.

He marches me over to Cleo's table and directly cues her:

'So, Cleo, you were just telling me how Luca and Dante became friends . . .'

'That's right,' she seems happy to reiterate the story for my benefit, inviting me to take a seat beside her and her string of empty cocktail glasses. 'Well, it actually began with Dante's wife. She went to school with Luca in Naples. They always remained friends even when she moved to Venice. Initially Luca and Dante were just casual acquaintances but when she died—

'She's dead?' I gasp. 'Dante's wife is dead?'

'So sad, isn't it? Apparently they were known as the ultimate couple. So unfair.' She shakes her head.

'So then . . .' Kier prompts her.

'Well, shortly before the funeral Luca's wife had left him – finally!' She rolls her eyes. 'So there they were, both single parents and they became a long-distance support system for each other.'

'That's very sweet,' I mumble, still feeling Dante's loss. And Chiara's for that matter . . .

Kier gives me a look. 'So I was saying to Cleo that I understood now why Kim and Luca would accept us strays from The Love Academy as last-minute guests at their wedding and she said . . .'

'It wasn't last minute at all.'

'This has been planned for months.' He looks at me with great significance.

I furrow my brow. 'I'm not sure I understand what you're getting at.'

'Dante is the only Venetian connection to the wedding party.'

Why did I have that last Bellini, I just can't think straight! 'And?'

Kier sighs impatiently and then has another go at spelling things out. 'I told Cleo that surprised me because as far as I knew Dante had only been an Amore for a week.'

Oh! Now I get it.

'So you're saying he lied. He's actually been an Amore for months . . .'

'Oh no, this is definitely his first time,' Cleo cuts in. 'Up until now he's just been involved with the management side of things.'

Kier gives me another look as if to say, 'Now do you see?'

'The management side of things?' I am officially a dunce.

'You know he's the co-founder of The Love Academy, don't you?' Cleo blinks at me.

Now I've gone beyond getting it, straight through to incredulity. I look for Dante on the dancefloor, now with Sabrina, looking very pally now I come to think of it.

'When I saw the two of you dancing together . . .' Kier tails off. 'I just thought you should know.'

I sit back in my seat, not knowing what on earth to do with the information I've just been given.

Dante is the co-founder of The Love Academy.

'Are you ready for me now?'

'Not yet Joe,' I apologise to the man who, a few minutes ago, I was desperate to get back to. 'I need a quick word with Dante.'

'I thought you were done with him,' he complains.

'Not quite,' I mutter as I burrow through the shimmying bodies to get to him. I have to find out the absolute truth ASAP.

'Can we talk?' I bluntly enquire, avoiding Sabrina's gaze.

'Of course,' he motions for me to take a seat at the nearby table.

'Not here. In private.'

He looks around. There are people everywhere.

'My room is close by,' he offers.

'Okay, whatever,' I'm getting testier by the second. 'I just can't believe it!' I splutter as soon as the door closes behind us.

'Kirsty, what is it?' he looks concerned.

I take a breath, not quite believing I'm going to ask this question: 'Are you, Dante Soranzo, one of the founders of The Love Academy?'

His mouth opens and then closes. He looks awkward and then puffs, 'Yes.'

'Oh my god!' My hands raise to my head as I yelp, 'Why did you pretend that it was all so new to you?'

'Why did you lie about being a reporter?' he rallies back.

Now it's my turn to be speechless.

'How long have you known?' I ask in a much quieter tone of voice.

'Since the first day.'

Stunned, I take a seat at the foot of the bed. 'Is that why you put yourself with me?' I ask. 'To control the story?'

'Not exactly. When I met you—' he pauses. 'Let me tell you the events in sequence so that you are clear.'

'Clear would be very welcome right now,' I admit.

He tentatively takes a seat beside me and then begins: 'It is a long time since I have been involved with the day-to-day running of the Academy. For the past year I have been coming in only for the welcome reception so that I can help choose which Amore to put with which client. It turns out I have something of a talent for matchmaking.'

'Oh really?'

'Your brother and Cleo, by the way, very good together.'

'Seriously?' I feel a leap of hope and then realise I'm being too easily distracted. 'So you go in once every nine days or so . . .'

'Supervise the matches and then leave everyone to it. That was my plan the night you arrived. I had already made my observations and suggestions and was on my way to deliver—'

'You were there, at the reception? I didn't see you!'

'I was wearing a mask. The Phantom of the Opera.'

'That was you!' I gasp. 'I spoke to you!'

'I know,' he smiles.

Oh this is all too much to take in. I take a breath before continuing with my questions, 'So then you left . . .'

'. . . with my package, to make my delivery. At which point I was assaulted most violently!'

'I really am sorry about that,' I cringe.

'And there was just something about you . . .' he shakes his head. 'I decided to escort you back to the reception. At that point it still wasn't in my mind to become your Amore, I just wanted to make sure you were alright, you seemed very flustered.'

I was – by him! 'And then what happened?'

'Sabrina took me to one side and told me that you were a reporter from a British magazine.'

'How did she know that?' I despair.

'A woman called to speak to you, Sabrina accidentally cut them off so she dialled the number that was on the screen and it went directly to *Hot!* magazine.'

'Oh god!' I flush.

'She hadn't got the name of the woman who rang so she

asked if someone was calling for Kirsty Bailey at which point she was told that Kirsty Bailey was on assignment in Venice and wouldn't be back until the following week.'

'So much for undercover.' My shoulders slump. 'I can't believe you've known the whole time. You must think I'm a terrible liar.' I look up suddenly. 'If you knew I was with the press, why did you take me to George Clooney's villa?'

'I knew you wouldn't exploit the situation.'

'How?'

'You passed the test with Elton John's chandelier at the Bubacco studio,' he replies.

'That was a test?'

'Of a kind. I knew anyway. Like I say, I am a good judge of character.'

I expel a long sigh. 'I suppose I should take that as a compliment?'

He shrugs. 'You do know that you are in the wrong job?'

'I am becoming increasingly aware of that fact.' I confirm. And then I look up at him. 'But you . . . Was The Love Academy ever an actual job to you? I mean, how did it start? And, I've been meaning to ask, who did you co-found the Academy with?'

His face illuminates. 'My daughter.'

'Chiara?

He nods. 'The whole thing was her idea.'

'But she's only eighteen now—'

'She was sixteen at the time. She had been on an exchange programme in London, staying with a family with five daughters all under thirty and all she heard them talk about was their disappointing love lives. She came back home and she said, "Papa, you need to teach the British men how to treat a woman, they have no idea."'

I laugh.

'But of course, the whole point with most British men is that they don't want to know! They don't see it is in their interest to please a woman.'

I experience a small flash of pride for Joe – he gets it! It may be recent wisdom but my Joe is a convert!

'So that's when she came up with the idea of pairing English women with Italian men,' Dante continues. 'And then, after some time, we began to get some interest from men who wanted to experience romance in Venice. We had to vet their applications a little more thoroughly but it appealed to us that some allegiances may be made outside our initial match. This time we thought that Kier and Megan would—'

'Oh me too!' I blurt, cutting him off. 'I totally could see them together.'

'But now I see him with Cleo . . .'

'Even better!' I pip.

'Exactly.'

My mind is racing with all this new information. 'What about Tiffany? Why did you subject poor Lorenzo to her?'

'He actually made the request,' Dante informs me. 'He sees the best in everyone. He was sure that with the right kind of nurturing, a more gentle spirit would emerge.'

'You know, there was a little glimmer of that one night at the Dei Dogi dinner – do you know Alessandro, the bar manager there?'

'Yes I do. And I would say he had a similar sensibility to Lorenzo, wouldn't you?'

'Yes!' I agree. 'Both are so ardent in their sweetness.' Then I frown. 'So why did he get through to her and Lorenzo didn't?'

'I think because her guard was up with Lorenzo. As soon as she realised he was poor—'

'Temporarily!' I hoot.

'You heard about the inheritance?'

'Yes, I did. But don't worry, I won't tell her. Sorry, you were saying . . .'

'Just that I think Tiffany is somewhat contrary by nature and there was no real possibility with Alessandro because he is devoted to his girlfriend so she was free to feel real warmth towards him.'

'Aren't emotions the darnedest things?' I tut absently and then face Dante head on: 'So tell me, what *is* the real deal with the Amores? I know it's above board, but are they essentially just dating coaches?'

Dante smiles, 'Dating coaches need love too. All of our Amores are single to avoid any complication. There needs to be chemistry otherwise the dates would feel forced, and if a deeper connection develops, that's excellent.'

'Yes it is,' I concur. 'You really are providing a good service.'

Dante grins fondly and then adopts a more businesslike pose. 'So, now you know all this. How will this affect your story?'

'Well. As it just so happens . . .' I roll my eyes. 'There is no story. It's been axed. I don't know if you heard about Adam's article in the UK tabloid?'

Dante nods. 'We have had to make many, many refunds as a result.'

'Oh no!' I howl. 'But he painted such an inaccurate picture!'

'Our reputation has been tarnished,' Dante looks sad. 'Only time will tell if The Love Academy can survive.'

I feel anguished. 'I wish more than anything I could write

what I really think, to properly do you justice . . .' I sigh. 'But I just can't see it happening. My editor is not one for negotiations . . .'

Dante leans back on his elbow. 'Did you have any other questions for me?'

I think for a moment and then mirror his pose as I ask, 'Out of curiosity, who did you originally have me matched with?'

'One of the men you never met. He had the red mask with the two facial expressions – happy one side of his face, sad the other . . .'

'I don't remember him.'

'Lucky for me.'

For a second we just look at each other.

Then in a soft voice Dante tells me, 'When my wife died I had no intention of looking for new love. In my heart I will always be married to my Gabriella. Just the memory of her love can sustain me from now until the day I die. But for a moment it was nice to feel the warmth of another personality. When I heard you had come to the Academy for work, I knew that you weren't as open-hearted as the other girls so I wouldn't hurt you. And I could sense that you were holding yourself back – you are not available are you?' he enquires.

'No,' I say simply, deciding it's time I start telling the truth.

'I think that's what made me feel safe to enjoy your company. I can't be with anyone. Not yet. Not for many years from now.'

I nod understandingly, thinking of the beloved couple at the San Michele cemetery and then I find myself smiling, realising how apt it was that Dante and I should have spent this time together. 'We really were the perfect match, weren't we?' I decide.

Dante beams back at me, leaning to give me a final kiss on the cheek when the door bursts open.

'Kirsty?' A concerned voice calls.

I turn and see Joe – his concern quickly morphing into disgust. 'And to think I was checking to see if you were okay!' he spits.

'Joe! Wait!' I scramble up from the bed but he's already bolted.

I turn back to Dante. 'There's just a little bit more to my situation than I mentioned . . .'

# 33

*'There is no revenge so complete as forgiveness.'*
*– Henry Wheeler Shaw*

It's the last song of the evening and Joe is dancing with Valentina, very much on purpose. I try the old 'May I cut in?' line but he's having none of it, simply spinning her around until the two of them create their own Kirsty-repelling force field.

I decide to let him have his little tit-for-tat retaliation and return to my former table to wait for him to skulk over – now sheepish and conciliatory – in his own time. Of course I can see how things looked with Dante but I'm not going to panic and over-react; tonight at least, my conscience is clear.

As he continues to ignore me and downs his drinks with ever-more vigour, I suspect it is going to take more than a playful tweak to his cheek and a 'Don't be silly baby! Nothing was going on, you know I love you!' to make things right. I want to get to him before he gets too drunk to reason with but suspect I may have missed my window of opportunity, seeing as he has just sat on the spare knee of the old fella that Tiffany is chatting up.

'I think your clutch bag is ringing,' Megan informs me, snug within the arms of Stefano.

I take a peek at the display. *Hot!* calling. Oh what now?

Even though the cat is out of the bag in terms of Sabrina and Dante knowing I'm from the magazine, I don't want to alarm the rest of the party, especially since the article has been nixed, so I decide to head back to my hillside suite to take the call.

'Hello?' I answer en route.

'Kirsty, it's Helena. Please tell me you're still in Venice, please, please!'

'Hold on a mo!' I put my hand over the receiver as I pass my brother and Cleo. 'Kier, if you see Joe can you get him to come to the suite so I can talk to him? It's very important.'

'Will do,' he nods.

'Manhandle him if necessary,' I insist.

'Okay!' he gives me a mock salute.

'Helena?'

'I'm still here. Where are you?'

I wince. 'Florence. What did you need in Venice?'

After cursing effusively she sighs, 'Ruth only wants the bloody Love Academy piece re-instated. I was hoping against hope that you hadn't left yet.'

'Well,' I begin cautiously. 'I haven't actually left the Academy at all. This trip to Florence is part of the course – we're here for a wedding.'

'Then it's not too late?' she gasps.

'Well, that depends . . . why does she want to run the piece now that Adam has beaten us to the punch?'

'Answer me one question,' Helena demands. 'Do you think The Love Academy is legit and for real?'

'Yes, I do,' I tell her, thinking of Dante and his daughter. 'More than ever.'

'Perfect!' she whoops. 'Then we're good to go.'

I frown down the phone. 'What exactly is going on?'

She takes a breath. 'Okay, well you didn't hear this from me but Ruth's love life has taken something of an upturn.'

'What do you mean?'

'You know she was just out in the Bahamas? Well she met a man there, one of the masseurs at the spa and they got together the night before she flew back. He made lots of promises to keep in contact but of course being the cynical old hag that she is, she didn't believe him. Then, today, he turns up in the office!'

'What!' I shriek, suitably amazed.

'You should have seen her face! Anyway. She's done this massive about-turn on all the features we had planned for the next issue saying she now wants it to have a True Love theme!'

'Oh my god!' I gasp. 'It's going to be like a collector's edition!'

'So are you up for it?' Helena enquires.

'YES!' I cheer.

'When do you think you can have it for us?'

'Well, tomorrow is our last day, so if I go full-tilt I could get it to you first thing Wednesday?'

'Brilliant! You're a star!'

Wow. Talk about unexpected. I think I might actually start writing now because who knows how long Ruth's romance is going to last? The sooner I get it in, the better chance of getting it published and potentially saving The Love Academy.

I take out my laptop and start clicking away at the keys. Finally some inspiration! I begin by answering all of Adam's negative observations and as I start going through the elements of the course I realise how much I've learned along the way – the 'accentuate the positive' principles of *bella figura*; Raeleen's observation that a romantic relationship should be the dessert not the main meal (because the main course has to be you!); Maria Luisa's urging for us to embrace the present moment; Lorenzo's thought that romance isn't so much poetry and chocolates as it is paying close attention to what makes your special someone happy; the Italian faith that "Love will always find you again!"; Alessandro's notion that if you consistently think bad thoughts about love, you will not be able to see a possibility when it is in front of you; Dante's conviction that romance begins inside yourself and of course, Sophia Loren's insight that love is more like a wildflower than a long-stemmed rose. Not to mention the Italian proverb that a rained-on bride is a lucky bride!

I glance at the clock. Forty minutes have passed but no Joe. I step out on to the terrace to see if I can spy him but no luck. Probably best I don't go in search of him in case he's on his way up and we miss each other. I'll just go back to my work until he gets here. Maybe I'll even take the laptop over to the bed and get really comfortable.

The next thing I know it's 5 a.m. and Kier has returned, setting my laptop on the floor beside me, I'm guessing as I step out of bed and tread on it. Cautiously I put on one of the small lamps and scour the room for a note of any description.

'What are you doing?' Kier croaks, raising his head.

'Did you see Joe?' I ask him.

'What? When?'

'You know last night, I asked you to get him to come up to the suite and talk to me? What did he say?'

Kier's head flumps in to the pillow. 'Oh shit! I totally forgot, I'm so sorry!'

I open my mouth to berate him but realise that the reason he no doubt forgot was that he was so embroiled with Cleo, and besides, fixing my love life is not his job.

'Don't worry about it, just go back to sleep.'

Now I'm really starting to feel anxious. As far as Joe is concerned I just buggered off into the night. I can't bear to think of the hours he's spent with erroneous images of me and Dante playing in his head. Surely he wouldn't take it any further with Valentina just to spite me? I feel sick just thinking about the two of them together. I try to calm down, assuring myself that everything will be resolved, but the thought of losing Joe feels distinctly real. Even though this is an innocent misunderstanding, at the very least a sour aftertaste will remain – not the ideal circumstance to be telling him that I want us to go ahead and try for a bambino. Right now he'd probably tell me he didn't think it was a good idea. He'd certainly hardly respond with the boundless joy I was hoping for.

Again, I look at the clock. I know it's early but I have to go and find him. If I wait until breakfast everyone else will be around and then we'll be in a car full of people and then there's whatever activities the Academy have planned for our last day . . . I have to set the record straight before the day gets going.

I quickly dress and tip-toe out the door. He's in one of the suites on the next layer, so up this path . . . oh my god! I stop in my tracks.

Valentina is emerging from one of the gated entrances – high heels in one hand, last night's dress hitched up in the other, no doubt in preparation for a sprint back to her own accommodation.

'*Mio Dio! Che spavento mi hai fatto prendere*!' she exclaims when she sees me.

I'm just about to collapse in a pool of wretched tears when a man in blue boxer shorts, most definitely not Joe, comes running after her. 'You forgot your earrings!' He too stops when he sees me.

She takes her jewels and he quickly retreats.

'Please don't tell Joe!' she implores as she hurries to my side. 'He would be so disappointed if he knew you'd seen me with another man! I was supposed to be making you jealous!'

'Then you know . . . ?' He must have confessed that we're a couple!

She nods. 'He drank so much he could not keep his secret any more. I told him that it was most unlikely that anything was occurring with you and Dante but he would not believe me. He thinks any man would find you impossible to resist!'

'Really?' my face brightens.

'He was very hurt and confused. I do not think the alcohol he consumed was of great assistance.'

'No,' I shake my head, inadvertently glancing to the door behind her.

'Oh no,' she tuts. 'That was not alcohol, that was love!'

I grin back at her. 'Who is he?'

'I don't know his name!' she looks a little giddy. 'But did you hear that Welsh accent?'

I chuckle to myself, always having wondered what would make an Italian swoon.

'I was just going to try and talk to Joe now,' I explain my early morning stroll.

Valentina pulls a face.

'You don't think it's a good idea?'

'If he is sleeping and you wake him and his head goes boom-boom, I don't think he will hear what you have to say.'

I chew my lip. I certainly don't want to compound his hangover, that's not in either of our best interests.

'You could write a note,' she suggests. 'Slip it under the door and if he is awake he can respond.'

'That's what I'll do,' I say, thanking her for her advice and waving her on her way.

I take a moment to think of what to write, having my usual trouble with succinctness, and then return to my suite to get a piece of paper and a pen.

'My darling Joe,' I write. 'I want you to know that I was simply having a private word with Dante regarding the magazine article (which by the way has been re-instated, now from a positive angle) as it turns out that he is co-founder of The Love Academy. As Valentina may have explained to you, he is not looking for love as he is still mourning the death of his beloved wife.

'Now you know the facts, I hope we can have a romantic reconciliation! I love you so much and I can't wait for us to return to our life together in London, with renewed appreciation for each other and some fabulous new hopes for the future.'

Is that a bit twee and simplistic? I know he won't wade through pages of waffle and what I've said gets to the crux of the matter, doesn't it? I can go into more detail when we talk. I slide the note under the door, blowing a little kiss through with it and then return to the room. There's no point in going back to sleep now, we have such an early start back to Venice, I'm just going to get ready and continue working on my article up until breakfast.

In the end we order room service so Kier can eat while he's getting ready. Apparently he was up until 3 a.m. with Cleo. He talks chirpily of her and even mentions the fact that there's a gardening job going in Bute Park in Cardiff, which he would definitely consider applying for.

'Apparently there's an equestrian school within the park grounds – I've always wanted to learn to ride!' he enthuses.

For the first time, he doesn't try to play down his interest in a woman or hide his fantasy of their future. He's too happy to try and contain his optimism! What a result!

While he's in the shower, I do a word count on the document I've been working on – 1800 words already! All I need now is the ending to the piece and I can't write that until the end of play today. I feel good though – like everything is in order and heading in the right direction. All I need now is for Joe to get on board and all will be well.

There's a knock at the door.

My heart leaps and I hare over only to find Tiffany on the other side.

'Oh hello!' I say, masking my disappointment with excessive pep. 'How are you this sunny morn?'

'I've been sent to gee you up, are you ready to go?' she cuts to the chase, clearly not feeling overly joyful herself.

'Five minutes,' I reply. 'Kier's almost ready.'

'Alright, well don't dilly-dally, the others have already left.'

I frown. What others? Tiffany was in the 'other' car on the way here . . .

'Sabrina has gone ahead with Melvin, Filomena, Joe and Valentina,' she clarifies.

'What?' I baulk.

She shrugs. 'They were all ready to go. It's no big deal. Just don't be more than ten minutes because there's some big event we've got to get back for . . .'

I can't believe it! I can't believe he's gone without me! I stomp over to my phone and dial Joe's mobile number but it goes straight to voicemail. He surely can't still be sulking? Doesn't he believe that nothing went on with Dante? I'd hope that Valentina would set him straight, and tell him that I went looking for him this morning but then that would blow her cover so I can't see that happening with Sabrina within earshot.

I sit heavily on the edge of the bed. Why, when Joe and I should be leaving The Love Academy on a love-high, are we at our all-time lowest ebb? I just hope that this oh-so-romantic trip to Venice doesn't have us drifting home in separate gondolas . . .

# 34

*'There is no remedy for love but to love more.'*
*– Henry David Thoreau*

Everyone in our car seems to be suffering on the way back to Venice: Megan and Stefano with his 'n' hers hangovers; Dante from a jarred ankle having tripped over Ethan's yacht left on the steps outside his suite; Kier at having to leave Cleo too soon, Tiffany with some internal struggle causing her to bite a person's head off at the merest hint of concern, and myself on account of my unresolved issue with Joe.

I spend the majority of the journey thinking of all the things I love about him – not to mention all the things I'll do differently if I get the chance, like relieve him of the duty of making me happy.

Dante is a tingle on the surface of my skin, but Joe is rooted to my very core. When I think about the kiss with Dante at Villa d'Este I remember the fireworks and the unspeakably romantic setting but with Joe, I can be standing in our kitchen with a potato peeler in my hand and he'll grab me and kiss me and I feel a sense of contentment throughout my entire body.

Meeting Dante certainly has been life-enhancing but Joe I can't live without. And I really hope I don't have to.

When we arrive back at Piazzale Roma our luggage goes back to the Academy while we are shipped directly to the Dei Dogi to catch up with the others, awaiting us in the hotel bar.

'Did you get my note?' I go directly to Joe, unconcerned with what people might think.

'I did, yes.' His response is way too non-commital for my liking.

I want him to envelop me in his arms and tell me that he knew deep down I'd never cheat on him but I know he can't do this, not least because I've forbidden him to indulge in any give-away intimacy in front of the group. All the same, just some tiny inkling that we're going to be alright would be most welcome at this time.

'So how did you leave it with Cleo?' he talks across me to Kier.

Clearly he's not in the mood to resolve our issues so I decide to bow out and leave them to it, gratefully accepting a fancy hair-of-the-dog cocktail from Alessandro. Though she is hanging back, I sense Tiffany watching the barman's every move, almost as if she wants to see if what she thought and said about him before could be true when she is sober and he is standing in direct sunlight.

'*Buon giorno*! How is everyone?' We turn to find Maria Luisa entering the room, bringing with her a halo of exuberant light. She really is one of the most glowing individuals I have ever encountered. '*Bene, bene*!' She nods, acknowledging the successful couplings of Megan and Stefano and Melvin and Filomena before turning to Kier. 'You have called her, haven't you?' she enquires, seemingly already apprised of the Cleo situation.

'Yes,' he nods with a broad grin.

'And she agreed?'

He nods again.

'Good, good.'

Hello? What's going on here? I have no time to speculate further as Maria Luisa's eyes are now upon me. And then Joe. And then me again. 'Hmmm,' she says contemplating us. I'm willing her to sprinkle us with fairy dust – make everything sparkly and happy before we depart but I'm hoping in vain. She simply shrugs her shoulders as if to say, 'I'm leaving you two to sort yourselves out!' before moving on to embrace Dante like a son. I wonder if he has told her about us? Not that he is entirely *au fait* with the details – when I did have a moment alone with him before leaving the Villa San Michele, I chose to tell him the good news about *Hot!* magazine featuring a positive article on The Love Academy, rather than discuss my domestic glitches.

Finally Maria Luisa approaches Tiffany, linking arms with her as she instructs, 'You can walk with me, *mia cara*.'

The pair of them lead us through the garden, talking intently as they go and stopping just short of the jetty where Raeleen gave us our sunset talk four nights ago. I was expecting some kind of graduation ceremony, maybe a little parchment scroll to say that we have met The Love Academy's stringent standards of romance but it looks more like we're going to be baptised in the lagoon.

'What are all those boats on the horizon?' Kier asks as he gazes beyond her.

Maria Luisa looks exceedingly pleased with herself as she announces, 'Today is the annual Vogalonga boat race.'

Is that why the Academy requested we wear sporty attire today? Are we going to be taking part? There are no immediate answers as Maria Luisa chooses instead to explain the connection with today's event and a ceremony from the past.

'The race is held each year at this time to commemorate the Doge's symbolic marriage to the sea,' she tells us. 'Every Ascension Day he would lead a solemn procession of boats out beyond the lagoon and cast a consecrated ring into the water with the words, "*Desponsamus te, mare*."'

'We wed thee, sea,' Sabrina translates.

'And thus Venice and the sea were one,' Maria Luisa smiles.

How can you not love this city – even the politicians are romantic here!

'As your time with The Love Academy concludes, we hope you feel at one with your hearts' desires,' Maria Luisa continues. 'And we hope that each of you in your own way has experienced love during your stay.'

I can't help but glance at Dante – his eyes seem to tell me that he has. I'm so glad to have been a part of that.

'If you keep believing, your love will continue to grow,' she assures us all before handing over to Sabrina for the low-down on the practicalities of the race.

'Everyone is welcome to compete in the Vogalonga provided they have a rowboat – and just in case you didn't pack your own, we have a supply,' she grins as she leads us on to the jetty where an assortment of vessels await at the mooring. 'The race is thirty kilometres long – eighteen miles – but we have special dispensation to allow you to join at this point and continue down Grand Canal to the finishing line in Piazza San Marco.'

As amazing as it sounds, I can't help but whimper, 'Is this absolutely compulsory?'

'Not at all,' Sabrina replies, to my great relief. 'What is a sportsman without a spectator to cheer him on? Now, all those who *would* like to compete please raise their hands?'

All the boys – Kier, Joe, Stefano, Dante and even Melvin – volunteer without hesitation.

'Ladies?' Sabrina turns to the rest of us.

Filomena and Valentina decide to take their own boat, somewhat wisely as their boobs alone could count as four extra passengers. But the rest of us – Tiffany, Megan and myself all politely decline, concluding that our skills are best put to use cheering from the sidelines.

As Sabrina hands out red sashes branded with The Love Academy logo, Maria Luisa pairs Stefano and Dante, setting them head-to-head against Joe and Melvin which seems more than a little weighted in the natives' favour. I look to Kier to ask why he can't team up with Joe but he is emphatic that he wants to sail solo.

'We have one more canoe left,' Sabrina offers. 'Are you sure none of you ladies would like to make a *maiden* voyage?' she quips.

Megan and I shake our heads but Tiffany does the most extraordinary thing – she raises her hand and proclaims, 'I do!'

'Really?' Sabrina looks suitably shocked but Maria Luisa cheers effusively as Tiffany steps out of her not-remotely-sporty high heels and hands them to me, wasting no time in getting prepped. 'Do you have any kind of hairband I can borrow?' she asks, voice a-tremble.

I scrabble for one in my handbag and she duly sweeps up her highly styled tresses into a top-of-the-head ponytail.

'I can't believe you're going to do this!' I gasp. 'What made you change your mind?'

She looks back in the direction of Alessandro, casts an appreciative glance at Maria Luisa and then confides, 'You know that chap I was talking to last night at the wedding reception?'

'The millionaire?' I whisper back.

'Do you know how old he was?' Tiffany enquires.

I shake my head.

'Eighty-two!' she exclaims. 'At one point when I was in the middle of talking he fell asleep and for one awful moment I thought he'd died.'

'Five minutes,' Sabrina gives Tiffany her departure time while the other competitors swing their arms round in circles to loosen their joints.

'Go on,' I urge her to continue with what she was saying.

'All I could think for the rest of the night was *I can't live like this anymore!*' She looks earnestly at me. 'The other day when you suggested I earned my own money to pay for my own treats, I dismissed the idea because it seemed too far-fetched – I've spent my whole life waiting around for someone to take care of me, someone to make me feel valued, someone to pay my bills! I don't know how to do things differently! Then, just now, Maria Luisa asked me if I wanted to go back to Miami the same Tiffany as I arrived and I felt this panic – I *don't*! I *can't*!' She glances down at the fibreglass vessel that awaits her. 'This may only be a baby step but,' she takes a breath: 'I want to know what it feels like to paddle my own canoe!'

I can't help but enfold her in a big booster hug.

'Shouldn't you be saving the congratulations until the end?' she laughs.

'No, I'm proud of you right now!' I tuck a stray loop of hair behind her bejewelled ear. 'Do you want me to look after your bling while you're on the water?'

'Oh no,' she declines my offer. 'If I'm going to do this, I'm going to do it in style!'

As she slides her slim frame into the canoe and takes the paddle, I note how surprisingly confident and adept she looks.

'My dad used to take me out on the water a lot as a kid,' she reveals, looking wistful. 'I actually used to really enjoy it . . .'

And then she's off. As I watch her even, smooth strokes and perfect posture I smile again – there really is hope in the world. Something tells me that the next course Tiffany signs up for will be an outward-bound white-water rafting adventure. And she'll have the time of her life.

'Go, Kier!' My brother is next to set off, with a fierce determination I haven't seen in years. I always forget how strong his lean body is until I see him in action and recall that he toils on a daily basis. He overtakes Tiffany without a backward glance – I never had him down as competitive but he seems highly motivated today.

Dante and Stefano are now in position with Joe and Melvin bobbing at a slight angle to them. Joe is still studiously avoiding my gaze but as they prepare to make their first stroke I summon the fullest breath to my lungs and bellow, 'Go Joe! Go Melvin!' In the split-second Joe turns to look at me, I take the opportunity to mouth, 'Love you!' and give him a big thumbs-up of encouragement but he looks more confused than pleased.

Megan meanwhile, may be surprised at who I have chosen to champion but quickly shrugs off her meek demeanour to holler, 'Stefano! Dante! *Avanti, avanti*!'

We giggle as we attempt to clamour over each other, following the chaps' progress as they begin to merge with the stream of other competitors. There has to be a thousand boats out there, ranging from pencil-thin darts to great hulks of timber, all manually propelled. As I watch, I notice a variety of rowing techniques, principally the sit-down stylings of the Oxford and Cambridge Boat Race brigade versus the traditional Venetian mode of rowing standing up.

'So they can watch for mudbanks,' Sabrina explains the origin of style.

The Venetian interpretation does lend a certain unique charm to the proceedings. Not least because they are rowing in costumes that wouldn't look out of place in an Asterix comic strip – primary bolts of red and blue and yellow with cute little neckerchiefs. One particularly colour-co-ordinated vessel – propelled by six women in green vests, white knee-length skirts and towelling headbands – looks like half a dozen gym teachers out for the day. I notice that some of the longer crafts have a petite drummer at the back, banging out a booming rhythm, lending a primitive vibe, whereas the scattering of solo canoeists brings us back to the present day.

'This way,' Sabrina takes us on a series of short-cuts, sometimes leading us inland to cut off a corner and then gaining a new vantage point where we pogo up and down amidst the crush of observers, trying to keep track of our assorted voyagers.

It's always easy to locate Tiffany, Filomena and Valentina – we just listen for the wolf-whistles. Overall the atmosphere is of teamwork and camaraderie – at one point a fellow loses his oar just before the Rialto Bridge, fearlessly dives in after it and is retrieved by the next boat who claim him for their own!

The one person who seems to be paddling like he's got

something to prove is Joe. Whereas Dante is zen and focused, concentrating on moving swiftly and calmly towards the finishing line, Joe's eyes flick constantly to the man who has become his arch-rival. Ironic that this should happen *after* Dante has ceased to be any kind of threat to the relationship, at least from my point of view.

'Not far to go now!' I try to egg him on, though it's unlikely he can hear me.

I can't help but feel for him – he's certainly set himself quite a task: attempting to beat two Venetians, half-amphibious by birth, with only a pint-size accomplice. Well those fictitious squash games of his seem to be paying off – when we leave them at Riva del Carbon, it's still level-pegging.

Keeping quite a pace ourselves, Sabrina, Megan and I career through Campos Manin, San Anzolo and San Stefano to get to our next vantage point on the Accademia bridge. As they pass beneath us, the strain is really starting to show, but there is a noticeable surge when the Doge's Palace comes into their view. It's agony but we have to leave watching their progress for a good few minutes as we make our way in a hand-holding chain through the inland streets to St Mark's Square. At the finishing line there is such a chaos of people and boats, it's hard to make anyone out but Maria Luisa calls to us from a raised platform and, having been studying the waves intently for the past hour, directs our gaze to the approaching red sashes . . .

We rally and cheer and I get hoarse from whooping as the first of The Love Academy team crosses the line – it's my brother, Kier!

'Yay!' I hug him vigorously. 'That was *amazing*! What was propelling you with such force?'

He gives a shy smile. 'I was trying to impress a girl.'

I look around me, following Kier's eyeline to a certain vision in courgette-blossom yellow. 'Cleo!' I yelp, amazed. 'What the—'

'She said she'd never been to Venice so I offered to show her around.'

'But we leave tomorrow!'

'Actually I thought I might stay on a few days . . .'

'Really?' My eyes widen.

Kier nods as he accepts a hug from the object of his affection. 'Maria Luisa said we could stay on at the Palazzo Abadessa.'

I find myself beaming. He has reclaimed his love for this city and is intent on replacing sad memories with happy ones – I couldn't be more thrilled! Or could I . . . ?

'Here come the others!' Maria Luisa alerts us.

We turn to find Dante and Stefano on the approach, barely breaking a sweat alongside a dishevelled but perfectly synchronised Joe and Melvin, noticeably willing their boat forth. I'm particularly impressed with Melvin's fortitude – it's like he's doing this for every time a tall, handsome man ever stole his girl.

'Come on Filomena!' He even manages to rally his half of the 'Vali Girls' as Valentina's team has been nicknamed.

'I'm coming!' she yodels back at him.

The cheering of the crowd crescendos.

'Tiffany!' I wave wildly as she comes into view. Her ponytail is now lopsided but she's never looked more beautiful – there's a healthy flush to her complexion and her eyes look wonderfully vibrant and alive.

'Dante!' 'Stefano!' 'Joe!' 'Melvin!' All the names are chorused with increasing volume and urgency as they approach the finishing line. Who's it going to be?

'Come on Joe!' I give one final holler of encouragement.

But, ultimately, it is Dante and Stefano who triumph.

Cries of *'Congratulazioni! Ben Fatto!'* ring around them.

I'm trying to get to Joe to praise him on a valiant effort but I can't get through the crush of well-wishers. All I see is flicker-book glimpses of his dejected face and his exhausted body being jostled by the mob. But then his hand extends in my direction and for a second I think he's reaching for me . . . but instead his palm meets Dante's in a manly handshake and I hear him murmur, 'I guess the best man won.'

'I simply won the race,' Dante asserts, simultaneously locating me and pulling me through to his side. 'You, Joe, won the prize.'

He looks at the two of us, more distraught than ever now, and goes to turn away but someone is standing forcibly in his path – my brother.

'You're headed in the wrong direction, buddy,' he growls like a New York cop.

'Kier, are you meddling for me?' I can't help but gasp, oh-so-gratefully.

He gives me the quickest nod of affirmation before returning his attention to Joe. 'Well?'

Joe expels a weary, defeated breath. 'Your sister deserves better than someone who's in the loo when the first dance of the wedding is announced.' He casts a glance back at Dante. 'She should be with a true romantic, not a pretend one.'

Oh, he's not getting away that easily.

'Did you just pretend to fly to Venice?' I challenge him.

He half-turns his head in my direction. 'No,' he concedes.

'Because, to me, a man who would suffer airport security during the peak of the holiday season just to be with his girl, sounds pretty darn romantic.'

'Really?' His eyes beseech Dante, seemingly searching for the Master's approval.

'Don't look at me!' Dante laughs. 'Everything you need to know is right here, in her eyes . . . '

Finally Joe looks directly at me and as my gaze warms him with the full glow of my love, I see his eyes get misty and he swallows back a lump in his throat as he croaks, 'I thought I'd lost you again!'

'I'm right here!' I tell him.

And with that we fall into the Valium Hug that I've been longing for – and he holds me closer, tighter, longer than ever before. So long, in fact, that the others all drift on their way and now it's just me and Joe, standing in contemplation of the majesty that is the Grand Canal.

'I can't believe you just rowed those jade waters!' I marvel. 'I wish I'd had the nerve.'

'Maybe next year we can Vogalonga together?' Joe offers. 'In a canoe built for two.'

It's then we spy a just-vacated gondola – the long, black limousine of the rowboat world.

It's a particularly sleek specimen with ultra-glossy jet woodwork, ornate gold flourishes and an invitingly squooshy red leather seat. With tassles.

'I suppose you've already . . .' he nods towards it.

'Actually I haven't . . .' My eyes meet his.

'Is that too much of a cliché to count as romantic?' he tentatively enquires.

'Not with you,' I grin.

'Signore!' He calls to the straw-boatered gondolier. 'May we?'

*'Si, si,'* he beckons us over. 'My name is Milo,' he greets us as we step aboard.

'I love that name!' I enthuse, nudging Joe. 'What do you think?'

He gives me a quizzical look. 'Yeah, it's cool.'

'Cool enough for our first baby boy?'

Joe gawks at me. 'Are you serious?'

I nod.

'You mean . . . you're really ready to try . . . ?'

I add a grin to my nodding.

'Oh Kirsty!' he breathes as he presses me into the squishy heart-shaped cushion and kisses me and kisses me and kisses me.

'You know, when we get home, I'll even take a dance lesson for you,' he smiles indulgently.

I laugh as I stroke his face, 'Now *that's* amore!'

ALSO AVAILABLE IN ARROW

# *I Love Capri*

## Belinda Jones

**Sundrenched days, moonlit nights and Italian ice cream. What more could a girl ask for . . .?**

Kim Rees became a translator for the glamourous jet-set lifestyle. So, five years later, how come she's ended up in a basement flat in Cardiff translating German computer games in her dressing gown? Fortunately her mother has a plan to extract her from her marshmallowy rut: a trip to the magical isle of Capri.

At first Kim refuses to wake up and smell the bougainvillea, but as she starts to succumb to the irresistible delights of cocktails on the terrace and millionaire suitors, she's surprised to realise she's changing. And when she meets a man who's tiramisu personified, she finds herself falling in love. But how far will she go to win her Romeo?

arrow books

ALSO AVAILABLE IN ARROW

# *The Paradise Room*

## Belinda Jones

When Amber Pepper's jeweller boyfriend Hugh asks her to join him on a business trip to the paradise islands of Tahiti she's not keen – Amber loves big jumpers and rain. She'd rather be pedalling through puddles at home in Oxford than lolling in the gel-blue waters of the South Pacific. However, the prospect of sipping Mai Tais with her long-lost friend Felicity is incentive enough to coax her on the twenty-hour flight.

Within hours of touching down on coral sands the girls venture into a seductive new world of mesmerising music, exotic black pearls and sexy strangers. And for the first time Amber falls head over flip-flops in lust, only to receive an unexpected proposal of marriage.

Will she opt for a barefoot beach wedding or cast caution – and her coconut bra – to the wind? No easy decision for a drizzle-loving gal when it's ninety degrees in the shade . . .

'As essential as your SPF 15'
*New Woman*

'This is definitely worth cramming in your suitcase'
*Cosmopolitan*

arrow books

ALSO AVAILABLE IN ARROW

# *Café Tropicana*

Belinda Jones

Latte-lover Ava Langston knows exactly what she wants: her very own café in a Regency arcade in Bath and a life free of complicated relationships. But her plans go awry when her long-distance dad phones insisting she hop on the next plane to Costa Rica to meet his brand new wife Kiki.

Ava has no intention of jetting to Latin America to acquire a stepmother – until, that is, her father offers her head honcho status at a local beachfront café. The lure of frothing cappuccinos in a land where the coffee beans grow proves irresistible. But she hasn't planned on Santiago, her sexy-yet-stubborn business rival, or rugged Ryan whose idea of romance is swinging through the rainforest canopy at 6am. Both men give her butterflies, but only one will capture her heart . . .

arrow books

# Win a romantic break for two in the incredible city of Venice!

To enter, just fill in the form below and return to:

*The Love Academy* Competition,
Arrow Marketing Department,
Random House, 20 Vauxhall Bridge Road,
London SW1V 2SA

QUESTION 1: What is the name of Kirsty's brother?

Answer: ..........................................

QUESTION 2: What is the name of the magazine Kirsty works for?

Answer: ..........................................

TIE-BREAKER: (complete in 15 words or less)

I want to go to Venice because ..........................................

..........................................

..........................................

Name: ..........................................

Address: ..........................................

..........................................

Email: ..........................................

Telephone Number: ..........................................

☐ I would like to receive more information about books by Belinda Jones

☐ I would like to receive more information about Random House books

See overleaf for terms and conditions

# TERMS & CONDITIONS:

1. By entering this competition you agree to be bound by these terms and conditions and any other subsequent requirements. 2. This competition is open to residents of the UK, except employees of the promoter and their immediate families and anyone professionally connected with the promotion. 3. Entrants must complete the official entry form, in ink or ballpoint pen. 4. The closing date is midnight on 30th October 2007 5. The winner will be chosen by an independent judge on 1st November 2007 and will be notified within 14 days. 6. All entrants must be 18 or over and hold a valid passport. 7. Responsibility will not be accepted for entries lost, delayed or damaged in the post. Proof of posting is not proof of receipt. 8. Any number of entries per individual is acceptable but only one attempt per official entry form. 9. Entries will become the property of the promoter and will not be returned. 10. The prize will be awarded to the entrant who has answered the two questions correctly and who has, in the opinion of the judge, answered the tiebreaker, in 15 words or less, in the most apt and original way. 11. The prize is 2 nights in Venice for two people. The prize is based on two people sharing a double/twin room and includes: return flights from a UK airport, 2 nights 4* accommodation on a B&B basis. There is no cash alternative to the prize. 12. The prize does not include (and therefore the winner will be responsible for) any costs relating to: travel to and from the airport; airport transfers; visas; insurance ; passenger taxes; the flight tickets (including charges, fees and surcharges, the amounts of which are subject to change). 13. The prize is subject to availability and certain dates (including but not limited to 22nd December 2007 – 2nd January 2008) are excluded. 14. The prize must be completed by 31st May 2008. 15. The decision of the judge is final and binding and no correspondence will be entered into. 16. The winner and the winner's companion may be required to take part in any publicity relating to this competition and it is a condition of entry that the promoter's use of their names and photographs in relation to any publicity material is agreed. 17. Events may occur that render the awarding of this prize impossible due to reasons beyond the control of the promoter and the promoter may, at its absolute discretion, vary, amend, suspend or withdraw the prize with or without notice. 18. The promoter is The Random House Group Limited, 20 Vauxhall Bridge Road, London SW1V 2SA. 19. These terms and conditions are subject to English Law and the exclusive jurisdiction of the English courts.